One hell of a ride . . .

"We should have taken some pictures," Alicia pointed out.

"I can see it now." Frank grunted in disdain. "We could have the Blockers and the McIntyres over for a slide show." He raised his voice theatrically.

"Here we are in Hell—notice the demons at the tables? Observe the stuffed children mounted on the walls. Here we are on the highway that takes you off the edge of the world. This place that looks like Las Vegas? It's really on another planet. You can tell by the guy with the root growing out of his head and the lady with the purple fur on her face. Christ!" He slammed both hands against the wheel. "I don't wanna save the world. I just want to be able to keep selling Taiwanese baseball mitts at fifty percent markup. That's my idea of a reality worth fighting for!"

TO THE VANISHING POINT

Also by Alan Dean Foster

Alien
Aliens
The I Inside
Into the Out Of
The Man Who Used the Universe
Spellsinger
Spellsinger II: The Hour of the Gate
Spellsinger III: The Day of the Dissonance
Spellsinger IV: The Moment of the Magician
Spellsinger V: The Paths of the Perambulator
Spellsinger VI: The Time of the Transference
Starman

Published by
WARNER BOOKS

ALAN DEAN FOSTER

TO THE VANISHING POINT

POPULAR LIBRARY

An Imprint of Warner Books, Inc.

A Warner Communications Company

POPULAR LIBRARY EDITION

Popular Library®, the fanciful P design, and Questar® are
registered trademarks of Warner Books, Inc.

Cover art by Gary Ruddell
Cover design by Don Puckey

Popular Library books are published by
Warner Books, Inc.
666 Fifth Avenue
New York, N.Y 10103

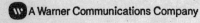 A Warner Communications Company

Printed in the United States of America

This book was originally published in hardcover by Warner Books.
First Printed in Paperback: June, 1989

10 9 8 7 6 5 4 3 2 1

To Cele Patterson,
the angel of Peter Cooper with love and affection

DESOLATION IS MAGNIFIED *at seventy miles per hour. At that speed, colors that are normally separate and distinct tend to blend together like the test pattern on an old TV. Sharply defined objects melt into one another, precluding identification, forestalling recognition. Landscapes adopt the illusion of reality.*

It's worse in the desert because there is so little to focus on. Those creatures that don't hide usually spend the daylight hours sleeping. For most of the year the plant life is dressed in a blistered gray hue that seems designed to confuse the eye. Nothing moves except the tormented air that rises in waves from the frying-pan pavement in front of you.

In summer, when the thermometer in the Mojave creeps past the 110 mark with threatening regularity, all activity ceases. Like the sidewinders and the kangaroo rats, the desert's human inhabitants have gone to ground by eight A.M., embracing the protection of dark buildings and overstressed air conditioners.

Once you get out past Barstow, driving east, civilization vanishes for hundreds of miles except for one tiny outpost called Baker. The map will insist you're still in the United States of America, but if not for the nondescript ribbon of concrete known as Interstate 40 you might as well be crossing the Gobi, or the Sahara, or the Namib. Brothers in emptiness. Parts of the Great

Southwest Desert are as deadly empty as Arabia's Rub' al Khali.

*If anything stands out it's the absence of black. Everything is
painted light or white. In the Mojave black is the color of fools;
sometimes dead ones. Now and again travelers convinced that
living in the twentieth century has endowed them with immunity
break down out in the desert. Travelers neglectful of water.
Transient visitors who perish of dehydration despite aerial surveil-
lance and thermos bottles and air-conditioning and CB radios.*

*Dull the desert can be, but it slays the thoughtless and
carefree as efficiently as any gilded Toledo blade. Indifference
makes it no less lethal.*

The Sonderbergs had no thoughts of dying, though there were
times since they'd left Los Angeles when Frank thought of doing
some killing of his own, if only in the metaphorical sense. It was
his own fault and he knew it. Normally they flew to Las Vegas.
He'd decided they'd do it differently this time. Among the things
that had inspired this changeling journey was the fact that Wendy
was now old enough to appreciate the beauty of their unspoiled
surroundings. That she had not the slightest intention of doing so
was no fault of his. He ought to have known better.

Straightening slightly in the captain's chair enabled him to see
her in the rearview mirror. Sixteen and pretty, she was convulsing
on the couch that folded out to make a bed. Her head snapped
from side to side, her torso twitched violently at the waist, and her
feet massaged the floor. Eyes shut in private rapture, she was
moving to the electrified rhythm of an unpronounceable group of
heavy-metal leprechauns, delivered exclusively to her ears via the
tiny wire that connected earphones and Walkman.

Though he would never have said so among peers, Frank
didn't consider his daughter's musical taste all that bad. It wasn't
so very different from what he'd been chastised for listening to
when he was her age. But it was one thing to appreciate, another
to be addicted. Wendy only removed the damn earphones to bathe
and to sleep, and he wasn't sure about the latter. Fascinating sights
were whizzing past outside the motor home and the only time his
daughter opened her eyes was to change tapes.

Even when she paused briefly between concerts it was difficult to get her to pay attention to the country they were passing
through. Worse, she was just old and smart enough to come up

with a new word each week to describe her father. The current pejorative-of-the-month was "droll." As in his telling her plaintively, "Why don't you watch some of this scenery? Why the hell do you think I took off the extra time and shelled out the extra bucks to rent this palace on wheels so we could drive and look and learn instead of flying?" And her rolling her eyes and replying, "Oh, Daddy. How *droll.*"

He would have welcomed the comment from Steven, who was ten. He would have welcomed anything from Steven, so long as it didn't sound like a whine. His son was two years too old to still be a whiner. Overweight, unattractive, he only displayed enthusiasm when they drew near the next Burger King or McDonald's or Carl's Junior. Anything but a Wendy's, because that was the name of his despised, contemptuous older sister.

Frank settled back into the thickly padded seat. Two junkies he was raising. One addicted to indecipherable music, the other to junk food. Glancing to his right, his expression softened. God knew Alicia tried her best. The children were just going through a phase, she would assure him. That was her favorite line and she clung to it like a talisman, reciting it like a prayer. Just going through a phase. No matter what the problem was it was just a phase. Heavy metal, it's just a phase. Overeating, a phase. Cats and dogs phasing out now. Scarred bass guitarists and Big Macs phasing in.

He was being too hard on himself, he knew. His kids could be worse. Steven might grow out of his gluttony, and at least Wendy wasn't into drugs. Not so far as he knew.

Alicia still had that glow. She'd never been truly beautiful, but there was a serenity about her he'd always found attractive. The maid helped maintain that aura, as did the money. She'd been much more hyper when they'd met. Success bred in contentment, bred out her early nervousness and uncertainty. They enjoyed each other's company, and that was more important than superficial physical attractiveness. Besides, he was no Cary Grant himself.

She'd been ambivalent about this project all along, but she'd agreed to renting the motor home and driving to Vegas instead of flying as usual because he'd been so enthusiastic. He knew she'd done it for that reason and not because she thought it was the right way to go. The warm feeling prompted him to reach over with his right hand and pat her thigh. She looked back and smiled that familiar half-certain smile of hers.

"Love you, too."

He returned his attention to the empty highway ahead. The big engine sang to itself beneath the hood. The outside thermometer read ninety-eight and rising. Other vehicles, even eighteen-wheelers, were scarce this morning.

"It's not working out."

She glanced back, then settled into her seat again. "You mean the kids? You can't really blame them. They'd rather be lying by the pool. At their age there's no vacation in getting there."

"I know. It's my fault."

The kids enjoyed Vegas. Wendy was old enough to enjoy watching the young men at the pool and in the casino. Steven liked the pool, too, and freaked over the selection of video games, not to mention being able to order room service. With the children occupied, Alicia spent the day soaking up the sun while Frank relaxed from the business. At night he and Alicia would take in a show or spend some time at the craps table while the kids relaxed in front of the TV, watching movies. They were pretty good about that, he had to admit.

Now Steven was whining constantly and Wendy had withdrawn to her private metal nirvana, and it was all his fault. Just this once he'd determined to do something different. Hoping for enlightenment, the result so far had been unrelenting discontent and alienation. Maybe he should have let Alicia stock the motor home's larder with Steven's requested cookies and chips and candy. At least he wouldn't have had to put up with the boy's continual whining ever since they'd left San Bernardino.

Wendy didn't whine. She just ignored him, as she ignored the barren landscape flashing past the windows while slipping fresh tapes in and out of her player as efficiently as any late-night DJ. Frank no longer tried to point out ocotillo or cholla, jumping cactus or paloverde. He could have counted on more response from a stone.

"You never thought much of this trip either, did you?"

Alicia Sonderberg tried to frame a tactful reply. Truth to tell, she'd been startled when her husband had first broached the idea. It wasn't like him. One of the traits she most loved him for was his predictability. She'd found him a welcome change from her own unsettled adolescence. Frank made her feel safe and secure right from the start, even during the early days when they'd lived in a cramped studio apartment in a run-down section of Santa Monica while he'd tried to start his business. He was dependable, reliable.

Then out of nowhere came his declared intention to deviate from their vacation plans, from the pattern they'd followed for years. Instead of flying to Vegas, let's rent a motor home and drive, he'd announced brightly.

She smiled to herself. It wasn't as if he'd proposed chartering a plane to fly to the North Pole so they could watch polar bears and walrus. Nevertheless, she'd quietly tried to change his mind, arguing that Steven wasn't old enough to appreciate whatever they might encounter and that Wendy wouldn't care. That she'd been proven correct so far was small comfort. She derived no pleasure from her husband's disappointment.

It was no way to begin a vacation. He'd always expected the truth from her and she'd always given it to him, but it was going to be hard to reply honestly. Oh sure, one or two things they'd seen had been of interest, but they had to consider the children. Frankly, Wendy and Steven were bored to tears. Wendy wanted boys to admire her new swimsuits and Steven wanted his snacks. Their idea of a vacation was not slowing down to watch a real live rattlesnake cross the road. It wasn't Alicia's, either. The closest she wanted to get to creepy-crawlies was watching them on PBS. She was even more of a city person than Frank. Thank God they could afford a gardener.

Seeing how genuinely distraught her husband was, she tried to work around the question. "Frank, you know how I always like to look my best for you."

He frowned. "What's that got to do with anything?"

"Cosmetics don't hold up too well in this kind of climate. That's why I don't go outside when we're in Vegas, except to go to the pool."

"You're being evasive, hon."

She smiled gently. "Maybe a little. Frank, you've got to admit this hasn't been very exciting so far."

"Did I promise excitement? Did I ever say it was going to be exciting? We're going to spend a week in Vegas, for chrissake. Isn't that excitement enough? Can't we take a few days away from that to have an educational experience?"

She looked toward the middle of the motor home. "I'm afraid the kids have had all the education they can take."

He grunted and leaned over the wheel. "The kids! My kids. The zombie and the human garbage disposal. The Jacksons they ain't."

"Frank, their summer vacation just started. They've been nine months in school. The last thing in the world they're interested in is an educational experience. Don't you remember what it was like when you were their age?"

"It should be fun for them, too." He was losing ground and knew it. "I mean, seeing that big diamondback cross the road. You know how many kids never get that close to a real live rattler?"

"Every kid in L.A. gets to the zoo."

"That's not the same thing as seeing it in its natural habitat," he protested.

"I'm not sure I-40 qualifies as a natural habitat, Frank."

He nodded to himself. "You're gonna fight me on this one, aren't you?" He swerved slightly to avoid a piece of broken crate littering the pavement, pulling into the fast lane to go around it. He barely bothered to glance at the sideview mirror. There'd been so little traffic since they'd left the outskirts of San Bernardino he felt they had the highway to themselves. In a sense they did.

The Sonderberg children attended private school. The public schools didn't let out for another two weeks. That was another reason why they always vacationed this time of year. The usual tourist destinations were still devoid of high school and college students and families traveling with kids. Only Wendy was upset, bemoaning the lack of boys her own age to chat with.

Frank worried about his daughter's preoccupation with members of the opposite sex, only to have Alicia reassure him that it was nothing but another phase. Wendy was no worse than any other pretty girl that age, and better than some. It was all part of growing up. Like her son's admittedly regrettable overeating problem.

Alicia had to admit that her son's junk food binge was lasting longer than was healthy. His continued inactivity wouldn't be so bad if he was, say, a computer genius or something. But he was quite average, well-meaning enough but in no way exceptional. In that regard he was much like his parents. Frank Sonderberg had risen above his station through sheer determination and hard work.

Maybe when Steven was older he would begin to show some skill, or at least a little of his father's drive. To date, however, the boy had proved himself relentlessly ordinary.

Nobody appreciated what he was trying to do for them with this trip, Frank mused. Not Wendy and Steven, not even Alicia. They knew only city life, the big house, the private schools, vacations, and shopping sprees. It wasn't right. He enjoyed all those things himself, having worked hard to gain them. But there ought to be some balance in a person's life. Frank was big on balance.

If you lived in the city then you should spend some time in the country, and if you were a country person you needed to experience the sophistication of the city. Balance. Television couldn't compensate. Watching the creatures of the desert on "Nova" or Disney or "Nature" wasn't the same as encountering them in the wild.

Their brief sight of a family of javelinas in a gully just the other side of Barstow had been instructive. Alicia couldn't get over how "cute" the two babies were. Wendy wondered why all the fuss over a bunch of hairy pigs, and Steven spent the whole evening at the RV park whining about bacon and pork chops. While there was something to be said for reducing an experience to its essential elements, his family had a way of doing it that transformed the extraordinary into the mundane.

Maybe he was expecting too much of them. Especially the kids. He doubted they were all that different from their friends. Everything had been given to them. Alicia knew better, but his decision to drive instead of fly to Vegas was clearly baffling to her as well.

Indifference and muted hostility. Those were his rewards for trying to act the responsible father. For trying to show his family something of the world beyond Los Angeles. Side trips to San Diego, San Francisco, and New York didn't count. He'd sired an urban family, pure and simple. To Wendy and Steven a wildlife expedition consisted of going to the beach and fighting to avoid anything organic while playing in the surf.

He looked up at the map secured by magnetic clips to the bare metal dash above the radio/cassette player. Fifty miles to go to Baker, the minuscule outpost of civilization that lay between

Barstow and Vegas. This was one of the emptiest spots in California. Nothing to the south, Death Valley to the north.

In point of fact, he reluctantly confessed to himself, it *was* pretty boring. Not like the Pacific Northwest or the bayous of the Deep South. Not that he was intimate with those regions, either. He was an armchair explorer, letting someone else's camera be his eyes. Until this trip.

He was ready to admit defeat, conquered by apathy. Already he'd discarded his original plan to take several days between San Bernardino and Vegas to explore side roads and beckoning arroyos. Not even the unblemished night sky had been sufficient to enthrall his offspring.

"We saw it all at the planetarium, Daddy." So much for his daughter's sense of wonder. As for Steven, he could only decry the absence of a laser show.

"Right," he muttered to no one in particular. "I give in."

Alicia glanced over curiously. "You give in to what, dear?"

Instead of replying he turned his head to the right, shouted toward the back of the motor home. "Hey! You kids!"

Steven looked up from his comic book. "What's up, Dad?"

"We're going to— Get that thing off your sister's head, will you?"

The boy shook his head violently. "Uh-uh. If I touch 'em she'll hit me. She's always hitting me."

Alicia finally managed to catch her daughter's eye. Wendy rolled her eyes and nudged the earphones back from her ears. Mötley Crüe drifted weakly through the motor home.

"What is it now?"

"You win." Frank kept one hand on the steering wheel.

Wendy glanced at her little brother, who shrugged. "What do you mean?"

"I mean I give up. I try to introduce you to a new experience, try to show you something unique, and I'm just wasting my time. I know when I'm beaten."

"Frank, watch the road," Alicia cautioned him.

"I am watching the road. Not that there's anything to watch." He waved his hand at the cream-gray concrete. "There's nobody else out here. We're the only ones stupid enough to drive this stretch of road in the middle of the day, right?"

That wasn't entirely true. Eager gamblers crammed into old

Chevys and Toyotas occasionally rocketed past the motor home, exceeding the speed limit by a good twenty to thirty miles an hour in their haste to reach the neon lights and gaming tables just over the state line. They vanished rapidly over the shimmering, heat-struck horizon.

"We're not making any more stops," he explained tiredly. "We're gonna drive straight through. When we get there we'll check in to a big hotel, just like everybody wants. I'll turn the motor home in to the rental agency and we'll fly home when vacation's up."

"Wow, that's great, Dad!"

"Thanks, Pops." Wendy slid her headphones back into position, closed her eyes. "That's really rad of you." Her upper body began to sway rhythmically.

"You're both welcome." His sarcasm was lost on them. He saw that Steven had abandoned his comic book in favor of a Transformer toy.

When he'd been a boy he'd had cap pistols and a football and a train. Immutable diversions. Now they had toys that turned into other toys. What galled him was that he couldn't figure out how they worked. He'd once spent a futile couple of hours fiddling with one of his son's Transformers and had achieved only a fine sense of feeling daft. Steven's pudgy fingers effortlessly turned the chunk of brightly colored plastic and metal into a succession of sleek gadgets.

"You look worried," said Alicia. "You're upset."

"Sure I'm upset."

"You've got that look on your face."

"What look? The look that says I'm forty and death is just around the corner?" He tried hard not to smile at her and failed. She reached over and caressed his right arm, squeezing gently. Both his expression and his voice softened.

"You've known me so long. I don't know what I'd do without you, babe."

"Same back at you, Sonderberg. Want to drive for another hour, or you want me to take over?"

"Naw. I'll stay with it awhile longer. After all, I'd planned on driving for another couple of days. You're not real disappointed, are you?"

"Would I lie to you, Frank? No, I'm not disappointed. A real bed and a real shower would be so nice.''

"So much for the natural experience," he grunted.

"If you want to expose the children to nature, maybe at the end of summer we can all go up to Yosemite together. I think they'd handle that okay."

"Sure they would. There's fast food machines everywhere, cable TV, and plenty of boys for your daughter to flirt with. We can stay in some fancy hotel and eat out every night."

Her smile faded slightly. "You know, Frank, keeping house even on wheels and cooking three meals a day on that little gas stove isn't exactly *my* idea of a vacation."

"All right. Point conceded. Look, I've already given in, haven't I? I said we'd drive straight on through and take the plane back when it's time to come home. Don't make me feel any worse about it than I already do."

"I know you better than that, Frank. You're protesting too much. Don't tell me you've been having such a grand time yourself. Be honest, now."

As usual with Alicia he was unable to muster a convincing lie. "Yes and no. I'm disappointed the kids didn't get to see more of this country. I'm sorry you and I didn't get to see more. But maybe they aren't old enough to appreciate it like I thought, and maybe it's the wrong time of year." Even though it was early summer it was already too hot to stand outside for long. "My intentions were good, sweetheart."

"I know that, Frank. I think the children realize it, too."

He was nodding to himself. "My intentions were good. It was just the actuality that stunk, right?" He held up a hand to forestall her protest. "Maybe we'll try it again another year." He stared out the bug-splattered windshield at the endless ribbon of highway, the sallow-colored hills, and frugal vegetation. "Yosemite probably would be more interesting. It's just that we were going to Vegas anyway."

"Education shouldn't be the main purpose of a vacation, dear. It's a lot like work. It's hard enough to get you to relax. You're thinking about work right now, aren't you?"

"I'm always thinking about work. Can't help it, hon. I'm trying to run fifty-six stores and get ready to open those four new ones in Oregon. Two in Portland, one in Medford, the other in Eugene. It's tough to leave stuff like that behind you. You don't know what it's like trying to run the company now that it's gotten so big.''

"No, but I know what it's like to try living with the man who does. That's exasperating enough. If not for your own sake then for mine, try to put it out of your mind long enough to relax a little. It'll do you good.''

"We go through this every time we go away. God knows I've heard the same thing from every doctor I've ever seen. You know what they say? They say it's a miracle my blood pressure isn't higher than it is. You're right about it, of course.''

"You're going to have to try to learn to relax in spite of yourself. You sure you don't want me to take over?''

"No, I'll drive for another hour, anyway. Alicia, when you've built up something like the business from nothing, it becomes a lot like a child itself. It's tough to put it out of your mind.''

"Well, you have two other children to consider. Sometimes it's important for us to think about what they want instead of what we want for them.''

He made a face. "You make it sound like I've been forcing them to sit through a ten-hour lecture on national monetary policy.'' He reached out to tap the map with a finger. "That ghost town yesterday was fun, wasn't it?'' He looked back. "Didn't everybody have fun at the ghost town?''

"They had great corn dogs.'' Steven tried to sound hopeful, aware that his father was less than pleased with him. He wasn't sure his reply had the desired effect, though.

"What about you?''

"Say what?'' Wendy slipped off the headphones.

"Calico.'' Frank spoke patiently, trying to watch the road at the same time. "The ghost town. Didn't you have a good time there?''

"Actually, Pops, I thought it was kind of a drag. The walk through the gold mine, that's just so *old*. And the bar where all they could sell was soda. I mean, come on, Pops. Get real.''

"You'd have preferred a beer, I suppose.'' She just smiled knowingly. "You've got a few years to go before you're legal, kiddo.''

"Maybe I'm not legal, but I'm cute.'' She was teasing him now, he knew. Demonstrating the social superiority of the

American adolescent. "I can get beer in Vegas, you know."

"Where? Who gave you beer?"

"Frank." Alicia spoke softly, trying to calm her husband. "Can't you see she's just trying to get to you?"

He turned grumpily back to his driving. "She's succeeding. If I find out someone in a casino is selling sixteen-year-olds beer, especially my sixteen-year-old . . ."

"Take it easy, Frank."

"I know, I know. Blood pressure."

"I mean," said Wendy, her attention and voice beginning to fade under the influence of the tape she was listening to, "it was a place for golden oldies, you know?"

Frank forced himself to keep both hands on the wheel. "Just remember it's the golden oldies up here who're paying for this trip, and for those invisible swimsuits you think you're going to wear poolside. I swear," he muttered, "the less material they put in those things the more they charge. I'm waiting for pasties and a fig leaf at fifty bucks a pop."

"Frank . . ." Alicia began warningly.

"What 'Frank'? You think I shouldn't talk like that in front of the kids? You think they're innocents? Your daughter doesn't listen to that metal crap all the time. She can hear when she wants to. And I'm not going to have her parading around some casino pool in those new suits. They don't hide anything. She can wear 'em in the room if she wants, but that's it."

"Frank, this is Las Vegas we're going to, remember? The hotels are full of showgirls and would-be actresses. You really think anyone's going to pay any attention to a sixteen-year-old?" She looked back. "No offense, darling."

"Oh, gee, Mom, none taken," said her daughter sardonically. "When we get there I'll damn well dress as I please."

"What? What was that?" Frank managed a furious glance backward. "What did you say, young lady?"

"Frank, please keep your eyes on the road." Alicia hastily examined the map, looked out her window with forced excitement in her voice. "Oh, look! See those mountains over there?"

Not really wanting to look but willing to change the subject, Wendy turned boredly without removing her headset to peer out the long window above the convertible couch. Steven scrambled onto his knees to do likewise.

"What about them?" She turned up the volume on the tape player slightly, willing to meet her mother halfway but in no mood for a geology lecture.

Alicia double-checked the map. "They're called the Devil's Playground."

Wendy slumped, burdened by the sheer weight of her parents' presence. "Whoopie."

"But just look at them." Alicia was trying real hard, Frank knew, and he loved her for it. "Isn't it fascinating to wonder how a place like that could get such a name?"

"Yeah, kinda," said Steven slowly, displaying interest in something other than food and his toys for the first time in the last hundred miles.

His sister eyed him in surprise. "Give me a break, little brother." She found herself staring through the glass in spite of herself. "There's nothing out there, Mom. Just like there's been nothing out there since we left L.A."

"But the *name*. Can't you just see some poor prospector or hunter struggling through this awful country by himself, without freeways and hamburger stands and gas stations to fall back on? That's who probably named this place."

"Maybe it was a thermometer salesman," Frank quipped, feeling a little better now that the decision had been made. "Or some old guy with a burro and a beard who spent his whole life looking to make the big strike."

"Yes," said Alicia. "This whole part of the country is covered with names like that, and the bones of the people who bestowed them."

"Honestly, you two." Wendy popped a stick of gum in her mouth, extracting it from its package as neatly as a woodpecker would siphon a grub from beneath the bark of an elm. "Probably named by some guy who inherited a couple thousand acres out here. Maybe he thought it would bring tourists. 'Come see the Devil's Playground. Pan for gold. Touch a cactus. Souvenirs, cold cherry cider, hot dogs, kids eat free.' That's where your weird names come from."

"You're not much of a romantic." Frank refused to let her upset him. "I thought all girls your age were supposed to be romantics."

"Oh, we are, Pops, we are. But not about nowhere dumpos

like this. Now, if Bon Jovi or Roger Hornsby were giving a concert out here, I'd get real romantic.'' She gestured at the blasted landscape visible through the window. ''Get real. The name's the only thing distinctive about this place. It looks just like the last hundred miles we've driven and just like the next hundred miles will look.'' She blew a bubble, let it burst, sucked the pink latex back through her teeth.

Alicia settled back in her seat, the expression on her face saying ''I tried.'' Frank had nothing to add. As a father he was coming to appreciate that the world-view of sixteen-year-old girls was somewhat limited.

Though Wendy's disinterest continued, her mother's hypothesizing had stimulated Steven. He was still staring avidly out the side window. So the line about the wandering prospector had been useful after all, Frank mused, though his son was more likely conjuring up visions of cowboys and Indians. Times had changed. These days all the kids wanted to be the Indians. He couldn't remember who'd once told him that history was like a flapjack. As soon as it was done on one side, somebody would flip it over to expose the untouched obverse, whereupon a new raft of eager revisers would set to rewriting a period anew. As soon as it got cold, it would get flipped again.

Pity they were driving from L.A. instead of, say, Utah. They could have driven through the Grand Canyon or Zion or Bryce instead of this boring, eventless terrain. They'd flown over the Mojave many times and, much as he wanted to believe otherwise, he was coming to realize that this part of the country was better viewed from the air. Mountains, canyons, even the plant life had a skeletal aspect. It was as if the upper foot of the planet here had been stripped away, as though the landscape had been scoured by an immense sandblaster.

Only the government had a use for this kind of country, chopping it up into military reservations larger than many states. One percent utilized, ninety-nine percent ignored. Only the air had real value, bright and clear. Mountains that appeared to crowd the highway were actually many miles away. It caused a man to concentrate on the little things. When you built an important business with your own hands you became a stickler for detail. Maybe that was why he spent so much time on each ocotillo, each Joshua tree and prickly pear.

Tough little suckers, he thought. He could appreciate them even if his family could not.

"How much further, Dad?"

Frank blinked behind his sunglasses. He'd been daydreaming. His gaze dropped to the odometer. "Twenty miles. Twenty minutes, kiddo."

Steven nodded, spoke hesitantly. "Do you think they'll have . . . ?"

"No, I don't think they'll have a McDonald's. The whole town of Baker is about the size of your school. Don't tell me you're out of food already."

"It's all cookies and stuff, Dad. I'm really hungry."

"It's close to lunchtime," Alicia pointed out, "and it would be nice to eat in a restaurant. I can throw something together, of course, but . . ."

"No, no, everybody's made their feelings perfectly clear. We'll see what they've got to offer, kiddo. If there's a halfway clean-looking café we'll stop. I promise."

"All right!"

Truth was, Frank was feeling hungry himself. Could be this journeying by motor home wasn't exactly as the salesman who'd rented it to him had described it.

Near noon and the sun was high overhead. Nowhere for man or beast to hide. The thermometer flirted with the hundred mark. Thank God it was only May. In a few weeks a hundred would be a cool day out here.

It was hot enough, though, for the sight of a lone figure standing by the side of the road to startle him. He began to slow down, barely realizing he was doing so.

2

I T TOOK A MOMENT for Alicia to react. She made his name into an extended question. "Frank?"

He nodded. "Some fool hitchhiking."

She leaned forward. The solitary shape was unmistakable now, motionless as a monument. "You aren't thinking of picking him up?"

"Why not? Everybody's so bored, maybe some company would add a little excitement. I could do with some conversation."

His wife didn't try to conceal her anxiety. "What kind of person would be hitchhiking way out here in the middle of nowhere?"

"Someone trying to get to somewhere." He took a perverse delight in her obvious unease. "That's something that would be interesting to find out. Besides, I wouldn't leave a dog on the side of the road on a day like this." He squinted as he rode down on the brake. "Don't see any luggage. Maybe he had a breakdown. Good thing we came along."

"Frank, I don't know if this is such a good idea."

Steven had his nose pressed against the window. Conscious that something out of the ordinary was taking place, Wendy had removed her headphones and had actually turned off her Walkman.

If he hadn't been so fed up with his family Frank would ordinarily have cruised on past, but he was ready to do anything to shake them out of their lethargy. Now he found himself wondering if maybe Alicia wasn't right and he was about to do something foolish. Certainly the absence of any luggage was peculiar. He scanned the ground bordering the road, but there was no place for malign accomplices to hide. The skinny bushes concealed nothing. There were no large boulders and the ground was flat.

If his supposition was correct and the hitcher's vehicle had broken down somewhere close by, their ride-to-be had already disobeyed the first rule of desert survival: namely, to stay with your car. The people who died out here were the ones who naively thought they could walk to safety. No sign of a stalled vehicle, though. An off-road machine, maybe, stuck somewhere out in the sand. He strained but could see only isolated plant growth spotting dirty beige terrain. A couple of beer cans slowly disintegrated in the sun amid a tiara of crumpled plastic packaging.

As he pulled over, the hitchhiker turned to face them. The right hand which had been extended in the classic hitcher's pose, hand out, thumb up, now fell to the figure's side. Wendy had come forward to lean between her parents for a better view.

"How old is he?"

Frank's eyes widened slightly. It was Alicia who replied. "It doesn't look like a 'he,' dear." She turned to her husband. "I apologize, Frank."

"What?" His eyes followed the lone figure as it walked slowly toward them.

"It's probably a good thing you stopped. She's in trouble or she wouldn't be out here alone like this. I wonder what happened. I wonder where her car is?"

"Bet she had a fight with her boyfriend," said Wendy. "Bet he kicked her out and left her here."

"If so, it wasn't long ago." Frank stopped staring. "She's not even sweating."

Alicia eyed him curiously. "I didn't think your eyesight was that good, *dear*."

Frank ignored the gentle dig. "Wendy, get the door for the lady."

His daughter nodded vigorously and moved to do so.

Compared to the air-conditioned interior of the motor home, the air that came flowing through the open door had the force of blast furnace exhaust. Wendy automatically retreated from it. As she stepped back, the hitchhiker climbed in, thoughtfully closing the door behind her.

She was Wendy's height and slim as a reed. It was impossible to tell if the purple and gold scarf she wore wound around her head was a separate piece of clothing or merely part of her sari-like dress. Wispy folds of multihued silk wrapped round and round her body, tenuous as cirrus clouds. They moved slightly in the blast of air-conditioning, like sleeping snakes. There was just a hint of dark skin beneath, and none of undergarments. Even as he stared, a layer of silk fell into place, leaving Frank to wonder if he'd seen anything at all.

He'd been wrong about something else. The hitchhiker had only looked cool. Beads of sweat hung like flattened pearls from her dark forehead. She used a hand to wipe them away. As she did so she moved some of the silk, revealing thin, brilliantly blond hair. It fell almost to her feet, a golden cascade incongruous against her olivine skin.

"No wonder she's hot," Alicia murmured. "Look at all that hair."

The woman must have overheard because she turned to look at them and smiled. Frank saw she had violet eyes. The only other woman Frank knew of who had violet eyes was Elizabeth Taylor. He'd always suspected it to be a trick of glamour photography. But this young woman's eyes were a light violet, the color of tanzanite. They were too large for that small, heart-shaped face, like the eyes of those Keene paintings that had been so popular back in the sixties. Big-eyed children and dogs. The mouth was tiny, the nose and chin almost nonexistent. Everything was overwhelmed by those eyes.

Her head and neck appeared almost too thin to support the weight of all that hair, but closer inspection revealed that while extraordinarily long, those gleaming blond tresses were thin and wispy, the ends trailing off to near invisibility.

"It's not so very uncomfortable," she said in reply to Alicia's observation. Her voice was high-pitched, ethereal. Not frail. Just soft and distant.

Quit staring, Frank told himself. She's just a small-boned little gal. No pointed ears and no tendrils sprouting from her forehead. Not much to her at all. What was it Spencer Tracy had said about Katharine Hepburn? "Not much, but what there is is choice." He felt himself flush, turned back to face the dash.

"I really like your clothes." Diplomacy is an alien conception to sixteen-year-olds. "And, oh, wow, check out these nails, Mom!" Wendy's eyes were wide, admiring.

The woman smiled and held up her right hand. Frank saw that each of her inch-long fingernails was painted a different iridescent hue. She raised her other hand, holding them side by side, the ends of her fingers forming a perfect rainbow from left thumb to right. Placed next to one another like that, the colors appeared to flow into each other. He wondered if her toenails were similarly decorated. Her feet were concealed by slipper-like shoes.

He was still trying to reconcile the Mediterranean coloring with that blond hair. Blondes were inordinately popular among his Hispanic employees. While her coloring it was a possibility, the pale golden hue looked natural to him. Somehow he doubted a woman wanting to dye her hair would take the color to such an extreme. He hunted in vain for buttons, zippers, hooks, saw not even a safety pin, and wondered how the loose assemblage of veils stayed in place.

Wendy hadn't stopped talking. "Do you do your own makeup?"

"Makeup? Oh, you mean these." She held out one hand. Light exploded off the glittering, almost transparent polish. "I do most everything myself."

That's when Frank took note of the lavender eyeshadow and faintly purple lipstick. On this woman it looked right, though he'd never been big on makeup himself. Neither had Alicia, though Wendy was a real bear on the subject. Good thing the woman's skin wasn't as fair as her hair, caught out on a desert highway the way she'd been. It struck him that the thin silk would protect its wearer from the sun's rays while still allowing any breezes to circulate.

She had backed up next to the couch. "May I sit?"

"Sure, sit anywhere," Frank told her expansively. "Don't mind the kids. They spend most of their time on the floor anyway."

The couch was directly behind Alicia's chair. Alicia swiveled around to face their guest, who extracted a tortoise-shell compact from the folds of her clothing and began to comb her hair.

"Could I do that?" asked Wendy eagerly.

"Thank you, but not now. Perhaps later." She was working on the ends, untangling them with the comb while the children gaped at her.

It dawned on Frank there was no reason to sit there idling in the middle of the desert with the air conditioner running on high. He checked the sideview mirror, pulled back out into the slow lane.

"Car break down?" The big Winnebago slowly crawled back toward cruising speed.

"No. I have been traveling with the helpful, as you found me, for quite a long time."

Alicia sounded disapproving. "You shouldn't be doing that. Especially way out here, and without any luggage."

"I always like to travel light." Their guest shook her head. A simple necklace of purple beads flashed light from her throat. Frank struggled to remember his high school geology. Amethyst, most likely. Unfaceted, it would be very inexpensive. She wore a matching ring on the long finger of her right hand. Hardly a target for prospective muggers, he mused.

That's when he realized she wasn't even carrying a purse. That was more than just peculiar. He could rationalize the absence of baggage, but he'd never seen a woman without a purse. Not even a poor woman down on her luck.

Inquiring would have been impolite and, besides, he was sure Alicia would notice it eventually and ask.

"Neat outfit," Wendy was saying. "I'll bet it's comfortable."

"Comfortable enough." The woman looked past her. "Might you have something to drink? I am a little thirsty."

"Inconsiderate of me." Alicia was honestly upset with herself. "I should have asked you right away."

"I'll get it." Wendy moved to the fridge. "What would you like? We've got Coke, cherry RC, kiwi soda, ginger ale, orange juice."

"Some cold water would be most welcome," said the woman gratefully.

"How 'bout some lemonade?" chirped Steven. "Hey, I'd like some lemonade."

"Get it yourself." Wendy made a face at him, replaced it with a wide smile as she looked back at their guest. "With ice?"

"Ice would be wonderful." The woman looked around,

taking in her surroundings for the first time. "These odd vehicles and their luxuries. Quite extraordinary." Her voice trailed away, each word not so much ending as fading like a puff from a silver flute.

"You interested in cars?" Frank asked conversationally.

"I am interested in everything."

Frank set the cruise control and relaxed. In a little while they'd reach Baker, pull off, and find someplace to have lunch. By tilting the overhead rearview mirror down slightly he could watch as Wendy handed the woman a plastic glass full of cold water. Ice cubes clinked against the yellow acrylic. The hitchhiker sipped delicately instead of gulping. She reminded Frank of a doe lapping at a forest stream. He knew about deer drinking from streams because his chain of sporting goods stores sold a lot of hunting rifles. His gaze traveled down their visitor's body, a petite enigma wrapped in rainbow silks.

Knock it off, he told himself. This isn't a wholesalers' convention and your wife and kids are with you. You're just giving a stranger a lift. That she happens to be uncommonly beautiful has nothing to do with it. Your thoughts were virtuous before you got a look at her. Keep 'em that way.

As the woman sipped ice water Wendy reached out to finger a trailing flap of orange fantasy.

"Ow—hey!" She drew back her fingers, shaking her hand. "I got a shock."

"Static electricity." The woman lowered her glass and smiled reassuringly. "Touch again if you want."

Wendy looked uncertain. "You sure?"

"It'll be okay. Go ahead."

This time Wendy was able to rub the thin material between thumb and forefinger. "It's so soft. Where'd you find it? Rodeo Drive, I bet. Or maybe San Marino? There are some neat new shops in San Marino."

The woman shook her head. "Not on Rodeo Drive and not in San Marino."

Frank struggled to place their passenger. She didn't look a day over twenty-six, but her manner of speaking suggested someone a lot older. Or non-American.

"It's really rad. How many pieces in it?"

The hitchhiker glanced down at herself. "Just one piece."

"Aw, c'mon! Really? How does it stay in place, like here."
Wendy tugged at the waistband of her jeans.

"Practice, and knowing what you're doing." Abruptly she
turned her head to look forward, straight at the rearview mirror
that was providing Frank with his view.

There was a brief flash of light, as though the mirror had
unexpectedly jerked around to catch the sun. Frank blinked.
Reflection from something in the road, he told himself. She hadn't
moved.

"I want to thank you, Mr. . . . ?"

"Sonderberg. Frank Sonderberg. My wife Alicia, our daughter Wendy, son Steven."

"Hi," said the boy.

"Hello yourself, little man." Steven beamed.

"How long were you waiting before we picked you up?"
Wendy wanted to know.

"Quite a while. I was beginning to think no one would stop
for me, and my destination is too far to walk."

"Anywhere out here is too far to walk." Wendy shifted on the
couch. "Couldn't you have found some shade?"

"There is no shade out there." The woman's voice was
solemn. "No place to hide."

"You're damn lucky we did stop." Frank glanced at his wife.
"Told you we were doing a good deed. How far you going?" he
called out.

"We're going to Las Vegas," said Steven helpfully. "I'm
gonna play video games all day and go swimming until I fall
asleep!"

"You are not going to play video games all day, Steven."
Alicia tried hard not to make it sound reproachful. "You need to
get some exercise."

You need to get off your fat little butt once in a while, Frank
murmured to himself.

"You wouldn't be interested in where I'm going," the hitchhiker
told him.

"I would!" said Steven.

The woman looked back down at him. "You might at that."
She held her glass out to Wendy. "Perhaps I will have some of that
lemonade."

"Sure. We have lots."

"What am I thinking of?" The woman rose from the couch in a single, flowing motion. "Let me help." She followed Wendy back into the compact kitchen. Alicia watched them dig the lemonade out of the refrigerator, turned her chair toward her husband.

"Frank, I wonder if we did the right thing."

"What . . . ?" He lowered his voice. "What are you talking about? You saw her, standing out there all by herself. If we hadn't picked her up she could be in serious trouble by tonight." He gestured at the road. "Rides look about as scarce as she said they were."

"Some trucker would have stopped for her," Alicia declared with conviction. "She's pretty. I'm surprised one hadn't picked her up already."

"You can't tell she's pretty until you see her up close," Frank pointed out, "and there haven't been that many trucks, either. As soon as it starts getting hot like this they try running at night. What's wrong with helping someone in trouble?"

"It's not like you, Frank. You never stop for hitchhikers."

"So this is my trip for doing different things. Don't tell me you're worried about her? Look at her. She's barely as big as Wendy."

"I don't mean that. It's the way she talks. So soft, you can hardly hear her."

"Kind of nice for a change, isn't it? Maybe the kids'll pick up on it."

"Those strange clothes she's wearing, and not having any luggage, not even a purse."

"Yeah, I noticed. So she's down on her luck or something. None of our business. We're just giving her a lift. That doesn't entitle us to know her life story."

Alicia turned her chair full around so she was facing forward once more. "Maybe she's a hippie or something."

Frank almost laughed aloud. "You've been watching too much TV, sweetheart. Hippies are like dinosaurs. They're both extinct."

"Then what if she's a drug addict or like that?"

Her husband made a disgusted noise. Alicia folded her arms, refusing to back down.

"I'm just saying there's something abnormal about her. You

can tell just by looking at her."

"Poor kid probably hasn't had a decent meal in no telling how long. Skinny as a rail."

"Not so skinny," said Alicia carefully, "though she is on the slim side. Doesn't that go with taking drugs?"

"So I've heard. It also goes with exercise, dieting, and good genes. A few days out in this country would sweat poundage off anybody."

"Hush. She's coming back." Alicia pretended to find something of interest in the unchanging scenery.

Frank shook his head. Funny gal, his Alicia. Calm, composed, charming, and ever ready to see a conspiracy in everything from a cluster of Libyans to a line of talkative nuns. A glance upward revealed that their guest had resumed her seat on the couch, holding her lemonade like a glass of rare wine. She was smiling and whispering to Wendy, who giggled and whispered back. He wondered what they were chatting about. As the thought left his mind the hitchhiker looked toward him. Guiltily he dropped his eyes from the mirror.

"Since all of you have introduced yourselves I suppose the turn is mine. My name is Mohostosocia." Her tongue twisted around the syllables, adding at least two impossible inflections. Frank tried and failed to place the accent. No linguist he. Central European at a quick guess, possibly Slavic. Certainly not Spanish, which he had a nongrammatical but efficient grasp of. "Now that we are all friends, though, you may call me Mouse."

Wendy giggled. Steven grinned. "We've got some cheese, if you want."

"Steven!" His sister took a swipe at him and he was forced to duck.

"It is all right. As a matter of fact," she said, staring at the mesmerized boy out of strangely transparent eyes, "I do like cheese. Swiss, colby, longhorn, Brie, Gruyère, Gouda, shannon—"

"I like American!" said Steven proudly, interrupting before she could finish.

"Most little boys like you do, I understand."

"I'm not a little boy. I'm eleven."

"Ten," Alicia said patiently.

"I'll be eleven in six months." Steven subsided, but only slightly.

"I stand corrected. You are not a little boy."

Steven looked mollified. Frank was straining to listen to the conversation. Though Mouse's couch wasn't far behind the front seats, her breathy voice tended to get lost in the motor home's copious interior.

With a start he realized that their guest was far more interesting than anything else they'd encountered since commencing this ill-conceived journey. He wasn't sure about Alicia, but he found her fascinating. So did his daughter. As for Steven, the boy was giving the woman the sort of attention he usually reserved only for fried foods and large desserts. It was easy to understand. That exquisite and mysterious face, the unknown figure enshrouded in yards of iridescent silk, the whispery, musical voice—those could hypnotize a ten-year-old boy as easily as they could a much older male.

"Frank, you're drifting over the center line again."

"What? Sorry, hon." He conscientiously eased the motor home back into the slow lane. Steven could freely fall under Mouse's spell. Frank had to drive.

Alicia looked back, made an effort to be pleasant. "Where are you from?"

Mouse turned slightly on the couch to wave indifferently at the rear of the motor home. "Back that way."

Los Angeles? It made sense, Frank knew. On Hollywood or Sunset boulevards her attire would be positively subdued.

"No. Farther than that. Farther"—she hesitated for a fraction of a second—"south."

He grinned to himself. Let her affect an air of mystery if that was her pleasure. "Where you headed?"

Once again Steven spoke before she had a chance to answer. "We're on vacation already 'cause we go to private school, so we get out earlier than the other kids."

"That's nice," said Mouse. "Myself hasn't had a vacation in quite some time."

"What is it you do?" Alicia asked her.

"I help others out of their troubles."

Frank guffawed. "In Vegas? No wonder you don't get any time off. That's a town where just about everybody needs help."

"No, not in Las Vegas. I'm not going there. I am going to the Vanishing Point."

"Vanishing Point." His brows drew together in thought. "A lot of little towns up the interstate between Vegas and Salt Lake. Never gone that far north ourselves, but I see them on the map. Cedar City, St. George, Littlefield, even a place called Hurricane." He tried to see the fine detail on the map stuck to the dash. "Vanishing Point doesn't ring any bells."

"It's quite small and very big." Mouse wasn't smiling and Frank couldn't tell if she was making a joke or not. "I would not be surprised if your map omits it, though one never knows."

"What's in Vanishing Point?" He drove with one hand resting easily on the wheel, the cruise control doing the drudge work.

"My task."

"Helping somebody with a problem?"

She nodded. "I must try to regulate the Spinner."

"You a psychologist of some kind?" He'd always envisioned psychologists, male or female, in severe business suits. Of course, there were all kinds of unorthodox philosophies of mental health abroad in the land, especially if that land was Southern California. "Vanishing Point. Nevada or Utah?"

"Yes," she said, replying without answering. "I am afraid I am the only one practiced enough to do it."

"You wouldn't expect to see a psychologist hitchhiking," said Alicia tartly.

"It is not my preferred mode of travel. In this instance circumstances compelled me to adopt this method of reaching my destination. I really cannot thank you enough for picking me up."

Her gratitude was so obvious and heartfelt that Alicia's suspicions were dampened. Frank kept trying to read the small print on the map.

"I bet I've seen it on the Utah map."

"We're only going as far as Las Vegas," Alicia informed their rider.

"I understand. I will travel with you as far as you will take me and go the rest of the way on my own. I am used to traveling on my own."

"Then the least we can do is take you all the way into Vegas." Frank gave Alicia a the-matter-is-settled look.

As her father concentrated on his driving, Wendy moved closer to their guest, lowering her voice to an anxious whisper.

"C'mon, now, where'd you get all that great stuff?" She tentatively ran fingers over the material again. "I bet this is imported. Indian?"

"Not Indian." Mouse ran an index finger down the front of her dress. "My clothing is woven from the fabric of existence, which is very fine and light and quite stable." Her hand rose. Delicate, dark fingers touched the single strand of purple beads that hung from her neck. "This is the blood of past transgressions. The past is always bleeding, I fear. At long intervals I have to add a new bead, so that my emotions keep pace with what has gone before. I remember when this necklace was but a bracelet." She extended a leg, revealing ankle and slipper.

"My shoes are very strong and very soft, so that my passing disturbs the earth as little as possible. I am careful not to touch it any more often than is necessary. Floating is easier than walking anyway." She smiled at the girl next to her. "Have you ever tried floating?"

"Not me, but some of my friends have. You know, you're really weird. But I like you."

"I like you, too, Wendy." She surveyed her surroundings. "I like all of you."

"Except for my little brother," Wendy added distastefully. "Nobody can like him."

Mouse laughed; fingertips teasing the keys of an electric piano. "I suppose it is not the nature of elder sisters to like younger brothers. Nevertheless, you should be nice to him. What elder sisters fail to realize is that little brothers have a tendency to become very big brothers as they mature. Big brothers of any age can be very nice to have around."

"Yeah, that's what Mom keeps telling me." Wendy studied the radiant material of her new friend's dress. " 'Fabric of existence,' huh? There's so many brand names around these days, you can't keep up. Not Indian, okay, but I still bet it's imported."

Mouse nodded slightly. Her every movement was barely more than a suggestion, yet in no ways uncertain. "You could say that, after a fashion."

"After a fashion—hey, a joke, right? You like punk?"

"I like anything that makes people smile or feel better about themselves."

Alicia was trying to make small talk with Frank and listen in on her daughter's conversation at the same time. Though she had excellent hearing, she was unable to make out more than an occasional word or phrase. Wendy seemed to have lowered her own voice to match that of their guest. Whatever the hitchhiker was saying it appeared to enrapture the teenager.

She would have felt better about the situation if she could have heard more. No telling what sort of nonsense this half-wild young woman they'd picked up in the middle of the desert might be pouring into Wendy's ear. There was no point in trying to forbid the conversation. Wendy would ignore any directive so blatant and the motor home was too small to isolate someone anyhow. Alicia decided she was being silly. Strange their guest might be, but she'd been nothing if not friendly and polite, not to mention effusively grateful for the lift. She had a strange but captivating personality, like some exotic fish washed up on a public beach amid the empty beer cans and plastic bags. Certainly she'd captivated Frank and the kids.

If only she could be sure their guest wasn't into drugs. Wendy was at an impressionable age.

If I can't forbid conversation, she thought, at least I can participate in it.

"You said you help others but that you're not a psychologist. That doesn't leave a whole lot. Are you some kind of traveling social worker?"

"Something like that." Mouse was unable or unwilling to answer any personal inquiries directly. "I just help others feel better."

"I know. You've already said that." This time Alicia was determined not to be put off. "But just how do you go about doing that? I mean, exactly what kind of therapy do you employ?"

"Musical. I am a singer."

"A singer, wow!" said Wendy.

"A singer." Steven sounded disappointed. He'd been hoping their beautiful visitor was something much more mysterious. A spy, like, or a lady commando. Although spies and commandos usually didn't help people to feel better.

If Alicia had been hoping that pinning a specific profession on the hitchhiker would dilute her daughter's interest, she found Mouse's admission had just the opposite effect.

"I've never met anyone who sang professionally before,"

Wendy was saying rapidly. "I mean, I've got friends who want to and a couple of the kids at school have parents who are pretty big in show business, but they're not singers. What do you sing? I know! The way you dress and the kind of voice you've got, I bet you're a lot like Stevie Nicks."

"Who is Stevie Nicks?" asked Mouse politely.

"You don't know who Stevie Nicks is?" Wendy hesitated, then grinned broadly. "You're putting me on, right? Sure you are. Hey, could you sing something for us?"

"Oh, I don't think it's right to ask something like that." Alicia was beginning to wonder if she mightn't have pressed her inquiry too far.

"Your mother's right." Frank had been listening while driving. "We don't want to embarrass our guest."

"Besides," said Steven snidely, "she doesn't have a band. Every singer's gotta have a band."

That's my boy, Frank thought admiringly. An overweight junk food junkie he is, but he's got brains. He listens to stuff between the commercials.

"I do not use a band," said Mouse. For a moment her expression turned dreamy. "It helps, but it is very rare I find musicians who know how to play just the right music. I usually have to sing a cappella."

"A cappella? What's that?" Steven wondered.

"Without accompaniment." Mouse stared down at him, then back at Wendy. "I would be happy to sing you a little tune. It is what I do."

Alicia's bluff had been called, but once Mouse began to sing she no longer minded. She was as enthralled by the music as the rest of her family.

It was a wordless song Mouse sang. Alicia's formal musical education extended to a single music appreciation class taken in the tenth grade. Despite that, she knew the hitchhiker's range was extraordinary. The soprano that flowed from Mouse's throat was pure as spring ice, and just as clear. In actuality Mouse's voice was effortlessly spanning six octaves. This was quite impossible, but no one in the motor home knew enough about music to realize it. They knew only that the sweet sounds that filled the motor home were achingly lovely.

Mouse sang without visible effort. Beneath the folds of silk her chest did not seem to rise and fall with each breath. Sometimes her song imitated the sounds of waves lapping at a beach. The slower sections reminded Frank of pictures he'd seen of South Pacific lagoons, pristine sheets of water, flat as mirrors, disturbed only by the fleeting musical ping of a fish breaking the surface.

Individual notes rippled and flashed through the underlying melody, like brightly colored tropical fish darting among a coral reef. Bells and chimes echoed in the air, lingered in the ear. Certain notes were like pebbles tossed in a pond, each initial sound framed by spreading, decreasing vibrations.

As the last of the song faded to silence an exquisite yet disturbing chill ran through his spine.

Mouse closed her eyes. She'd kept them open while singing. Now she gathered herself as she relaxed. Throughout it all her body had hardly moved. Steven and Wendy sat as if gently frozen. Even television couldn't hold Steven like that. No one spoke until the last echo of the final note had finally died, dissipating itself against the metal walls. Frank cleared his throat, was surprised how dry it was. It was almost as if he'd forgotten to breathe or swallow for the duration of the song.

"That was one of the most beautiful things I've ever heard in my life," he said slowly. "Maybe *the* most beautiful thing. I mean, I'm no music expert or anything like that, but I know what I like. And I liked that."

"I am pleased you did." Mouse sipped her lemonade. "I like to sing. To sing for pleasure, as now, is fun. When I do my work it can be something of a strain. The notes you cannot hear are difficult to sing."

Frank chuckled good-naturedly. "Now how can you sing notes nobody can hear? If we can't hear them, that means you can't either, and if you can't hear them, then how do you know they're being sung?"

"Vibrations. Those are the most beautiful notes of all. You must feel what you cannot hear."

"I don't know about that, but I know I heard what I felt. How about it, kids? Not heavy metal, but..."

"It was amazing." Wendy was gazing at their guest out of worshipful eyes.

"Yeah, pretty," said Steven, equally overwhelmed if not as descriptive.

Wendy's expression turned sly. "I just figured it out. You *are* going to Las Vegas."

"She said she wasn't, kiddo," said Frank.

"I'll bet she is, Pops. I'll bet she was just too shy to tell us. That's why you didn't recognize this Vanishing Point place. In art class they told us the vanishing point is where all the lines on a drawing meet. It sounds like a perfect name for a club."

The Vanishing Point. You had to hand it to his daughter, Frank thought. Considering where their old man had come from they'd turned out damn bright. Of course it was a nightclub, or something similar. Mouse was a young singer, maybe just trying to get started. She'd landed this important gig in Vegas but didn't have the bucks to get there. So she'd decided to hitch it across the desert.

"I mean," Wendy was saying, "it's so *obvious*. Anybody can see you're good enough to sing professionally. I'm right, aren't I?"

Mouse smiled enigmatically, then abruptly put a small hand to her forehead. Those expansive violet eyes closed tightly. Lines appeared on that perfect face.

"What's wrong?" Wendy was suddenly concerned. "You okay?"

Mouse's hand fell from her forehead and she managed another smile. "I just need to rest. My journey thus far has been a long and difficult one. Singing is exhausting."

"Standing out in that heat would knock anyone for a loop." Frank glanced at Alicia, who spoke up reluctantly.

"The big bed is in the back. It'll be quieter there." She tried to set her suspicions and concerns aside. "You lie down for as long as you like. Shall we wake you when we get to Baker?"

"Whatever you will be comfortable with," Mouse replied as she stood. "I just need some sleep. And this." She hefted the half-empty glass of lemonade.

"There are holders for glasses and stuff built into the headboard," Wendy informed her. "They're kinda neat. You won't spill anything if we hit a bump. I'll show you." She scrambled to her feet.

Mouse followed, pausing and turning outside the bedroom door. "Thank you many times afresh. For your kindness and caring."

"Hey, enough already," said Frank. "We've got plenty of room and we were going the same way anyhow, right?"

"The same way. Yes." Mouse wore an odd expression as she spoke.

"Thanks for the song."

"I hope I may be able to sing for you again some time soon." She followed Wendy into the bedroom.

Alicia waited until she was certain their guest couldn't overhear before muttering to her husband. "Now no matter what you think of her musical talents, Frank, that is one peculiar young woman."

"Who'd you expect to find hitchhiking in the middle of the Mojave? Someone from your bridge club? Encounters like this are what make life interesting." He was feeling pleased with himself.

"More than interesting," Alicia argued. "You're fascinated by her. So are the children."

"Aren't you, sweetheart? Who knows? We may have given a helping hand to a budding star. With a voice like that she could be on the Carson show in a couple of months. Then we can say we picked her up in the back of beyond and gave her a hand when nobody knew who she was." He paused, then added, "Don't tell me she's still got you worrying?"

Alicia leaned back in the captain's chair. "Not worried, exactly. It's just she's so *strange*."

"This from a woman who lives in L.A.? The rest of the country thinks everybody who lives in Southern California is strange."

"She must have some luggage somewhere."

"I don't remember that being in the Constitution. And in spite of what you've been thinking, she's no doper."

"How can you tell, Frank? How can you be sure?"

He thought fast. "If she was on something, regular, like an addict, there's no way she could sing a song like that. You need real breath control and concentration."

"You're right." Alicia sounded relieved. "I hadn't thought of that." Frank had the knack of always saying the right thing. Her husband wasn't particularly brilliant, but he had a way of going right to the heart of a problem. As he'd once told her, he wasn't smart enough to be distracted by subtleties. It was one of the things that had made him such a successful businessman. No, Mouse couldn't have sung like that if she'd been high.

"Then let's relax. We've decided what we're going to do and everybody's happy and we've even managed a good deed for the day. I wonder," he said thoughtfully, "if she'd let us record some of her music. We can borrow your daughter's tape recorder, if you can pry those earphones off her head for an hour or two."

"If she's really serious about a show business career she might not want somebody taping her compositions, Frank."

He shrugged. "No harm in asking. I might even be able to help her out when we get home. We've got some pretty big names who shop in the Westwood and Valley stores. I could try to make a few contacts for her."

"Let's not get too involved, dear. We really don't know anything about her yet."

"There you go, worrying again. How could that hurt? You've seen how grateful she is just for a lift. She's an interesting young gal who's having a hard time making it. Her being a singer explains a lot. Some of these young people trying to break into the business can't afford but one decent set of clothes. They travel in it, audition in it, perform in it, and sleep naked." He lowered his voice further. "Wonder when's the last time she had a decent meal."

Alicia gave it one last try. "Frank, you're a good-hearted man. It's one of the reasons I fell in love with you." She reached across to pat his arm. "But you can't go involving yourself in the problems of everyone you meet."

"I've no intention of involving myself in the problems of *everyone* I meet. But I can be selective, can't I? I wish there'd been someone to give the two of us a helping hand when we were starting out. Just because there wasn't doesn't mean I can't help somebody if I'm given the chance."

"You've helped already. You picked her up and you're taking her closer to her destination. If Wendy's right and this Vanishing Point is a club, I'm sure she'll tell us when we get to the city. We can drop her off right by the front door. That's a big enough favor to perform."

"What's the matter, Alicia? Don't you like her? She could be our Wendy ten years older."

"God forbid! Are you sure you haven't been talking to those 'big names' you mentioned?"

He shook his head. "Relax, hon. I'm interested in stomach crunchers and basketballs and running shoes. Show biz ain't for me. I'm smart enough to know that. People are always trying to get me to invest in their 'projects.' The only projects I'm interested in investing in are newer and bigger stores." He blew her a quick kiss. "You're all the bright life I want."

They were both silent for a while. Then Frank gestured cheerfully toward the sign coming up fast on their right. "What we need is a break."

Alicia frowned at the sand-scoured marker.

DEVIL'S PLAYGROUND
1 Mile
GAS—EAT

"I thought we weren't going to stop until we got to Baker?"

"This'll be more interesting." He was slowing gradually, lining up with the off ramp. "The station in Baker'll be full of screaming rug rats and overheated people with overheated tempers. This looks quiet."

Alicia strained to see as they rolled up to the stop sign at the crest of the off ramp. "It looks dead. I don't see anybody at all."

3

THE STATION LOOKED like it
had been built in the twenties
or thirties, walls of local vol-
canic rock mortared together, an archaic arch reaching out to the
twin pumps like a dirty stucco hand.

"Bet this was here on the old highway before the interstate
was put through," Frank commented as he pulled across the access
road and up to the pumps. "We need some gas anyway if we're
going to run the rest of the way straight through to Vegas."

Alicia checked the gauge and frowned. "But we just filled up
back in Barstow. We haven't come anywhere near far enough to
burn up that much gas."

Frank put the transmission into park. "We've been climbing
all the way and running the air conditioner on high. It's a lot hotter
here than it was in L.A. You know how these things burn fuel."

"I didn't think we'd come up that far, but you're right. What
do I know about motor homes?" She leaned forward and studied
the station through the window. "Doesn't look like it's been very
well kept up."

"Ahhhh, c'mon," he chided her. "You're intrigued and you
know it." He leaned close, trying to see past her. "I'll bet whoever
runs this place has rattler skins on the walls and a stuffed deer head
over the cash register. I could do with a cold beer."

"We have a whole refrigerator full of beer," she reminded him.

He sat back, disappointed. "There you go, taking all the romance out of it. Anyway, we do need the unleaded. Then it's a straight shot all the way across the border and into Vegas. I promise. This is my last chance to show the kids something different, the last time we'll stop."

"Not if we keep gulping gas at this rate," she pointed out as she moved her legs so he could pass.

It was pretty run-down, he had to admit as he stepped out of the motor home and into the heat. One of those ancient old gas stations that used to line the state highways of the Southwest made redundant by the bypassing interstates. This one had managed to hang on because it was fortunate enough to sit next to an off ramp. Closer inspection confirmed his initial appraisal.

It was all dark volcanic rock and cement, the pitted round stones garish in their setting of faded concrete. The twin gas pumps looked brand-new, though, in striking contrast to the cracked cement island on which they sat. Whoever owned the place had enough sense to maintain his equipment if not his home. The neglect could be intentional. The thick stone walls probably stayed cooler during the day than modern slat and steel. He didn't see an air conditioner. Probably in the back.

Poised atop the station was one of those flame-red flying horses that had been common in Frank's parents' day. Like the pumps, it looked new. It was also probably worth more than the station. He sensed movement behind him, glimpsed his children filling the doorway.

"Check it out, kids." Shading his eyes with one hand, he used the other to indicate the flying horse. "Major brand gas and a real antique."

Wendy had slipped off the earphones, proving anew they weren't rooted to the bone. "Why are we stopping?"

"Because I thought this would be an interesting place to stop."

"Looks like trash to me."

Frank tried not to growl. "It's not trash. It's history. We're going to get something cold to drink, and we need to get some gas."

"We just filled up in Barstow, Pops."

I don't even have to watch the gauge, he told himself sourly. The women in this family monitor everything for me. "In case you haven't noticed, young lady, this ain't exactly a compact wagon we're driving." He let out a sigh of resignation. "If you don't want anything you don't have to get out. Steven," he asked none too hopefully, "you coming?"

"Sure, Dad." To Frank's surprise his son hopped out and scuttled past him, heading for a high chain-link fence that enclosed a small area between worn house trailer and station.

"Hey, Dad! They got snakes in here, and I think I see a Gila monster, and a chuckawalla, an' a . . . !"

The attendant or owner would probably want a dollar in payment for Steven's looking. Frank would gladly fork it over. At last his son was showing some real interest in something besides billboards.

"Look all you want, kiddo, but don't touch. And keep your hands outside the links, okay?"

"Okay, Dad." Steven quickly and guiltily withdrew his fingers from one gap.

Frank checked the pumps. Somewhat to his surprise he found premium unleaded. Considering the location, the prices were quite reasonable. He unhitched one of the pumps, glanced toward the station office. No one had appeared to greet them. The door that secured the repair bay was closed.

Surely the place wasn't deserted, as Alicia had suggested. The door to the office was ajar and there were no padlocks on the pumps.

"Anybody home?" he yelled.

There was no response. Not even wind to reply at midday. He shrugged and turned to the motor home. No doubt as soon as he started pumping gas someone would show up fast enough. He flipped the pump switch up, saw the digital readout on the machine's flank flop to zero, and unlocked the motor home's filler cap, setting it carefully aside. The nozzle rattled its way into the tank. As he squeezed the trigger, gas began to flow.

The digital readout counted the cost silently. He missed the friendly musical *ding* gas pumps had made when he was young. Steven was walking slowly around the chain-link enclosure, intently surveying something inside.

"Fingers!" Frank shouted.

"Sure, Dad," his son replied in that special tone children utilize for acknowledging parents' admonitions without actually devoting any attention to them.

The sharp, vaguely threatening aroma of gasoline stung Frank's nostrils as he topped off the tank. Except for the gurgle of gas it was silent outside the motor home. You could hear a mouse gallop out here, he mused silently. Not a leaf stirred on the salt-tolerant trees that shaded the old station. The petals of a single paralyzed fuchsia drooped tiredly in the sun. Listen hard enough and you could hear ants scurrying underfoot, the slither of a king snake off in the bushes. And one other sound.

Frowning, he slipped the pump back in its steel saddle, then bent to check the tires. An intermittent hissing sound. The tires on this side looked full. Bending toward the ground he spotted a pair of legs walking past the wheels on the other side of the motor home. Rotting dirty denims were stuffed into scruffy brown boots. Boots used for work, not dancing. He still didn't know the source of the hissing, but at least he'd located the station's attendant. The legs kept coming. Frank straightened.

"Howdy."

"Howdy yourself." Frank returned the appraising smile.

The old man was tall, well over six feet, and thin as a fencepost. A weathered scarecrow, Frank thought. Shaving was a casual affair and he had stubble the consistency of beach sand. Bright, unblinking eyes stared out from beneath brows fashioned of steel wool. Perched on his head was a filthy baseball cap with a John Deere emblem sewn to the front. Like its wearer the cap's original color had been overwhelmed by generations of fossilized grease and oil stains. As threads had broken and unraveled, the torso of the jumping deer had parted company from its legs.

A short-sleeved work shirt was loosely tucked into faded coveralls. Gloves concealed both hands. Frank decided this emaciated ghost of the modern West was old enough to have preyed on migrating Oakies back in the thirties, before the interstate had usurped old Route 66.

"Glad to have your business," the relic declared cheerily. "Most folks go on through to Baker. Got three stations there now. A real metropolis." He chuckled. Maybe he'd gone batty living alone in the desert, but he'd retained a sense of humor.

"We thought your place looked interesting. I like stopping off the beaten track." Frank nodded at the sky. "Thought we'd make a stop before sundown."

"Glad you did." The old man was standing close now. A soiled handkerchief protruded from a pocket of the coveralls. For a change the stains weren't from oil or grease. Red or maroon paint, Frank decided.

"I heard a funny noise. Kind of hissing, or sniffing like."

"That was me, all right." He still hadn't blinked, Frank noted. "Thought you might've had a gas leak." A gloved hand patted the motor home's flank. "These self-propelled trailers got so many pipes and lines crisscrossing underneath 'em you never know when one's going to rub against another and make a hole. First you get a leak, then you get friction, and then"—the old man's eyes went startlingly wide—*"bwoom!* Charcoal time."

"Yeah." Charming sense of humor, Frank thought.

"Where you folks staying in Vegas?"

"How'd you know that's where we're going?"

A soft chuckle. "Where else would anybody be going east on this road?"

"We're not sure yet." He jerked a thumb at the motor home. "We were gonna stay in this, but the kids and wife don't think that's much of a vacation. I got outvoted."

"Nothing personal, but I'd side with them." Stepping past Frank, he used the soiled handkerchief to wipe gas from the still open filler cap before flipping the cap cover shut. "Folks these days in such a hurry they don't take the time to appreciate the world around 'em. One of these days the end'll come and then they'll be damn sorry for what they missed."

Uh-oh, Frank thought, detecting the first faint whiff of an oncoming sermon in the air. Time to be moving on. He reached for his wallet.

"I don't see the stickers. You take credit cards?"

"Ain't really big on plastic around here. Usually like for folks to pay in kind for what they owe. But I'll make an exception for you, you being such a relaxed customer and all. Most folks get to this point, they're pretty nervous and upset. Not you, though. Coolest one I've seen in some time."

"Thanks." Frank felt flattered without knowing why. "American Express okay?"

The ancient shrugged. "Good as any of 'em, I expect." He

took the card, then seemed to freeze. As Frank stared, the man sniffed ostentatiously, tilting back his head and flaring his nostrils. He walked toward the back of the motor home and sniffed a second time. "You smell something funny?"

Frank joined him, took a few sniffs himself, feeling foolish as he did so. "Just the fresh gas."

The attendant straightened. "Reckon you're right. Just me and my suspicious nature, I expect."

"If you think there's a leak why not take a whiff underneath?" Frank asked curiously.

"Fumes would rise. The underchassis'd stink without any leaks. Get a truer appraisal standing up." He waggled the card at Frank. "Be right back with your bill. Got to get an authorization number, you know." He hesitated. "You didn't by any chance pick up anybody down the road apiece? Somebody stranded, somebody's car broke down? Like maybe somebody hitchhiking?"

Most people would have responded instinctively to the casual inquiry. Frank Sonderberg had spent too many years in business, too much time listening for the real meaning behind obfuscatory soliloquies to offer a straight reply without giving the matter careful consideration. Instead of answering, he evaded.

"That's a funny thing to ask." He turned and gestured at the highway. "I mean, who'd be dumb enough to stand out on that stretch of road and hitch this direction, when it'd make more sense to go back to Barstow?"

"Depends how anxious they are to get somewheres besides Barstow." The old man was staring at him with perverse intensity, unexpectedly alert. And he had yet to blink. Of course, Frank had looked away from him several times. He could have blinked then.

Instead of replying, Frank checked his watch. "Getting late." He'd planned to accompany the old man inside the station, hoping for a glimpse of such treasures as antique bottles and fifties-era advertising posters. Now all he wanted was to regain the comforting interior of the motor home and gun the big Detroit powerplant. It occurred to him they hadn't passed or been passed by a highway patrol car all day.

The oldster slumped slightly. "Guess so. Be dark soon. Don't want to hold you up. Just that sometimes folks come through this way, they ask to use the facilities and then they just kinda walk off with something. You know, forget to pay for their soda or candy.

Not that many people pull off here. Somebody swipes something from a small dealer like myself, it hurts."

"Are you saying somebody stole from you recently?"

"Maybe, maybe not." The brown-toothed smile made a curtain call. "That ain't your problem, though, is it? I'll get that authorization number and be right back with your card."

Frank discovered he'd been holding his breath. Now he exhaled as the attendant sort of loped toward the stone building to be swallowed by the single door. With the old man gone he could hear Wendy and Alicia chatting inside the motor home.

What's with the nerves? he asked himself. So the old fossil's peculiar, so what? Living out here alone would set anybody slightly off kilter. He found himself remembering the stained handkerchief that hung from the coverall pocket like a linen leech. Red or maroon paint—except it didn't really look like paint. But what else could it have been? And the John Deere cap with the familiar image of the leaping stag. With the legs separated from the body. Those legs had been sewn in awfully strange positions. Skewed, as if they'd been torn away only to be replaced haphazardly beneath the jumping torso.

Not much of an imagination, he told himself, but what little you've got is making a break for it. He rubbed at his cuticles, a nervous habit he'd failed to break in twenty-five years of trying. At least he didn't bite his nails anymore.

Old fart's taking his time. Of course, phone service to an outpost like this might not be in the best of repair. Even in downtown L.A. it could take awhile to get through if the volume of calls to the authorization center was heavy. Probably had to use a rotary phone without an automatic redial, for chrissake.

"Hey, Dad!"

"What?" Frank looked down, saw Steven flinch. The boy had come up quietly behind his father. "Sorry, kiddo. Find something interesting to look at?"

"Sure did. Birds and lizards. Something else, too. I went around the back and there was a place where it looked like something had tried to dig under the fence. I saw some stuff sticking out—it was on my side of the fence, honest, Dad—and so I sorta picked it up. See? Neat, huh?"

He held up a handful of old bones. They were deeply scored

and mostly detached from one another. Too big to be chicken bones. Most likely from a holiday turkey. Not hog or cattle.

Frank accepted the offering, nudged them with his finger. "Interesting. But maybe the gentleman who owns this place doesn't want strange kids digging around in his yard. That hole under the fence could've been an exit for a rattler. You could've been bit. Did you think about that?"

Steven looked downcast, his initial enthusiasm muted. "Naw. But it's all right, Dad. I was careful. Besides, you said snakes and stuff don't come out this time of day 'cause it's too hot. I didn't see anything moving."

You had to hand it to the kid, Frank thought. He remembered. Then a cold chill ran down his back and the waistband of his shorts was suddenly tight against his skin.

Not all the bones were disconnected. A few were still attached to others. Three of them in sequence, which he carefully held up to the light. At the tip of the last small bone was a suggestion of something besides bone. It was broken and brief, but unmistakable.

A nail.

Frank was no anatomist, but he was pretty sure he was holding most of a human finger. A small finger, bigger than an infant's, smaller than a man's. A woman's, perhaps, or a teenager's. There were spots on the bit of nail, but too old and dirty to tell if they were polish.

Fighting to contain his emotions he let the amputated finger bones fall back among the others. "Steven, I want you to listen to me very closely." The boy's eyes got wide, as they usually did on those rare occasions when his father turned solemn. "This is private property and should not have been disturbed. So I want you to put them back exactly where you found them." He glanced toward the station office. Still no movement there.

"I want you to put them back in the ground, quietly and quickly." He handed back the bones.

"Aw, gee, Dad. I was kinda hoping that if the man didn't want 'em maybe I could . . ."

"Put them back." Frank kept his voice low. *"Now."*

Steven stared up at him. "Is something wrong, Dad? I mean, I didn't mean to do anything wrong."

"It's not a question of right or wrong. You just don't bother

other people's property, understand? Go on. Go bury them back and then get your butt back here and inside. We're leaving.''

''Okay, Dad.'' Steven shrugged, turned to scamper back to the enclosure. Frank noticed for the first time that the fence was a high one. Higher than was needed to keep snakes and lizards in and the prowling coyote out. High enough to keep strangers from climbing over to disturb the inhabitants. Or to keep anyone from climbing out. The four posts that held the chain link taut were oversized and sunk deep.

His head jerked around to see the attendant emerge from the office. He wore the smile he'd first used to greet his customers. One gloved hand held Frank's credit card and the unsigned receipt. Steven was out of sight behind the enclosure. Trying to look casual and relaxed, Frank moved to the front of the motor home. The old man changed direction to meet him without breaking stride.

''Here you go, sir. Eighteen even. Guess she wasn't quite empty.''

''Not quite.'' Do I sound normal? he wondered. Though his thoughts were in turmoil his fingers were steady as he signed for the gas. Just let us get out of here, he thought wildly. Just let us get away from this place and I swear to God I won't stop until we're on the Strip.

The old man's back faced the enclosure. Frank tried not to stare past him, tried not to locate Steven. He wondered if Alicia was in her seat, staring down at him. He didn't look to find out for fear she'd notice the strain on his face. He signed very carefully, not wanting to tear the fragile paper and have to start over again.

''Here we are.'' He handed back the pen and clipboard. The oldster didn't so much as glance at it.

''Thanks.''

''Guess we'll be on our way.'' He turned to go.

''Don't forget your card.''

''Right.'' Frank grabbed at the plastic, shoved it back in a pocket without bothering to replace it in his wallet. There was still no sign of his son.

''Something the matter, sir?'' The old man hitched up the coveralls.

''No.'' An awkward moment of silence passed. ''Just looking for my little boy. You know kids. Always underfoot until you're ready to go someplace.''

"Yeah, I know kids."

"You have children?"

"Naw. Never been married. Never appealed to me. I'd just rather bang 'em and leave 'em, y'know?" He opened his mouth and laughed, an unpleasant sound, like cats fighting inside a garbage can.

"Right, sure." Frank forced a smile. It turned to one of relief as Steven reappeared. "Here he is. Go on, kiddo. Get inside."

The boy just nodded. He glanced quickly at the old man, who grinned down at him. Then he was safely back inside the motor home.

"Thanks again." Frank didn't extend his hand to shake the old man's because he wasn't sure he'd get it back. "Have a nice day," he finished lamely.

"I'll sure try to." Gloved hands plunged into coverall pockets. "Drive careful, now. Don't take any wrong turns, and watch out for hitchhikers. All kinds of unpleasant folks try to get picked up along this stretch of highway."

"We'll be careful. We're driving straight through. I wouldn't pick anybody up. I've got a family to watch out for."

"That's right. You've got a family to watch out for." With a final nod, the attendant turned and strolled back toward the station office. Relieved, Frank turned to re-enter the motor home.

What the dickens was wrong with him? He'd been watching too much TV, especially the kind of gruesome R-rated horror videos his son and friends were beginning to favor. The station's isolation, the soiled handkerchief, the emblem on the hat of the deer with the four dismembered legs, all had other, more plausible explanations than the one that had made evil connections between them in his thoughts. Been out in the sun too long, he told himself. Alicia and the kids were right, after all. What they needed were not stimulating encounters but air-conditioning, neon, television, and prepared food.

So what about the bones?

Yeah, what about them? What did he know about bones? They could have come from anything. Or they might have been plastic fakes planted there as a gag. That would fit the attendant's sense of humor. Buy some from a medical supply house and bury them near the enclosure to scare prying kids like Steven. Furthermore, if anything illegal was somehow involved, that didn't mean the old man had a part in it. It made no sense. Anyone wanting to dispose of a body and who'd take the time to dismember the bones wouldn't bury the incriminating results only a few inches deep.

As he reached the entrance to the motor home he spared a last look for the subject of his musings—and paused. There was something moving at the back of the old man's pants, up near the beltline. He squinted. The bright sunlight made it difficult to concentrate. A tuft of black attached to a wire or stick protruded from a corner of the coveralls. Funny he hadn't noticed it before, but he'd been looking the old man in the eyes, not staring at his backside. Despite the fact it was still blazing hot outside a chill ran through him.

The twitching black tuft looked just like the tip of a tail.

You *have* been out in the sun too long, he admonished himself.

Alicia greeted him as he slid back into the driver's seat. "Everything all right, dear? You were out there a long time."

"Fine," he muttered as he fumbled with the ignition key. "Everything's fine."

The engine grumbled. Come on, dammit, he thought tensely. Catch, you steel bastard! Don't you die on me here.

With the third wrench on the key the big engine came to life. Frank let it idle for a minute, then put it in drive. The motor home exited smoothly from the station. As soon as they were clear he leaned slightly forward so he could see the whole image presented by the rearview mirror on Alicia's side. Nothing stirred behind them. The station and its attendant trailer home appeared as still and lifeless as they had when he'd first pulled in.

He turned onto the on ramp, flooring the accelerator. The motor home picked up speed like a runaway juggernaut, roaring onto the deserted sanctuary of the slow lane.

Alicia didn't speak until her husband set the cruise control. "Frank, you look like you've seen a ghost. Is something wrong?"

"No, nothing's wrong. Everything's fine."

"You're lying. I can always tell when you're lying."

He clung to the wheel, didn't look around at her. "Tell you later. It's no big deal, okay? We're on our way again and everything's fine. Just don't press me about it right now."

Maybe she saw the tension in his face. Certainly she heard it in his voice. "All right. You'll tell me about it when you're ready."

"Right."

He ought to have been able to relax then but could not. The landscape was beginning to bother him as much as his memories. For one thing it seemed darker than it should have been outside. There wasn't a cloud in sight and the external thermometer hadn't fallen a degree, but suddenly it didn't look as bright as it had before they'd pulled into the strange little gas station. The interstate was unchanged, but the desert didn't seem right anymore.

The plants, the sandy shoulder pushing up against the pavement, even the mountains no longer looked the same. Steep slopes had acquired a rusty red hue instead of the familiar beige and brown. Several plants hovered over the barbed-wire fence that isolated the interstate from the surrounding terrain. Branches reached for the concrete. At sixty it was impossible to say for certain, but a few appeared to be dripping dark liquid. Probably creosote, Frank told himself. Creosote bushes were supposed to be common in this part of the world. But should a bush drip creosote?

The ocotillo looked shriveled and drawn, like anorexic octopuses. Then there were the Joshua trees, not as common here as elsewhere in the desert, with their contorted limbs that resembled broken arms. That was to be expected. All Joshua trees looked like that.

But they shouldn't have had faces with wide, imploring eyes and mouths frozen in mid-scream.

He thought about pointing them out, found himself wondering if he was the only one to notice what might not actually be there. All desert plants looked funny. Just because he was seeing their gnarled shapes as ominous didn't mean someone else would view them in the same way. They might find the distortions amusing, and laugh at his interpretations. So as badly as the sights unnerved him, he kept his observations to himself.

No one passed them from behind and there was no traffic in the oncoming lanes. That was starting to worry him as much as the appearance of some of the vegetation when something rocketed past in the fast lane. The low jet-black sports car must have been traveling well in excess of a hundred miles an hour.

Damn highway patrol's never around when they should be, he grumbled silently.

The truck convoy that passed a few minutes later was moving at a more sedate velocity. There were three of the big eighteen-wheelers. He tried to see the drivers, but the three cabs were wrapped in smoked glass. All were painted a bright red-orange and were devoid of company logos or identification except for the big crimson H stenciled on each side. Very catchy, Frank mused.

The last truck had vanished over the horizon when he pulled hard on the steering wheel, forgetting that he wasn't driving a sports car himself. Wendy squealed and was immediately angry at herself for doing so, while Alicia let out a startled gasp. Then the motor home steadied again. Frank clung to the wheel, trying to drive and stare at the rearview mirror at the same time. There was sweat on his forehead.

"Snake."

Alicia gaped at him. "You almost wrecked us to avoid hitting a snake? I know you love animals, Frank, but . . ."

"Not a snake. I thought it was at first, but it had legs. Short, stubby legs, and it was about eight feet long."

"I don't care how big it was! You"—she hesitated, leaned toward him—"Frank, you're sweating."

Reflexively he drew a forearm across his brow, sopping up the moisture. "It had stripes, Alicia. Legs and orange and black stripes. Eight feet long. And it had—a face."

She stared uncomprehendingly. "A face? Oh. You mean, like a lizard face."

"Yeah, that was it. A lizard face."

Except it hadn't looked anything like a lizard. It had been distorted, the expression a frozen alien grimace, but humanoid. Much too human. As the motor home had roared down on it the wide mouth had parted in a hiss of fear and loathing. He'd barely avoided it, careening wildly into the fast lane, fighting weight and wheel as he'd brought it back under control.

A crawling abomination, a stripe-slashed monstrosity born of some fevered nightmare, that's what it had been. Nothing so normal and healthy as a snake. What was happening?

The gas station. That heat-ravaged gas station with its damned attendant. That's where it had started. Had they taken a wrong turn somehow? Had he driven onto the wrong on ramp, the wrong highway? They'd driven into a part of the desert people didn't know about. Perhaps a desert that lay just under or parallel to the real Mojave? Or maybe he was going a little crazy from all the driving and the heat. The latter explanation was the more reasonable of the two.

A glance revealed Wendy locked in the blissful catatonia provided by her tape player, Steven absorbed in a comic book. Say nothing to them, don't involve them. So far the nightmare was still a private one. Alicia had only been brushed by the horror. Leave her out of it, too. The snake that was something less than a reptile and the station attendant who might have been something more than a man had him seriously unsettled.

"I'm going to lie down in back for a few minutes." Alicia climbed free of her chair. "Just a few minutes so I can rest my eyes. Then I'm taking over. You've been driving too long, Frank."

"Yeah. Yeah, maybe I have." He nodded his thanks, followed her with his eyes as she moved toward the back of the motor home. "Steven? Hey, come on up and sit with your old man for a few minutes, kiddo."

Silence, then a resigned sigh as his son reluctantly set the comic aside. "Okay, Dad." Moments later a rotund little form plopped itself down in the big captain's chair next to his. Father and son watched the passing scenery quietly for a while.

"Tell me something, kiddo. What do you see out there?"

Steven had to sit up straight in order to be able to see out the window. He gazed for a moment before turning back to his father. "Same old shi—stuff, Dad. Sand and rocks."

"That's all? It doesn't look different to you? I mean, different from when we started out from Barstow."

"Different?" Steven frowned, wondering as he made a second survey of their surroundings if this was some new kind of game. He pressed his face against the glass. "I dunno. Some of the plants look kind of funny. Weird-like. Isn't that how desert plants always look?"

Frank stiffened in his seat. So he wasn't imagining everything. "How do you mean, 'weird-like'?"

"Sorta twisted." Suddenly he was on his knees on the seat, his head turning to look back the way they'd come. "Hey, neat!"

"What?"

"There went one that looked just like a little kid!"

"Really." Frank kept his voice even. "A kid, huh?"

"Yeah. It looked like it was running. That's what was so neat. I mean, lots of these plants have branches that look like arms and hands, right? But this one musta had two trunks. They looked just like legs, like they were running. Too bad you missed it."

"Too bad." How deeply did he want to involve his son in this nightmare? Did he have any choice, or were they all already deeply involved? If his son was seeing similar apparitions, then there was nothing personal about the nightmare. If it was a nightmare.

It had to be. *Had* to. "Remember the gas station where we just stopped?"

"Sure, Dad." The boy looked simultaneously small and overweight in the oversized, velour-upholstered chair. "What about it?"

Frank struggled with the words. "Did you notice anything, well, funny there? Besides the bones you found?"

Steven thought a moment before shaking his head. "Naw." His expression brightened. "Well, maybe one thing. You know the old weirdo who ran the place?"

"The elderly gentleman, yes."

"When we first got there and I was over lookin' around at that pen or whatever it was, I saw him trying to peek inside the motor home. He was standin' on his tiptoes trying to see in one of the back windows. I didn't think about it 'cause I thought he was helping you, Dad. He had his face right up against it, real close like." Steven demonstrated by putting both hands in front of his face and pressing his nose against them. "He was like sniffing or something. I guess that was pretty funny, huh? Is that what you meant?"

Frank nodded slowly. "Funny enough. He was standing up and sniffing? Not looking underneath?"

"Nope. Just sniffing along the side, like a big dog." The boy laughed at the memory. "That's pretty silly, isn't it?"

"Hysterical. Do me a favor and go get your mom."

Steven looked around the seat. "But she just went and laid down."

"Just get her. Tell her I need to see her for a minute."

"Okay." Steven shrugged, slipped off the chair, and jogged toward the rear bedroom. A few moments later Alicia appeared, blinking and rubbing at one eye.

"That wasn't much of a rest, dear." She settled into the chair. "But if you're ready for me to drive I'll take it."

"It's not that. There's something wrong."

She was suddenly alert and awake. "With the motor home?"

"No. I don't think that's it. I think it's something else. I'm not exactly sure what it is, but I'm tired of wondering about it and I think I've figured out how to fix it." He tapped the map clipped to the dash. "In a few minutes we'll be in Baker. That's where our hitchhiker is getting off."

"In Baker? I thought you wanted to take her all the way to Vegas?"

He nodded vigorously. "That's what I thought at first, yeah. On reflection I think maybe we'd be better off dropping her sooner. I have this feeling we're getting ourselves too involved in someone else's personal business, some kind of business we don't know anything about and that we're better off not knowing about. I'll think of some reason. It's not like we're dumping her in the middle of nowhere. She ought to be able to get a ride out of Baker easy if she just hangs around one of the gas stations."

"You're not making a whole lot of sense, Frank. That's not like you."

"Didn't you want to get rid of her?" he asked challengingly.

"Well, I wouldn't put it that way." She glanced toward the back bedroom. "She looks so frail and innocent when she's sound asleep. What happened to change your mind?"

"Tell you later. You agree we should put her off, then?"

"I don't know. I know what I said when we first picked her up, but we've agreed to take her all the way to Las Vegas. I don't feel right about changing my mind."

"This is our vacation, isn't it? She oughta be grateful that we brought her this far instead of leaving her standing where we found her."

"If you think this is the best way, Frank."

"I do."

There was silence between them for a while before she spoke up anew.

"Frank?"

"Yeah."

"Can't you tell me what's going on? Please?"

He chewed at his lower lip. "Hon, I'm not sure I know what's going on. I just know that she's involved somehow and that I don't want us to be a part of it. She still sleeping?" Alicia nodded.

"I think what's going on is she's in some kind of trouble. She may be a singer like she claims. I mean, we know she can sing, but we don't know that that's her profession. Now, you know me. I'm always ready to go the extra mile to help somebody out of a jam. But not if I think it's going to touch my family."

"Us?" Alicia was genuinely puzzled. "How could any problems Mouse might be having affect us?"

"Like I've been saying, I'm not sure. It's just that there are a number of things that don't feel right."

"Your funny-looking snake troubling you again?" She half smiled, uncertain whether she was expected to be taken seriously.

"Among other things. You remember the old attendant who sold us gas?"

"Not really. I hardly got a look at him. I was talking to Wendy."

"He asked me if we'd picked up any hitchhikers. He tried to be casual about it, but I could tell he was real interested in my answer."

She frowned. "Why would he ask a question like that?"

"He said something about having problems with people swiping stuff, but I don't think that had anything to do with it. I think it's something else, something a lot more serious. Steven said he saw him trying to sneak a look inside while I was pumping gas. Sniffing around, you might say."

"You think he was looking for Mouse?"

"I don't know, but he sure as hell was looking for something, and I don't want any part of what's going on. He wouldn't give me any straight answers, and she''—he jerked his head in the direction of the back bedroom and their sleeping guest—"hasn't given us any straight answers and I think the best thing under the circumstances is to let people like that work out their problems among themselves. Let her find another ride. I've had enough of her and enough of this."

Then maybe life would return to normal, he thought desperately. Whatever else Mouse might be, she wasn't normal. Her appearance wasn't normal and her voice wasn't normal and her whole aspect was slightly skewed. Once they were rid of her maybe the world would return to normal. Unless he was the only one who'd gone crazy. But Steven had seen the attendant sniffing.

Alicia thought her husband was overreacting, but she kept quiet. She accepted his change of heart gratefully. Not because she didn't like Mouse. She just didn't like strangers. Obviously Mouse's presence was putting a strain on their vacation. That was reason enough to ask her to find another ride.

It had nothing to do with funny-looking snakes and curious gas station attendants.

4

ACCORDING TO THE MAP Baker was less than ten miles ahead. They drove the ten miles, then fifteen, without sighting the little desert town. Frank hadn't paid much attention to the odometer since they'd left L.A., but he watched the slowly revolving numbers intently now.

Admittedly Baker wasn't much. A couple of hundred inhabitants, a few gas stations, a convenience store or two. But it was definitely too big to overlook. He drove another ten miles, searching the salt plain north of the highway. They had yet to see so much as a sign.

At least the sky had brightened. The unnatural darkness had vanished. The absence of their intended destination, however, mitigated the relief he felt at the return of the sky to normalcy. He checked the map. Baker should be twenty miles behind them by now.

"Sweetheart?" Alicia shifted uncomfortably in her chair. "Shouldn't we be there by now?"

"According to the map." He nodded at the dash.

"Could we have gone past it somehow?"

"You can't go 'past' a whole town out here," he shot back irritably. "Maybe it ain't Manhattan, but there's at least one off ramp. I don't see how we could have missed it. We've both been watching and there are no wrong turns out here. I don't under—"

She interrupted excitedly. "Oh, there's a sign!"

Sure enough, they were coming up fast on one of the familiar big green highway signs that were posted on the shoulder. He could read it easily.

LAS VEGAS—152 Miles
HADES JUNCTION—6 Miles

The sign came and went at fifty-five miles per, leaving him little time to ponder the implications. Hades Junction but no Baker. He squinted at the map. There was no town by that name anywhere along I-40.

"They don't always show the real small towns, Frank," Alicia said, replying to his concerns. She leaned close to the dash, looked satisfied when she sat back in the chair. "This map's a couple of years old. They're always putting in new stops."

Not in the Mojave, he told himself, but how could he be sure? Since when had he become a specialist in desert real estate? Anyone who wanted to build a new station, maybe a motel, could lobby for state recognition as a town. If you paid for your own off ramp the state would probably grant you any kind of designation you wanted. He stared at the map.

He could have purchased a more detailed one, but what for? Why worry about the location of details you had no intention of visiting? None of which explained how'd they'd managed to drive right past Baker without seeing it. Baker had been here for a long time. Could it have been renamed Hades Junction since the map had been printed? He almost smiled. Certainly it would be a more descriptive moniker for a community located in the middle of the desert. If he'd been on the local Chamber of Commerce he would've voted for such a change. Hades Junction might attract a few more tourists than the bland Baker. Maybe that was it.

As for it lying twenty-six miles farther east than it should have, that could be his mistake. Or the odometer might be defective.

"Maybe you're right," he said at last. She had to be right. There was no other explanation. "Either we missed Baker or they've gone and renamed the place."

"I don't know." Alicia was brooding now. "I don't like the idea of letting anybody off in a place with a name like that."

He couldn't keep himself from laughing. "With a name like what? Half the places in the Southwest have names like that. Bad Water or Devil's Hole or Perdition. We just passed the turnoff to Bagdad yesterday. Bet Hades Junction is a paradise compared to that."

"You're probably right. As long as it's a place where she can find another ride."

"Pretty lady like her," he murmured, "shouldn't have trouble getting a ride anywhere." But hadn't she insisted she'd been waiting a long time until they'd paused to pick her up? Or had that just been a line? Here he was worrying about a total stranger again.

As they cruised eastward he kept an eye on the odometer. It looked to be functioning properly. When they'd gone six miles from the sign they'd just passed he was by God going to stop and find himself a town, or a gas station, or something. Otherwise he'd have a few choice words for the highway department and the manufacturers of their so far inadequate road map.

The sky was darkening again, but this time with obvious reason. Clouds were gathering overhead. Peculiar clouds, though. Rain clouds. What was unusual was that they took the form of long, thin tendrils instead of thick, puffy masses. Streamers of storm.

So now you're a meteorologist, he chided himself. First you decide the plants have gone crazy, now it's the clouds. He glanced speculatively to his left, out the window. Sword-leafed yuccas pressed close to the barbed-wire fence that bordered the highway limit. Ocotillo waved their tentacle-like arms in the absence of wind. Feeling unexpectedly queasy at the sight, he turned away.

Since the three big trucks and the single sports car, not a single vehicle had passed them. Unusual, since he was doing fifty-five and out here it was normal for most drivers to ignore the speed limit. You'd expect to see trucks, if not a lot of cars. As a lifelong Angelino, the absence of traffic made him uneasy.

Alicia was leaning forward. "Oh, look, Frank! There are animals on the overpass!"

No off ramp here. Just an elevated crossing for an unknown country road. He tried to identify the shapes as they bore down on the overpass. "Not deer," he declared with certainty. Then they were passing beneath and the single brief glimpse was lost.

What sounded like a deluge of empty beer cans danced on the motor home's roof.

"Hey!" Steven put his comic aside to look ceilingward.

"Must've been kids," Frank decided. "They must've thrown something down on us."

Except that couldn't be the cause because the noise continued. It didn't sound like beer cans or garbage rattling around the luggage rack. It sounded a lot like feet. Small feet.

"Some idiots jumped onto us." His knuckles whitened where he gripped the wheel. He knew what he ought to do was pull over and step outside for a look. Something in his gut insisted that that wouldn't be a good idea.

Whatever was up there, scuttling around among their rented patio chairs and spare tires, there was more than one of them. The cold feeling he'd felt when he'd seen that black tuft at the rear of the gas station attendant's coveralls now returned. He thumbed a switch. The luxurious, brand-new motor home came equipped with power everything. It took only the quick gesture to lock all the windows and doors.

Almost immediately the main door began to rattle.

"Dad?" Steven's voice had gone hollow. "Hey, Dad, there's something trying to get in."

Frank said nothing, trying not to let his imagination get in the way of deciding what to do next. He should have brought the gun. But Alicia hated guns. Besides, of what use was a pistol on the busy interstate between L.A. and Vegas?

That's when Alicia screamed. Frank let out an oath and fought the wheel, fighting his own panic simultaneously as something came crawling down the windshield. It descended from the roof by clinging to the metal shaft that divided the windshield in two.

It looked like a big rat, complete to reddish-brown fur and naked tail. A rat with a feral intelligence gleaming in its oversized eyes. Halfway to the hood it paused to stare in at them, grinning to display razor teeth. In its right paw it held a crude blade about two inches long.

As Frank tried to keep the motor home from crashing, the verminous passenger crawled the rest of the way down the windshield support. Safely on the hood it squatted on its hind legs and turned to regard the motor home's inhabitants with a murderous gaze. It was soon joined by a companion. Instead of a miniature knife, the newcomer carried a tiny pickax.

Alicia had stopped screaming to hold her breath. The rat-things were chittering animatedly to each other. When they finished they began using their sharp utensils to dig at the insulation that ran around the windshield's perimeter. Meanwhile the rattling at the door had not ceased. Scraping sounds began above Frank's head. They were coming from the rim of the skylight a foot behind his seat.

"My God, Frank—what is it? What *are* they?"

"I don't know, Alicia. I don't know!" He could hear Steven whining anxiously somewhere behind him.

"Mom, Dad?" Wendy was whispering. "What's going on?" All of a sudden she sounded neither cocky nor composed.

Frank swallowed, found his voice. "Alicia, you and Wendy get the big kitchen knives out of the drawers. Look around under the stove. Maybe there's a firewood ax, too. Anything that can be used as a weapon. Understand?" There were half a dozen of the rat-things on the hood now, cutting and chopping around the windows and vent flaps, hunting for a way in.

"Okay. Okay." Alicia started to rise, then yelled and pointed.

The vent door that was built into the metal next to the accelerator was opening.

With a curse Frank jammed his left foot down hard, slamming the six-inch-high louver shut. There was a tiny, inhuman screech and the pop of small bones crunching.

"Hold the wheel!"

"Frank?"

"The wheel, hold the damn wheel!"

Alicia grabbed at it, kept the motor home more or less steady as Frank bent over to throw the manual latch on the vent cover. Then he straightened and instructed Alicia to do the same to the vent on her side. She managed, though her hands were shaking badly.

It sounded now like a small army was scurrying all over the roof and sides of the motor home. Wendy sat huddled in a corner next to the bathroom while her little brother's eyes flicked nervously from one window to the next.

It took Alicia a few minutes to find all the knives. There was no firewood ax. "The toolbox!" Frank glanced into the overhead rearview mirror. "It's under the fridge. Take out the hammer and the screwdrivers!"

The rat-things weren't big, but there were dozens of them and they were fast. If they found a way inside he'd have to pull over to fight them, and if they stopped here who knew what other nightmares might be lying by the side of the road, crouching behind the mutated prickly pears and boulders, just waiting for the opportunity to get their hands on the motor home's defenseless inhabitants?

A sharp cracking sound filled his ears. Wendy shrieked as the small window opposite her was partly shattered. There was a fixed screen inside the window. It blocked the entry of a furious, frustrated rat-thing long enough for Alicia to smash the baseball-sized skull with the toolbox hammer. Wendy screamed again as blood and brains went flying. The little monstrosity fell away and another took its place. Alicia battered at clutching hands until tiny clawed fingers had been beaten to pulp.

"Get out!" she screamed as she flailed with the hammer. "Out, out, out!"

One on one, Alicia had the advantage of size and determination. No longer was she defending the integrity of the motor home. She was protecting her children now, protecting them from the unadulterated, unmitigated evil that wanted to hurt them. Though they kept trying, none of the rat-creatures managed to slip through the screen or past her bloody hammer.

"Everybody hang tight!" Frank yelled. "I'm gonna hit the brakes hard! Maybe we can throw some of them off!"

Risky to slow to a stop, he knew, however briefly. Surely in that one abrupt, unexpected moment they wouldn't be able to disable the vehicle. It was the only thing he could think of.

My God, he thought suddenly. What if they're under the hood? He could envision them swarming over the engine, slicing away with their little knives, chewing with their sharp teeth. If they cut through the alternator or fan belt the motor home would die from lack of power, or overheat. If that happened he knew they couldn't hold back the furry tide for long. But he couldn't stop to check under the hood.

Hit the brakes. That was their only chance. Maybe he could throw half of them off, or even more. They wouldn't be expecting the maneuver and . . .

A new sound filled the motor home's interior. It rose cleanly over the bloodthirsty chittering outside and the panicky screams and cries of the imperiled family within. It soared above the still-smooth hum of the engine.

Mouse stood by the door to the rear bedroom. She had her head back and mouth open, and she was singing a song unlike anything Frank had ever heard. It contained echoes of the song she'd sung for them earlier, echoes only. Compared to the edgy, vaulting lyrics, his daughter's heavy metal sounded positively pastoral, and Mouse achieved the effect without any instrumental backup.

At times the sound disappeared, but you could tell by watching the singer that she was singing as powerfully as ever. You couldn't hear with your ears, but you could feel it in your bones, a high-frequency vibration that set your teeth on edge. It was all overpowering and wonderful and frightening. Words in a language Frank didn't recognize were interspersed with stretches of pure music. He discovered he was shivering even though it was warm inside the motor home and the air-conditioning thrummed dutifully in the background.

It did more than make the rat-things shiver. Dropping their weapons they pressed paws to their ears, squealing in agony. Then they broke and ran, forgetting about the soft, warm, meaty things locked in the steel box on wheels. Mouse continued her apparently effortless song, her lithe body arrow-straight, the music pouring out of her as if from the depths of a high-powered speaker. Claws skittered across metal as the attackers fled, leaping from the roof and hood, some landing safely, others breaking and splattering on the unyielding pavement. Something in Mouse's song drove them insane. Dozens crunched beneath the big steel-belted radials. Their bodies were small enough so that the impact didn't interfere with the motor home's progress.

The scratching and skittering faded while the song remained strong and pure, until the last little carnivore with its glaring red eyes and piranha-like teeth had vanished.

Frank studied the view presented by the rear-facing side mirrors. He saw nothing and did not expect to. At the speed they were traveling they would already have left the tiny army far behind. Meanwhile Mouse concluded her saving song with an impossible triple trill that sounded more like the product of a synthesizer than a human throat. When it died away it was once more peaceful and calm inside the motor home.

Alicia held both arms across her chest as she stared silently forward. Wendy was still sobbing fitfully in back but was beginning to regain some self-control. Her little brother just crouched motionless against the couch, watching their guest.

"What the hell were those?" Frank drove- mechanically, afraid to slow down, unwilling to release his convulsive grip on the wheel. "What the hell is going *on*?"

"This isn't happening." Alicia's voice was very small. She was shaking her head slowly from side to side. "It isn't happening. It's all a dream."

"Not a dream." Mouse came toward them. "I'm sorry. For your sakes I wish it was."

Frank noticed that she kept her balance no matter how severely the motor home leaned or swayed. She kept her balance, and he'd kept control. He sat a little straighter. Plenty of guys would've panicked back there, would've let go of the wheel or pulled over and run screaming into the desert. He'd held together better than a lot of would-be heroes in the face of unexpected, unimaginable horror. Alicia'd always told him he responded well in a crisis, like that time her mother had been visiting and had suffered the bad heart attack. Five minutes from now he might go completely to pieces, but for the moment he was fine.

Better try to find out what was happening now, then.

"Who are you? Nothing's been right ever since we picked you up. Has the world gone nuts, or have we?"

She sighed. "I am very much afraid you are all still sane. Madness would make it easier for you to cope. As we strive constantly to hold back the madness we are concurrently forbidden the luxury of descending into insanity." Vast lavender orbs gazed directly into his eyes. They held nothing back, and concealed everything.

The last vestiges of hysteria had faded from his voice. "While you were sleeping in the back we stopped for some gas. The guy at the station was, well, 'weird' would be an understatement. He did a lot of sniffing around the motor home. I mean really sniffing, like a bloodhound or something. As we were getting ready to leave he asked me if we'd seen or picked up any hitchhikers. I thought that was a real peculiar thing to ask, just out of the blue like that.''

"And you didn't tell him.''

"No. Now I'm not so sure I should've lied. What have we gotten ourselves into by giving you a lift, Mouse? Or Moscohotcha, or whatever your name is? Who are you, and what's going on, and why do I have this funny feeling this 'Vanishing Point' of yours isn't a nightclub? Dammit, you owe us some straight answers!''

"Nightclub?'' She looked puzzled. "I never said anything about a nightclub.''

"You haven't said anything about anything. Business partner of mine once said that in the absence of information it was natural for people to speculate. So we've been doing a lot of speculating. Me, I'm fresh out of speculations. I don't understand those rat-things that attacked us and I don't understand that attendant and I especially don't understand *you*.''

"I am . . .'' she began, then stopped and started again. "It has to do with Chaos.''

Frank turned back to stare at the unwinding ribbon of highway, growled, "Oh, well, that explains everything.''

"Try to understand what I am going to say to you,'' she continued anxiously. "There is a problem with the Spinner. The One Who Spins. Who Modulates.''

"Spins what?'' Wendy had come forward to listen. She was frightened and exhilarated and scared and exultant all at once. Mouse turned to smile at her. Though the difference in their ages did not appear great, Wendy was conscious of an immense gap between them. For some reason it didn't intimidate her.

"The fabric of existence.'' Mouse plucked at her rainbow sari dress. "This stuff, only new. This is fashioned of old existence; forgotten memories and lost history. Places that were but are no longer. Thoughts no longer vital. I wear the echoes of what was once. The Spinner weaves the threads of what is and will be.

"There lies the trouble. Almost always the Spinner spins smoothly and without interruption. Only very, very rarely does it suffer distress. When that happens the fabric of existence becomes tangled, begins to unravel in places. Instead of unwinding in intricate patterns of logic, lines of existence twist and tangle. It is a matter of stress.''

"How do you fix something like that?" Wendy asked the question without being sure what she was asking about.

"By relaxing the Spinner. By soothing it. By helping it resume its former natural rhythm. You cure such problems among yourselves, infinitesimally minor, with medicines. There is not enough medicine in the universe to adjust the Spinner's rhythm. It requires something much more powerful and elusive." The corners of her mouth turned up slightly. "It requires music.

"On the line of existence where I come from, music is our art and our science rolled into one. We are the consummate musicians of our age. And since music is very much a universal constant, something your people are only just coming to discover, we can survive the crossing from one line of existence to another. Among those of us who are considered gifted, I was the one chosen to try to reach the Spinner to soothe it. To regulate it with song. I was told it would be difficult and dangerous. In this I have thus far not been disappointed.

"I am not alone. Others will strive to reach the Spinner by other lines. But I was given the best chance. I cannot fail. I cannot assume that if I do so another will be successful. And time is growing short."

"And this 'Spinner' whatsis, it lives at this Vanishing Point place?" Frank asked dubiously.

"Where else would the Spinner exist?"

"Beats the hell out of me," he muttered sarcastically.

"What happens if you don't get to this Vanishing Point in time?" Wendy wondered.

"Then," Mouse declared solemnly, "the fabric of existence will continue to tangle and unravel. Some lines will abruptly cease to exist, while many will cross and intertwine, to the destruction and detriment of all." She moved forward until she was standing close to the back of Alicia's chair. "That's why the countryside here has appeared different to you."

"What about those—creatures," Alicia asked. "Why did they attack us?"

"Because my journey is opposed. I was told it might be."

"So those things were after you, not us," Frank said. "Same with that station attendant." She nodded.

"But if what you're trying to do is for the good of everyone, why would anyone want to stop you?" Wendy wondered.

"Not for the good of everything." Mouse turned her gaze to the road ahead. "There is Chaos. To it the tangling and unraveling of the lines of existence would be a final fulfillment. Once, eons ago, it almost achieved this, but the Spinner was modulated and the fabric of existence saved. Periodically, small lines of existence do break or knot. Your own line has several knots in it. Once when plant life appeared. Again when the creatures you call dinosaurs became extinct. But these were only knots, not breaks. Small interruptions to an otherwise intact and undamaged line."

"'Small,'" Frank mumbled.

"Each time a line knots, or breaks, or tangles, the Cosmos moves a little nearer utter Chaos. When the lines are straight and smooth, when logic and reason rule the Spinner's actions, civilization advances everywhere. Chaos is pushed back, its dominion reduced. One day in the unbelievably far future it may be eliminated altogether. Then peace and understanding may pass between the lines, and all organized intelligence everywhere may come to know one another.

"Chaos is a poor pursuer. Relentless, but by its very nature disorganized. That is its weakness and our strength. Unfortunately, it has an ally. What you would call Evil. In all its forms it serves as an ally and friend to Chaos, for where Chaos reigns, Evil prospers. So Chaos seeks, by means we are not certain of, to enlist Evil in all its forms to aid it. That is one reason why singers such as myself do not travel in groups where we would be conspicuous. Individuals can slip and slide and hide themselves among various lines of existence, escaping the notice of Evil."

"That attendant!" Wendy said with a start.

Mouse nodded. "He was certainly searching for me, but my smell was submerged among your own." She looked down at Frank. "Even so he would have found me out if not for your quick thinking."

"How come I don't feel better?"

Mouse put a fine hand on his shoulder and then he did feel better. Warm, and admired. He thought about shrugging it away but did not. "It is a great thing you are doing, Frank Sonderberg. Greater than you know."

"Don't get melodramatic. I'm just trying to get my family and myself to Las Vegas. For a vacation." He snorted in frustration. "At the rate we're going we're gonna need a vacation from the vacation. 'Lines of existence.' 'Spinners.' 'Chaos and Evil versus reason and civilization.' Gimme a break. I'm just a successful businessman. My idea of a major crusade is buying season tickets to the Dodgers.''

"I am sorry, Frank. You have committed yourself."

"To getting to Vegas," he muttered.

Wendy rose, tugging at the waistband of her jeans. "What would've happened if that old man at the station had figured out you were in here with us?"

"He would have raised a great alarm. Others would have responded. Minions of Evil far more dangerous than he, infinitely more vicious than the rat-things that assailed us. I think they attacked because they saw in you easy prey, not because of me. At least, I am hoping that is why they attacked.

"As to my fate if I had been discovered, I have no doubt I would have been slain on the spot. Then Chaos would have rejoiced. The Cosmos would have grown a little darker, the stars a touch more ominous at night."

"What about us?" Alicia swallowed hard. "What would have happened to us?"

"I can imagine for you. Are you sure you want me to?"

Alicia turned away from those bottomless orbs. "No, never mind. I guess that's not necessary."

"I know what *is* necessary." Frank was grim. "Next stop, whether it's Baker or Needles or wherever, you're getting out. I'm sorry if you've got a problem, but it's none of our business."

"Of course it is your business. Your line of existence is as much in danger as my own, or anyone else's. As I said, you are already committed."

He frowned uneasily. "I heard what you said. What's that mean, we're 'already committed'?"

"By helping me you have entwined yourselves with my line. We are bound together now, by circumstance if not choice. If I were to leave you now the servants of Evil would still seek you out. You are involved, Frank. You are all involved. I did not plan it this way. Remember, it was you who stopped to assist me."

"Just to give you a *ride*, fer chrissake."

She nodded. "Without me to guide and protect you I fear you will never reach your destination. *Any* destination."

"Does it have a name?" Steven asked.

Mouse turned in surprise. "You're a precocious little fellow, aren't you? I suspected as much. Does what have a name?"

"This Chaos thing that's after us." To Steven it was all a game, albeit a serious one.

"We call the antisoul the Anarchis. Think of it that way if it pleases you." She turned back to Steven's parents. "The great danger is that it realizes it need only prevent me from reaching the Spinner. If it can do that by placing obstacles in our path, then the fabric of existence will continue to unravel by itself. It need but rest and wait as the Cosmos comes apart around it."

"Like melting Jell-O," said Wendy thoughtfully.

"And you're the number-one Anarchis-fighter, huh?" Frank no longer made any attempt to keep the bitterness out of his voice.

"Not Anarchis-fighter. Through thought every sentient being does battle with it every moment. It is not a question of defeating the Anarchis but of soothing, of modulating, of re-regulating the Spinner."

"You can sing. I'll grant you that. Otherwise you don't look so hot to me."

"Not all is exactly as it appears to be, Frank Sonderberg. You too are more than you think you are."

"Never mind what I am," he said, embarrassed. "What matters is that according to you even if we drop you off somewhere we're still stuck with fighting this whatever-it-is because we're somehow sensitized to this battle from picking you up."

Mouse was genuinely contrite. "I am sorry for that, but if you had not helped me the fabric of existence would continue its unraveling. I promise that would soon affect you and your entire world. But help me you have. Now I am on my way again to the Vanishing Point. Hope is born anew. All we must do is get there."

Frank was shaking his head. "You're real big on this 'we' business, aren't you?"

"Drive me to the Vanishing Point and I will take care of everything. Once there you need no longer be involved, nor will you be an object of interest to the forces of Evil any longer."

"That's all we've got to do, huh? Where is this Vanishing Point, anyway? I take it somewhere close to Vegas?"

"It moves around. At the moment it is indeed in the vicinity of the place you call Las Vegas. Its motions are complex and difficult to predict."

"I'll bet. And this Spinner, it's at this Vanishing Point?"

"Yes." Mouse looked relieved. "Now you understand!"

"No, I do not understand. I don't understand a damn thing. But I didn't understand those rat-creatures that tried to get at us, either, and they were real enough." He glanced back. "You're real enough. So even though I don't understand, I guess at least part of what you're talking about must be real, too.

"How do I know we can trust you? How do we know you're not lying about all of this? It'd be easy just to kick you out, right here, and forget about you."

"Easy enough, until your whole world accelerated its descent into madness and destruction."

"Look, why should I have to take that kind of responsibility? I didn't ask for it. I don't want it!"

"Frank," said Alicia calmingly, "we're going to Las Vegas anyway. Aren't we?"

He slumped in the padded seat. "I used to think so."

It was still unnaturally dark outside. Nothing else materialized to assault the motor home. After a while the peculiar thin storm clouds began to break up and fade away.

"What happened to Baker?" he asked.

Mouse blinked. "What?"

"Baker," he repeated patiently. "We were supposed to have passed a little town called Baker."

"Then we probably did, only we are no longer on its line of existence. Your reality has already begun to fray."

He shook his head dubiously. "I can't get used to this idea of reality coming to pieces like an old suit. What about Las Vegas? Are you saying it doesn't exist for us any longer, either?"

"Oh, Frank." Alicia started to chide him. "Of course Las Vegas still exists!" Her expression dropped and she turned uncertainly to Mouse. "Doesn't it?"

"I would think so. It is the small things that change first. They are more brittle. Small things. A few plants, an animal or two, the color of the sky, a small town sooner than a large one. Your road has not yet changed, has it?"

Frank had to admit that I-40 looked as monotonous as ever. The smooth concrete stretched out unbroken before them. The barbed-wire fence lining the limits of the state's right-of-way held back the desert. The culverts they occasionally passed over were still fashioned of corrugated steel—though after detecting motion in one of them he found he no longer glanced in their direction.

"All right. We'll take you in to Vegas, but no farther. No matter *what's* happening to the 'fabric of existence.' Got it?"

"I am grateful for your aid. Though you know it not, you are helping yourselves as you help me."

"Yeah, sure." Frank didn't hide his displeasure as he hunched over the wheel.

5

THE FABRIC OF EXISTENCE, unraveling like a ball of twine. Chaos yclept Anarchis. Sirens with lavender eyes who came from a civilization of eerie musicians and sang like whole choirs of electronic instruments. Armies of oversized rodents that fought with tiny knives and axes and gazed at you out of eyes wet with malevolent intelligence.

Somewhere between Barstow and Baker Frank had unknowingly taken an off ramp named Madness. But he couldn't be going mad because his whole family was seeing the same things. It was all much too real. Certainly his fear was. His fear and frustration.

Why him? Why innocent, ordinary Frank Sonderberg? Hadn't he worked his butt off all his life? Hadn't he been a good father and husband, not hitting the kids any more than absolutely necessary, not cheating on his wife except maybe once? Wasn't he understanding even of his daughter's freako friends and his son's alarming passion for junk food and candy? Why did the damnable fates have to go and pick on him and his family when all they wanted was a little safe, clean excitement and to sit by a pool for a few days? He knew he was nothing special. Why not pick on the President, or a general, or some brilliant scientist? Why the owner of a chain of sporting goods stores?

He knew why. It was all because He was the One who had Stopped. Him, Frank Sonderberg and kin. They were the ones who stopped for Mouse, thereby aligning themselves with her and her mission. According to her, if they hadn't stopped and she'd been left standing riderless by the side of the highway much longer, the world would soon perish in a cataclysm of unraveling reason.

Had she maybe overstated the situation just a little to keep them from throwing her off? Might her theorized Armageddon not have come in his lifetime?

No use supposing, as he'd told his kids on more than one occasion. The fact of the matter was that they *had* picked her up. She was real, as were the gas station attendant with his hidden tail and the syrupy bleeding vegetation they'd passed and the rat army. So how could he dispute everything else she'd told them?

She'd given no guarantee she was any better than the other unnatural creatures they'd encountered. No guarantee at all, except— he'd seen the evil in those compact rat faces, had heard it in the old attendant's chuckle. And she'd driven off the rat-things. That meant she could protect them from similar attackers. Perhaps there wouldn't be any more attacks. Perhaps they'd drive straight through to Vegas, drop her off somewhere, wave good-bye, check into their hotel, and start pumping quarters into slots. The only narrow, pinched faces he wanted to see from this point on were those belonging to the habitual gamblers who packed tight around the craps table.

They'd take in Wayne Newton and maybe he'd even let Wendy persuade him to go see Tina Turner. When they were suitably relaxed and tanned they would take a limo to the airport and fly home. He'd completely lost his desire to explore this damnable, ominous desert. Fine with him if the next time he saw these blasted mountains it would be from thirty thousand feet.

"I don't have time to save the world," he murmured to himself. "I've got a family to look after and a business to run."

He'd whispered it under his breath, but Mouse heard nonetheless. "That's the trouble with you people. You don't have any time for your world. You've time for your business and time for your religions. You've time for your families and time for your fun. But you don't have time for the fish and the birds, for the land and the air. No time for the trees. No time for—"

"Spare me the eulogy," Frank said, interrupting her. "I said we'd get you to Vegas, and Frank Sonderberg's not a guy who goes back on his word. Ask anybody in sporting goods west of the

Mississippi. East, too, pretty soon. I'm thinking of expanding into Chicago.''

Alicia turned in surprise. ''Frank! You didn't say anything about that.''

He tried to sound casual about it. ''It came up at the executive meeting about a month ago. Carlos and Garrison agree with me. They think it's time. I sent Garrison into Chicago a few weeks back to start scouting locations. Got to keep moving if we're ever going to be nationwide.''

''I'm so proud of you, Frank.''

''Yeah, well, I guess it won't mean much if this young lady doesn't make it to her Vanishing Point.''

''I assure you, Frank Sonderberg, that all your hopes and dreams will be for nothing, as will everyone's, if the Spinner is not soothed.''

''You know something?'' he said suddenly, surprising even himself. ''I've never been afraid of any challenge that's been put to me. Never. And one thing I'm for sure not afraid of is chaos. Because if you'd ever seen what goes on in my headquarters you'd see that I have to deal with it every day.''

As they drove east he found himself feeling better about their situation. Nothing else had materialized to attack the motor home. The sky had become normal once more, and even the plants lining the shoulder were looking healthier. It would have been nice to write it all off as a dream, but he knew he couldn't do that. He was nothing if not realistic. To run a nationwide business you had to be. No, they hadn't dreamed any of it.

Perhaps the worst was behind them. Maybe Mouse's singing had frightened off any other potential assailants. Or maybe Evil was hunting for them elsewhere. Maybe even on another line of existence. Hadn't their passenger told them that Chaos was bad at organized pursuit?

They passed another sign indicating they were coming up to Hades Junction. It didn't matter whether it was the renamed, misplaced Baker or not because he had no intention of stopping. Not until the sky was stained with neon. Having filled the motor home's tanks at the threatening old man's station, they could cruise straight in to Vegas without a break.

The desert sky was bright and reassuring. No fog, no rain

clouds, no unnatural dimness. It was ninety-five degrees outside, baking hot, and that was how it ought to be.

So relaxed had he become he didn't even get excited when the engine began to cough and sputter and the big vehicle started to slow. Pumping the accelerator only intensified the coughing from beneath the hood.

Alicia eyed him uneasily. "Frank?"

"Relax, sweetheart. Sounds like a clogged fuel line. Maybe the gas that old fart sold us was as old as he was. It's starting to mix with the good stuff we bought in Barstow. No big deal."

Of course, if they'd been close to empty when they had filled up at the ancient station with bad gas, the motor home would have died a mile or two east of it. Could that have been what the old man had had in mind all along for them?

If so, he'd miscalculated. Frank had only stopped to add a few gallons to tanks more than half full.

"Could be the filter, too," he said cheerfully. "Whichever, should take just a minute or two to clean it out."

He carefully checked all three rearview mirrors, expecting the highway behind them to be empty. It was actually more of a relief to see the big rig coming up fast behind them. It rumbled past as he pulled off onto the shoulder. A packed station wagon followed close on the heels of the truck. Both were additional signs of normalcy.

He set the emergency brake, rose from his chair. "Have a cold drink or something, darling. I'll have us back on the road in a jiff."

She was trying hard, he saw, not to panic. "All right, but don't take any longer than you have to, Frank."

"Don't worry. I mean, it's hot outside, right?"

She moved to join him. "Would you like something cold when you finish?"

"Anything with ice and caffeine." He gave her a quick kiss and they exchanged smiles. As he headed for the door she moved to the refrigerator.

The hot sun felt good on the back of his neck. Maybe, he mused as he made his way around to the front of the vehicle, I shouldn't get on Steven's case so much about all the junk he eats. He glanced in the direction of his own inescapably mature gut. It wasn't that many years ago that he could still see his belt. Now, even when he inhaled deeply, it was difficult to locate the leather band that held up his pants. Whoever had made dining so enjoyable had a lot to answer for.

Slipping his left hand under the Winnebago's hood, he flipped the security latch and raised the metal cover. A single support rod held it in place. The big engine smelled warm but not overly hot. Ignoring his suspicions for the moment, he took the time to check the oil level, coolant overflow tank, even the brake fluid. Only then did he hunt for the fuel filter. If it was just the filter, they'd be back on the road in a couple of minutes. If he had to clean out the line they might have a problem.

The little plastic cylinder looked like the carbon-loaded filters Alicia used on the den aquarium. Using a pair of pliers he detached it from the line, resisting the urge as he worked to look over his shoulder every thirty seconds. But there was no elderly, grinning gas station attendant hovering nearby ready to offer advice of an uncertain nature.

He could hear the welcome whoosh of other cars and trucks racing past, glad of the familiar sound. Birds get nervous when they become separated from the rest of the flock, he told himself.

Alicia looked up from the refrigerator. "Where are you going, dear?"

"Just outside for a minute, Mom." Wendy paused impatiently in the doorway.

"I don't know if that's such a good idea. What if some of those horrible little rat-things are still out there?"

"Naw. They're all gone. Mouse sang 'em all away. There's nothing out there anymore. Everything's back to normal again. *Dad's* been outside for a while and nothing's bit *him* on the leg. Come on, Mom! I've been cooped up in here for *days*."

"Just for a few minutes, then, and stay close to the motor home."

Wendy sniffed boredly. "Why not? There's nowhere to go out here anyway."

Slipping on her headphones, she turned up the Walkman's volume a notch and stepped outside, squinting at the bright sunlight. A glance forward showed her dad working quietly, his head hidden by the open engine compartment.

Might as well circumnavigate the world, she told herself glumly. Pivoting neatly, she danced toward the back of the motor home. Maybe one or two of the ugly rodent-things that had attacked them had been caught up in the back axles and bumper. It would be interesting to see one of them close up, to see if they'd really been carrying little axes and knives or if it had been all an invention of their overactive imaginations. Maybe they'd just been regular rats all along. It had been dark and hard to see during the attack, and everything had happened so fast.

There were damp stains all over the motor home's undercarriage, and a few really gross chunks of unidentifiable flesh, but nothing resembling a complete corpse, rodent-like or otherwise. So intent was she on the chassis she didn't see the tall figure that came up quietly behind her until she happened to notice the moving shadow on the ground nearby. With a start she whirled, only to relax as the figure smiled down at her.

He was a hunk. More than that, he was almost beautiful, with delicate features like Michael Jackson's. His hair was blond and straight. Altogether a striking combination. If she'd studied harder in English she could have labeled him saturnine.

"Sorry," the young highway patrolman said apologetically. "Didn't mean to startle you." He peered past her as she straightened self-consciously. "You folks having a problem? Too bad. You almost made it to town. Travelers usually don't break down this side of town anyway. Most everybody who makes it this far usually makes it all the way without any trouble, but I guess you can break down anywhere, isn't that right?"

She nodded, furious at her muteness but terrified of saying the wrong thing. He was a lot older than she was and she didn't want to start out with him thinking of her as some dumb kid.

He was clearly puzzled. "Fact is, I don't recall ever seeing anyone break down right hereabouts."

"An old man sold us some bad gas," she explained, not knowing what else to say. At least it wasn't dumb. "My dad's trying to fix the fuel thingy right now." Twenty-three, she thought. She stood as straight as possible, wishing she was wearing something more flattering to her figure than a T-shirt and jeans, though the jeans were tight enough.

Looking past him she finally noticed the patrol car parked on the shoulder. She hadn't heard or seen it drive up, but then she'd been poking around beneath the motor home in search of rat bodies. She turned down the Walkman and the rhythm in her head eased. Now she could hear him without straining.

"Jack's already up there." He nodded toward the front of the motor home. "Helping your dad, I guess. He'll fix whatever it is. Jack's swift with mechanical things. Me, I'm still learning the route. Oh. My name's Joe."

"At least it isn't Jill." She put her hand to her mouth, giggling. "I'm sorry. I wasn't making fun of you."

"Hey, that's hot. Important thing is you've got a sense of humor. Most of the folks we meet out here are pretty uptight about the heat and their destination." His smile was just this side of overpowering. "You're a refreshing change."

"Thank you." She knew she was blushing but hoped he'd put it down to the effects of the sun. "I never saw a highway patrol car like that before."

He looked back at the parked cruiser. "Like it? It's the latest model."

"Pretty sharp. What is it? A Camaro or Firebird?"

"Naw. Want to see? You're going into town anyway."

She frowned slightly. "I don't think so. I think my dad's going to want to go straight through to Las Vegas once he gets the engine fixed."

The patrolman laughed uproariously, as though she'd just made the perfect joke. "That's beautiful! You're too much. Just meeting you has made my day."

Instantly she forgot her initial and obviously unwarranted suspicions. "I'm glad I was able to make somebody's day. Ours hasn't been exactly perfect."

"How could it be, headed the way you're headed, on the road you're on?" He put a gentle arm around her shoulders. "Come on, let me show you the car. We've got a communications system you won't believe."

Wendy allowed herself to be nudged along. "My mom said I should stay near the motor home."

He stopped, took his arm away. "Hey, you're not afraid of me or anything, are you?"

"Of course not. Why, should I be?"

He nodded. "Somehow I knew you wouldn't be. I'm looking forward to meeting your folks. You're really a special family."

"We aren't all that special."

She had to admit the patrol car intrigued her. It was low and sleek and looked like it was doing a hundred standing still. It wore a full complement of roof lights, the yellow ones rotating brightly as they approached. The emblems on the doors were kind of funny, but if it was a local sheriff's car it wouldn't wear the familiar California Highway Patrol symbol.

The paint job made up for the odd insignia. Yellow on crimson, she decided, was much cooler than white on black.

"Fuel filter."

The resonant voice brought Frank's head around fast. He breathed easily when he caught sight of the uniform, badge, and the smiling, clean-shaven face of someone his own age looking concernedly back into his own.

"Didn't hear you drive up."

The sergeant jerked a thumb backward. "Parked behind you. Don't like backing up when I don't have to."

"Neither do I. Especially in this sucker." Frank indicated the motor home.

The other man chuckled appreciatively, nodded at the filter Frank had removed. "Why don't you let me do that?"

"It's all right. I can handle it."

"Please? As a favor. Playing with combustion's a hobby of mine. Don't get much of a chance to get my hands dirty working patrol."

Frank shrugged, stepped aside. "Suit yourself." He handed the sergeant the plastic cylinder. "Get many breakdowns hereabouts?" he inquired conversationally.

"Not a lot." Sunlight flashed from his mirrored sunglasses.

His smile was bright as the sunshine, which surprised Frank. You'd think a cop forced to work this featureless, miserable stretch of interstate would be in a bad mood most of the time, especially with summer coming on fast. But this one appeared downright ebullient.

"What trouble we do have is with folks who try turning around once they get this far. They pull out into the median and get themselves stuck. Then we have to call a tow to pull 'em out. You should hear the wails and screams when they get the bill."

"You mean they get this far and then they try going back to Barstow?"

For some reason this struck the sergeant as insanely funny.

When he finally stopped laughing he could only shake his head weakly at the memory of it. After wiping his eyes he held the filter up to the sun. He kept it there, studying it intently, until Frank started to worry for him.

"Better watch it."

"No sweat. Light doesn't bother me." He lowered the cylinder, rolled it between his fingers. "This is your problem, all right. Clogged."

Frank nodded. "Thought it might be. Old fart down the road apiece sold me some bad gas."

"Tall, skinny, ugly son of a bitch?"

"You know him?" That was a stupid question, Frank thought. Of course he'd know him. Anyone working this piece of highway would know every full-time and semi-permanent inhabitant within a dozen miles, probably by name.

He wondered if the sergeant would know anything about intelligent rat-things.

"Tell me something. How'd he ever get an off ramp put in out there? It doesn't show on the map." He took back the fuel filter, examined it himself.

"Guess he's got some pull," the sergeant theorized.

Frank put the filter to his mouth and blew. A few bits of road grime flew out the other end. Embarrassed, he took a deep breath and blew harder. More grime was expelled, but the filter was far from cleared.

"Really bad gas," he murmured, breathing hard.

"We've had plenty of complaints about that guy. I guess you can't blame him. Most of the business goes straight into town. He has to work for everything he gets. Here, let me have a go." Frank passed the cylinder over, curious to see what the patrolman could do. He wasn't particularly big and if he possessed unusual reserves of lung power they weren't visible from the outside.

Lung power didn't enter into it. To Frank's shock the sergeant put the cylinder to his lips and *inhaled*. He kept sucking until a stunned Frank thought the man's face was going to collapse in on itself. Only then did he remove the cylinder from his mouth and smile hugely.

Even then Frank didn't suspect something was seriously wrong until the sergeant sniffed appreciatively—and swallowed.

"Here." The patrolman extended the hand holding the now

perfectly transparent filter. When Frank made no move to take it, the man added, "You'll need this back."

"Yeah. Yeah, right." Not knowing what else to do, his thoughts churning furiously, Frank gingerly took the cylinder and moved to reinsert it on the fuel line. "What—what did you do with all that gunk? You didn't *really* swallow it, did you?"

"Sure! You don't think I'm going to waste it, do you? That old stuff may not be so good for your engine's digestion, but when it's aged like that it acquires a real tang." He licked his lips approvingly. "Premium unleaded. Wasn't sure I'd like the stuff when they started switching everything over. Turned out to be an improvement. Taking out the lead changed the flavor, but this way you get more of the original hydrocarbon essence. Not to mention the additional distilling it's undergone." He threw back his head and roared anew, this time producing not only rich, deep laughter but a gout of blue flame pure enough to have issued from the nozzle of an acetylene torch. It shot four feet into the air. Frank felt the heat of it keenly.

As laughter and fire faded, the sergeant removed his silver sunshades and Frank saw his eyes for the first time. Vertical pupils set in irises of intense yellow. Cat's eyes. He wanted to scream, dared not.

A finger dug road grit from one eye, then the glasses were slipped back in place. "I'm no connoisseur." As Frank fought to still his trembling hands, the otherwordly officer methodically checked the positioning of the filter. "Can't afford the really good stuff. Racing fuel, top octane. Nice to sneak a swig now and then. Keeps you alert and on your claws. Of course, we're not supposed to drink on duty, but a quick shot now and then's not going to upset anybody's applecart, right?" Frank nodded numbly.

"Besides, back at the station they really don't know what the hell's going on out on the road. All they know is what they read in our reports. They've got enough vices to deal with at the Entrance without worrying about the staff's. That's one of the compensations of this assignment. You have some privacy." He coughed and blue flame exploded in a narrow stream from his lips. Wiping his mouth with the back of his hand, he glanced at the surrounding desert and said conversationally, "Starting to warm up again. First time in months it's been comfortable out here."

Frank retreated as inconspicuously as possible. "Thanks for the help."

"Hey, no problem. That's what we're here for."

Both turned as the patrol cruiser sidled up next to them, out in the slow lane. A tall, much younger officer partly rose from his seat on the driver's side to shout over the top of the car. Frank couldn't tell for certain, but he thought the younger patrolman's eyes looked normal.

"Hey, Jack!"

"What's up, Joe?"

The younger officer glanced briefly at Frank. "Seems we've got a problem here."

"Problem?" The sergeant turned apologetically. "Excuse me a minute."

"Sure thing."

As the sergeant moved to check with his partner, Frank hurriedly re-entered the motor home. Panting hard, he locked the door behind him.

Alicia was staring at him. "What is it? What's wrong now?"

Without replying he threw himself into the driver's chair and started the engine. It spat a few times, clearing the last of the bad gas from the fuel line, before turning over.

"Nothing," he told her, grim-faced. "It's nothing."

She moved up next to him. "Don't give me that, Frank. I know you better."

A tapping on the driver's window made Frank jump in the seat. The sergeant was standing outside, his voice barely audible through the glass. He made rolling-down motions with one hand. Trying to stay calm, Frank nudged the power window control, lowering the small vent window.

"Something the matter, officer?"

To Frank's surprise, the inhuman sergeant appeared uncomfortable. "I'm afraid I'm going to have to ask you to come into the station, sir."

"Why? What've we done wrong?" Once the motor home was up to speed Frank had no intention of slowing down or stopping at any station, no matter how many guns or what kinds of allies the officer produced. But motionless as they were, stuck off on the paved shoulder, they were vulnerable.

"I don't know that you've done anything wrong, traveler. But there's an irregularity. Nobody's sure about it, but we ran a computer check and your license and vehicle aren't in there.''

"Then somebody's not checking the right place. We rented this outfit in Torrance. I can give you the name of the rental outfit, the salesman who turned it over to us, and any other identification you need. If there's some problem with the plates that's the rental company's concern, not mine.''

"It's nothing like that.'' The thing tipped its cap back on its head. ''But I'm still going to have to ask you to follow us in.''

"I'm not sure I want to do that.'' He had a hand on the shift lever, ready to throw it into drive on a second's notice. ''We haven't done anything wrong. You've as much as said so yourself.''

"That might be.'' The officer sounded genuinely apologetic. If only, Frank thought frantically, his eyes had been normal and his taste for flammable liquids not so pronounced. ''I have to insist. Like you say, this probably has nothing to do with you, but it's not my place to decide blame or responsibility. We just patrol this section of highway. Don't make things difficult for me. It's been a tough week.''

Turning, he nodded in the direction of the patrol cruiser. When he saw what the thing was looking at, Frank rose halfway off the seat.

"Wendy!''

His daughter stared back at him from the front seat of the cruiser. Her eyes were wide, but she didn't seem especially frightened.

"If you'll come along peacefully, please,'' the sergeant said, repeating his demand.

"What's my daughter doing in your car? You have no right to—!'' But the sergeant ignored him as he climbed into the back of the cruiser. Flashing its red lights but no siren, it rolled twenty yards forward before stopping. Only then did the driver run the siren a couple of times. It sounded distinctly like a human scream.

Frank clutched the wheel for support. Alicia had come up beside him, worry in her voice and in her expression.

"What's going on, Frank? Why is Wendy in that police car?''

"I don't know what's going on and I don't know why Wendy's in that car, but they want us to follow them and with Wendy there we don't have a lot of choices.'' The siren raced again, a terrifying sound. "Get Mouse. Tell her what's going on and ask her what we—"

"I already tried. She's asleep in the back. I can't wake her up. I've never seen anyone sleep so soundly."

"Yeah, singing's hard work," he said sarcastically. A rising wail came from the police cruiser, like a pig being butchered alive. "Keep trying."

Pale, Alicia nodded and rushed to the back of the motor home, ignoring Steven's queries. With a wrench almost hard enough to break the shift lever, Frank pulled out into the slow lane. Automatically, he checked the rearview. There were two cars coming up fast, but as he pulled out they both changed to the fast lane.

He caught a brief glimpse of the passengers in the second car. A young man and woman. The woman was pounding on the inside of the rolled-up window. Her expression was wild, her hair disheveled. The driver of the car sat motionless behind the wheel, both hands affixed to the plastic circle. They went by so quickly Frank couldn't be certain, but it looked to him like the driver had no face.

The two cars vanished over the horizon. The police cruiser accelerated, and Frank, feeling utterly helpless, fed gas to the motor and followed.

"What's happening?"

Frank saw Mouse, still sleepy-eyed, standing behind Alicia's seat. Somehow she kept her long hair from tangling while she slept.

He explained and when he was through she nodded knowingly. "Another thread has broken. The end has entwined with your line of existence."

"They've got Wendy with them. They ordered me to follow."

"You're doing the right thing. If your daughter was here I might be able to help." She stared at the patrol cruiser keeping ten car lengths in front of them. "Now we can do nothing until we have her again."

"They're not going to hurt her, are they?" asked Alicia. She was fighting back tears, fighting to keep control, Frank saw.

"From what your husband has told me they have no reason to. That is not a guarantee, but it offers reason to hope."

"This is what you meant about this Evil allying itself with

Chaos, right?" Frank wanted to accelerate, to pull around and use the motor home's greater weight to run the ominous cruiser and its occupants off the road. Wanted to see the car roll over and over among the weeds and Joshua trees until it exploded in a ball of flame. Instead he followed meekly. "They were waiting for us."

"You told me they were not expecting you."

He sat a little straighter. "Yeah. Yeah, that's right. That's what the sergeant said."

"Then we are still an anomaly to them. We must break away before they learn who I am."

"Who are they?" Alicia asked. "What is this place?"

"An outpost of Evil. That much is certain. What kind of Evil we do not yet know."

They fell silent, following. Other vehicles passed them regularly now. Frank tried not to look in their direction, hoped Alicia did not. Steven remained in the back, absorbed in his comic books, for which Frank was grateful.

Each car featured the same blank-faced driver, gray robots immune to everything but their driving. Chauffeurs on a concrete Styx. Like the cars and trucks, the passengers they were convoying came in all sizes, colors, and shapes.

Frank watched as an open-topped Jeep went bouncing past, towing two middle-aged men behind it. Both were naked and obviously had been dragged a considerable distance. Their bodies were raw and bloody and yet they acted lively enough. Probably more alive than they wanted to be. A big blue Lincoln cruised by smoothly. An attractive woman of middle-age hung out the rear back window. She was screaming and waving both arms frantically. He had a quick glimpse of her companions in the back seat. They were ugly and alien enough to stop a sensitive man's heart.

The Jeep and the Lincoln were exceptions. The majority of vehicles which roared past had all their windows rolled up. Their human occupants were visible only as jerking, gesticulating silhouettes, tormented shadows riding in the back of Chevrolets and Mercedes and VWs. Frank wondered if there was a formal relationship between the class of vehicle and its passengers, as well as the kind of tortures they were undergoing.

Only the motor home drove in the slow lane. We're normal, he thought. Maybe that's why these cops find us abnormal. A check of the speedometer showed they were doing fifty. Their captors were driving cautiously.

The landscape commenced a radical metamorphosis. This time it wasn't a matter of a few stunted, distorted plants. The sky had turned a pale greenish hue, sickly and unhealthy-looking. Pools and ponds of molten sulphur and other unidentifiable acrid fluids pockmarked the terrain on both sides of the highway. He turned the air-conditioning up all the way. They might freeze, but at least they could breathe. The air outside stank of rotten eggs and burning flesh. The distant mountains were now obscured by steam and mist rising from pools of boiling mud.

Once Frank thought he glimpsed a line of at least fifty men, women, and children yoked to an enormous four-wheeled wooden cart. The cart had barred sides through which twisting, contorting bodies tried to squeeze. Blood and excrement formed a noisome trail behind the great wheels.

Squatting atop the front of the cart wielding long metal whips were a pair of nightmare faces with bulging eyes and long fangs. They had no legs and bounced up and down on a pair of muscular arms. All in a nightmarish glimpse as the motor home cruised past, its air-conditioning humming efficiently. After that he ignored the terrain on both sides of the highway and concentrated on the road ahead.

Whatever else might happen he did not want to break down in this country. Alicia rested a hand on his leg. Even going fifty with the air conditioner running on high he could still hear occasional pitiful screams from the passing cars. The shrieks of the damned filled the air beyond the barbed-wire fences that delineated the limits of the highway.

Only the cactus had done well here. They had ballooned to enormous sizes, with spines like swords. Prickly pear and jumping cactus, cholla and devil's tail covered the ground. Everyone he'd seen beyond the fence had been naked and barefoot.

It took him a moment to recognize a different humming sound. A glance in the rearview showed Mouse cuddling a frightened Steven. Apparently he'd forsaken his comics for a look outside and had been traumatized by what he'd seen. Now she was doing her best to reassure and comfort him.

"It's all right," she was telling the boy over and over. "Everything will be all right."

."But I want to go home." Steven's voice was barely audible. "I don't like this place. I want to go home."

"In good time we shall all return home."

Alicia raised no objections to Mouse's maternal exertions, realizing that their visitor was doing a better job of calming her son than she could herself. She had enough trouble fighting down her own hysteria. All she could do was concentrate hard on the taillights of the police car in front of them, concentrate and not think.

Once she'd made the mistake of looking to her right, at the land beyond the highway. She'd seen half a dozen creatures, each no taller than four feet, stockily built and clad in black pants striped with yellow. They surrounded two women, a mother and daughter. Each time the women would try to run through the circle, two or three of the imps, or devils, or whatever the creatures were, would grab the naked figures and throw them back into a pile of bed-shaped cacti. Both women were thick with imbedded spines, and blood trickled endlessly down their bodies. Beyond them two young men fought to escape a similar circle. It struck her then that the men were trying to reach the women, and the women the men. Shuddering, she turned away from the ghastly sight, praying that the four were not related.

The smooth unbroken concrete roadbed was a white slash of normality in the midst of nightmare. That, and the police cruiser ahead that held her daughter.

"Frank, what's going to happen to us?"

"Nothing's going to happen to us." He said it because he didn't know what else to say, and because he strongly suspected that to give in to pessimism in this would be to give in to madness. "We'll get out of this all right. Wendy, too. It's just a mistake on somebody's part. Like the patrolman told us."

"He's not a patrol*man*."

"I know that!" Immediately he apologized for snapping at her, conscious how close he was to the breaking point. He lowered his voice. "I just don't know what else to call him."

She was sobbing now. Softly, not hysterically but steadily. "What's going to happen to us, Frank? What is this place? Where are we?"

"I think you know where we are, Alicia. I think we've both known for several miles. It can only be one place, and it isn't Baker."

A N OFF RAMP LOOMED just ahead. Frank wasn't surprised when the police cruiser's turn signal began flashing.

There were two lanes. The right one was backed up onto the highway with cars and trucks. The left was empty until the patrol car started up it. As they followed close behind Frank saw that the land surrounding the highway was still barren but full of red buildings. The plethora of architectural styles was astonishing. There was no rhyme or reason to the town that he could see. Victoriana slumped next to early medieval, Islamic alongside Frank Lloyd Wright, Balinese beside early Russian.

There was a stop sign at the top of the off ramp. A crossroad ran right, through part of the town, and left via an overpass to the other side of the highway. Directly ahead lay an on ramp. Part of him desperately wanted to take it, to chance pursuit by the patrol car, which had already turned right onto the crossroad. They'd have a slight head start and the down ramp would let him build up speed quickly.

But not without his daughter. Not without Wendy. She might be something of a rebellious airhead, but no more so than many teenage girls her age. He loved her even when he yelled at her. No way was he leaving her in this place.

There was a big parking lot off to the left, fronting a squat, single-story building. Feathery antennas protruded from the roof, giving the edifice the appearance of a bloated caterpillar hugging the ground.

Frank had no trouble turning across the road since there was no oncoming traffic. It was all one way. The lot was full of police cruisers and vans, all the same color as the one carrying Wendy. Above the main entrance a sign unsurprisingly proclaimed:

HADES JUNCTION POLICE

The cruiser they'd been following parked. Its driver turned off the spinning red lights and exited. A moment later Wendy emerged in the firm grasp of the sergeant. Her headphones hung from her neck. Fear and confusion vied for dominance on her face.

The older officer held on to her as he beckoned toward the motor home.

Frank rose, unlatching his seatbelt. "You stay here."

"Not a chance, Frank. I'm coming, too."

"I think we'd all best go." They both looked at Mouse. She indicated the waiting police. "Their company offers official protection, at least until they find out more about us. I'd rather not stay out here alone."

Frank hesitated, then nodded. "All right. I'm taking your advice because I don't know what else to do. Steven comes, too?"

"Especially Steven." She put an arm around the boy's shoulders. Alicia noted the gesture but said nothing.

After checking to make sure the doors and windows were locked, Frank followed them outside. He paused atop the steps, his attention caught by the long line of vehicles backed up in the lane they'd just exited. They crawled slowly toward an imposing gate a couple of hundred yards down the road, inland from the highway off ramp.

He couldn't read the symbols atop the gate, but he had no trouble with the big steel sign just down the road from the police station parking lot. It was painted cherry red and only confirmed what he'd already guessed. The three words were a contradiction in terms.

WELCOME TO HELL

He hurried after Alicia and Mouse and Steven, not wanting to be left behind outside. As he hurried he wiped sweat from his cheeks and forehead. It had been hot by the side of the road, but not this hot. The paved parking lot was a frying pan, Death Valley's Furnace Creek in high summer. He fancied he could hear his sweat evaporating into the air.

If anything it was hotter inside the station.

The sergeant was waiting for them. "If you'll all just follow us we'll get this business cleared up straightaway." He turned and led them up a corridor, chatting with his taller, younger subordinate.

Frank went straight to his daughter. She wasn't crying, but there was panic in her eyes and she was trembling visibly. He opened his arms and she sagged gratefully against him, her hair disheveled, her blouse torn from one shoulder.

The slimy-looking officer behind the front desk was staring at them and grinning. His teeth were filed to fine points. His desk, like the floor and walls, was fashioned of cut stone. There wasn't a sliver of wood to be seen in the building.

Trembling a little himself, Frank started to step around his daughter. Her arms tightened against his.

"No! No. It's okay, Dad. I'm all right." She glanced back over her shoulder to where the two officers had stopped to wait on them. "He didn't do anything much. Just got me scared, that's all."

"You sure?" He searched his daughter's eyes, was immensely relieved not to find what he'd feared there.

She nodded. "Daddy, where are we?"

He remembered the sign, didn't have the heart to quote it. "A bad place. Very bad. But we'll be out of here soon, you'll see. As long as we keep our cool and stick together we'll get out all right. We have to keep our composure, though. Understand?" He gripped her shoulders hard.

"I understand."

"Okay. Now wipe your face. We don't want to let these things think they're getting to us, right?"

She nodded again, managed a feeble smile.

They followed the two officers up the corridor.

It might have been any office building in L.A. except for the intense heat and the fact that everything was made of stone or metal. No air-conditioning in Hell, he thought. Only heat and hotter. Officers and non-uniformed help passed them in the halls. Doors opened onto busy rooms full of clerks and technicians. Many of them were far less human than the two patrolmen who'd picked up Wendy. Steven stayed between Alicia and Mouse while Wendy hung close to her father. The station's personnel ran the gamut from near-human to semi-human to utterly alien grotesqueries equipped with multiple tails and horns. Some had more than the usual complement of eyes and arms. Others sported fangs borrowed from saber-toothed cats. There were computer operators with forked tongues and filing clerks with long, narrow skulls that showed more bone than flesh.

They stopped outside a door while the sergeant vanished into the office beyond. The younger officer picked his teeth while something seven feet tall slumped down the hallway, long arms dragging the floor, knuckles turned inward. It did not turn to inspect them, for which Frank was grateful. He had no desire to encounter those vast yellow eyes with their tiny black pupils nor to see what might live inside that cavernous, bulging mouth. It held a sheet of plastic in one immense paw. Two red chevrons gleamed on the six-foot-long sleeve of its tunic.

Two more modest monsters flanked a water cooler in the room opposite. The cooler jug contained an amber-colored liquid. Gasoline? he wondered. Or something equally volatile?

The sergeant emerged from the office he'd entered, took the younger patrol creature aside and whispered to it. Frank wanted to smash in both smug faces. He might've tried it in L.A., but not here. Not in this place. A stupid, probably futile gesture that would do neither him nor his family any good. He wasn't afraid of the younger officer who'd tormented his daughter, but he was damned afraid of the other things that lurked throughout the building. Besides which it wasn't a smart idea to take a poke at a cop inside a police station, no matter what kind of things populated the place.

The sergeant turned back to them. "We've done some checking. The lieutenant wants to see you." He turned and they followed him inside. Frank kept a protective arm around his daughter. The younger officer kept staring at her and grinning. She avoided his gaze.

In the outer office they passed something like a shell-less tortoise. It had a uniform and a face like a demented wild boar. The sergeant spoke to it and it grunted a reply before waddling past.

They halted outside a door of frosted glass, except the design in the glass wasn't frost but rather flames. It was very artistically done, even to the details of the human hearts that floated in the midst of the flames.

The lieutenant was waiting for them. He was four feet across at the shoulders and weighed in the neighborhood of a quarter ton. His oversized desk barely accommodated his enormous frame. It was dominated by piles of plastic sheets, which he was perusing as they entered.

Frank's gaze rose to the pictures that filled the wall behind him. There were several framed certificates, including a crimson diploma. A miniature gold pitchfork was mounted on an engraved brass plate. Obviously symbolic rather than practical, it looked like the sort of thing you'd give a retiring judge, only he'd get a gavel.

He preferred not to study the actual photographs, would have given a lot to keep Steven and Wendy and Alicia from having to look at them at all. He could only hope that they were too stunned by what they'd encountered already to pay much attention to them. They'd ignore the long string of preserved human organs that hung above one file cabinet, twisting slowly in the hot air of the office, only because their attention was drawn to the mounted, stuffed, perfectly preserved figure of a four-year-old boy that sat regarding them blankly out of glass eyes from its marble base atop another cabinet.

The lieutenant's saucer-sized eyes were pink with red pupils, framed by towering bushy eyebrows that resembled dancing flames. His orange hair had recently undergone a severe crew cut. The uniform he wore could serve as a tent for any three normal men. Whether it was his natural body odor or some grisly cologne Frank had no way of knowing, but the great body stank like the backside of a slaughterhouse.

The uniformed monster put aside his plastic sheets and regarded the arrivals with interest. His was not a pleasant stare and Frank would have given a lot to be out from under it.

"Well," a voice rumbled, as if from somewhere deep beneath the ground, "it's clear you shouldn't be here."

Frank hadn't made it close to the top of the business world by being meek and deferential. This wouldn't be the proper place to show weakness, he decided quickly.

"Of course we shouldn't be here! We were just cruising along, observing all the local laws, minding our own business, not in the flow of traffic at all, when these two pulled us over and insisted we follow them." He indicated the sergeant and younger officer, who stood off to one side. "And that one," he added for good measure, "tried to take advantage of my daughter."

"Good," the lieutenant growled. "Glad to know my people are doing their job. As for pulling you over, what else would you expect them to do? I've read the transcript of their report and you're right about not being in the regular traffic pattern. Around here that's more than unusual: it's exceptional. There *is* only the prescribed traffic. Casual travelers just don't end up on that piece of highway. It's reserved for the departed who've been assigned this as their final destination."

"We did our own determining," Frank insisted. "We must've taken a wrong exit somewhere. We were on our way to Vegas and—"

The lieutenant interrupted him, nodding to himself. "That could explain it. Las Vegas is as close to Hell as humans can get in the real world. I can see how there could've been a mixup. An interchange under repair, some fool places a detour sign improperly— not impossible. You're certain you were going *to* Vegas, not coming from there?"

"That's right."

Great craggy eyebrows bunched together. "Damn peculiar. I knew when Joe described you to me we had a real problem here."

While he pondered the fate of those before him, the young officer had worked his way next to Wendy. He grinned down at her while she tried to move away from him. Frank wanted to shout in his inhumanly beautiful young face, to order him to stay away from his daughter, but he held on to his temper. The slightest wrong move might upset the lieutenant's fragile objectivity. So far he'd been courteous, even polite. But not apologetic. Frank could not risk getting on his bad side, assuming he wasn't all bad side already.

He kept his mouth shut until he heard Wendy whimper.

"Look, if this situation's beyond your authority I'll be glad to speak to your superior officer."

The demon's face twisted into an unexpected, horrid smile. He leaned way back in his couch-sized chair and filled the room with his laughter. His elephantine bellowing bounced off the rock and shook the pictures and plaques on the walls. Steven clung to Mouse's waist while Alicia turned away and tried to shield Wendy.

By the time he regained control of himself the lieutenant had tears rolling down his cheeks. They didn't roll very far, evaporating with tiny sizzling noises before they fell as far as his mouth.

"The Chief? You *want* to see the Chief? Now that's really funny! Anybody would know you people don't belong here or you'd never say anything like that." Abruptly he leaned forward across his desk. He seemed to take up the whole room that way, shoulders and chest and face of planetary dimensions, glowing pink eyes continents adrift in a sea of unwholesome flesh. His tone lowered and it sent shivers through Frank's entire being.

"You don't *really* want to talk to my boss, do you?" he growled softly.

"Not if we can solve this business without bothering him, I guess," Frank said bravely.

"I thought you might reconsider." The demon sat back in his chair, which creaked beneath his enormous weight. "I don't like to have to deal with the Chief under any circumstances. The more you can avoid him, the more pleasant your sojourn in Eternity will be. I guarantee you wouldn't enjoy the meeting."

Out of the corner of an eye Frank could see the tall young officer's hands roaming over his daughter's body. She stood motionless save for her trembling because she didn't know what else to do. Frank didn't know what to do, either.

Steven had left Mouse's side and retreated to the far end of the room, as far from the two patrol-things as possible. Instantly three squat creatures popped into existence, surrounding him. They were smaller than adults but bigger than Steven. Each wore sneakers, jeans, dirty shirts. One had on a leather jacket. They began poking and kicking, trying to trip him. All had mean, narrow little faces, believably human save for the brightly glowing eyes. Three schoolyard bullies, a precocious, overweight youngster's worst nightmare come to life.

So far Alicia had been ignored, and Mouse might be immune, but it was becoming clear that the longer they lingered in this place, the less reluctance the inhabitants felt about abusing them. Demonic inhibitions were breaking down while he and this officer argued. If they didn't do something to get away soon, their presence here might become a fait accompli instead of a matter for debate.

"We don't belong here because we haven't died yet," he argued desperately. "It's not our time, or whatever it is they call it. This is a big mistake."

"I tend to agree with you," the lieutenant rumbled. At that declaration the schoolyard trio paused in their bullying. The young patrol-thing stepped away from Wendy. "Yet it remains that however you got here, you are here, and must be dealt with. I don't know what kind of leeway I have in a situation like this. I'm going to have the records checked for precedents. If there is one, it will guide me in the disposition of your case.

"Meanwhile"—he turned to the sergeant, who stiffened beneath that relentless glare—"put these people somewhere comfortable so I can find them when I want them."

"First Level?" The sergeant's voice was eager.

"No," replied the lieutenant with obvious reluctance. "Can't do that until it's official. Someplace neutral but secure. Your enthusiasm for your work is commendable, Sergeant, but we have to follow correct procedure. Don't worry. If this works out the way we all hope it does, I'll see to it you and your partner receive proper credit."

"Thank you, sir."

"Can I take charge of this one while we're waiting, sir?" The younger officer had advanced to put both arms around Wendy. He held her easily in spite of her struggles. She moaned in his grasp. "She's a squirmer. I like squirmers."

"Corporal, you're a patrolman. You asking for a transfer to field operations?"

"No, sir. But it'd be nice to have something to play with between handing out tickets and keeping the traffic moving."

"Don't count your bonus until it's approved. But I'll note your request." The lieutenant turned back to Frank, who clung to his remaining composure with great difficulty. "Sorry about this, but you've got to see my side of it."

"I'm sure you'll do the right thing," Frank replied through clenched teeth.

"The right thing?" The demon found this amusing, though not as hilarious as Frank's request to meet with his superior. "We never do the right thing here. That's not my business. What I do is the appropriate thing, which isn't the same at all."

"Yeah, right." Frank's voice fell to a mumble. "That's what I meant. Thanks."

The two patrolmen escorted them out of the office. Trailing the crying, battered Steven, the three young bullies kept up a relentless barrage of taunts and kicks, pinching and punching him hard enough to cause pain but not injury. Wendy's patrolman devoted equal attention to her, easily warding off her rejecting blows. Possibly sensing a favorable forthcoming decision, the sergeant was eyeing Alicia with intense interest.

Frank suffered persistent visions of arteries tightening like cords around his brain, of little wiggly worm-things swarming into his eyes and nostrils like sentient cholesterol in search of his stroke center.

Only Mouse remained unaffected and aloof. Frank wondered how long her immunity might last. Not that it mattered what they did to her. All that mattered was that she would be trapped here along with them, prevented from reaching her Vanishing Point. It occurred to him that if the fabric of existence came apart completely, Hell might go to pieces along with everywhere else. Somehow that was no comfort at all.

With obvious reluctance they were shoved into an empty room. Frank heard the sergeant lock them in.

The room was identical to the sort you might find in any government building. A couch, several battered chairs, a couple of end tables boasting lamps fashioned from what looked like human bones, and a magazine rack next to the single coffee table. Frank glanced at the magazines, quietly scooped them up, and dumped them behind the couch so Alicia and Wendy wouldn't see them. He couldn't do anything to conceal the scratches on the walls and door or the gouges that had been dug in the floor.

Wendy sat down on the couch next to her mother, who tried to comfort her as best she could. Steven had stopped crying and was rubbing his eyes.

There were no windows and only the single doorway. A shadowy alcove suggested the presence of a bathroom. There was a drinking fountain bolted to the wall just inside.

Steven put his lips to the spigot and pressed the lever. Frank paid no attention to him until the boy screamed in pain. He jerked sharply away from the fountain, holding his mouth with both hands and bawling anew.

His parents were at his side in an instant. Forcing his hands down, they examined him. His reddened, burned lips were already beginning to blister.

"They let me bring my purse," Alicia murmured. "I've got some chapstick." Frank nodded wordlessly, moving to examine the fountain. A flick of the lever brought forth a stream of clear water. As might have been suspected, though not by a ten-year-old, the liquid was boiling hot.

"All we can do is wait," said Mouse into the silence.

"Wait?" He turned away from the diabolic fountain. "Wait for what? Can't you get us out of here? I wouldn't want to bet that lieutenant or whatever he reports to is going to end up deciding anything in our favor."

Her expression turned sorrowful. "I have the ability to heal and to soothe, to regulate and relax, but I cannot work miracles. If I could do such things I would not have to stand by the side of strange highways begging for a ride. It may yet be that when they realize we do not belong here we shall be sent on our way."

"Sure. I know we can rely on that lieutenant's inherent good nature." He watched while Alicia applied balm to their son's seared lips. Wendy had found something to look at.

He'd missed one of the magazines. She was gazing at it transfixed by horror. Covering the distance between them in a single step, he wrenched it out of her hands and threw it across the room. She stared at him in shock, then let him take her in his arms. It had been a long time since she'd allowed that.

He held her for a long while. When he let her go she managed a slight, hopeful smile. But as she resumed her seat he saw she was staring worriedly at the hallway door, perhaps remembering the intentions of a certain uniformed demon.

An hour passed, then another. Somehow they endured the stifling heat. There was a metal cup in the bathroom. Frank filled it with boiling water from the tap, let it stand until it was cool enough to drink. Lukewarm water was better than none.

No one checked in on them. Whatever procedure the lieutenant was having to go through was evidently complex and time-consuming.

Of course, if they all perished of heat stroke in the interim it would solve all his problems.

He longed for the motor home's well-stocked pantry, but all they had to eat was a package of crackers Alicia found in her purse. While providing some nourishment the crackers also intensified their thirst. Frank also had to go to the bathroom, but after his son's experience with the water fountain he wasn't sure he was ready to try the dark alcove's facilities.

Fifteen minutes later the door clicked as it was unlocked from outside. Wendy and Steven retreated to their mother's side. Frank took up a stance in front of them, ready to confront whatever entered.

It was only a man. Tall and powerfully built, he wore stained dungarees, flannel shirt, and battered cowboy boots. A red headband controlled his shoulder-length straight black hair. One hand pulled the handle of a galvanized metal cart that contained two mops, a wire broom, and a bucket of steaming, soapy water. The intruder silently soaked one mop in the bucket, ignored them as he began swabbing the bathroom floor.

Other than being the size of an NFL lineman, the janitor looked perfectly normal. Normal eyes and face and no more than the accepted number of appendages. He worked silently, moving the mop back and forth, pausing only to wring it out and resoak it.

"Hey, Dad," Steven whispered urgently, "he looks like a real Indian!"

"Be quiet. Nothing here's what it appears to be." He kept his voice down, but not enough.

"Now that's where you're wrong, friend." The mop-wielder spoke with a soft, Southwestern drawl, his enunciation almost too precise. "Everything here's exactly what it appears to be. No need for subterfuge."

Something in the man's manner, in his tone, impelled Frank to take a chance. "You don't look like one of *them*." He nodded toward the hallway beyond the door. "You don't talk like one of them, either."

"Probably because I am not one of them." He smiled. Frank was immensely relieved to see that his teeth were not pointed. "Name is Burnfingers Begay. First thing now is you will ask yourselves how I come by such a name."

"Oh, no, we wouldn't—" Alicia began.

He answered before she could finish. "When I was born I came out so hot in the delivery that I burned the doctor's hands." Still smiling, he turned back to his work.

Alicia wasn't sure if he was being serious or not. Wendy didn't care. She just laughed, until her mother shushed her. What if the janitor didn't find it amusing?

"Go ahead and laugh. It *is* pretty funny."

She gaped at him. "Can you read minds?"

"No. But after a while you get a pretty good idea how folks are thinking, even if you don't know for sure what they're thinking."

Frank was eyeing him dubiously. "I don't get it. You seem normal to me."

"Oh, no. Not normal at all." He paused, leaning on his mop. "You see, I am crazy. Very much out of my head. Major wacko. Isn't that obvious? What sane person would be working here?"

"But you're not a devil, or a demon."

"Only to a few folks who've gotten in my way. Actually I am Navajo and Comanche. Begay is Navajo. Burnfingers is the Anglo transliteration of my Comanche name, which you could not pronounce. My mother was visiting the all-Indian powwow in Gallup one year, where my father was exhibiting. They begot yours truly." He laughed softly. "Half of me wants to settle down and make jewelry and the other half wants to go on the warpath. No wonder I am crazy."

"You don't sound crazy to me," said Alicia hesitantly.

He raised a cautionary finger. "Ah: the sign of the truly mad."

"Is this your torment, your punishment?" Frank asked him curiously.

"Punishment? This isn't punishment. I was on my way to L.A. when my pickup broke down. Going to meet a girl. The local police gave me a ride."

"Us, too," Frank told him dourly.

"Of course I was kinda surprised at first. I think I puzzled these locals. They used all kinds of creatures and critters and sights to try and upset me, but all it did was remind me of Disneyland, so I laughed. You see, we have no equivalent of your kind of Hell. That is when they decided I did not belong here in this place."

"That's what they're doing now, trying to decide what to do with us," Frank said eagerly. "What happened then?"

"There was a lot of talking going on. While they talked I saw how filthy this place was. Myself, I am a stickler for cleanliness. My father's mother kept the cleanest hogan in the whole Four Corners area, until we all moved into the big house. So while they all talked I just started to clean things, to keep busy. When they saw what I was doing they offered me a job. They're not very good at cleaning up after themselves and when they assign some of their own kind to do it they end up making a worse mess or pulling off one another's arms and things like that."

"A job? Here?"

"Why not here? Have you ever been to the Four Corners area, friend?"

Frank shook his head, added absently, "Sonderberg. Frank Sonderberg." He proceeded to introduce the rest of the family, leaving Mouse for last.

Burnfingers nodded. "Four Corners boils in summertime, but in winter and fall it's such a cold place you cannot imagine. Something in me could not tolerate the cold. My family thought it was funny, big fella like me always being cold. One thing about this place here: it never gets cold. The pay is good, too. They pay me in gold, any kind of gold I want. Spanish doubloons, Imperial Roman coinage, Persian ingots—I have quite a collection now."

"Where do they get all the gold?" Steven wondered, wide-eyed.

"I don't know for sure, but I think a lot of it comes from some of the people who are given permanent residency here. Those kind of people always seem to acquire gold. Many are carrying it when they are brought in. Trying to take it with them, I guess. It doesn't get any farther than the main gate."

"Don't you worry about accepting that kind of gold?" Alicia asked him.

Burnfingers moved his mop across the marble floor. "Why

should I? Metal is innocent of its makers." He gestured to the left. "I got a nice room here, private. So long as I do my job nobody messes with me. Also got a TV. I can get all the L.A. and Vegas stations. They must have a pretty good antenna around here somewhere. For keeping track of future guests, I guess. They even let me comfort some of the ladies who end up here."

"They let you do that?" said Frank.

"They think it's pretty funny. Tears make them laugh hysterically. But I don't deceive anybody and they're glad for a little last human contact. Some of the people I have met would surprise you. Some probably would not. Fewer politicians than you would think. More artists than you would suspect. A lot of bankers."

"Doesn't being stuck here worry you at all?" Alicia asked earnestly. "What if they changed their minds about you?"

"Got a contract."

"Well, what about your soul, then? Your immortal soul?"

"If I got a soul it's not around here. Don't have a shadow, either. Too hot for it, I think."

"Everyone has a soul." When she spoke like that, Frank thought admiringly, she looked like a suburban madonna.

Burnfingers shrugged. "Maybe so. Maybe I'll run in to it again one of these days. In meantime I'm getting along okay without it. Nobody's asked me about it, so I guess they're not interested in it. Or me. I'm kind of a neutral here, not part of this world or the other. One thing, they appreciate my work. That's nice. I've worked plenty of places in the real world where people just yell at you and call you names behind your back." He smiled slightly. "Nobody's ever called me a name to my face. Well, one fella. I think he's around here now someplace."

"They don't call you names here?" Frank wondered.

"Oh, sure, but that's different. Part of their work. In a way it's almost affectionate."

"You don't sound mad to me."

Burnfingers's smile faded and he turned to stare intently at Mouse. "Now you are one enigmatic little lady. You I haven't got figured out yet. Of course I am crazy. If I was not, living here would have driven me mad by now. Since it hasn't, I must already be. If you need confirmation, go down to any of the Levels and ask the people there for eternity what their opinion is of the mental condition of someone who would remain here voluntarily."

While Burnfingers and Mouse appraised each other Frank had been thinking furiously. "Are you saying they let you go anywhere? That you've the run of this place?"

"More or less. I pretty much work around the station. Messy as your average imp and demon is, there's enough to keep me busy here. And I don't like going past the Gate, down to the Levels. Even though it's pretty much an Anglo idea of Hell it's still not very pleasant to look upon. Besides which it's an impossible place to clean. Take me centuries just to make a start on the brimstone stains. This place I can handle."

"I still don't understand why they'd hire you in the first place," Alicia murmured.

Burnfingers smiled thinly. "Apparently admissions are way up. Personnel hasn't been able to keep pace, even with a lot of the staff putting in extra overtime. Being so close to Las Vegas, this is one of their busiest checkpoints. The Gate here is open round the clock and the traffic never dries up entirely, though I'm told things slow down some around Christmas."

"How long have you been here?"

He moved his cart out of the bathroom. "Hard to say. Time never much interested me and I don't own a watch. There are clocks all over the station, but they don't have numbers on them. I have had to let my own biorhythms set my pace."

Frank relaxed enough with Begay to take a seat. "What did you do before you ended up here? You sound pretty sharp to me."

"They tested me once, back when I could stand school. My IQ is, I don't know. Two hundred and ten, something like that. I was off their scale. Unfortunately, being crazy I can't do much with it. Grandfather, now, he was smarter than me. They wanted him to run the Nation. The Navajo Nation, that is. But he would not have any part of it. He was only interested in sheep and corn and watching the weather.

"The schoolteachers kept trying to interest me in different subjects. When I was in high school I got interested in something they call amorphous silicon. I thought you could make high-efficiency solar cells from it. My teachers would not listen to me, so I forgot about it. Then for a while I thought I wanted to be a diesel truck mechanic. There was much talk of a football scholarship, too, until I found out I preferred avoiding people to running over them. That is not the kind of attitude that turns on college recruiters.

"Finally I just picked up and went my own way. Traveling suits me best." He winked. "This is not the only interesting place where I have worked."

"And you don't find this kind of work, your situation here, degrading?" Frank asked interestedly.

"No hard work is degrading. Ask yourself sometime who you would rather have go on strike: the physicists or the garbage collectors? I have done both kinds of work. I spent much time in a plant in northwest Texas assembling nuclear weapons."

Steven's eyes got real big. "Atom bombs?"

Burnfingers nodded. "My job was to help with the final assembly and checkout. When no one was looking I made improvements to each warhead I worked on."

Frank tried to envision a self-proclaimed crazy assembling nuclear devices. It made him sweat harder. "What kind of improvements?"

"On the ones that I helped prepare for shipment I adjusted them so that if they were set off, all the radiation would be confined within a quarter-kilometer radius. The rest of the energy released would take the form of harmless fireworks, like big Fourth of July sparklers." He grinned.

"That's sabotage!" Frank said angrily. "You've weakened our national security."

"Oh, I always even things out, Frank. I did the same work for a time in a Soviet assembly plant near Lake Baikal. The Russian bombs will make red and yellow sparklies, the American ones red, white, and blue." He allowed himself a chuckle. "If they are ever used there are going to be some very surprised generals on both sides."

"I love your bracelet." Alicia gracefully changed the subject. "Is it Navajo?"

Burnfingers raised his left arm. The flannel sleeve slid back from his wrist to expose a mass of worked silver and turquoise. "My grandfather gave it to me. It is old pawn. Myself, I prefer to work in gold. That is why I am collecting so much of it. I have a mind to make something one day."

Abruptly, the hall door opened to admit the three demonic

juveniles who had been tormenting Steven earlier. They entered laughing and cackling.

Steven saw them, let out a scream, and fled to the bathroom. One of the demons got an arm and leg between the closing door and the jamb and forced the door open. His companion resumed picking on the hapless ten-year-old.

"Hey, that's about enough!" Frank moved to aid his son.

One of the juveniles whirled on him. "You keep out of this, blood bag!" He had pupilless red eyes and when he hissed, two narrow streams of flame shot from those inhuman orbs. Frank reeled back from the heat. The creature chortled nastily and turned to join in the fun.

Burnfingers Begay took a step toward the bathroom. "This is a holding area. You do not belong in here."

"You stay out of this, too." Eyeballed flame reached toward the tall Indian.

Begay ducked the fiery blast. One hand reached back to grab the water bucket, brought it around to smack the demonic bully square in the face. A noise like a big boiler letting off steam filled the room together with a ragged shriek. The other two demons stumbled clear of the evaporating puff of steam that had been their companion. All that remained of Steven's principal tormentor was a small pile of red and black ashes.

Burnfingers tossed the empty bucket aside and picked up the wire broom. "Now you two both get out."

Watching him warily, the survivors edged rapidly around the far side of the room. Though they spoke threateningly, they were obviously frightened of the janitor.

"You'll hear about this!" one of them squealed. "You'll be sorry—ouch!" Burnfingers's broom caught him across the seat of his jeans and lifted him a foot off the floor.

"We're gonna tell, we're gonna tell the supervisor!" its companion moaned as he retreated down the hall.

"Go right ahead. I'll tell him you were operating in a restricted area." Burnfingers closed the door behind them. He put down the broom and entered the bathroom, smiling reassuringly. "It is okay now, little fella. You can come out. They are gone and will not come back soon."

A hesitant Steven peeked out, rubbing at one eye with a fist. "Thank you, Mr. Begay."

"Me, too," said Frank, holding out a hand to his son. "Thanks."

"You are welcome. They did not belong here doing what they were doing and they knew it."

Alicia was staring in amazement at the pile of ashes.

"Now maybe you folks ought to tell me what you are doing here," Burnfingers suggested.

"With pleasure." All suspicions gone, Frank proceeded to explain as best he was able.

7

AFTERWARD, Burnfingers stood thinking for a long time. Then he muttered something angry in Navajo and gave the water bucket a kick that dented the metal.

"Wrong. All wrong. If you were not sent here, then you should not be kept here. They should confess a mistake has been made."

"But will they?" Alicia dared to sound hopeful. "If they don't, is there anything you could do for us? You say they let you move about freely. Can you help us get away from here? Or maybe you could intercede on our behalf with whoever's in charge."

Burnfingers shook his head. "He does not concern himself with small matters. In any case, you do not want to bring yourselves to his attention. One time I saw him, riding by in his limo, and even though I had a long hot way to travel I did not consider asking for a ride." He paused, added thoughtfully, "I had not really realized it until this minute, but I think I am tired of mopping floors. Some of the staff is okay, but your average demon or imp is a real slob. They just do not care about keeping things neat.

"I have accumulated enough gold here. With what I have acquired before, I think I have enough to do my work. So I suppose it is time to move on." He regarded them somberly. "Crazy I may be, but I still like my sleep. It is hard to sleep here, what with all the screaming of the Damned. If I agree to help you, then you must agree to trust me.''

"Trust a crazy man?" Frank murmured.

"You will get out of here only by trusting someone crazy. But if you would prefer to rely on the kindly nature of the lieutenant and his advisors, I will not interfere.''

Alicia clutched at her husband. "Frank, he can help us. Let him."

"I dunno." He stared at Burnfingers, who waited patiently. "We might be getting ourselves in deeper than we already are.''

"You will find yourselves in deeper when they send you through the Gates to the First Level. Once past that point, nothing can help you."

"That lieutenant admitted we don't belong here. Maybe when they finish checking their records they'll just let us go.''

Burnfingers nodded thoughtfully. "They might. But if they let you go, then they are going to have to fill out a big stack of special forms. They all hate paperwork. Just stopping you on the highway and bringing you in will tie up half a dozen clerks for a week. Letting you go will mean ten times as much work. I do not remember it ever happening before. I admit that the lieutenant is not bad, for a demon, but when he figures out how much extra work he is going to have to authorize to process a release, he may find it better to lose you in the shuffle. Hell is an easy place to lose people. After a week or so down on the Third Level or lower you will none of you be in any condition to think of filing a complaint or anything else. Think hard, friend. Do you really expect to receive justice here?''

"Frank, please, let's do as he says." Alicia was pleading with him now. Her daughter joined in.

"Daddy, if he can get us out of this awful place, let him!" She was looking at the door. "I don't want to have to see that creature again!"

His daughter's stark terror convinced him. "Okay. We'll take a chance on you, Begay."

The big man was pleased. "Good. It has been awhile since anyone had to take a chance on me. You really have no other choice. If this is passed on to the higher-ups they will find a way to keep you here. A nice, contented middle-class family like yours would be a coup for the boss here. So if he finds out what's going on here he'll have you booted through the Gate and damn any subsequent difficulties.''

"Can you do that trick with the water every time?" Alicia asked hesitantly.

"Those were just minor imps, class-four grade-school bullies. What I did was comparable to swatting a fly."

"Fire-breathing flies," Steven whispered to himself.

"A few of your major demonic personages, now, you toss a bucket of water in their direction and they'll laugh and spit napalm back at you."

"Then how are you going to get us out of here?" Frank challenged him.

"How did you get in?"

"We've got a motor home." Alicia gestured indecisively behind her. "It's parked out in front of the station. At least, it was."

"Don't worry," Burnfingers told her. "They won't bother it. They aren't interested in machines unless they're built in their own shops. Parked out front, you say? Since they have not figured out what to do with you yet, I am sure they have not figured out what to do with it. It should be as you left it." He placed his damp mop in its slot on the bucket cart. "Now, I want you all to follow me."

Frank put out a hesitant arm, felt it bounce off ribs that felt as if they were sheathed in stainless steel. "How can we do that? Maybe they won't question your movements, but we're not staff here. Surely they'll stop us."

"They must see us first. Then someone must make a decision. The lower echelons shy from doing that because if they make a wrong one it can get them in trouble. Demons and imps have their own punishments." He nodded at the door. "My room is not far. There are a very few things I want to take with me. I do not plan on returning to this place. It may be that I am not breaking any rules by helping you, but I do not think it would be healthy for me to remain to find out."

He cracked the door. The hot air that came pouring in made Frank flinch.

"You folks are lucky," Burnfingers told them. "They turned up the air-conditioning for you."

"Air-conditioning?" Alicia whispered, crowding close to her husband. "It must be a hundred and twenty in here."

"Remember where you are, earth mother. For recreation some of the supervisors here put on winter clothes and go sand-skiing in the Danakil Depression." He opened the door wider, peering out into the hall. "Not a busy day. We're lucky. Keep close behind me, but act unconcerned. If we should pass anyone, appear resigned to your fate. Show any unease and you will be lost."

"Has anyone ever escaped from this place before?" Frank asked him.

"It is not common, but there are stories. Some years ago a minor trusty named Adolph tried to organize a big breakout. Only a few of his people made it and they returned here soon after. As punishment he spends Eternity cleaning bathrooms and waiting on tables in the Jewish section of Level Seven." He continued talking softly and urgently as he opened the door the rest of the way.

"Quickly now, before someone comes to check on you."

They exited into the stifling corridor and trailed Burnfingers closely. A minor female imp wearing the red-orange uniform of Administration appeared in a side corridor. She barely acknowledged Burnfingers's existence, gave the family clustered close behind him a disinterested glance, and continued on her way.

Only when she'd turned a corner and vanished behind them did Burnfingers take a moment to explain her indifference.

"There is so much paperwork to keep up with, hardly anyone knows what the demon in the next cubicle is doing, let alone the ones in the next department. Act like you belong out here." For the second time his gaze locked on Mouse. "You aren't part of this family, are you?"

"I was hitchhiking. The Sonderbergs were kind enough to offer me a lift. I am on my way to the Vanishing Point to try and regulate the Spinner before it allows the fabric of existence to unravel completely."

"Something to do with weaving, is it? You'll have to tell me more. We Navajos make the finest rugs in existence, just the best there is. Especially the medicine rugs. I've seen some; a Two Gray Hills, a Seven Yeibichai, and a Teec Noc Pos, with plenty of the fabric of existence woven through them. Miracle Yazzie's work would astonish you." He turned left up a cross corridor. "One of her medicine rugs had dancing figures in it that shifted whenever you looked away. By the time you looked back the pattern was different.

"But pure fabric of existence, without wool or cotton, that is something I have never seen. If it is coming apart and they find out who you are and what you intend, they will try to stop you. Such unraveling would inspire jubilation in this place."

"That's what Mouse told us!" said Wendy in surprise.

Burnfingers Begay favored her with a wide smile. "All the more reason for helping you folks away from here."

"It's nothing to do with us," said Alicia. "We're just on our vacation."

"Not anymore, you're not." Abruptly he halted and unlocked a door. "My room," he said helpfully.

Frank didn't know what to expect. A simple bed, perhaps a table and chair, possibly even a rug of the type he'd described to Mouse. All those were present, and more, but what took everyone's breath away was the vast and highly detailed work of art that occupied the whole far wall.

Rummaging through a box he extracted from beneath the bed, Burnfingers noticed their rapt stares and commented indifferently.

"Sand painting. My father taught me how to do them."

"It's beautiful!" Alicia told him.

"Totally awesome," Steven added admiringly.

Burnfingers was filling a small backpack. "It gives me something to do in my spare time. One thing I have no trouble acquiring in this place is plenty of sand." He nodded in the painting's direction. "But making the sand stay in place on a vertical surface, that is the real art."

Frank was confused. "You mean it's not glued on?"

"No glue can last long here. It is a matter of placing the grains of sand one at a time and making sure the internal planes of the various crystals are correctly aligned."

That didn't make sense, but Frank had no reservations about the painting itself.

Four lines radiated from a common center. These served to isolate yeibichais, plants, animals, and highly stylized representations of the forces of nature. Creatures and gods, lightning and stars, combined into an immense whirling shape on the wall. Though the figures were simplistic in design, the overall effect was quite awe-inspiring. It drew you into an alien but warm world.

Burnfingers frowned. "The lower right-hand corner has been giving me a lot of trouble, but it doesn't matter now." He was watching Mouse as he explained. "That part contains a representation of Chaos. Not easy to paint."

"The Anarchis." Mouse sounded approving. "A most remarkable and revealing portrait. You are quite an artist, Mr. Begay." She stared at the intemperate mass of black and yellow sand that occupied most of the right-hand corner of the painting.

Burnfingers shrugged off the compliment. "When I don't have time for making jewelry I like to play with sand. Keeps the fingers nimble. And the mind."

"What's this?" Steven had walked around the foot of the bed to examine the painting more closely. Before Frank could stop him, the boy touched the portion of the painting that had piqued his curiosity.

A rush of wind blew through the room, unexpectedly cool in that hottest of regions. It was the kind of wind that caressed beaches and mountain buttes. On contact with Steven's finger the entire intricate construction collapsed. Where an elaborate work of art had hung an instant earlier there was now only a blank wall with an uneven pile of multicolored sand heaped at its base.

Alicia's hands went to her cheeks. "Oh my God."

"I'm sorry!" Steven stumbled backward. "I'm sorry, I'm sorry. I didn't mean it."

"It doesn't matter." Burnfingers smiled at him as he slung a battered canvas backpack over his shoulders. "We are leaving anyway. Sand paintings are not meant to be permanent. They are intended to instruct and reveal and entertain. The permanent ones you can buy in places like Arizona are for tourists to take home and hang on their walls." He put a comforting arm around the boy and hugged him. "When I have time I will make another, just for you. One you will be able to take to school to show your friends."

"Okay. Just as long as they don't ask me what I did on my summer vacation." Steven managed a weak smile.

"That's the spirit. You have quite a little fella here, Mr. Sonderberg. Right now he is a bit too much of a good thing, but I think that will change as he grows older.

"Come now." He led them to the door, checked the hallway beyond, and stepped out into the intense heat. Mouse followed, then the Sonderbergs. They left a small room occupied by simple furnishings and one collapsed painting of the entire universe.

"I hope this doesn't make things worse."

Frank whispered to his wife, "What could be worse than this?"

She looked up at him out of doe eyes. "Fleeing police custody."

"I think you were right the first time, hon. We're not gonna find much kindness and sympathy here."

"I wish we knew more about Mr. Begay, though."

"We know he's human. In a place like this that's good enough for me. And Mouse trusts him."

"I thought you didn't trust Mouse."

"I don't, yet. Not entirely."

Burnfingers had stopped. They crowded close behind him.

"Wait here." They complied as he disappeared around a corner. Minutes ticked toward oblivion. Frank was starting to worry that they were being set up when their newfound friend finally returned. "All clear. Come quietly."

Following him into another hallway, they passed something that lay in a heap off in a corner. It wore a red-orange uniform over bright green skin. A single fang protruded from the upper jaw. Both eyes were closed tight and the row of spines that ran from the base of the skull to the sacrum lay limply against the monster's back. Green blood trickled from the misshapen forehead.

"Did you do that?" Fear and admiration mixed in Wendy's query.

"Had to. He was on station here and I couldn't talk him away. So I waited until he looked elsewhere and then I clobbered him."

Frank's gaze lingered on the unconscious beast as they hurried past. "He'll be pissed when he comes to."

"This whole place will be in an uproar when you are discovered missing. They will search the station first. That should allow us a good head start."

"Won't they see the motor home leave?" Alicia wondered.

Burnfingers shook his head; a terse, economical gesture. "Not unless some are standing around out in the parking lot. There is no reason for them to do so. They will expect you to be wandering around lost inside the building, which is exactly what you would be doing without my help."

"It just occurred to me," Frank said, "that if they find out you've helped us and this doesn't work, what they do to us will be nothing compared to what they'll do to you."

"Don't worry about me. Remember, I am crazy."

"You can still feel."

"Pain is only a different state of mind. You sound like an old woman, Sonderberg. They are not going to catch me, and they are not going to catch you, either."

Then they were running past the solid quartz door Burnfingers opened for them, out into the lot. Across the road, the endless line of vehicles containing the Damned awaited their turn to pass through the Gates. Screams and moans emanated from within as panicky, fearful faces hammered on locked windows.

A few patrol cruisers were parked nearby. There was also something that looked like a giant toaster on wheels. Which, Frank mused uneasily, it might well have been. Their motor home gleamed whitely against the stark surroundings, as out of place in that parking lot as a beluga whale in a school of salmon.

Frank was relieved to find it still locked. He dropped the keys twice before he got the door open. Everyone piled in. Still no sign of alarm from within the station. The lot was devoid of officers, while the demons who worked the line of traffic across the street were too busy to pay attention to anything going on behind their backs.

Frank slipped gratefully into the driver's seat and jammed the key into the ignition.

"What if it doesn't start?" Alicia whispered tensely.

Frank growled at her as he turned the key. The engine turned over immediately, a warm, purring sound.

Burnfingers was standing between the two captain's chairs, watching the station. "Okay. Move out, but not too fast."

The lot was big enough to give Frank plenty of room to maneuver. He'd backed up, swung around, and was about to pull out into the road when something with four eyes and vestigial leathery bat wings came running toward them, waving its clawed hands urgently.

"What should I do?" Frank said tightly.

"Stop."

"Stop? But we—"

"Be calm, Mr. Sonderberg. Roll down your window."

Frank complied reluctantly, forced himself not to recoil from the stinking monstrosity that leaned close for a look at them. It could do so easily because it was at least nine feet tall. The nasty expression it wore relaxed when it espied a familiar face.

"Janitor, what you do here with these humans?"

Burnfingers grinned. "These here tourists took a wrong turn back up the highway apiece. Honest mistake. I'm giving them a guide out."

"That so?" The winged apparition made an unpleasant gurgling noise. "I heard somethin' about that." It rested a clawed hand on the windowsill. Frank did not look at it. Those thick scaly fingers could easily pluck him right out of his seat. "Whatsa matter? Don't you folks like our hospitality?"

"We're on vacation." Somehow Frank found the wherewithal to talk calmly and rationally. "We were on our way to a warm destination, but not one quite this warm."

Again the gurgling laugh, followed by a display of four-inch-long teeth in a gaping mouth. "Let you go, huh?"

"That's right," said Burnfingers, nodding. "No reason to keep them. It was a mistake in traffic control."

"All right." The tall demon's drool dripped down the inside of the door. Frank quietly moved his left foot clear of the noisome liquid. "Seems a shame to havta let such sweet people go." It shrugged, an unexpectedly human gesture. "But if that's the decision, it not my business. What you going do with them?"

"They're a little nervous," Burnfingers explained easily, "so I'm just going to show them the on ramp. I'll walk back. I can use the exercise."

The demon nodded once, leered at Frank. "See you folks in a few decades, right?"

"You never know," said Frank, astonished by his facile reply.

The hand which looked capable of lifting the motor home off the pavement released the windowsill. "I'd tell you to be good, but that would be bad for business. Right, Burnfingers?"

"Not really my department." Burnfingers smiled and waved as the demon returned to his duties across the road. Still smiling and waving, he whispered to Frank. "Okay. Now go like hell, Frank Sonderberg."

The partly paralyzed Frank put the motor home back in drive and thromped the accelerator. Kicking up sand and gravel, the big vehicle clawed its way back onto the access road. Their lane was deserted, that opposite bumper-to-bumper. Frank was glad all the traffic was on his side so Alicia wouldn't have to see what was taking place inside some of the cars and vans waiting their turn to deliver the condemned to their fate.

"Here," said Burnfingers. "Don't miss the ramp. There is no other."

"I'm on it." Frank swung the wheel to the right. The motor home plunged down the on ramp, picking up speed as it descended. They were at fifty by the time they hit the empty freeway. No traffic on their side, but plenty headed in the other direction, slowing as it prepared to exit.

"Made it!" Frank shouted gleefully, pushing them up to sixty.

"Maybe." Burnfingers was staring back the way they'd come, his eyes narrowed.

A moment later they heard the sirens.

"Oh, God," Alicia was mumbling, "oh, God, not again, not now!"

Grim-faced, Frank tried to shove the accelerator pedal through the floor. The motor home raced past sixty-five, heading toward a futile seventy. The tri-axled beast couldn't outrun a family compact, much less a highway patrol cruiser fueled by Lord knew what.

"We aren't going back with them," he told his wife quietly. "No matter what. Tell the kids to strap in. Get everybody secured." She nodded, left her seat to comply. Frank kept his eyes fastened to the highway ahead as he spoke. "Burnfingers?"

"Very right, Mr. Sonderberg. You keep going. I do not think I could talk to them anymore." Frank sensed rather than saw the big Navajo straighten and turn curiously. "Hey there, missy, what are you doing?"

A rush of warm air reached the front of the motor home. Someone must have opened the big rear window, back in the master bedroom. Frank was about to protest when his ears were filled with a high-pitched quaver. The single note rose and fell but slightly, hardly varying at all in pitch or intensity.

His attention was diverted by something that *spang*ed against his sideview mirror. The top half, glass and metal alike, had been melted. He wondered what kind of bullets their pursuers used.

Enough of the mirror remained to show the half-dozen patrol cars that were pursuing. Sirens wailed, rotating lights flared threateningly, and the sickly sunlight gleamed on bright red-orange hoods. Rising above the hellish cacophony was Mouse's single, unwavering note. No mysterious words to this song, no elaborate contrapuntal harmonics: just one note sung with all the power at her command.

Their pursuit began to fall by the wayside, one car after another pulling over or stopping dead on the pavement. Two brushed past each other at high speed, causing the one on the left to veer sharply. It slid onto the sand shoulder that bordered the slow lane and rolled several times. Behind the retreating motor home a dull *boom* was chased by a pillar of smoke.

By now the relentless unvarying note was sending shivers through Frank's whole body. He clung determinedly to the wheel. Everyone else was trembling, too, but the effect on the pursuing demons was far worse. Even so, one last cruiser hung grimly on their tail, closing ground between them even as the last of its companions screeched to a halt behind it.

Pulling alongside, the screaming din of its siren penetrated the glass to claw at Frank's soul. Knowing that the motor home was ten times heavier, he considered swerving sharply in an attempt to shove their assailant off the road. Even as the thought occurred to him, Alicia was letting out a warning shout.

He ducked and something smashed through the glass where his head had been a moment earlier, forming a perfect hole half an inch in diameter. There was a thump atop the roof. Frank jerked instinctively and they slid across into the fast lane, tires screeching in protest. The move forced the remaining cruiser into the sandy median strip. It spun out and stalled.

Mouse had stopped singing, unwilling or unable to hold the saving note any longer. Scratching sounds moved from the roof to the walls. Then he saw it, clinging to the side of the motor home and grinning at him through Alicia's window. Two long, vampirish fangs protruded from the lower jaw of the man-sized cadaver. It stared at him out of tiny, evil button eyes. Then he saw the red revolver. He saw why Mouse's song had not affected it.

It had no ears.

"No," he whispered as the decaying finger tightened on the trigger.

The shot wasn't fired. A look of surprise came over the creature's face as it turned toward the rear of the motor home. As it tried to re-aim the gun, its head exploded. Green blood and bits of steaming flesh splattered the window. The decapitated body clung to the metal a moment longer before dropping away.

A dull roar had preceded the execution. Burnfingers Begay closed the rear window he'd been leaning out of and came forward, his expression one of solemn satisfaction. In his right fist he held a handgun the size of a small cannon. While Frank tried to slow his heart, the Indian removed a box of cartridges from his backpack and calmly reloaded the massive pistol.

"Four-fifty-four Casull," he announced in reply to Frank's unvoiced question. "Not as pretty as our lady singer, but effective in its own way. Even the most eloquent sentence can benefit from proper punctuation."

He finished the loading and slipped the pistol into a leather holster, which he carefully placed back in his pack. Frank caught a brief glimpse of the holster. Arcane Navajo symbols and floating stars had been engraved in the cowhide.

"I wouldn't think that would be very effective in a place like this. I thought you had to use black magic or something special, like Mouse's song."

Burnfingers let out a grunt as he closed the cartridge box. "There are all kinds of magic, my friend. Cold lead works very well in Hades."

"Another gift from your father?"

Burnfingers smiled. "No. This I bought for myself, in a pawnshop in Flagstaff. It is not traditional, but I find it comforting. Its chant is short."

Alicia sat up in the seat opposite her husband's, moaned when she got a look at what had smeared itself all over her window.

"They let you bring a gun in with you?" Frank's tone was disbelieving.

"It was part of my personal goods. Why take it away from me? They knew I dared not use it back there."

Mouse was gulping lemonade from the refrigerator. The effort of holding the single note for so long had put a severe strain on her throat. "This will not stop them. They won't give up so easily."

Burnfingers leaned forward for a look at one of the rearview mirrors. "I know they will not, but we have a good start now. In a little while I think we will be out of their jurisdiction."

"That's no guarantee of safety. Not when the fabric of existence is coming apart. Nothing is as it should be. Realities are crossing unpredictably. Not even Hell is stable anymore."

"Maybe not, but we have someone who I think can drive his way even out of Hell." He clapped a huge hand on Frank's shoulder.

Frank felt as though he'd just been knighted.

After a while he was able to stop glancing at the mirrors. There'd been no indication of further pursuit for some time. Wendy and Steven filled glasses with ice and soda for everyone. The longer they drove, the more the land outside grew normal. The endless procession of the Damned shrank until the oncoming lanes were empty again save for the occasional car or truck. Cacti straightened, green and brown, once more healthy succulents instead of human beings frozen in poses of eternal torment. The sky brightened and there were no unwelcome stains on the pavement.

"Check it out." He gestured forward. They were coming up fast on another road sign. It gave only the distance remaining to Las Vegas and several small intervening towns. There was no mention of a Hades Junction or anything like it.

"We'll make it by tonight." He settled back against the padding, the feeling of relief almost painful. "Everything's okay again. No gambling for a few days, though. I think we've done enough gambling for a while." He laughed, but it was a forced sound. Alicia knew it but smiled back anyway.

He glanced around. "Wendy! Why don't you put a tape in and turn up your machine so we can all hear?"

His daughter didn't try to hide her surprise. "You want to listen to *my* music?"

"Why not? Come on, put something really radical on. After what we've been through a little heavy metal would be soothing."

"I don't listen to that much metal, Pops."

Pops. How delighted he was to hear that mildly contemptuous appellation once more. "Well, then, whatever you're into right now."

"Okay, you asked for it." She removed her earphones and turned up the volume on the compact recorder. Soon they were rolling down the highway to the accompanying strains of Huey Lewis, Bon Jovi, and Cyndi Lauper.

"Real food." Frank whispered as he drove. "Gaming. Television. Civilization."

"It's funny," Alicia was saying, "but we can't ever tell anybody what happened to us. No one would ever believe."

"I'm having a hard time believing myself." He raised his voice. "Hey, Steven! Why don't you come up here and join your folks, kiddo?"

"That's cool, Dad. I'd rather stay back here for a while, if it's okay."

"Sure it's okay." Despite his son's smile Frank knew the boy had suffered badly from their experience, maybe worse than any of them. Just seeing parents threatened could traumatize a sensitive child deeply. "There's ice cream in the freezer."

"I know, Dad." The boy smiled wanly. "It's all right. I'm okay."

Mouse started to turn. "Perhaps I can help him."

"No." Burnfingers stopped her. "It's been a long time since I had the chance to talk to a worthy child. The few who passed me in that hot place deserved to be there."

Mouse stared up into his eyes, then nodded sagely. "You are crazy. No wonder you were able to keep your sanity."

Burnfingers just smiled cryptically and walked back through the motor home until he came to Steven's couch. He sat down on the floor and crossed his legs.

"Troubles, boy?"

Steven glanced past him, toward the front of the vehicle where his parents sat. He lowered his voice conspiratorially. "I'm still scared, Mr. Begay."

"Burnfingers will do." The boy's knuckles were white where his fingers clutched at the upholstery. "They cannot bother us nomore, Steven. Mouse's singing made most of the bad things give up. I took care of the rest."

"You sure did." Steven's grip relaxed slightly and a flicker of interest replaced some of the terror in his eyes. "You shot 'em, didn't you?"

"That's just what I did. Want to see my gun?"

The boy drew back slightly. "No! I'm afraid of guns."

"No reason to be afraid, if you know what you are doing. You're not afraid of a hammer, are you? Or a saw?"

"N-no."

"Well, a gun is just another kind of tool."

"I never thought of it like that before."

"That is because you live in the city, where people think of guns wrongly. Tell me what else you are afraid of."

"Fire. I'm scared of fire. That's one reason why I was so frightened back there."

Burnfingers shook his head and chuckled. "Another tool. Fire is a gift the gods gave man long ago. If you learn to know it and how to make use of it, then it will be your good friend forever. There is no reason to be frightened of it."

Steven sounded uncertain. "Mom always warned me to be careful of matches and the stove and things like that. I just don't feel comfortable around them." Burnfingers noted that the boy's hands had finally relaxed, no longer dug for dear life at the fabric of the couch.

"Be careful, of course. But friendly, too. There's more than one reason why I am called Burnfingers Begay. Want to see a trick?" He lowered his voice to a whisper. "Just between you and me. Not for your mom or dad or anyone else."

Steven peered past the big stranger. His parents were in the front seats, chatting to each other. Wendy had her eyes closed as her feet tapped time to the music. Despite not reacting to the rhythm, Mouse looked as if she was listening. He turned back to the powerful, soft-spoken man who had saved him and his family, and suddenly he was no longer afraid.

"All right. Sure."

"Good. Put out your hand like this." Burnfingers extended his left hand, demonstrating how to place the thumb against the tip of the forefinger.

Steven struggled to position his much smaller fingers. "Like this?"

"No. Cross them a little more." Burnfingers gently adjusted the boy's hand. "Now you do—this." He snapped his fingers. A tiny dancing flame burst from the tip of his thumb, burning merrily.

Even for a ten-year-old, Steven's eyes became very wide. "Wow, that's neat! How'd you do that?"

"Practice, and knowing how things are." He gestured with his burning thumb. "Blow it out. Go on, go ahead."

Steven leaned forward, hesitated a moment, then exhaled sharply. The flame vanished. Where it had danced was no darkening of the skin, no scorch mark.

"It's a trick."

Burnfingers smiled. "Didn't I say so? Most of life is a trick, Steven. Physics is a trick, and chemistry a trick, and mathematics the neatest trick of them all. Now you try it."

"Okay," the boy said dubiously. He concentrated hard on his thumb as he snapped his fingers together. They popped cleanly, but several attempts produced only sore fingers and no flame.

"You do right with your fingers but not with your head. That's where the trick part is." He leaned close and whispered in the boy's ear. Steven listened intently, nodding as he did so. "Now try again."

Steven did so, repeatedly. The fourth attempt brought forth a tiny but unmistakable puff of smoke. "Gee!" Steven started to smile, staring at his hand in wonder.

"You see?" Burnfingers sat back, satisfied. "Like most tricks it is just a question of practice and getting your head straight. Concentrate now."

Steven leaned forward eagerly, trying to set his mind the way the Navajo had instructed him. As he concentrated, he relaxed, and as he relaxed, the fear and terror of the past hours faded from his memory.

Which was what Burnfingers had intended all along.

8

FRANK DROVE EASILY. Alicia had swiveled her chair around in order to talk with Wendy, who kneeled on the floor next to her mother.

"He was so good-looking I didn't see his eyes," she was saying. "Or maybe I did and I just ignored what was there."

Alicia stroked her daughter's hair. "It's all right. It doesn't matter now."

Mouse stood nearby, staring out the windshield. "Do not berate yourself, child. It is difficult much of the time to tell devils from men. Most devils have a little man in them, and most men a little devil in them. What one has to learn is how to judge proportions."

Alicia smiled tolerantly. "A very clever metaphor."

"Oh, no, not at all," said Mouse innocently. "It's the literal truth."

"I take it, then, you've had a lot of experience with men?" As soon as she said it Alicia was sorry. That wasn't her style at all. It was one of the main reasons she hated attending the parties thrown by Frank's business associates. The women who came had raised bitchiness to a high art, and she wanted no part of it.

She needn't have worried. It affected Mouse not in the slightest. "As a matter of fact I do know quite a bit about men. I've known men who were intelligent and handsome, men who were witty, men who were evil, a few who were everything. I've also known some devils, and I say again there are times when it is hard to tell them apart." She smiled warmly down at Wendy.

"Don't think you are the first woman who has had trouble making the distinction. The only difference in your case was that the differences were more clear-cut than usual."

"I can tell you've had a lot of experience," Wendy replied, "but really, how old are you?"

"Four thousand two hundred and twelve."

Alicia laughed: a short, sharp giggle that brought her hand quickly to her lips. "Sorry. I didn't mean that."

"Laughing is good for you. Now especially."

Alicia didn't dispute that. It had been awhile since she'd laughed aloud. You had to appreciate the joke. Given the talents Mouse had already demonstrated, a figure of fifty or sixty might have been acceptable. After all, Lena Horne was in her sixties and didn't she look wonderful? Four thousand, though, made the gag work.

"You don't look a day over three thousand. What's your secret? I'm having cellulite trouble already."

"The secret," Mouse told her somberly, "is to see time coming and to step around it. Laughing at it helps a great deal. Time is very sensitive, you know. It can cope with almost anything except laughter." Vast violet eyes turned back to Wendy. "Remember that always, girl. When you see time coming at you, laugh at it and it will retreat. You see, it knows how absurd it really is."

Wendy considered this, though it was impossible to tell if any of it stayed with her. "What happens if you don't make it to this Spinner? Will the fabric of existence keep unraveling?"

Mouse nodded. "Completely. As you have seen, it has already begun, like a rope fraying at the edges. Right now we are on an intact thread, though it's impossible to tell whether it is running true or twisting about another line entirely."

"What happens if it all unravels?" Alicia asked her.

"Then the Anarchis will have final victory and order will dissolve into Chaos. Confusion will reign supreme forever, nothing will be certain or stable, and logic and reason will become naught but memories, themselves unsecured."

"You mean the world will come to an end," Wendy said.

"Not to an end: rather to a confusion. All the threads will break and intertwine and twist and contort about themselves."

"I think I understand. Everything would stay the same only it would be different. You wouldn't be able to be sure of anything. Like driving to Baker and ending up in Hades Junction instead."

Mouse nodded. "Only it will be worse than that. Much worse. The little things will be as severely disrupted as the big things."

Wendy nodded solemnly.

Burnfingers Begay had lumbered forward, ducking to clear the ceiling of the motor home. He gazed at the dash. The instruments were partly obscured by Frank's body.

"How are we doing on gas, my friend?"

"If the stuff that old guy sold us is burnable at all, we'll be okay. This dinosaur has double tanks. Should be able to steam right through to Vegas without stopping. The fridge is full. Poke around near the back, you might even find a beer."

"I would appreciate that," said Burnfingers gravely.

Alicia was staring past him. Her son sat on the convertible sofa. He was bending forward concentrating on his hands. "What were you telling Steven?"

Burnfingers glanced back at the boy, then forward again. "Nothing, really. Little tricks to keep him amused. Desert survival techniques. One or two amusements I have acquired in my traveling."

"So you've been around?"

"Yes. He is a traveler." Mouse was eyeing the big man appraisingly. "An experienced traveler."

"I have spent my life trying not to be bored, Ballad-Eyes."

"How old are you, Burnfingers?" Alicia asked.

"About forty-five. Why?"

"Nothing." Alicia sounded disappointed. Perhaps she'd been hoping he would respond with another outrageous claim the way Mouse had. "That's what I'd guessed."

"Drat. I was hoping you would think I was thirty-five." He touched a rough hand to his cheek. "Genetic wrinkles. White people think every Indian they see looks 'dignified.' We do not understand that."

Wendy settled her legs under her. "If you've traveled, where have you been?"

"Everyplace, just about. I've fought alongside African rebels, worked rice paddies in a Communist commune in China, dived with great white sharks off Dangerous Reef in Australia. I've circumnavigated Greenland and found remnants of a civilization the archaeologists don't know existed, buried deep beneath the ice, where their instruments haven't reached. One of these days they are going to be surprised, boy. I've lived with the Inuit and their Siberian relations, gone swimming off the Ross Ice Shelf, and crossed the Rub' al Khali in the dead of summer, when the Bedu insisted it couldn't be done without frying your brains. Of course, being crazy, that did not worry me much.''

Wendy laughed and Alicia, though she disapproved of such facile prevarication, couldn't keep from grinning herself.

''Your home, now, I have yet to visit,'' he concluded, looking down at Mouse.

''If you can get there you will not soon forget it.''

''Bet you've met some interesting people,'' Wendy said.

''Soon-woman, I have been with sturgeon fishermen in the Black Sea and Lake Superior both. I've talked with representatives of every Indian tribe on both the north and south continents, including some the anthropologists don't know about. In Patagonia a tribe keeps young ground-sloths for pets and hides them from visitors. I've gathered giant pearls with divers from a lost linguistic group on an uncharted island in the South Pacific, dug out sapphires the size of hen's eggs from river gravel in the mountains of Sri Lanka, and spent time with a lama in Bhutan who insisted he could teach me how to levitate.''

Wendy's eyes widened. ''Could he really do that?''

''Oh, that he could, but only upside-down.'' Burnfingers shook his head sadly. ''It's not a very useful thing to know. After a while all the blood rushes to your head and all you want to do is throw up.''

Alicia smiled easily this time. Another joke, clearly one of many, cleverly designed to amuse them and relieve the tension in the motor home. Burnfingers knew what he was doing.

''What will you do now? I mean, once we drop you off in Nevada,'' she asked him.

''Find another job.''

''In Las Vegas?'' Wendy wondered.

''Why not? It is a very interesting place, good for studying people. That always interests me. A good place to find people like myself."

"You mean other Indians?" said Wendy.

"No. I mean other crazy people. Vegas is like the Mad Hatter's tea party, only with neon."

Wendy giggled. This charming older man was helping her to forget the unhappy ordeal she'd suffered at the hands of their hellish captors. It all seemed like a bad dream now. Maybe she would wake up and find out that that was just what it had been. Only if that turned out to be the case, Burnfingers Begay would vanish like part of a dream, too, and she didn't want that.

"Know anybody in Vegas?" Frank inquired casually.

"Don't worry about me. I can get a job anyplace."

Frank didn't doubt Begay's word. He checked his watch. Hades Junction lay far behind them. Probably below them as well, if half of what Mouse said about reality lines twisting and bending was accurate. The cars that passed them in the fast lane were filled with people. Anxious certainly, but not yet damned. Maybe they weren't going to go mad, after all.

"What time do you think we'll hit Las Vegas, dear?" Alicia appeared to have completely recovered from their recent other-worldly encounter. A resilient gal, his spouse, Frank mused. He checked the clock on the dash.

"If we don't run into any more detours, we'll be at the hotel before midnight."

"Want me to drive for a while?"

"Naw, not yet. Lemme take it for another hour. Then we'll switch."

"If you folks get tired, I'm a pretty good driver."

Frank glanced back at their oversized companion. "Thanks. I think we can manage." Despite everything he'd done for them, Frank had no intention of letting Burnfingers Begay behind the wheel of the motor home. Wasn't he a self-confessed crazy?

As for Mouse, she anticipated his next thought. "I am not very good with mechanical things. I'm far more comfortable with what you might call the citizenry of the natural world."

"Everyone to their taste," Frank jibed. "Give me a four-forty any day." Of them all, only the motor home itself had emerged untouched by their experience. He found himself wondering what happened to old machines when they passed on. Was there a mechanical hell, a place where devilish mechanics ran sugar through engines and deliberately overtightened nuts and screws?

There he was, doing as Alicia did, ascribing human characteristics to inanimate objects. She had a word for it. Anthro— anthrosomething. The habit infuriated him. "Oh, that poor chair!" she'd wail when it was time to discard a crippled piece of furniture. "It's been in the family for years!" At such times he would have to try to explain patiently that the chair was not dear old Uncle Ned but simply a collage formed of wood and plastic. A soulless assemblage.

Like Burnfingers Begay? But if Begay was right and soulless, could not a machine have one in his place?

He wasn't aware when he did it that he'd given the Winnebago a comforting pat on the steering wheel.

Steven was hungry, a sure sign everything was back to normal. Wendy had slithered back into her headphones and was twitching to some unheard electronic rhythm. And Alicia, sweet Alicia, was humming to herself.

But when the hour had come and gone and it was time for her to drive he did something he hadn't done previously. Instead of stopping he made certain the road ahead was clear, then rose and stepped behind her, holding on to the wheel until she was able to take his seat, letting the cruise control handle the accelerator for them. When he'd said earlier that they weren't stopping until they reached Vegas he'd meant exactly that. And when they got there he was going to drop his family off right on the main steps before parking the motor home. Though Hell had been painfully bright he planned on avoiding dark places for some time to come.

"As it seems all is well again would you like for me to sing you a song? One of delight and relaxation this time, not of rejection and defense."

Burnfingers answered her before his host and hostess had a chance to reply. "I would like that very much. A cappella."

She looked at him in surprise, but only a little surprise. "Yes, of course. I'll sing you a song," she murmured, her expression turning dreamy, "of the far places you've never been. Wispy landscapes visible in dreams alone, seascapes beyond any blue paint, the worlds writers fight for words to describe. I'll sing of the shadow folk who live on the fringe of reality, and of my own people, my own land. My home.''

And as she sang she soon had all the adults humming softly along with her. Wendy's music remained hers alone and Steven went unnaturally silent, munching like a chipmunk in the woodwork on a sack of chocolate-covered raisins. Within the solid, middle-class rectangular world on wheels all was peace and contentment.

It relaxed Frank's spirit if not his determination. One of the reasons he was rushing Vegasward was to be rid of their strange little passenger. Be it club, garbage can, manhole, or bus stop on the way to somewhere else, they would find her Vanishing Point and deposit her there. Let the fabric of existence unravel around *her*. He was convinced that if they could separate themselves from her, despite her warnings, they could distance themselves from her problem. Hadn't she confessed to being some kind of focal point on which Evil and Chaos concentrated their efforts? If she needed to travel beyond Vegas, let her find another ride. She'd as much as promised to do that and he intended to hold her to her promise. So while he absorbed her wonderful music and smiled frequently and tapped his fingers on the steering wheel in time to the subtle melodies that poured effortlessly from her throat, the true joy he felt sprang from the vision of finally being rid of her.

No one suggested stopping in Needles for dinner, despite the tempting beacons of the billboards and road signs that announced the town's presence like so many frozen TV screens. They roared past both off ramps, the gas gauge holding steady and the engine running cool. As they accelerated into Nevada the desert night descended on them, clothing everything except the starry sky in black velvet.

Frank was driving again and the onset of night troubled him, though he didn't show it. It was impossible to tell now if anything was crawling or flying or hopping toward them out in that vast dark emptiness. He was glad he wasn't a particularly imaginative man. Better to be persistent and hard-working. This way he was able to drive steadily onward without glancing too often out the window in search of improbable manifestations. The road led northeastward, comfortingly eggshell-white in the glare of the headlights.

He decided he preferred the near total darkness to the shadows a full moon would have thrown up. The motor home droned on, trailing the scent of its own high beams.

Steven was sound asleep in back and Wendy drowsed in her own bed. Their original intention had been to use the motor home as a mobile hotel room, moving from trailer park to park. The hotels maintained elaborate facilities for visitors who preferred to spend their time on wheels. Now he couldn't wait to turn it in to the local representative of the rental company. Even though it was paid for, they were going to check into a hotel tonight. He'd ask for a noisy room, in the middle of the hotel, surrounded by hundreds of other rooms and thousands of people. He wanted to bathe in light and conversation and mumbled banalities. In his present state of mind, turgid reality was far preferable to the least excitement.

They'd had enough of that to last a lifetime. For the next ten days he planned to bury himself in activities utterly devoid of social value. Alicia could buy all the junk she desired and he wouldn't say a word. His daughter could display herself in her less-than-there swimsuit and he wasn't going to complain. Steven might personally send the price of sugar futures soaring without a single objection from his father. Let them all indulge themselves. He would derive his pleasure from watching them. It was an attitude that made him a good husband and father.

As for himself, he'd lounge around the pool squinting through his sunshades at showgirls and rich men's mistresses and beauty-contest runners-up from Iowa and Tennessee, trying to keep his gut sucked in while not perishing from self-induced asphyxiation. Alicia would smile tolerantly on such behavior, knowing that all her husband would ever do was look.

They would be safe in Las Vegas, that mildly risqué middle-class Disneyland. Even the temptations of the casino posed no threat. Frank could gamble sensibly. He was too good a business-man to lose severely. Hard work was the best vaccination against gambling fever. So he would usually break even at craps, Alicia would lose on roulette, and he would make a little of it back at blackjack, where years of manipulating figures gave him a slight edge over his fellow gamblers.

The long miles tired him, but he became wide awake when the glow from the lights of an approaching city lit the underside of lingering clouds not far ahead. Alicia sat up straighter in her seat.

"There it is. There it is." The reality of it put paid to the last lingering memories of nightmare.

Sleeping soundly, the children didn't react. Burnfingers Begay didn't look up from the book he was reading as he sat cross-legged on the floor near the kitchen. Mouse might have nodded as she stared out a side window at the night. Big as her eyes were, Frank mused, maybe she could see in the dark.

A big green highway sign loomed up out of the darkness. Frank leaned slightly forward, grumbling, "Now what?"

The detour was clearly marked. Uneasy at the thought of leaving the main highway, he thought of running the barricade, but there were ample signs of heavy equipment at work not far ahead. Arc lamps illuminated a distant section of road. It made perfect sense. Naturally the highway department would try to do all its repair work at night, when it was cooler and there was less traffic.

A vehicle had paused just ahead of him. Now he followed it as it turned right to travel the detour. It was a sleek, expensive-looking sports car. Ferrari or Lamborghini or something like that. In seconds it had accelerated into the night and was gone, though he could still see its lights moving long after the car itself was no longer visible. Ahead, the narrow road was so bright it might have been lit from within. Brand-new paving, he told himself.

"Must be a new way into town, or they've upgraded an older road to take some of the traffic off the highway," he surmised aloud. "Not even oil-stained yet."

There was a distinct absence of traffic. Of course, it was well after midnight. And what did he know of traffic patterns in and out of Las Vegas? They were used to flying in, not driving. Probably most drivers were already busy pumping their hard-earned quarters into hungry slots, or groaning over craps tables.

They could see the city now, coming into view off to the left. Alicia stared and sounded mildly disappointed.

"Won't we drive in down the Strip?"

"If it's lights you want to see we can take a cab and do it tomorrow night. Right now I just wanna get rid of this tank and find us a hotel."

Mouse had come forward to join them in gazing at the distant, glowing towers. "Is something the matter? I heard you talking."

Funny, he thought. Your ears don't look as big as your eyes. "Main road into town's all torn up. We're on a detour." As they began curving toward the city, the lights of the Strip receded, their place taken by the silhouettes of dark, squat structures from which few lights gleamed.

"Looks like we're coming in the back way. Vegas isn't all gambling."

"Industrial park, maybe," said Alicia thoughtfully.

They were alone on the road. As they moved among the buildings, Frank found himself wishing they'd spent more time driving around the city on previous visits. He had no idea where he was. In this dark, dingy part of town it would be easy to miss a road sign. Detours didn't always provide adequate directions, especially for strangers.

Fortunately they couldn't get completely lost. The lights from the distant Strip were a constant glow against the sky. All they had to do was keep going in that direction.

As he was consoling himself with that thought, the road abruptly came to a dead end. He braked, angry at himself for obviously having missed the right turn. Ahead, the roadway became a driveway leading into a large factory lot.

Not quite a dead end, he told himself. Narrower but perfectly passable roads split off to right and left, paralleling the factory. But which way? The lights of the city illuminated the air directly ahead, and that way was denied them.

"Damn! Don't know how I missed the turnoff. If they're going to detour you off the highway, you'd think they'd put up more signs."

"What's going on?" A glance in the center rearview mirror showed Steven sitting up and rubbing at his eyes. After hours of steady highway cruising, their coming to a halt had awakened both children.

"We're here," said his sister tiredly. "Isn't that obvious?"

"That's right." Alicia tried to see past the dark bulk of the factory. "But your father seems to have missed a turn somewhere."

In his frustration he spoke more sharply than he intended. "I did not miss a turn!" Then, more gently, "All right. So maybe I did. Any suggestions?"

"Go left, I think. The lights look brighter over that way."

He shrugged. "Good enough." He backed up slightly to

make sure the motor home would have enough space to clear the curb, then tugged the wheel to port.

Several blocks on, they found themselves driving slowly past a dark park. Strangely thin trees sprouted from among blades of thick blue-green grass.

Walking on the edge of the grass was an elderly gentleman clad in a thin coat of some shiny, silvery material. It would have to be thin, Frank knew. This time of year Vegas was warm even late at night. His shoes matched his coat and he carried a cane, which he was giving a jaunty twirl. Golden tassels trailed from the back and one side of a gray beret.

The outfit would have drawn laughs in south L.A., but this was Las Vegas. He might be a visitor out for an evening's stroll, or a casino employee enjoying his mid-morning break. Many of the bigger hotels required the wearing of special uniforms by their employees, the flashier the better.

"Let's ask him," Alicia said.

The same thought had already occurred to Frank. He slowed and pulled toward the curb. Alicia lowered her window.

The old man stopped to look up at them. There was no concern in his expression, only curiosity. If he lived or worked in this neighborhood he was probably used to encountering lost tourists.

Alicia leaned out. "Excuse us, but is this the right way to downtown?"

He nodded. With his full mustache and beard he resembled a slightly anorexic version of that old character actor, Monty Woolley.

"Sure is." Funny accent, Frank thought. European of some kind. The man was pointing up the street with his cane. "Just keep on the way you're headed. The road will curve to the right, then fork. Take the left-hand fork. That'll put you right back on the main road." Now he turned his attention to the motor home.

"Interesting contraption you got there. Internal combustion, is it?"

Frank could take a joke as well as any man. "Naw. Nuclear-powered."

The riposte didn't faze the nightwalker. He sniffed. "Don't smell nuclear. Can't tell much anymore." He touched the side of his nose. "Sinuses. You know what desert pollen can do to you when it's in season."

"Tell me about it," Frank replied. "We've been to Vegas every year about this time for the past five years."

The oldster's eyebrows drew together and the mustache twitched. "Vegas?"

"Las Vegas," said Alicia encouragingly.

Suddenly Frank saw the light. No wonder the old guy was out walking by himself in the middle of the night. He was slightly off.

"We had to take a detour," his wife was saying.

"Must've been some detour." The oldster scratched at his nose, sniffed again. "Never heard of this 'Las Vegas.'" He gestured with his cane once more. "This is Pass Regulus."

"Maybe in your language," Frank told him, positive now of the man's foreign origins, "but it'll always be Vegas to us."

The old man thought about it for a moment, then shrugged. "Like you say, it's that kind of. town. Guess there are lots of names for it, depending on where you hail from."

"Exactly," said Frank with satisfaction. "Depending on where you're from. That was straight on, curve right, take the left-hand fork?"

Their guide nodded. "You got it."

"Can we give you a lift?" asked Alicia. Frank growled and she pretended not to hear him. It didn't matter.

"No, thanks. I'm on duty."

That at least explained what he was doing out here all by himself in the middle of the night. "What kind of duty?" Frank inquired.

"Night watchman. You folks have a nice time, now. Try not to lose too much money."

"We'll do our best. We're not big gamblers anyway. I'd rather sit by the pool and people-watch."

"That's the way to do it." The old man nodded approvingly. "Take care now, and remember: left-hand fork."

"Thank you." Alicia sent the window up as Frank pulled back out into the middle of the street. "Didn't you think he was kind of old to be working as a night watchman, dear?"

"Naw. Some of those old guys might not be able to run down purse snatchers, but that doesn't mean they still can't shoot straight."

She nodded, then said thoughtfully, "I wonder what language Pass Regulus means Las Vegas in?"

"Beats me, sweets. Hungarian or something." He glanced at the rearview. "Mouse?"

"The name is unfamiliar to me, Mr. Sonderberg."

"What about Italian, Pops?" Wendy suggested.

He shook his head. "I don't think so."

"How would you know?" His daughter's voice had regained its normal, healthy smart-ass tone.

"Because your mother and I have eaten at Mama Genovese's over in Long Beach ever since we were dating, and this guy didn't sound anything like Mama Genovese."

The argument over accents continued as Frank followed the curving road until they came to the fork, just as the old man had predicted. The city lights were brighter than ever. Frank turned left. A few minutes later they found themselves out of the industrial area and cruising down a main street.

Alicia stared in puzzlement at the casinos and hotel towers. "I don't recognize any of this."

Frank didn't reply immediately. They were surrounded by slowly moving traffic and he was trying to concentrate on his driving. "I don't, either, but remember we usually come straight from the airport to the hotel. We've never been in this end of town."

"Maybe that's why everything looks so different. But you'd think we'd have seen at least one familiar place by now. The Golden Nugget or Silver Dollar or *some*place."

"Any minute, now. You'll see. Maybe there's been a lot of redevelopment in the past year."

Alicia looked dubious.

"Oh, wow, look at that, look at that!" Wendy was gesturing excitedly to the sidewalk on their right. "There must be a science-fiction convention in town!"

Frank managed a brief glimpse of the crowded sidewalk beneath the neon. Scattered among the mass of people were a few visions lifted from a fever dream. Two figures a good head taller than the rest of the crowd boasted eyes on the tips of wobbling stalks and orange-hued skin beneath loose green vests. Behind them strolled a dozen tall bluish shapes. White stripes ran down their backs and they wore robes of saffron satin. No heads were visible.

Hari Krishna asparagus, Frank thought, laughing to himself.

Other figures wore thick fur despite the warmth of the night. Dog-faced dwarfs that must have been children in costume wore incongruously bright kilts. He tried to penetrate the exquisitely designed masks, but it was difficult, what with having to concentrate on driving. Whoever had fashioned the masks and costumes had done a superb job. They looked loose and natural.

Only then did he let his gaze shift to the humans in the crowd. That was at once more reassuring and more disturbing. They were undeniably people, but not one wore anything familiar. If this were New Orleans at Mardi Gras it might have made sense, but this was Vegas, where visitors tended to the outré in their habits, not their attire. The street people's clothing was as outrageous as the alien costumes.

For that matter, the hotels and casinos didn't look quite normal. Alicia was right about that. Oh, they were every bit as flashy and glitter-plated. But at the same time they were somehow different. Some of the neon signs appeared to float in midair, attached to nothing, like holograms only brighter. Instead of mere concrete the sidewalks were paved in spots with bright tiles that flashed different colors and filled the air with music when they were trod upon.

As they cruised slowly down the road, hemmed in by smaller vehicles on all sides, he searched in vain for the Tropicana, the Flamingo, the Dunes. There was no sign of the older hotels, Vegas landmarks since the fifties. As for the newer ones, they were remarkable and elaborate. Only the names were missing. Most had signs in languages other than English. Those that did identified themselves as the Gloryhole and Eruption and Coraka. At that moment he would have given a hundred bucks to see a sign reading Hilton.

As if in response to his unvoiced wish they came up on still another grandiose structure. The huge glowing sign seemed to drift unstably twenty feet above the sidewalk. It read HULTON, but for Frank that was close enough. As he pulled out of the street into the parking lot he saw that the bottom floor was perfectly transparent. Beyond he could make out strange fish and other sea creatures, along with more swimmers in costume. They wore no scuba tanks.

The knot that was growing in the pit of his stomach doubled in size.

Forty stories of hotel were mounted on water enclosed by

glass. As they drove farther into the lot they could see people traveling between floors in glass elevators. Fish scattered to avoid the moving lifts.

"It's like Vegas." Alicia's tone was soft, hushed. "But it's not. It's someplace else. Where's Circus Circus?" She leaned forward. "It should be near here, near the end of the strip."

"It better be." He pulled back out into the street, continued westward.

Circus Circus wasn't where it ought to be. In its place was an equally outlandish casino-hotel complex. Instead of the long pool intended to imitate an ancient Roman bath, they found a stream filled with pure blue light. Yellow steam rose from the liquid like dry ice from a tropical drink. The stream was flanked on both sides by tall statues of beetles and reptilian things in formal suits.

A long line of vehicles was waiting to unload passengers at the main entrance, beyond the spring which fed the stream of blue light. Some cars had wheels, others did not. A long low bus sported a pair of humming wings. No wonder the old watchman they'd encountered had been curious about the motor home.

"Gee, Dad. Do you see that?" Steven had his face pressed up against one window as he stared. He was gazing not at the hotel or the strange vehicles but at the night sky.

Trying to control his trembling, Frank leaned forward and twisted his head to peer up and out. What he saw were four moons, each a different size, all hanging in an impossible sky. He wondered what the sun would look like when day finally broke over this place. Would it be yellow or some other alien color? And would it have cousins, like the moon? His hands clung tightly to the wheel lest it metamorphose beneath his fingers.

"Let me guess," he said quietly. "Another thread twisted?"

Mouse nodded, though he couldn't see her. "Another thread."

"Right." He sat up straight, so sharply Alicia was startled. He began turning the wheel. "I've had enough! I don't give a damn where the real Las Vegas is or what this place is, but we're going home. Now, tonight."

"Aw, Dad!" Steven whined. "This place looks neat!"

"We're going home, like your father says." Somehow Alicia held on to her composure, not to mention her sanity.

While Steven folded his arms and pouted, his father accelerated away from the taunting lights of the city. "Airport. Gotta be an airport. Every city has an airport. We'll fly home, right now."

Half a mile past the last casino they found the sign. It proclaimed, in perfect English: AIRPORT. An arrow pointed down a road leading out into the desert.

Frank sent them skidding wildly around the corner. The lights of the city continued to shrink behind them. That's when he saw the thing that made him slow, then pull over to the side of the road and park. He ignored the profusion of remarkable vehicles that alternately whizzed, whistled, squeaked, and roared past the idling motor home.

Rising in the distance was a tower of cool purple flame atop which sat an elaborate flattened dirigible. Bright lights glistened along its side like the running illumination of some deep-sea fish. It was at least as big as the Empire State Building. As they stared it tilted to its right. When it was climbing at a forty-five-degree angle a loud *boom* echoed across the desert and it vanished into the night.

A moment later two smaller ships took its place in the sky. They were only as big as 747s. Ovoid-shaped, their lights were concentrated along the top. They were descending instead of rising, on puffs of bright red light.

"I cannot be certain," said Burnfingers Begay quietly, "but I do not think you will be able to get a plane to Los Angeles from here."

Frank let out a long slow breath, slumped over the wheel. Alicia was instantly concerned.

"Hon, are you all right?"

He looked over at her without straightening. "No, I'm not all right. I'm sick and tired. Aren't you?"

She hesitated. "I guess, I guess I am. I guess none of us is all right."

Wendy's voice was a mixture of awe and fear. "Daddy, where are we?" Her father finally sat up, staring blankly through the windshield at the distant spaceport.

"Pass Regulus. Wherever the hell that is."

"I know a star called Regulus," said Steven.

"Star. That's a big help." Steven looked hurt and Frank was instantly contrite. The kid had little enough self-confidence as it was. "Sorry, kiddo. I'm just a little upset right now, understand?"

Steven spoke reluctantly. "Yeah, sure. I understand. Gee, Dad, don't you think since we're here we oughta look around a little?"

"Doesn't look like we have any choice. But I'm still going to concentrate on getting us home."

A metallic squeak indicated the side door was being opened. He glanced around sharply, but it was only Burnfingers Begay leaning out for a look. Satisfied, he shut the door behind him.

"Constellations are all mixed up. I don't recognize a one my grandfather taught me. Maybe one of them up there is our sun. Or maybe this is our world and it is all changed around."

Frank was learning that when reality was dissolving around you like a pat of butter in a baked potato it was best not to try to define anything too precisely.

"So what do we do? Grab the first ship to Pluto or someplace close? What the hell am I supposed to *do*?" He was too tired to raise his voice.

"We must keep close to the road," declared Mouse. "It is the nearest thing that remains to a constant. Like all roads, this one is a thread of sorts."

Alicia turned to her. "What do you think we should do? Should we try and drive back to Los Angeles?"

"No. It is more important than ever for me to move quickly to the Vanishing Point. Reality is degenerating ever more rapidly. It is regrettable," she concluded apologetically, "that the Anarchis has chosen to concentrate its efforts on me, but that only proves how close I am to reaching my goal of soothing the Spinner. My fellow singers must be in even more difficulty than I am."

"Aren't we just lucky we happened to pick you up," said Frank sarcastically.

"It is a grand thing you are doing in helping me."

"Let me guess. You said this Vanishing Point was near Vegas. Am I right in assuming it isn't actually *in* Vegas, after all? Or this Pass Regulus place, either?"

"No. I said it lay in this direction. This is true. It lies onward. That is the way we must go. If we retreat now we run the risk of encountering the same twisted thread that nearly destroyed us before."

He nodded resignedly. "I thought it might be like that. So we can't go back, either. Unless we want to pay another visit to Hell."

"We must go on."

"To where?" He shifted in his seat. "To this Vanishing Point? Next big town is Salt Lake City. I suppose you're going to tell me it lies beyond that, too. Then what? Cheyenne?"

"No." She concentrated, closing her eyes. "Not that far. Surely not that far."

"I suppose I should be relieved, right?"

"So what you're saying," said Alicia, "is that if we can get you as far as this Vanishing Point, you'll be able to make everything right again."

"If I can soothe the Spinner, yes. If it is not already too late."

Alicia turned to her husband. "We have to go on, Frank. I thought maybe we could walk away from this, but we can't. Not if everything's going to keep changing. I thought it would be all right when we got to Las Vegas. Now we aren't even going to be able to do that. We don't have any choice."

"The hell we don't! I'm not heading out into nowhere again tonight. I can't drive anymore, and you shouldn't, either."

"I could drive, Dad," said Wendy.

He smiled at her. "Thanks, sweetheart, but I think I'd rather be behind the wheel myself in case we run into any new surprises. This boat's a little harder to handle than your XR-7."

"Then what are we going to do, dear?" Alicia asked him.

He sighed. "A city's a city."

"Perhaps it would be best for us to rest awhile," said Mouse.

"Frank's right." Burnfingers nodded back toward town. "Maybe Pass Regulus is not Las Vegas, but it looks to be a close facsimile. They should welcome us at one of the hotels."

"What about money?" Frank asked him. "They may not take credit cards here."

"What they take might surprise you. If nothing else we always have my gold."

"But you've been saving that for something special," said Alicia. "To make your jewelry, or whatever it is you intend to make."

"I can always get more gold. When we are safely back in our reality you can pay me back."

"You'd do that for us?" said Frank.

"It will be a cold day in Hell when Burnfingers Begay shies

from helping his friends. I am looking forward to seeing what kind of entertainment this city offers.''

Mouse eyed him. ''There's no guarantee gold is worth anything on this reality line. It might be quite common.''

''Not my gold. Mine is uncommon gold. Though I cannot dispute what you say.''

''It's worth a try, anyway.'' Frank checked the road behind them. Both lanes were empty. He swung the big motor home around, kicking sand from the opposite shoulder, and headed back toward town. Momentarily he found himself wondering at the difference between common and uncommon gold. Then it was forgotten as he concentrated afresh on the traffic that began to gather around them.

9

NOT FAR BEYOND THE Hulton he pulled into the parking lot of what appeared to be the biggest hotel around. Four metal and glass wings protruded from the crown of the immense cylindrical tower. Each wing contained a huge glass-bottomed pool in which guests were invited to swim. Their distance from the ground eliminated any temptation anyone in the motor home might have felt to do so.

The reservations manager was as human as they were, especially when it came to his attitude toward money. As he'd feared, Frank found that his credit cards and cash were utterly useless.

Or as the manager put it, "If you're trying to pull some kind of gag, my friend, this is the wrong place to do it." He wore a one-piece powder-blue jumpsuit with an exotic white and black flower sprouting from the buttonhole. His shaven skull was elaborately painted. The composition continued down both sides of his neck to vanish beneath the jumpsuit's shoulder straps.

"What about this?" Burnfingers fumbled inside his leather pouch and extracted a Spanish piece of eight. Frank didn't get a good look at it, but it gleamed like new.

The manager held it up to the light. "Pretty, but malleable. Not worth much, I'm afraid."

A discouraged Frank turned away from the desk. "So we're stuck. We'll have to sleep in the motor home after all."

"Wait." The manager's eyes narrowed. "What's that noise?"

Since the lobby fronting the desk was active with people and other creatures coming and going, not to mention the din rising from the nearby casino, his query could have stimulated several different answers. Except that he was looking straight at Wendy, who was standing behind her parents rocking to the sounds from her Walkman. Evidently the manager's hearing was more than acute.

Sometimes, Frank thought, it helps to be experienced in commerce.

"Just some of my daughter's music."

The manager listened a moment longer, licking his lips. "Could I hear closer?" he finally asked hesitantly.

"Sure." Frank turned to yell at his daughter. "Wendy!"

She made a face, slipped off the earphones. "What's up, Pops?"

"Let our friend here have a listen."

She looked dubious but passed over the Walkman and phones. The manager slipped them on carefully. A look of pure bliss transformed his face. Frank was becoming impatient when the man finally removed the phones. He looked around to make sure none of his fellow employees was near, leaned over the counter. He wore avarice like a cheap cologne.

"How much do you want for this?"

"Now wait a minute, Pops. That's *my* Walkman," Wendy protested.

The two men ignored her as Frank showed the manager how the little machine operated. He nudged the eject tape and the cover popped open.

"The music is recorded on this strip of plastic material?" The manager ran a finger over an inch of tape.

"That's right."

"This is wonderful. The archaic melodies, the astonishingly primitive rhythmic arrangements, the pure tone-deafness of the singers, not to mention the exquisite inanity of the vocals. Where did you buy it?" He looked up from the Walkman, studying their appearance, their attire. "Where are you people from, anyway? Canatolia? Marsecap? Notil?"

"Just tell me what it's worth to you."

"I don't know. This is just a hobby of mine." He swallowed. "Do you have more tapes like this one?"

"Yeah. There's a whole bunch out in the mot—out in our vehicle."

"How many is a 'whole bunch'?"

"Beats me." He turned. "Wendy?"

"C'mon, Pops," she protested. "You can't."

"Never mind. I'll buy you a whole new setup when we get home. Anything you want. Then you can spend a whole day shopping at Tower Records. All the tapes you can carry."

She still sounded reluctant. "Well—okay. But only if we have to."

"We have to."

"I guess," she mumbled, not looking at the desk manager, "I brought a couple dozen."

"A couple of dozen?" The man's eyes widened. Sensing he was overreacting, he tried to appear disinterested. "I guess we could trade. I could let you stay for a little while, maybe throw in a meal or two if you're hungry."

Frank hadn't become a major player in the sporting goods business by selling himself short. "Forget it." He reached for the Walkman. "We'll try somewhere else."

The manager's hand jerked forward to stay him. "Okay, okay. I just wanted to see if you knew what you had here." He glanced uncertainly at Wendy. "Several dozen, you say? All different?"

"All different," Wendy admitted.

"I'll give you a suite." The man was whispering now. "One of the best in the house. Not the best. I just can't. Those are strictly for the high rollers who come in from the major worlds. But you'll be comfortable, I guarantee it. And I'll give you an open line of credit to in-house services. Food and miscellaneous."

"What about shows?"

"Included. Anything at the hotel."

"And gambling," said Alicia suddenly, "we'll want to do some gambling."

The manager winced. "All right," he muttered after a moment's hesitation. He eyed Frank calculatingly. His subject managed to appear bored and indifferent. "I'll give you a ten-thousand credit line. No more. You aren't professionals, are you?"

"Professionals? Professional what?" asked Alicia.

"Gamblers."

"Heavens, no."

That satisfied him. "Fine. You'll lose it all back by morning, then. It's all I can do. I have a lot of discretion where food and board is concerned, but not actual credit. You understand?"

Frank didn't know how much ten thousand credits was, but he wasn't going to argue about it. "Deal. I don't think we'll be staying here more than a day or so anyway."

"Then we are agreed." The man looked relieved, as though he'd just pulled off a grand coup but was trying to conceal his elation. "Give me a minute and we'll register you. I'll do it myself." He winked. "Can't have you formally signing in, now can we?" He wore the smile of someone who'd just bought the Hope diamond for twenty bucks and a handful of subway tokens.

Let him celebrate, Frank thought. They'd had the better end of the deal. Tonight—today, rather—they'd sleep in a real bed and eat well. They'd have their vacation, if only for a day. Much longer than that and Mouse would be nagging at them to move on.

As soon as their surreptitious registration had been completed, the manager turned his duties over to an assistant and took them up to the room himself. The elevator they entered was cylindrical instead of rectangular. There was no sense of motion as it ascended, only unattached numbers crawling through the air where the door had been a moment earlier. As they rose, the manager enthusiastically recited a list of celebrities currently appearing at the hotel. Frank and Alicia recognized none of them.

Wendy continuously bemoaned the loss of her Walkman. "I said I'd buy you a new one," her father reminded her. "Soon as we get back to L.A."

"Yeah. If we ever get back to L.A."

Alicia put an arm around her daughter. "Of course we're going to get home. Aren't we, Frank?"

He nodded as their eyes met, and he could see the concern there.

Both of them felt better the instant they entered the expansive room.

"This is more like it," he murmured. "Maybe we ought to stay on this thread for a while."

"Frank!"

He grinned at his wife. "Just kiddin', hon."

"I am going to lie down for a while." Mouse's voice was wispier than usual. "I must conserve my strength for singing."

"Sure, go ahead," Frank told her magnanimously.

A quick survey revealed two sleeping rooms located off the main sitting area. Mouse crawled onto the first bed she encountered and was instantly asleep.

As for the rest of them, they could have spent the whole morning learning about the remarkable room, but Frank planned on seeing as much of Pass Regulus and their hotel as possible. So after several hours' sleep he roused his family and prepared to go exploring.

Controls on a round table in the center of the sitting room generated three-dimensional images a yard above the polished, mirror-like surface. By late afternoon Steven and Wendy were fighting over the buttons as naturally as they would over those of a television set.

"What about you, Burnfingers?" Frank inquired of their tall companion. "What are you going to do?"

"Guess I'll go downstairs and have a look around. No telling when I might find my way back to this part of wherever it is we happen to be."

"My feelings exactly. You kids watch it, you hear me?"

Neither bothered to look up. An eagle and a girl were dancing in the air above the center table. They moved in response to the children's commands.

Frank shrugged, went through the door with Alicia in tow. Burnfingers Begay followed close behind.

The hall was a tube lined with zigzagging neon lights. No, not neon. Closer inspection revealed that the lights hung by themselves in the air, dark as wine and quite tubeless. Frank passed his hand through one, certain no hotel would place dangerous lasers where a careless guest could stumble into them. He felt nothing, not even a tingling. The amazingly intense light was perfectly harmless.

The elevator took them back to the ground floor, deposited them in the casino. They found themselves surrounded by alien sights, smells, and sounds. None of the games being played was recognizable, though a couple came close. At one table, guests were playing something like craps with half a dozen dice suspended in midair. Nearby were intersecting wheels that juggled tiny arrowheads and fragments of script. As they looked on, one of the arrowheads collided with a drifting letter. There was a flash of light followed by a cheer from the spectators down front.

"This might not be as much fun as I'd hoped." Frank tried to find something they could play. "We've got credit, but we don't know how any of these games operate."

Alicia put her arm through his. "We don't have to gamble. Let's find a show." Reluctantly, he followed her lead.

A hotel employee directed them to an auditorium. It was tastelessly decorated in velour and crushed velvet, but considering its proximity to the casino it was astonishingly quiet inside. An assortment of nearly nude creatures was cavorting on the distant stage. Some of them were human. Frank found the display of alien anatomy less intriguing than the acrobatics the troupe was performing. Since several of the aliens possessed more than feet and hands to work with, some of the results were spectacular, especially when they interacted with their human counterparts. Frank and Alicia were properly enthralled.

"You were right to come down here." Alicia's eyes were shining. "It's wonderful! What a shame no one will believe any of it."

"Maybe they'd believe Burnfingers. What about that, Burnfingers?" Frank turned, frowning. There was no sign of their friend. He'd been standing close behind them only a moment earlier.

Straining on tiptoes, Frank barely caught a glimpse of him over the top of the crowd. He was being led away by three huge aliens in dark attire. Frank couldn't be sure, but he thought Begay was resisting the convoy.

"Hey, somebody's taking Burnfingers."

"Taking? He's probably just going to talk with some people he met."

"I don't think so."

"Well, it isn't our problem," she said determinedly.

He eyed her in surprise. "What do you mean it isn't our problem, sweets? If it wasn't for him we'd still be stuck back in Hell. Permanently, maybe."

She looked up at him. "This isn't Hell, and we're free to leave anytime."

Frank hesitated, tried for another glimpse of Burnfingers. A door opened in the side of the auditorium and the trio of aliens hustled him through. The Indian was definitely putting up a fight. He started toward the doorway.

Alicia tugged on his arm. "Frank, he can take care of himself."

"Sorry, hon. I have to check it out."

She was pleading now. "Please, Frank. Don't risk your life, don't risk all our lives, for a crazy man."

Burnfingers was no longer in view. If he didn't go after him immediately, Frank knew, he probably wouldn't be able to locate him again. Would that matter so much? Would it matter even to Burnfingers Begay? If he was half as crazy as he claimed to be, by tomorrow he might well have forgotten the Sonderbergs. Trouble was, Frank wouldn't forget him.

Though not a particularly brave man, and certainly not a foolhardy one, Frank had never shied from a fight. As much as anything, he was curious why anyone in this place would want to talk to Burnfingers, why they would single out a stranger in a crowd. Of course, Begay confessed to having been around some. Had he been here before, too, wherever here was? Or had he been truthful up in the room when he'd claimed he didn't know where they were?

What it came down to was not where they were, but what kind of people they were.

"I've got to see what's going on, sweets. Got to see if I can help."

"No, you don't. It's probably friends of his, or some kind of minor misunderstanding."

He gently disengaged himself. "You wait here. Or go back to the room and check on the kids. I'll be back in a minute. I just want to find out what's going on. I'm not going to do anything stupid. You know me better than that."

She nodded slowly. "I know that tone. But I'm not staying here and I'm not going upstairs. I'm coming with you. If there's no danger then there's no harm in it."

He didn't want to waste any more time arguing. "Come on, then." He turned and led the way through the crowd, oblivious to the fact that more than half of them weren't remotely human.

They left the raucous cheering of the auditorium for the comparative quiet of a circular lobby. Frank just managed to glimpse one alien and black hair turning up another hallway. Several corridors connected with the lobby like the spokes of a wheel.

"There they go!"

"Shouldn't we notify security or something?" Alicia's reluctance hadn't abated.

"Not until we find out what this is all about. Security might make things worse for Burnfingers."

They hurried across the lobby and into the hallway opposite—only to find themselves confronting a dead end. There were no doors lining the cul-de-sac, only inscriptions on the walls. Frank tentatively brushed a hand across the wall beneath one such label. The script above glowed briefly, but no entrance appeared.

Alicia hung back. "I don't know about this, Frank. Following's one thing. Breaking and entering's another."

"I'm not going to break anything," he assured her impatiently.

There couldn't be more than three doors off the dead end, he suspected. It was too small for more than that. One on each side and another at the far end. He began feeling his way slowly around the hallway wall, paying particular attention to the spaces beneath the inscriptions. It made no difference. The walls remained inviolate.

"They must've gone through here somewhere," he muttered under his breath. "We saw 'em come down here."

"You tried your best, dear. I'm sure Mr. Begay can take care of himself, wherever he is." She didn't entirely believe that, but what else could they do? They had their own troubles and children to worry about. Burnfingers had been a friend and good company, but she wouldn't be wholly displeased to see him fall by the wayside. It was feeling crowded in the motor home.

Frank didn't like the idea of giving up, but there didn't seem anything more he could do, unless he took Alicia's suggestion and notified hotel security. As he stood there debating how to proceed, there was a rush of air and a door-sized opening materialized just to his left. A second later bodies filled the gap, arms and legs pinwheeling around the flailing form of Burnfingers Begay as he fought with his three abductors. Alicia gasped as the pinwheel sucked up Frank. Despite the beer belly he'd acquired over the years, he still knew how to fight. He began kicking and punching wildly, realizing he had a three-in-four chance of hitting someone beside Burnfingers.

The combative quintet slammed into the far wall and came apart under the impact, which dazed two of Burnfingers's attackers. Frank extricated himself, bruised but unbowed, while the Indian wrestled with his remaining assailant. The two trying to rise from the floor and rejoin the fight owned ugly faces, short sharp teeth, pointy ears, and a fringe of porcupinish spines that presently lay back flat atop their heads. Frank became aware that Burnfingers was shouting at him.

"Go get Mouse and the children! Warm up the motor home. And do not forget my luggage!" His fist impacted on a blunt snout and his attacker fell limp. One of the two rising from the floor was trying to extract a steel whip from a pocket.

Frank stood paralyzed, puffing hard, realizing he was ill-suited for this sort of activity but unwilling to flee. "You heard him, hon! Get the kids and our stuff into the Winnebago!"

"But you—?"

"Go on, now!"

With a last helpless glance in Burnfingers's direction she whirled and raced for the elevators.

The thing without the whip weighed at least three hundred pounds. It threw itself on Begay's back. Burnfingers executed a deft little move and threw the monster into the far wall. As its companion raised the thin steel, Frank hopped forward and kicked it in the groin. That part of its anatomy was apparently analogous enough, because it promptly collapsed to the floor.

Burnfingers put an arm around Frank's shoulder and launched him down the short hallway. "Come on, my friend!"

"Call—hotel security!" Frank managed to gasp.

"Cannot. We can't stay here any longer, not even to answer helpful questions. Still got that credit with you?"

"The stuff the manager gave us?" He pulled out a spool of quarter-inch gold tape. "Yeah, right here, but—"

Burnfingers yanked it away. Glancing back, Frank saw two of the massive abductors pounding hard after them. Abruptly he realized how out of shape he was, wheezing and struggling to maintain the pace.

They charged into the casino, their pursuers closing the distance with every stride. Drawing startled looks and oaths in a dozen languages, Burnfingers leaped atop a gaming table. Before anyone could pull him down he unwound the secure end of the spool and threw it as far into the crowd as he was able. The gold tape trailed its spool like a berserk kite string, glinting in the lights.

Shouts and squeals of excitement filled the air as the gamblers and tourists scrambled for pieces of the tape. The crowd packed in tightly, rendering the aisles between gaming tables impassable, a living wave that smashed up against the pair of thugs and carried them backward.

Burnfingers was grinning as he jumped down from the table. "That ought to slow them down for a while. Let us leave now, before security does indeed put in an appearance. They would want to question us, and I don't want to be questioned." Grabbing Frank, he half led, half dragged him through the mob.

"Where are we going?"

"To the motor home, which your fine woman will hopefully have warmed up and awaiting us outside."

"What if she's late?"

"I think your woman is more resourceful than that. I don't think we will have to wait for her."

Whistles and sirens filled the room as the hotel's security forces finally put in an appearance. The effort required to try to control a crowd battling for possession of pieces of a ten-thousand-credit tape left them no time for chasing fleeing tourists like Frank and Burnfingers Begay.

"What's the deal, anyway? What'd those guys want with you?" Frank found it hard to run and talk simultaneously. Fortunately, whenever he slowed down, his companion all but carried him along.

"They wanted my gold, of course."

Frank's gaze rose to the backpack that bounced on the bigger man's back. "They didn't get it?"

"Of course not. Do you think I would wander around a place like this with a load of gold in my backpack? I may be crazy, but I am not stupid."

"Then, where is it? The gold, I mean?"

"I thought your luggage would be the safest place. I switched it when you were showing the children how to work the dimensional projector. I knew you would not mind."

"Me, mind? Why should I mind? So the gold's with Alicia and the kids?"

Begay nodded. Frank wanted to tell the Indian what he thought of him for placing Alicia in such danger, but he couldn't spare the wind and right now he was more interested in leaving Begay's assailants far behind. He didn't ease off until they'd left the auditorium-casino section.

"Wait a minute. How could anybody here know about your gold?"

"They sensed it, because it is special. It has the odor of history upon it. Other things besides wine can improve with age. There is a mystique to old gold that has been much handled. An aura, a sense of power; call it what you will." He nodded back the way they'd come. "*They* sensed it."

Frank didn't understand. "You mean they wanted your stash because it has antique value?"

Burnfingers shook his head. "No. They wanted to prevent me from making something of it."

Something still didn't make sense. "Why should they or anyone else care if you want to make some bracelets or watch-bands out of the stuff?"

Burnfingers smiled at a private thought. "Perhaps they are afraid I may make something out of it besides a bracelet or watchband." He gestured. "We made it. There is an exit."

As they plunged through the emergency door, Frank forgot to ask Burnfingers who *they* might be.

He seemed to know exactly where they were going. As they ran around the side of the hotel and entered the main parking area Frank bent over and rested his palms on his knees.

"Gonna have to slow down. Fast walking's about all the exercise I get anymore. Spent the last ten years behind a desk. Remember, I don't use jogging shoes. I just sell 'em."

"It's all right, my friend. We are nearly there. See?" Burnfingers pointed. The motor home stood out like an iceberg among the sea of leaner, sleeker vehicles in the parking lot. Lights blazed within and a slim figure stood silhouetted in the door.

"Hello, Mousewoman," Burnfingers said in greeting as he helped Frank stagger the rest of the way.

"Hello, Burnfingers Begay." She was eyeing him strangely. "Alicia told me you ran into some trouble."

"All over now. Everyone here?"

"Yes." Alicia pushed Mouse aside. "What happened? Why were those thugs beating up on you?"

"Tell you all about it later. Are the children all right?" He tried to peer past her into the motor home as Frank pulled himself through the door.

"They're fine. Confused, like the rest of us, but fine. They weren't happy about leaving in such a hurry."

"I am not happy about it, either. You brought all the luggage?"

"Naturally we brought all our luggage."

He smiled relievedly. "That's very good." He followed Frank inside.

Alicia closed the door behind them. Frank stood fighting for breath, paused as Burnfingers strode past him and took up residence in the driver's seat. He extended an open hand.

"Give me the keys, Frank."

"No. No way." He shook his head, exhausted by the long run. "I've gone along with you far enough. I risked my life to look for you."

"I appreciate that. I will explain everything eventually, but we cannot hang around here. Those unpleasant people will find us. Give me the keys."

Frank fumbled through his pockets, finally produced the handful of metal. He held them a foot from Burnfingers's outstretched hand. "Why should I let you drive? A crazy man?"

"I am a good driver, Frank. On the reservation, every day is demolition-derby day. We count coup in pickups now instead of on pony back. Compared to that, highway driving is a snap." He nodded toward the far window. "You better make up your mind quick."

Frank joined his wife in staring through the glass. The three near-humans who'd been fighting with Begay were standing in the brightly lit main entrance of the hotel. Even at a distance Frank could tell they were searching intently.

"In moments they will locate us," Burnfingers was saying. "Then they will shoot to disable our transportation. Hopefully they will not kill anyone in the process." Frank handed him the keys. "Thank you."

Burnfingers started the engine, raced it once, then pulled slowly out of the parking lot, heading for the main drag. Frank shifted his attention to the side window. As they pulled out into the street he thought he saw the three figures vanish into the lot.

Horns blared, whistles screeched, sirens wailed as the big motor home made room for itself amid the traffic. As they headed out of town and gained room to maneuver, Burnfingers accelerated, weaving around the remaining vehicles in front of them. Frank sat down next to him.

"Better slow up or you'll wreck us."

"No way, my friend." He kept his eyes on the road ahead, grinning. "You've done most all the driving so far. Now it is my turn."

Steven was whining because no one was listening to him. Wendy sat morosely off to one side, obviously frustrated by their precipitate departure. Alicia and Mouse were all the way in back, staring through the wide rear window.

"I think someone's following us!" Alicia shouted, raising her voice so she would be heard up at the front. "There's a big van or something back there and it's weaving in and out of traffic just like we are."

Burnfingers glanced at his sideview mirrors. "I see them. Don't worry. We'll lose them."

"In this tank?" said Frank worriedly. "This ain't no Corvette, you know."

"Don't worry." Burnfingers winked at him. "I once had to lose two busloads of tourists in Monument Valley." He continued to accelerate, recklessly disregarding the presence of the other cars on the road ahead. Frank moaned and closed his eyes, but they didn't hit anybody. Burnfingers handled the motor home like a Jeep, until they'd left the last of the city traffic far behind.

"They're still back there!" Alicia declared in a high voice. Her announcement was followed by a faint *whoosh*ing noise as something like a runaway skyrocket shot past overhead. It vanished into the night.

"Shooting at us," Burnfingers announced imperturbably. "I thought they would hold off awhile longer." He swung the motor home hard left.

Frank stared forward. "Why'd you turn off?" The road ahead was two lanes, narrow but paved, like a snake's tongue leading out into the desert. The main highway quickly fell behind. Dark mountains loomed against the night. "If they catch us out here they won't have to worry about witnesses."

"They won't catch us." Burnfingers spoke with assurance, staring straight ahead and holding on to the wheel with both hands. Occasionally he stole a glance at the rearview.

Another light flashed by, off to the right this time, fading into the darkness like fluorescent cola.

"If they've got a full tank they can just run us down." Frank was peering at the mirror on the passenger's side, barely able to make out the lights of the van pursuing them. "We'll run out of gas out in the middle of nowhere!"

"I thought this road angled right about here." Burnfingers was talking to himself, not Frank. "Ah." His face broke into a wide smile.

Frank's pupils became as big as grapes.

Everything they'd encountered so far—the incredible creatures, the impossible places—paled to insignificance alongside what happened next. Burnfingers shoved the accelerator to the floor and the motor home leaped forward. Steven stopped whining and raced to the nearest window, staring out.

"Oh, *wow!*"

"Steven! Steven, you come away from there!" Alicia hurried forward to put her arms around the boy. When she saw what he was looking at, her hands dropped slowly to her sides. Wendy had moved over to stand close to her mother, while Mouse stood behind them, saying nothing.

The road had become a pale, thin ribbon stretching across void. A soft pink light emanated from the pavement, a strip of cellophane trimmed with glowing fiber optics. Theirs was the only vehicle traveling the fairy road. Mountains, cacti, the barbed-wire fences that had lined both sides of the pavement: all had disappeared.

All that remained was the pure perfect night, and the myriad of stars overhead. Also to left and right. Also below.

They could clearly see radiant nebulae and supergiants, bright clusters and comets, through the semitransparent surface of the road.

A DIVIDING LINE still ran down the center of the highway. Further proof that two lanes remained was provided moments later when something like a runaway meteor came exploding toward them, only to scream past in the oncoming lane and vanish aft. Steven turned to follow its passage.

"Geez, what was that?"

Burnfingers was whistling softly to himself as he drove. A paralyzed Frank finally moved, straightening in his seat, accepting what he saw outside while fighting to avoid staring at it. There was no shoulder, no solid border to the narrow roadway. If Burnfingers lost control, there was nothing to prevent them from driving right off the pavement, to fall endlessly, forever, through the abyss that enclosed them on all sides.

The sign that came up fast on their right almost sent him over the edge inside his head.

SALT LAKE CITY—212 Miles

The sheer sameness of the speckled wonderment outside finally brought Alicia forward, just in time to catch a glimpse of the sign before they rolled past.

"Surely that can't be right."

"Why not?" said Burnfingers cheerfully. "Miles or light-years, what's the difference? It's all a matter of perspective."

"I don't know how much more of this I can take," said Frank in a low voice.

"You can take as much of it as you have to, my friend, because you have no other choice."

"Couldn't we, maybe, pull over and rest for a while?" Alicia asked hopefully.

"Pull over?" Frank gestured outside. "Pull over where? I mean, I like the wide open spaces, but I like solid ground under them."

"Nothing's solid anymore," Alicia observed thoughtfully. "You can't count on anything being real anymore." She turned to the diminutive figure on her left. "Isn't that right?"

Mouse nodded. "Reality flexes."

Frank half turned in his seat. "That's nuts."

"In and out, in and out." Mouse moved her hands to illustrate. "Like a bellows. Here reality has been stretched thin enough to see through."

"Wonderful." He slumped back down in his seat.

After a while Burnfingers finally gave in to Frank's repeated requests to let him drive. At first he was nervous, but a few minutes behind the wheel found him cruising easily. All you had to do was stay on the road, he told himself. Despite their success in escaping from Pass Regulus, he still had more confidence in his own driving than Begay's.

The last thing he expected to see was an off ramp.

It was coming up fast on the right, and he slowed quickly. The sign nearby said CEDAR CITY. Alicia was sitting across from him now and he looked anxiously at her.

"Seems okay." She glanced back. "Burnfingers?"

Begay came forward, studied both the sign and ramp. "Might as well. If it's half right we're a long ways from Vegas and longer still from Regulus."

Licking his lips, Frank flipped his turn signal and slowly started down pavement no thicker than plastic wrap.

There was a stop sign at the bottom of the off ramp. A normal-looking, battered red and yellow sign. As he hit the brakes the light changed, late afternoon replacing the awesome universal night around them. It was reality, snapping back like a rubber band.

"We've fallen through a crack," said Burnfingers.

"We're back." Alicia let out a long sigh. "Thank God, we're back!"

"Maybe," said Burnfingers, but to himself.

The sign by the dirty asphalt read WELCOME TO CEDAR CITY, UTAH. Ahead they could see structures of wood and stucco, clinging to the lower slopes of snow-capped peaks. On a telephone pole nearby, a hawk sat examining the motor home. As they approached, it took wing in search of vermin. The air was warm but not desert hot, refreshingly devoid of pollutants or other surprises. Frank lowered his window, sucked in mountain air.

"Smells right. Looks right. Could we be back where we belong, back on the right reality line?"

"Reality is rife with off ramps," Mouse replied gently, "but I admit it does appear promising. There is no need to try to find the interstate again. We can continue along this state highway."

"You mean *you* can continue along. I've had it. I know I promised, but I can't take this anymore, lady. Not even if we're, like you said, linked together. No more."

Mouse regarded him for a long moment. "I understand, Mr. Sonderberg. It has been harder than I thought. There will be dangers to you, but perhaps when I depart your company they will not manifest themselves. I will make my way alone the rest of the way to the Vanishing Point."

Frank seemed confused by her ready acquiescence. "Well, okay. That's more like it." Alicia said nothing.

"What will you do?" Mouse asked him curiously.

He considered, hardly daring to believe their ordeal was nearing its end. "I dunno. I guess we'll find a motel." Now Alicia smiled. "An ordinary chain motel where we can get some rest. Then I'm calling a taxi, or a limo, or something. The outfit that rented us this machine can come and get it. I don't give a damn if the taxi has to come all the way down from Salt Lake. I ain't doing any more driving. We'll head for the nearest airport. I'll beg, borrow, or steal a charter plane to fly us home. We're not even going into Salt Lake for a regular airline. I just want out of here as fast as possible."

"I do understand. I hope all will be well with you."

"Put me in the air headed toward L.A. and I'll be well, all right."

They entered town. A small Western town, salubrious in its ordinariness. Burger King, McDonald's, a Kentucky Fried slid past, until their mouths were watering. They were followed by a small shopping center anchored by miniature Sears and J.C. Penney stores, then a K-Mart. It was so much like Los Angeles on a smaller scale that Alicia started crying. Best of all, it didn't change as they cruised up the main street. Frank pulled into the first motel with a Best Western sign out front.

The vacancy–no vacancy sign wasn't working. That didn't matter to Frank, who could have spotted the lifeless neon letters a mile off. He pulled up alongside the fenced swimming pool and parked.

"Guess I'll be leaving you here, too," said Burnfingers. He raised a hand to forestall Frank's protest. "It's all right. I know this country well and will have no trouble here. You have been good people. I did not thank you properly for rescuing me back at that casino. Maybe someday I may even be able to explain it to myself."

"Didn't exactly rescue you," Frank replied. "All we did was help distract those guys who were beating on you and give you a chance to rescue yourself." He checked his watch. "Least we can do is buy you something to eat."

"That's kind of you. I would enjoy a proper meal. It has been a strenuous couple of days."

"Now there's an understatement." Alicia smiled for the first time in a while. Wendy, too, had recovered, though she wasn't twisting and tossing her body in time to the music inside her head with quite the same abandon as before. She missed her tape player.

Maybe a cheeseburger and fries would serve as a temporary substitute, her father mused. "Just let me check us in first." He headed for the door. "Maybe the manager can recommend a place to us."

They must have presented an interesting sight as they crowded into the modest waiting room. There was a stone fireplace, cold this time of year; a smaller color TV on a stand on which a young man with too many teeth was giving away large appliances; a pile of magazines; a couple of couches for the use of guests only; and the counter with the omnipresent revolving postcard rack and boxful of local giveaway pamphlets advertising attractions in Salt Lake City, Las Vegas, and points in between.

The manager/owner was in his early sixties, a large man with a tired paunch and a flowing white mustache. Thin white rimless glasses framed his eyes, and suspenders struggled to keep his waistband even with the bottom of a striped white shirt. He grinned as he inspected his visitors.

"Well! You folks look like you've been through the wringer!"

"We do?" Frank didn't realize it showed that much. "Just been driving a long time."

The manager grunted. "That's tough on anybody. Y'all stayin' here?"

"No. Just the four of us. Our friends will be looking for separate transportation out of town."

The man shoved a registration form across the narrow counter. "Greyhound stops once in the morning, Trailways in the evening—they been kind of irregular lately."

Alicia tried to make conversation while her husband filled out the registration form. "Pretty country."

"That's why folks're livin' here." The manager chuckled. "Quiet. You want excitement, you're in the wrong town. Wrong state, far as that goes."

A woman juggling a glass and dishrag against each other appeared by the back door. "Hello, folks."

Alicia smiled. "Good evening."

"Yes, it is a good evening, isn't it?" She frowned slightly at the glass, worked the rag a little faster. "Where you folks from?"

"Los Angeles," Steven piped up.

"Oh?" She left the doorway to peer over the counter. "Didn't see you down there, sonny."

"We're on vacation," Steven told her brightly, "and you should'a seen some of the things we've seen!"

His mother glanced sternly down at him. "That will be enough, Steven."

"Awww." Disappointed, he turned to stare at the TV.

Frank turned the completed registration form around. "Want a credit card imprint now?"

"Neh. Don't need it—unless you want to charge long distance calls. Local are free."

"All we want now is something to eat."

Taking his cue, the manager leaned forward and looked to his left, toward the street. "You go up Central about two blocks and you'll hit downtown. 'Bout half a dozen good places to eat."

"Which one would you recommend?" Alicia asked politely.

"Oh, none of 'em. They all pretty much stink. Dave's Diner's a real tourist trap and Judy's Country Kitchen's anything but."

"That's right," said his wife cheerfully. "They all suck."

"I see." Alicia regarded the pair of homey smiles askance. Frank stepped in.

"Then where *would* you suggest we eat?"

"There's another hotel up the street. The Gables. Rooms are awful; full of roaches." The woman made a face. "And sometimes they don't wash their linen between guests, but the kitchen is run separate. My husband and I go there ourselves sometimes when we want to eat out."

"That's very straight of you. Thanks."

"Don't mention it," said the manager. "Glad to help."

They went back to the motor home and began gathering clothes and toiletries for their room. "That's the kind of honesty you don't find anymore," Frank was murmuring.

Alicia was less sanguine. "I wonder. It was more than just honesty. They were so open, it was like they couldn't lie if they wanted to."

Frank grabbed a pair of clean socks. "Maybe it would've been different if they had a coffee shop of their own."

"Wouldn't it be neat if everybody was like that?" said Wendy.

"Bad for business." Frank looked toward the back of the motor home. "Burnfingers, Mouse: dinner's on us."

"I can pay," Begay told him. "I have gold."

"Which you need for your jewelry work," Frank reminded him. "Our treat, and I don't want to hear any more about it."

They walked, since it was only a few blocks to the hotel's restaurant. A few locals were out enjoying the evening sunshine. They chatted easily among themselves, occasionally waving to the cluster of tourists.

It was early for supper and they had the restaurant largely to themselves. Frank found it hard to relate to a dinner menu after hours of fleeing through permanent night. In jumping threads, they'd lost most of a day. Reality lag instead of jet lag, he told himself.

The place wasn't fancy, but it was clean. Flower-print tablecloths covered each dining area. Their waitress was young and attractive.

"Anything special?" Alicia asked as she studied the menu.

"Not really, but don't ask me. I eat here all the time. I'd change that color combination if I was you, though."

"What?" Confused, Alicia laid her menu down.

"Color combination. That yellow top really doesn't go with those jeans."

"I thought bright colors were in."

"Maybe for some folks. They just make me kind of nauseous, you know?"

"Hey," Frank said, "how about taking our order instead of criticizing my wife's clothing, okay?"

"Sure." The waitress sounded genuinely puzzled at Frank's tone. "Hey, kid, if you gotta blow your nose rub it on your sleeve instead of my clean tablecloth, will you?" Steven gaped at her. "And you," she went on, talking to Mouse, "we get some weird types in here, but you look like you just dropped out of some traveling freak show."

"How about me?" Burnfingers asked politely.

"I don't much like Indians."

"That's all right," Burnfingers responded studiously. "I do not care for blondes who bleach their hair and try to look younger than they are."

Frank held his breath, expecting to have to duck pad and pencil if not something weightier. But the woman just smiled at Burnfingers, who smiled back.

Alicia was right. He felt a by-now familiar tenseness in his gut. Something was wrong here. He noted that Mouse was paying more than casual attention to the conversation.

One by one they placed their orders. Frank found himself expecting additional comments and he wasn't disappointed. The waitress found Wendy's selection of lemonade to accompany her hamburger profoundly disgusting and didn't hesitate to say so, to his daughter's obvious surprise and chagrin. When Frank requested his steak well done, the young woman promptly told him what she thought of anyone dumb enough to order good meat burned. He would have shot back with a reply save for a cautioning look from Burnfingers Begay. So he bit back his natural response. Only when she left to turn their order in did he lean over and whisper.

"Why'd you shush me? What the hell's going on here, Burnfingers?"

Mouse interrupted. "I fear that despite appearances we may not have returned to your reality line after all."

"That can't be." Alicia gestured around them. "Everything here's normal: the people, the street signs, the brand names in the windows—everything!"

"I'm afraid not quite everything," Mouse replied somberly.

"You'd better spell it out for me," said Frank angrily. "Just because we run into an honest motel and a snippety waitress, you're trying to tell us we're still not 'home'?"

"What she is trying to tell you," Burnfingers Begay put in, "is that only one thing is different, but that this difference is significant. To put it another way, where reality is concerned, 'almost' don't make it."

Alicia was looking around worriedly, as though she expected a host of long left-behind demons to walk in through the front-door. "What one thing is so different?"

Burnfingers looked at Mouse, who simply gazed back. Finally he sat back in his chair. It groaned under his weight. "Maybe we're wrong. Let us just enjoy our food. Do me one favor, though, Frank."

"If I can."

"If the young lady who took our order, or anybody else, says something to upset you, do not get mad."

"Okay," said Frank slowly. "She's probably just an exception anyways."

"Somehow I do not think so."

As the unexpectedly silent evening meal proceeded, Burnfingers's prediction was borne out by the conversation around them. Other diners exchanged vicious, pointed insults and commentary with their neighbors, without trying to hide their opinions from anyone who might be listening. Their waitress smilingly insulted everyone in turn, offering her observations of their personal hygiene, taste in attire, appearance, and whatever else struck her fancy. They replied in kind. Neither restaurant staff nor customers appeared in the least upset. Later they were able to overhear her exchanging similar comments with the cook and cashier.

This biting verbal byplay was not restricted to the visiting adults. Children chatted equally guilelessly, and teenagers exhibited great ingenuity in putting down their companions. When a couple of girls Wendy's age passed the table and all but reduced her to tears with their comments about her coiffure and clothing, she responded in kind. They smiled, nodded, and walked on. It was as though the words had no effect on them, or at least none of the intended effect.

"Not quite our reality." Burnfingers was finishing his Coke.

"I think I understand." Alicia pushed peas around on her plate. "It's just like our world, except everyone here says exactly what they're thinking. Nobody lies."

"There's no tact or diplomacy, either," muttered Wendy darkly.

"Everyone here speaks the truth as they see it," said Mouse thoughtfully. "A different social system has evolved. It would probably be impossible to insult anyone in this place unless you accused them of telling a lie, and they very well may not know what a lie is."

"That's why the people back at the motel were so blunt with us," Alicia murmured. "An honest opinion is all they can offer."

Wendy crossed her arms and leaned back in her chair, glowering. "Well, I don't like it."

"No inhibitions. No restraints," said Burnfingers.

"It doesn't bother you?" Frank asked him. "Doesn't get under your skin just a little?"

"I do not have any illusions to shatter. I know exactly what I am. And also I am—"

"—crazy. Yeah, we know," said Frank tiredly.

"Then we're still lost." Alicia was wonderfully calm in the face of the crushing disappointment. "We're still not back where we belong. We still aren't—home."

"An almost perfect off ramp," Mouse observed, "but as Mr. Begay tells us, 'almost' does not count."

"We must be close, though." Alicia sounded suddenly eager. "Aren't we close? Wouldn't this be good enough?"

"I dunno," said Frank. "If we stayed here I'd have to learn a whole new way of doing business. I don't know how it works here. I don't think I'm ready for a reality where everybody tells the truth every time. Bet politics here are interesting. I wonder if our reality is exactly the opposite of this one. I mean, where we come from, it sometimes seems like you get elected for telling the biggest lie." He looked sharply at his wife. "Are you ready for all your friends to tell you exactly what they think of you?"

She hesitated, slumped slightly. "No. No, I guess not. I guess we better not stay here."

"If we're this close, then surely the next off ramp will be the right one." He tried to sound encouraging, reading the discouragement in her face. "At least this line isn't dangerous." He cut a chunk of steak. "The food's normal enough. Downright good."

So was the motel, as its managers would have honestly admitted. They had real beds with thick mattresses, a full-sized shower-bath, and strangely honest television to watch.

Not wanting to send their friends off in the dark, Frank insisted Burnfingers and Mouse spend the night in the empty motor home. Both accepted, albeit Mouse tentatively. As always she was anxious to be on her way. As he prepared to climb into bed Frank found himself checking the clock, almost laughed out loud. Time meant nothing to them until they made it back home. The numbers on the plastic face bore no relation to their experiences of the past couple of days.

Yet despite his exhaustion and the warmth of Alicia's slumbering form next to his own he found he was unable to fall asleep. The memories were too immediate, too strong. Alicia could sleep anywhere, anytime. The children had dropped off quickly. Only he was left to gaze at the ceiling, at the sweeps and curves in the stucco feebly illuminated by the light from the motel parking lot that filtered into the room around the edges of the curtains.

Now that they were close to the right reality line, near to home, he found himself pondering all they'd been through and experienced. Bad dreams, the stuff of nightmares. Tomorrow they'd find the right off ramp and take it all the way to Salt Lake or L.A. Tomorrow they would drive back to reality. In the morning they would rid themselves of the enigmatic child-woman who called herself Mouse and the wandering maybe-crazy Burnfingers Begay.

Meanwhile it was silly to lie here trying to decide how much of the past was real and how much hallucination. If he couldn't rent a plane or taxi, they'd have to drive all the way into Salt Lake. He rolled over, forced himself to close his eyes.

It was a quiet room, especially for someone used to traffic-laden L.A. He thought he heard a coyote howl out by the city limits, near the mountain slopes. Probably only a dog.

He was nearly asleep when he heard something else.

At first he thought it was a bird, singing at the moon. The longer he listened the more unlikely that seemed. Though no naturalist, he did watch a lot of nature programs on TV, and he'd never heard of any bird holding a single note for so long.

Alicia's back was ivory in the dim light. She hardly moved, deep in sleep, and he was reluctant to disturb her for an opinion. Yet as he started to lie back down the sound came again, a thin, lilting melody halfway between a song and a cry. It was weak with distance but still unmistakable.

Tension and curiosity had conspired to bring him wide awake. Frustrated, he pushed back the covers and quietly climbed out of bed. He donned jeans and shirt as silently as he opened the door.

It was much cooler than it had been in the desert. The mountain air chilled his skin like alcohol as he carefully shut the door behind him. Around him hung the silence of Utah night.

He stood motionless, listening. Just as he began to wonder at his foolishness he heard it afresh. Out in the parking lot the motor home squatted like a shipping container on wheels. The sound didn't come from its vicinity or from any part of the motel.

The concrete walkway that bordered the front of the motel led him to a deep arroyo which cut through forested land. A small creek gleamed like silver ribbon at the bottom, coursing toward the culvert that would lead it beneath the road. Abandoning the walkway at its terminus he followed the running water into the pines.

As long as he watched where he put his feet, the three-quarters-full moon provided ample light to walk by. Pine needles and leaves from other growths formed a stale carpet that crunched underfoot. Trees made a wall that soon obliterated the motel from sight.

There were no houses here at this end of town. Conscious of his increasing solitude, he would have turned back if the song had not continued to grow louder. It hung in the air between the trees, hypnotic and insistent.

A petite form appeared in the moonlight, standing by the water where the creek slowed and broadened to create a small pond. Silken tresses and folds of silk fluttered aura-like around it, despite the absence of a breeze. As he drew close a gentle wind sprang from the earth itself, curling about him. It was as if he were undergoing inspection by a ghost.

Head tilted back, the figure was singing to the sky. Stars of especial brightness twinkled through the atmosphere as though responding to that song, as if replying with light via some mysterious stellar Morse code.

She sensed his approach, or heard his footsteps compressing the forest detritus, because she stopped and turned to look straight at him. The silenced song hung in the night air like a physical presence.

"Be careful here, Frank Sonderberg."

"Mouse, what are you doing out here? I mean, you're singing: I can see that. But I thought you needed to save your voice for the Spinner?"

She smiled understandingly. "Sometimes I simply have to sing, regardless of other considerations. It's like breathing to me. It relaxes me and keeps me whole." As he continued toward her she put up a warning hand. "Truly be careful, Frank, or you will fall."

A yard away from her he halted, grinning in the weak light. "Where? The creek?" He gestured to his right. "Not much of a tumble."

"Not into the creek." Her head cocked sideways and those enormous violet eyes shone like amethysts. "Are you a brave man, Frank Sonderberg? Do you have real courage?"

After all they'd been through recently he thought it was an unnecessary question, but he answered anyway. "Depends how you define 'brave,' I guess. I've made it this far. I built up a nearly nationwide business on guts and determination, and I've never avoided a challenge. Never had to shoot anybody or anything, but I think I could if I had to."

"Weapons do not make a man brave. True bravery is here" —she touched a finger to her head—"and here." She repeated the same gesture, this time touching her hand to her chest above her heart. "Are you afraid of heights?"

"No more or less so than the average guy, I guess. Why?"

Off to his right the creek rang like water from a dripping faucet. He doubted it was more than six feet deep.

"Not there," she told him. She appeared to hesitate for a moment, then turned and gestured. "Here. But watch your footing. If you slip I'm not strong enough to catch you."

"I'll be careful." He tried to stand a little taller and keep his gut sucked in, always a strain and one that grew worse each year. In a moment he was standing alongside her. Though only of average height he towered above her slight form.

The wind was much stronger now. He turned away from her and looked toward his feet.

Six inches in front of his toes the earth vanished, along with the trees, mountains, and moonlight. A few incredibly distant objects fought vainly against the void, though what those minuscule pinpricks of light might be he could not tell. It was emptier than the night through which they'd driven to reach this place, an unholy abyss hard by his left foot.

He inhaled sharply. His brain screamed at him to step back from that awful infinity, but mindful of Mouse's words he was determined to hold his ground. As he felt her left hand on his arm he knew what she'd said was true: if he fell she wouldn't be able to drag him back. In spite of that her touch was immeasurably reassuring, the fingers warm on his bare skin.

"There are a few places where reality simply ends. Not just in this world but in every world. Places where nothing is, not even Chaos. The congruent void. This is one of those places. A dangerous place to stand, but an exhilarating spot to sing."

Frank wasn't afraid of falling anymore, perhaps because he was frozen to the spot. Astonishing how the utter and complete absence of anything could be so fascinating.

"When I was a kid we used to dare each other to walk to the edge of a roof at school and step off." He slipped another inch forward and felt her fingers tighten on his arm.

"This is no place for childhood pranks," she warned him. "If you step off this soil you will never stop falling. You'll never hit bottom because there is no bottom. You will just keep falling and falling until you perish of thirst or hunger or fear."

"What the hell. It's just like the second floor at Whitney Elementary. The only thing that's different is the scale."

Breathing fast, feeling the excitement course through him, he raised his left leg and stretched it out over emptiness. Then he lowered it, lowered it until his foot passed beneath the level of the ground on which he stood. As his right leg started to tremble he stepped back. At the same time the tension in her fingers eased.

"That was a foolish thing to do, Frank."

He shrugged, inordinately pleased with himself. "We're a foolish people. Besides, if you don't do something a little crazy once in a while life gets pretty damn stale. How many people can say they've stepped over the edge of the world? Wonder what Columbus's boys would've made of this. Maybe some of those old sailors were right all along."

She shook her head but couldn't keep herself from smiling. "Haven't you done enough crazy things recently to last you a lifetime?"

"Those weren't by choice. This was. You got to be in control to enjoy the craziness. Like in business." He looked behind him. The void was still there, threatening and infinite as before, however briefly conquered. "Call it juvenile if you want, but that felt pretty good."

"It was foolish. It was also a very brave thing for an ordinary man to try."

He was feeling slightly giddy and not a little wild. "Maybe I ain't as ordinary as you think. Wasn't I the one who stopped to pick *you* up?"

"That's so. Perhaps more than coincidence was at work."

He chuckled. "Don't get heavy on me. I'm just babbling. You ain't one of those folks who believes that everything's predetermined, are you? That we have no free will?"

"I believe," she replied evenly, "that certain deliberate confluences of people and places are possible." She'd moved closer to him. So near, her eyes were larger even than the void behind them. She smelled of faraway places and exotic ephemera.

There was something he couldn't define. He recalled her impossible claim of age. Certainly she was older than she looked. Five, maybe ten years. Not centuries. Not millennia. He didn't feel he was in the presence of an old woman. Quite the contrary.

Good God, she's beautiful, he found himself thinking. Not in the fashion of the aspiring actresses he sometimes encountered in L.A., nor in the classic sense of the portraits that hung on art museum walls. Like her silken dress, a kind of timeless elegance clung to her.

He discovered he was more nervous than he'd been when he'd suspended his leg over the edge of the world. He was more afraid of falling now, though it was an entirely different kind of falling that endangered him.

"Could you quit staring at me like that?"

Her gaze did not shift. "Why? Do I make you uneasy?"

"Uneasy, hell. You're driving me nuts, and you know it. This is crazy. I mean, I probably am just an ordinary guy like you said. The top of my head already reflects too much light, I'm twenty pounds overweight, and the only special talent or ability I've got is for making money, which is no big deal where I come from."

"There is more than that," she whispered huskily, "even if you refuse to recognize it yourself. You are kind. You have a stubbornness in you that translates into bravery. You are full of love for your family and your fellow man."

"Maybe so, except for Oshmans," he said, naming his major competitor.

His attempt to make light of her deadly serious comments had no effect on her. She put her arms around his waist. "It's easy to be brave when one is young and strong, much more difficult when one is not. Therein lies real courage."

"I told you, I'm not brave. I just like to do crazy stuff once in a while."

The evening chill had deserted them. It was downright hot there by the pond at the edge of the world. Despite all her denials she seemed to have considerable strength in those slim arms. Enough to pull him down toward her. Or maybe he bent. He was never sure.

The heat that seared him as they kissed awoke feelings and sensations dormant for twenty years. He found himself kissing back, unwilling to break the contact even though another part of him screamed for him to stop. She wouldn't let him back away, and he had to admit he didn't struggle very hard.

When she finally pulled away his whole body was on fire. She still wore that strange enigmatic smile as her hands slid away from his neck and the back of his head.

"Look," he told her, having to fight to find his voice, "I've never cheated on Alicia. Well, once, but that was a long time ago.''

"Life is short," she whispered.

"Not according to you it ain't. Of course, that was just a gag. Nothing lives that long. Maybe stars and sequoias and stuff. But not people." The fire was beginning to fade. He wanted it to linger and to leave. It had been much more than a natural kiss, much more. The brief, complete merging of two disparate individuals, a physical excuse for contact on a much deeper level.

"What did you do to me?"

"I kissed you."

"No. You did something else, something more."

"Only a kiss. Anything else you felt lay within you all the time. All I did was help you to unlock yourself. I am a key. I knew it would be worth it.

"The beautiful, the handsome people who bestride your world in awe of their own genetic good fortune are often dull and passionless, while those who do not match the artificial cultural ideal, who may be heavy or short, thin or dark, too light or too tall or too something, may have all manner of wondrous feelings bottled up inside them. Often they refuse to acknowledge their own potential. They are unable to recognize their true selves."

He was shaking his head. "That couldn't have been my true self. Not good ol' Frank Percivil Sonderberg."

"Why do you deny yourself? Why do you think you've been so successful at what you've tried?" She was chiding him the way she would a child. "You have achieved great things. There is greatness in all accomplishment. It's not necessary to write great music or draw beautiful pictures, to discover new medicines or plumb ocean depths to achieve, to accomplish. You have overcome your own limitations and have excelled. Only the direction you've chosen is different. That does not reduce you in stature. Visibility and popularity are not signs of greatness as often as they are of simply being loud. They are more often the signature of vulgarity rather than achievement. It is what we do with ourselves that makes us great, not the value others place on those doings.

"You possess hidden resources, Frank. Most people do, but yours run deeper than most. I had to find out what kind of man you are."

"And did I pass the test, teacher?" Despite his flippancy he was intensely interested in her reply.

She hesitated, thinking. Then the most marvelous expression came over her face, as though her entire body was smiling. It lit up the night and spilled over into the great abyss.

"You'll do."

He swallowed, then stepped past her, suddenly wanting to be away from the edge of the world. When he stopped and turned, the void had disappeared. There was only the moonlight shafting down between the trees and the distant shadowy ramparts of the mountains. He wondered if the void would reappear if he retraced his steps.

"I don't know what I'll do for," he said apologetically, "but while a lot of me screams to do otherwise, I'm afraid I won't do for you. See, I love Alicia. She's not as pretty as some and she's not as bright as some and she's probably not several other things as much as some, but then neither am I. So we make a pretty good match. We're comfortable with each other.

"You talked about merging. Maybe it's not the same kind of merging we just did, but Alicia and I merge on a lot of other levels. Pretty tight. So I'm sorry. If it's comfort you're looking for, why don't you try Burnfingers Begay? I'm sure he'd be happy to oblige."

She shook her head slowly. "I could never make love to a crazy man."

"You believe he's nuts?"

"He admits to it. Who am I to argue with him? Burnfingers Begay is a wondrous person I have yet to figure out. He is too much of a mystery for me to be intimate with. I prefer my love predictable."

She came toward him and he nearly panicked and ran. Because he knew that in spite of everything he'd said, if she kissed him like that a second time he wouldn't be able to resist, wouldn't want to resist.

"Burnfingers's spirit is pure and unencumbered by guilt. It's amazing to encounter someone like that in your corrupted world. I think maybe he's a yeibichai."

"A what?" They were making their way back through the trees, following the cheerful creek toward the motel.

"A Navajo spirit. What kind, I don't know."

"Come on. I mean, I know I just stepped over the edge of the world, but a spirit? Begay's about the solidest looking spirit I ever saw."

"You may be right. Perhaps he is only a man. A smart crazy man can fool people into thinking peculiar things. I am perceptive, but not perfect." She put her hand back on his arm, circling it through the crook of his elbow. "You cannot fly home to your Los Angeles, Frank."

"Don't tell me stuff like that. Please. I've just about reached my limit."

"Your limit is greater than you know. I'm sure of that now. I can only tell you no matter how painful you may find the hearing of it that if you try to leave me now you'll never see your home, your reality, again. You've come too far. Now I am your only link to that reality. You cannot abandon me any more than I can go on without you. I cannot prevent you from so doing, however."

"Yeah, yeah." He sighed heavily. "I guess I'm stuck with you. Got no choice, right? It's like Russian roulette. I can go ahead and pull the trigger, but if I guess wrong I don't get a second try."

"I'm afraid so. If you leave me and try to drive or fly home you might just make it. Or you might slip onto another thread of reality. Then I would never be able to find you again. You and your lovely Alicia would be lost forever."

"From here on it's all or nothing, is that it?"

She nodded. "You've crossed too many boundaries, jumped too many lines. There's no going back now until we reach the Vanishing Point."

"Which is somewhere between here and Wyoming, right?"

"As you would define it, yes. You're going to have to take me all the way."

"Just so long as you don't expect me to *go* all the way."

She smiled up at him. "You see? Only a truly brave man would be able to joke about something so serious."

"Yeah. Or else I'm crazier than Burnfingers Begay. Knowing you're in deep shit doesn't make you brave. Just realistic."

"I know it pleases you to demean yourself because you think of yourself as unattractive and not as intelligent as some. You do yourself repeated injustices, Frank." She took both of his hands in hers and squeezed tightly. "You must take me all the way to the Vanishing Point."

"What about my wife and kids? They ain't 'truly brave,' or whatever it is you're convinced I am."

"For that, I sorrow. I wish it were otherwise because of the great danger. I know how concern for their welfare preys upon your thoughts. Sadly, we have come this far together and so must continue to the end together. Console yourself in the knowledge that when the Spinner is soothed, reality will stabilize and you will be returned to a world no longer in danger of coming apart around you."

"Good thing I'm not paranoid or I wouldn't be able to handle any of this." She freed his hands. They burned from the contact, as his lips still burned. "When we get to this Spinner I'm gonna have some choice words for it. What business does it have screwing up reality anyway?"

"It is not a purposeful thing. Not even the Spinner is immune to illness and unhappiness."

"I hope we hit it off well. What's it like anyway? I know quite a bit about spinning. My stores only stock top-quality stuff. Jogging suits, sweat socks, uniforms, like that. Is the fabric of reality natural like cotton, or artificial like polyester?"

That made her laugh softly, as it was intended she should. It faded rapidly. When she spoke again it was in deadly earnest.

"The Anarchis will stop at nothing to prevent me from soothing the Spinner and realigning the fabric of existence. By now all the evil on every reality line will be watching and waiting, hoping to be the one that interrupts our journey. Evil thrives where Chaos reigns, remember, and nothing could do more to stimulate its expansion than the unraveling of order. Goodness requires the presence of stability, logic, and reason to do its work."

Frank considered thoughtfully. "You think maybe our little detours have been less than accidental?"

"It's difficult to say. My being marooned in the desert for so long before you stopped to pick me up was an unlikely happenstance, as was your subsequent shunting to Hell. As for our detour to Pass Regulus, only Burnfingers Begay's driving helped us escape from there."

Frank stepped around a tree. He ought to be exhausted, but there was no dozing in Mouse's presence. Not when she was keyed up like this. She exuded enough energy and sense of purpose to keep an army awake.

We're all the army she's got, he told himself. Myself, Alicia, and the kids, and one crazy Comajo. Or maybe Burnfingers would prefer Navamanche.

"I know this isn't a dream. I know it's all happening for real. But every now and then I find myself wondering if it's some kind of elaborate hallucination, if you're a terrorist or foreign agent or something."

"Think of me as a foreign agent if it makes it easier for you. Think of the Anarchis as a terrorist. The analogy is not so very extreme. All terrorists are agents of Chaos to some degree. All affect the fabric of existence. All alter reality or attempt to do so. It is the degree to which they achieve their aims that matters."

"You said the aim of the Anarchis is Chaos. What's the aim of Evil besides encouraging the spread of Chaos?"

"Extermination of the good. I'm sorry you've been put in this position, Frank, but I can't change that. More than just your reality is at stake here. Mine is endangered, as well. The fabric of existence weaves through all worlds. A single substantial rip anywhere"—she drew her hands apart sharply, as if ripping a sheet of paper in half—"can shock many worlds, many lines. The Anarchis will move quickly to exploit the smallest tear."

"Once reality gets ripped, how can you fix it?"

"I cannot. Only the Spinner can do that."

"What's this Spinner like, anyway? Is it like you?"

"Oh, no." She laughed gently, bells in the night. "It is difficult to describe. Whatever you imagine will be insufficient. Grand it is, and vast."

"Must be pretty damn overpowering."

"You will see for yourself when we reach the Vanishing Point."

"You know, I think I'm starting to get a handle on this. It's kind of like how a foul-up at a critical point affects a whole company. The ripple effect."

"You would be surprised how few differences there are, Frank, between existential philosophy and commerce."

"No kiddin'? I'm afraid my readings in philosophy don't go any further than Andrew Carnegie and Lee Iacocca's autobiography."

"That may be, but you have an instinctive grasp of how

things connect in order to work together. That is philosophical knowledge at its most practical. Reality is not so very different.''

"That so? You won't mind if I throw out the philosophy and just look at this as a question of getting from point A to point B without getting killed?''

"Think of it however it pleases you.''

"Hey, I may be crude, but I have shallow depths nobody's plumbed yet.''

"There you go, demeaning yourself again.''

"Yeah. But only among friends.''

W HEN PEOPLE HAVE BEEN married for a long time they develop the ability to sense their partner's presence or absence, even in the midst of deep sleep. Few scientists will admit to the existence of this marital telepathy—unless they themselves are married.

Alicia awoke and rolled over, squinting sleepily in the dark. "Frank?" She rose halfway, supporting herself on one arm. "Frank, you in the john?" She kept her voice down even though the children were in the other room behind a closed door.

No reply came from the bathroom, nor the chairs nor anywhere else. Enough light seeped around the edges of the curtain for her to make out the dim silhouettes of bed and cheap motel furniture.

It wouldn't be the first time. Frank was fond of nocturnal walks when he couldn't sleep. Certainly he had more on his mind than the future of their vacation.

With a sigh she slipped into her robe and went to the front door. The parking lot was mostly empty, dominated by the silent shape of the motor home. Moonlight enabled her to see clear across the street, to shuttered gift shops and real estate offices. The motel office was dark.

No familiar figure bestrode the concrete walkway in front of the rooms. If he wanted a soda he would've gone out to the motor home, she reflected. She retreated long enough to slip into a pair of sneakers, knotted the belt of her robe, and started across the lot.

The door to the motor home stood ajar, a figure seated on the lowest step. "Frank?" A face turned up to her and at the same time she saw that the shape was of a man much bigger than her husband.

"*Yatahey*, Mrs. Sonderberg. Or perhaps I should say good morning. The sun will rejoin us soon."

"Hello, Burnfingers. Have you seen Frank?"

"He's not with you?" Burnfingers tried to see past her.

She shook her head. "I thought he came out to talk or get something to drink." She looked back toward the motel, trying to remember where the vending machines were located. Even now he might be back in the room, wondering at the empty bed. Well, if he came looking for her this would be the first place he'd check. No point in worrying about it.

"You can't sleep, either?"

She could just make out Burnfingers's grin in the moonlight. "I never sleep. Waste of time."

"Oh, now really. Everybody sleeps."

"Not me. You know, if you spend eight hours out of every twenty-four asleep and you live to be eighty years old, you have wasted one third of your entire life."

"Well, *I* have to sleep." She wondered why she sounded so defensive. Burnfingers's claim was patently absurd, but of course he was crazy. It shouldn't have surprised her. Nothing he said ought to surprise her.

"Sleepy or not, what are you doing out here alone?"

"Talking to the moon. Watching the sky. Standing guard."

"Guard?" She turned sharply. "Is there something out here?"

"No. But if I wasn't standing guard, there might be."

"Like what?"

He turned to her. "After all you have seen these past couple of days, I would not think you would have to ask such a question, Mrs. Sonderberg."

"Just Alicia, please. It all has been real, hasn't it?" One hand clutched at the neck of the bathrobe, pulling it tight around her throat.

"Oh, very real. And instructive."

"Instructive?" She laughed nervously. "Didn't it scare you?

Weren't you frightened? But, then, maybe it wouldn't scare you. Not after working as a janitor in Hell.''

"Many things frighten me, Alicia."

She walked over to lean against the cool exterior of the motor home. "I bet you've seen a lot of strange things."

"More than you can imagine. I have worked with goblins as well as with demons, have danced with witches who were pure energy, have attended the Old Ceremonies. I have seen the sleeping places of the Great Old Ones and read the forbidden books. I've traded ice for gold with people who had no water and sat at the feet of all the prophets, trying to learn from them. Jesus and Buddha, Moses and Mohammed, Zoroaster and Confucius: all of them."

"Have you?" was all she could say.

"They like to get together and argue. Sometimes they get excited, but they never fight. That would be unbecoming to prophets."

Burnfingers's talk was starting to make her uneasy. Where the hell was Frank? To change the subject she pointed at his right wrist. "That's such a beautiful bracelet."

"So you've said." He raised his arm so it would catch more of the light. A huge turquoise nugget was set deep in a thick band of sand-cast metal. "Skystone and silver." With a finger he traced the recess in which the turquoise reposed. "This is called a shadowbox. The Navajo like to wear their wealth. I have more jewelry, but it can be awkward to travel with. This piece I wear because my father made it. He was very skilled. I keep it with me always."

"Kind of like a talisman?"

"No. To remind me of him. Sadly, he was quite sane. Not like me. That's what finished him. It is very difficult for an Indian to stay sane and live in your world, where insanity seems to be the normal state of affairs. Since I am mad, I have no difficulty coping."

"You've had a hard life, then." She'd moved nearer and was suddenly aware of his size and strength.

"I would say, rather, an interesting one. Many troubles I could have avoided, but to me boredom is the same as death. I would not have had it any other way."

His black hair was inches from her hands and she found

herself wondering what it would be like to stroke it, to run her fingers through it.

Abruptly she drew back. What was wrong with her? Here she was out alone in the middle of the night finding herself attracted to a madman. And he *was* attractive, dammit! The madness, the wildness she sensed in him, was part of it.

"I've got to go look for Frank," she found herself muttering. "I guess he's gone for a walk somewhere."

Burnfingers knew that Mouse had also gone for a nocturnal stroll, but since he was not completely crazy he sensed that mentioning this would have had a deleterious effect on Alicia Sonderberg's state of mind. So he kept quiet.

"Want me to come with you?"

"No. No, you stay here. I'm sure I'll run into him any minute now. I'll just go back to the room and wait." She left him sitting on the lower step.

As she turned the stern of the motor home she found herself confronting another male figure. "Frank! You startled me. Where have you b—?"

It wasn't Frank. It was over six feet tall and thin as a rail, and though it was obviously straining to look like a man it was having a difficult time of it, as though trying something without sufficient practice beforehand. Multiple fingers kept appearing and vanishing on each hand, like the tentacles of sea anemones retracting and extending in the current. The left side of the face kept trying to melt.

"Good evening," it said, the quavering voice a horrible parody of humanity. "Can I help you find your husbaaaand?"

Alicia took a step backward. As she did so a second figure appeared next to the first. It was much shorter and had stringy white hair that curled and contorted like a handful of worms.

"Is there a problem?" it inquired. It struggled to make itself taller.

She couldn't find her voice.

"It's all right." The first figure lurched unsteadily toward her. Instead of walking it seemed to shudder from side to side like a shorter creature toddling on stilts. Long, thin arms reached for her, the fingers rippling bonelessly. "We can take you to him."

Other shapes were materializing behind the first two. Alicia suddenly realized they were grotesque, distorted parodies of the motel manager and his wife. Only then was she finally able to scream.

"Burnfingers!"

The stringy fingers were grasping at her, pulling at her arms and robe, tugging her close. "No!" She tried to push them off, keep them away. "Go away, whatever you are, go away and leave me alone!"

Then Burnfingers was there, appearing like a wraith in their midst. He picked up the smaller of the first two things and threw it twenty feet into the night. Its companion growled and wrapped its arms around Alicia while two others jumped the intruder. Burnfingers ripped the first in half, cleanly, since there was no blood. The other climbed up his back, trying to get at his neck. The Indian leaped into the air, twisted, and landed on his back, crushing his assailant between his bulk and the pavement.

"Get inside!" he yelled at Alicia. "Get inside and lock the door!"

She fought against the monstrosity that held her tight, flailing at the thin body and trying to ignore the awful putrid smell that arose from it, the kind of smell she'd once encountered when she'd left some unwrapped chicken in the pantry for a week. The smell of death and rotten things.

Burnfingers was coming for her when a new shape silently emerged from the darkness behind him. The man-thing held a section of steel pipe in one hand. It made a sickening dull sound as it contacted the back of Burnfingers Begay's skull. The Indian staggered and turned, only to catch the pipe across his forehead. His eyes rolled up and he toppled forward.

"No, no!" Alicia kept screaming despite the attempts of the creature holding her to muffle her voice with one jerky hand. The fingers stank of decay.

Burnfingers lay unmoving on the pavement, blood forming an expanding pool around his head. Fighting down her nausea, Alicia tried to bite the hand that was gagging her. Her teeth went halfway through the rubbery flesh. The thing turned to other motionless shapes hovering nearby and croaked a command, ignoring the wound.

"Get—the—others."

Alicia redoubled her efforts, to no avail. Her teeth were stuck in the hand that muffled her screams. Despite the fact that she outweighed her captor, she couldn't break free. It was like being entangled in a spool of runaway bailing wire.

Frank halted, staring in the direction of the motel. "Did you hear that? It sounded like Alicia."

"I did hear it, yes, and I think it was your wife. Her voice was full of fear."

"Christ." He started running, somehow avoiding the trees that loomed up to block his path, trying to pace himself and not wanting to. Mouse kept up with him, her dress billowing around her slim form like a tormented cloud.

The motel was still there. It hadn't fallen off the edge of the world. They hurried around the side and up the path where not so very long ago he'd gone searching for a song. Once he slipped, felt something complain in his left knee, but regained his footing. By the time they reached the double room he was breathing hard.

The door stood ajar. He flipped the light switch, blinking back the artificial brightness. "Alicia? Damn! Alicia!" She wasn't in the bathroom, nor in the next room with the children. Wendy and Steven were also gone. There was no sign of a struggle.

"Burnfingers. I never should've trusted him. He *said* he was crazy. I should've taken him at his word and dumped him back on the highway."

"I am not sure it was..." But Frank was racing past her, pounding toward the motor home.

A light appeared in the motel office as a door opened. The manager stood silhouetted by the glow from within, squinting into the night. "Hey! What's going on out there? What's all that yelling about?"

"Call the police!" Frank shouted at him, not caring what line of reality they were on.

"Police? What d'ya want with the police?"

He was around the back of the motor home then, nearly tripping over a large shape lying on the pavement. His thoughts, which had been settling into a nice, comfortable, vengeful mode, were abruptly busted to hell and gone all over again when he saw what lay at his feet. He stood there, staring. Mouse joined him a moment later.

"Jesus." Considering the amount of blood, he was lucky he hadn't slipped. Bending over, he lifted one big arm, let it drop limply back to the ground. With Mouse helping him they were able to roll Begay over onto his back. -

"I think he's dead."

Mouse put an ear to Burnfingers's chest, then wet two fingers and passed them across his lips. "Dead he is."

"But if not him, then who . . . ?"

She rose. "Servants of the Anarchis. The forces of Evil. Had we been here they would have taken us, as well."

"I don't give a shit about that. If I'd been here maybe they wouldn't have taken anybody."

"You are a truly brave man, Frank, but you are not a fighter. If Burnfingers Begay could not prevail against them—do not berate yourself."

The elderly figure of the motel manager joined them. He was puffing hard, his robe hanging loose across his bony shoulders. "Holy Bejesus! What happened here? That guy looks dead."

Frank started to reply, until Mouse's stare induced him to swallow his words. "Could be."

"I'm going for the cops."

"Yeah, you do that." He waited until the old man was out of earshot, looked across at Mouse. "I'm going after them."

"It may be just what they want."

"You don't have to go."

She shook her head. "We are bound together in the rest of this, Frank. Wherever we go, we must go together."

"Then I guess you're coming with me, 'cause I ain't goin' anywhere without my wife and kids."

She sighed. "I know that. I will accompany you."

"Lucky me." He started across the pavement. "I'm gonna throw on some clothes, get my wallet and keys. Keep an eye on the bus until I get back."

"Hurry, Frank Sonderberg."

"Don't worry." He broke into a jog.

She followed him with her eyes until he vanished into the motel room. Then her gaze dropped to the motionless form at her feet. Poor, crazed Burnfingers Begay. Was he really as mad as he'd claimed? Or was he normal and the rest of the universe slightly unbalanced? She'd met Wanderers before, but never one who'd ranged quite so far or contentedly as he. That huge body had been home to an equally massive spirit. Had it fled, or did it linger still? Burnfingers was a stubborn man.

She knelt and leaned forward until her lips were only a few inches from Burnfingers's ear, and began to sing in a tremulous whisper. Across the street, the Doberman patrolling the back lot of a hardware store began to howl. He was not an animal easily spooked, but now he railed at the moon until his throat threatened to crack.

His cry was picked up by every dog in town, from poodles to stray mutts to the coyotes fighting over garbage they'd dragged up to their ravines, a mournful canine chorus accompanying the extraordinary sweet sound Mouse poured into a dead man's head. Its rhythm was subtle and serene, familiar yet unique.

A moment passed; two. The rhythm was echoed by the sudden movement of Burnfingers Begay's chest, then by a twitching of one hand, and at last by the opening of both eyes as he slowly sat erect. Letting out a long wheeze, he put both hands to his temples and rubbed hard. She sat down on the bottom step of the motor home and regarded him silently, the wind playing with the silken edges of her dress.

"Thank you."

"It was not all me," she explained. "There had to be something left to hear me. It works but rarely. You claim to have no soul. You are lying."

He sounded embarrassed. "I didn't say I never had one. I just said I didn't have one at the time. It floats around, like excess baggage." He struggled to his feet, feeling the back of his head. "A mule kicked me. What were they?" He described his attackers as best he could.

"Some local evil, or perhaps from a nearby reality line. They tried to fool you by imitating humanity, at which Evil is always poor. They came looking for a way to divert me from my course. It was only luck that enabled me to escape, but they may have achieved their purpose anyway. They took Frank Sonderberg's wife and children, didn't they?"

Burnfingers glanced reflexively at the motel, nodded.

"I feared so. When he returns we will try to find them. He will not go on without them. I did not think he would."

She didn't ask if he was coming with them. She was correct

in her assumptions, of course, but he would have appreciated the request nonetheless.

"I did not know Evil could be subtle, but I ought to. Native Americans know more about subtle evils than most people—though whatever put me on the ground was anything but subtle."

Frank rejoined them, slowing precipitously when he saw Burnfingers Begay standing in the moonlight caressing his neck. Frank's shirt hung over his belt, the buttons were unfastened, and he'd forgotten to zip his fly. He glanced quickly at Mouse, then back at Burnfingers.

"I thought you were dead."

"Was," said the Indian ruefully. "Colder than Spider Rock. Do not look so shocked, Frank friend. I have been dead before. It is different each time and always an educational experience, though on the whole I would have to say I prefer the alternative. Strange how darkness can be enlightening."

"But how, who...?" His gaze drifted back to Mouse. Burnfingers nodded solemnly.

"The little lady has some prickly tunes in her harmonic arsenal. I have been sung to sleep before, but never awake. I should not be so surprised. She is a special Mouse."

Frank hesitated the briefest of instants before pushing past him. "I'm going after my family. Who's coming with me?"

"I must," said Mouse, "but I would help anyway."

Frank paused in the doorway to look back at Burnfingers. "You?"

"Of course I am coming, Frank. What can they do but kill me again?"

"Yeah. Only maybe this time they'll cut off your ears so you won't be able to hear her songs." He headed for the driver's seat, Mouse's response ringing in his head.

"You don't need your ears to hear my songs, Frank. You don't need even a tympanum." She sat down next to him. Burnfingers settled himself between the front seats.

It should be Alicia sitting there, Frank told himself. Gentle, understanding Alicia, who was now being dragged God knew where by the hands of unmentionable things.

Mouse brought him out of his sorrowful lethargy, her hand on his arm, the contact as electrifying as before. "Drive, Frank

Sonderberg, and no matter where they have been taken, we will track your family."

"Sure you know what you are getting into?" Burnfingers asked him.

"No." He turned the key in the ignition, heard the engine respond. "I don't." He nodded out into the not-quite-Utah night. "But that's my wife and kids out there. Money, security, success—nothing means much without 'em. You wouldn't understand. You aren't married; you don't have kids."

"It is true I am not married, but I do have children. My sense of family is as strong as yours. Now shut up and drive."

"Yeah. Right!" Frank almost wrenched the gear lever loose as he put the motor home in drive.

He pulled out into the main drag, turned toward the interstate. As he did so, a blue and white police cruiser pulled into the parking lot behind them. Frank followed its progress in the rearview mirror.

"Just drive," Mouse instructed him, sensing his uncertainty.

"What if they could help?" His foot let up on the accelerator. The motor home slowed. "This reality line is almost identical to ours."

"Where we are going they cannot follow, and if they did they would not long survive."

"They would not follow, Frank," said Burnfingers, "but they will ask questions you do not want to have to try to answer. They will delay you with reports. They will kill your hopes with bureaucratese. Do not stop for them."

Frank considered the advice of his friends. Resolutely, he turned his gaze away from the rearview and back to the road ahead.

The officers who entered the motel lot didn't quite know what to expect, but when they saw the pool of blood where Burnfingers Begay had lain, their early morning lethargy was swept aside by professional concern. The motel owner was standing nearby, staring up the road.

"You the guy who called?"

"Yes." The old man didn't turn to look at the policeman. He was muttering to himself. "That fella was *dead*. I'm sure of it."

The corporal pushed his cap back on his head. "What man? Who was dead?"

"There was a man lying here and he was dead. His friends said he was dead. Then he got up and walked away."

Suddenly leery of what he'd walked in to at four in the morning, the cop walked around to where he could see the speaker's face. "Then I guess he wasn't dead after all, was he?"

"No," said the manager slowly, "I guess he wasn't." He looked down at his feet. "But there's the blood."

"Somebody's blood." The corporal turned to his partner. "Guess we better check it out. Where are these people?"

"Gone."

"Gone? Whattaya mean, 'gone'?"

"They left. With the dead man who wasn't dead. In their motor home."

The other officer spoke up. "Must be that big rig that was leaving as we were coming in."

"Yes. Yes, that's the one."

The corporal turned back to his car in disgust. "Let's go, Jake. Maybe the people in the motor home will make some sense."

They pulled out into the road, burning rubber as they drove off in pursuit of the vehicle they'd passed on arrival. The motel owner was left alone in his quiet parking lot. After a while he looked back down at the rapidly drying pool of blood. Then he went to get a hose to wash it away.

Frank saw the rotating red lights swing into sight in the rearview mirror. "Cops. What do I do now?"

"Keep driving," said Burnfingers.

"Keep driving," said Mouse. "We cannot waste time here, certainly not to answer questions."

"That's what I thought." He put his foot to the gas. "We won't lose 'em on the interstate. They'll catch up and pull us over."

"It depends which on ramp we take," Burnfingers told him.

"We must go the way your family has gone, and they have been taken to a different line. I sense it." Mouse had turned to observe the progress of the pursuing police cruiser. They weren't going all out. Not yet.

Beneath the hood the big engine rumbled. "They're catching up already."

"Relax, Frank." Burnfingers smiled confidently. "We will lose them."

Frank nodded ahead. "There's the on ramp. What do I do?"

"Ignore it. Keep going straight, through the underpass."

Frank sounded uncertain. "That's just a country road." Burnfingers's smile widened and that was enough to start Frank's heart a-pounding. He clung to the wheel for support.

The motor home shot beneath the freeway at sixty miles per hour. Now the police cruiser had its siren going as its occupants realized their quarry had no intention of pulling over voluntarily.

"Junction coming up," said Burnfingers. Frank stared into the night.

"What junction? I can't see a damn thing!"

He spoke too soon. It materialized out of the darkness, an unmarked fork in the road less than half a mile ahead.

"Left," Mouse yelled, "and don't slow down!"

"Okay, okay!" Looking in the sideview mirror he could see one of the cops in the pursuit car leaning out and waving wildly, his gestures unmistakable. He wanted them to pull over and stop. What, he wondered, if they started shooting? He was no stunt driver and the motor home no sprint car.

That's when he saw the fence, the barrier that blocked the road. A pair of yellow warning lights flashed like cat's eyes in the motor home's high beams. No wonder the police were frantically driving to stop him.

There was a roaring in his ears, like heavy surf banging a rocky shore. He hung on to the wheel, paralyzed. Mouse yelled at him again and it struck him that this was the first time he'd ever heard her raise her voice in anything other than song.

"Keep going, Frank! Don't stop now!"

Behind him the police cruiser swerved and twisted across the road, honking furiously, the two men inside doing everything possible to draw the attention of the motor home's occupants as they wondered why it refused to pull over.

Frank flinched but didn't cover his eyes. The motor home smashed through the flimsy highway barrier, sending splinters and warning lights and planks flying in all directions. They vanished like feathers in the night. The pavement vanished, too, and they found themselves screaming down a dirt road. At the speed they were traveling, the motor home's suspension was no match for rain ruts and potholes. Dishes flew out of cabinets to cartwheel wildly across the floor. Plastic glasses bounced and tumbled like debris from a New Year's party. Burnfingers Begay hung on as best he could while Mouse sat stiffly in her seat, gripping the armrests with delicate fingers.

"Where are we going?" Frank shouted. He heard a loud crack. Something breaking loose underneath, or were their pursuers finally shooting at them? The night-shrouded terrain was rushing by in a wash of headbeam light.

"I'm not sure," Mouse told him, "but wherever it is, we have to get there."

Another barrier appeared ahead, blocking the road. This one was smaller and had red warning lights flashing atop it instead of yellow. Beyond, the mountains and dusty landscape disappeared.

"Keep going," said Burnfingers calmly.

Frank stared at the barrier, his foot easing off the accelerator. "Keep going where? There's no more road."

Mouse leaned toward him, violet orbs flashing. "This is the way your family's kidnappers have come. Do you want to find them or not? If we hesitate here we may lose them forever."

His thoughts fought one another like a couple of tomcats in heat as the motor home continued to lose momentum. Behind him the wail of the siren lessened. Apparently the police were convinced he was finally going to pull over. After all, he had no other choice, did he? Frank turned to face her.

"How can I trust you anymore, after what you've dragged us in to?"

She stared steadily back at him and her voice dropped to its usual breathy whisper. "How can you not trust me?"

Frustrated, he turned to the motor home's only other occupant. "Burnfingers?"

The Indian shrugged. "The on ramps and off ramps we have to take on this journey don't always come clearly marked, Frank. This looks promising to me."

"And if it's the wrong way?"

"This world or another, what's the difference?"

Frank considered. "I guess the difference is that Alicia and the kids aren't in this one anymore."

He jammed the accelerator to the floor. The motor home roared forward, straight toward the barrier. This time he was positive he heard warning shots. As they struck the wood he closed his eyes.

The ground ended as cleanly as if it had been cut away with an ax. Far below the cliff he could see trees, a small lake, the lights of another town. A great calmness came over him as the motor home lost velocity and started to tilt down. Behind him Burnfingers Begay yelled a war cry—or maybe it was a prayer.

The police cruiser slowed, stopping well behind the ruined barrier that marked the end of the road. Its siren faded to silence, a dying beast encapsulated in a steel box. The red lights still pulsated atop the roof as the two policemen emerged to walk cautiously to the edge of the cliff. It wasn't a very high cliff: maybe a hundred fifty feet above the plain below. But there still should have been a smoking, twisted chunk of wreckage at its foot. They looked hard and saw nothing but a few pine trees, scrub brush, and bare rock.

A board that had been knocked loose from the road barrier finally fell from its persistent nail, making the older officer jump at the unexpected noise.

"Get the spot," he growled to his partner.

"But there's—"

"Just get it."

The younger officer ran back to the car, returned with a six-inch-wide spotlight attached to a long cord. Flipping it on, he played the powerful beam over the rocks far below. It wasn't really necessary. There was more than enough moonlight to see clearly by. Eventually he turned it off.

"Nothing down there. Nothing."

"That's right. Nothing."

"So where'd they go?"

The corporal raised his gaze from the base of the cliff. "I don't know where they went, but we're not going to ask anybody else, are we?"

"What about the report that old guy at the motel called in, about a dead man?"

"Can't have a dead man without a body." He glanced unwillingly back over the cliff. "Can't have anyone without bodies. Maybe they'll turn up somewhere else."

"Like where?"

"Find out where that thirty-foot motor home went and you'll have your answer. Me, I'm going to try real hard not to lose any sleep over it." He pushed past the younger officer, who favored the cliff with a last uncertain look before hurrying to join the corporal in the car.

He slid in, shut the door. "It wasn't a hallucination or something, was it?"

"I don't know what it was. If it was an illusion, then the motel manager saw it, too. If we try real hard, maybe we can convince ourselves that's what it was."   ·

The corporal turned the car around, headed back toward town. When they reached the place where the pavement started up again, the younger officer looked to his right. Pieces of wood and glass littered the side of the road.

"Illusions don't smash highway department barriers."

The corporal kept his gaze resolutely forward. "Shut up," he said.

THE MOTOR HOME BOUNCED once, hard, but the axles held. The jolt opened Frank's eyes wide. No cliff, no dirt road, no angry, anxious police car fading into the distance behind them. They were back on the interstate once more, cruising steadily northward.

Good thing he did open his eyes, because the pothole in the middle of the pavement that suddenly loomed in the headlights was big enough to swallow a Mercedes. Tires screeched in protest as he swerved around the crater. Then they were back on concrete.

He had no choice but to slow down, the road was in such bad shape. The crater had cousins, some so large there was barely enough room to squeeze past. What remained of the pavement was cracked and eroded.

Not potholes, he thought as they avoided another. Impact craters, the kind explosives would make. Though he let their speed fall to forty, the ride was still bumpy enough to jar the fillings out of your teeth.

"I've heard of infrequent maintenance, but this is ridiculous." The landscape looked normal in the moonlight. High mountains off to the right, trees and bushes scattered behind the shoulder, and off to the left, in the distance, a vast sheet of water gleaming like aluminum foil. The Great Salt Lake.

Some shortcut we took, he told himself. "Where are we now?"

"On the right road to the Vanishing Point." Mouse had relaxed back in her chair.

"I don't give a shit about the Vanishing Point."

"Gentle, Frank, gentle." She smiled at him. "This is the way your family came, too."

Burnfingers was staring out the windshield. "I do not like this. It feels all wrong, and I am not talking about the condition of the road. Do you want me to drive for a while, Frank?"

"No, thanks. I'll be okay."

They passed one road sign, but it was broken, knocked off its supporting posts as if by a high wind. Frank tried but couldn't make out what it said.

If anything, the road became worse as they neared the city's outskirts. They saw no other vehicles, a fact which might've been acceptable outside a town like Cedar City but which was full of ominous portents for a metropolis the size of Salt Lake.

"Ought to be some traffic." Frank scanned the road ahead. "Couple of trucks at least." He glanced to his right. "We're on another reality line, right? Burnfingers's 'on ramp' didn't just put us back on the same highway." Mouse just nodded. "Well, I don't think I like this one as much as the last, even if the people hereabouts lie like normal."

"It is not as bad as Hell."

"That a fact? We don't know that yet." He looked back over his shoulder. "Where's the chief?"

"In the back."

Burnfingers rejoined them moments later, having altered his appearance. He'd exchanged his flannel shirt for one of black cotton and his red headband for another of equally dark material. White and red lines decorated his face.

"War paint," he told Frank. "I had to improvise. I hope your woman will not mind my making use of her makeup kit. It was all I could find to work with."

Frank nodded his approval. "Seems appropriate under the circumstances."

"Mary Kay and Revlon." Burnfingers tried but was unable to repress a grin. "Not very traditional, but it will have to do."

"Getting ready for war?" Mouse inquired.

"I am always at war with something, little singer. This is serious business." Frank saw that Burnfingers had strapped on a holster that contained an enormous stainless-steel handgun. He was leaning on Steven's baseball bat. Burnfingers noticed his stare. "Somebody whacked me pretty good. I want to be ready to whack him back. Newton's Law. 'For every action there is an equal and opposite reaction.' Pretty smart dude, for a white man."

Mouse pointed out an intact sign.

SALT LAKE CITY—20 Miles

Frank was flipping through his maps as he dodged potholes. "What happened to Provo? We should be in Provo right now."

There was no sign of the college town. The highway curved around the sloping mass of a vast hill. Only when the sun finally put in a reluctant appearance over the mountains did they see that the ground had been turned to slag, as if the whole mountain had been melted and then crystallized out anew. Transparent lava covered the ground to east and north. There wasn't a tree or building to be seen.

"Glass," Burnfingers murmured. "Something has turned this whole section of country to glass."

An endless expanse of waveless water stretched from the edge of the highway to the western horizon. At least the Great Salt Lake hadn't changed. Or had it? Burnfingers frowned at the lake.

"I do not remember it being this big when I was here before. The lake has been rising for years, but not so fast as this. I wonder if the city is still here?"

"We saw the road sign," Mouse pointed out. "The kidnappers had to have a destination."

The interstate climbed a slight rise, arcing over the base of the glass mountain. Ahead lay what once was Salt Lake City.

"Oh my God." Frank pulled over and stared.

The rising sun illuminated a panorama of destruction and devastation seen only in disaster movies and the minds of distraught writers. Instead of a pale bluish-white, the Great Salt Lake was tinted an angry yellow-orange. High concentrations of salt could not account for the sulphurous stain that marred the quiet waters. It might have been a lake on Io.

The city itself lay in ruins. Jagged stumps of tall buildings protruded like broken teeth from what had once been the center of town. A caved-in square marked the location of the great Mormon temple. Not a single structure remained intact. There were only echoes, shadows of what had once been thriving suburbs and commercial districts. Nothing moved on the roads leading in and out of the city. Whole blocks had been flattened, the ground scoured to the foundations as if by a giant abrasive. In places the earth itself had been ripped away in long gouges.

Where it entered the city the interstate was broken and shattered. He took the first crumbling off ramp. As they descended, the concrete broke from beneath the rear right tires, but their momentum carried them safely the rest of the way to the surface of a city street.

It reminded Frank of the pictures he'd seen of Germany at the end of World War II. Only fragments of buildings still stood. The walls had been torn off apartment buildings, leaving the rooms exposed like broken honeycomb. Floors sagged like tired tongues. There was no smoke, no fire. Whatever calamity had struck the city was not of recent origin.

It had to have been more than a fire. No conflagration would crack stone or pulverize concrete or twist steel beams like pipe cleaners.

"This reality line is ill," Mouse declared. "Very sick."

"I know what line this must be," said Burnfingers quietly. "This must be one where they dropped the Bomb. I suppose if you have an infinite number of reality lines, then every possible reality is borne out sooner or later."

"No," Mouse insisted. "The number of lines is finite. There are only as many as the Spinner can control. That doesn't mean I dispute your analysis of what has happened here."

"If that's the case, then there oughta be a big crater somewheres downtown." Frank didn't realize how low his voice had dropped. "Couldn't have been too big a bomb or there wouldn't be this much standing."

"Maybe an airburst, or several," Burnfingers suggested. "In that case there might not be any craters."

Mouse was grim. "This is a line where Evil has taken control, where its servants would be likely to flee. A place where the Anarchis is already all but in command."

They drove through a crumpled intersection. "I can't believe it," Frank muttered. "I can't believe people would be this stupid on any reality line."

"The mind is the mirror of the Cosmos." Mouse pointed at the sky. "Out there Chaos wars unceasingly with Order and Reason. The same battle is refought every day in the mind of each thinking person. Logic does not always win out. There are lines where stupidity triumphs."

"It really happened here." Frank swerved to avoid the beetle-like hulk of a burned-out automobile. "This isn't a fake front, like on a movie set." He turned sharply on her. "Hey, this isn't *my* reality, is it?"

"When threads break and cross, nothing is certain—but it doesn't feel like your line, Frank Sonderberg."

"Thank Christ for small favors." He turned back to his driving, following Burnfingers's impressions and Mouse's hunches, trying to stick to those streets where the paving was relatively intact.

They were traveling through the western part of the city. Not every building had been flattened. A few structures boasted flimsy new roofs. Most had not been touched, remained eviscerated hulks that gazed with vacant window-eyes at the empty streets.

"How can we be sure we're not driving off onto another reality line?"

"We can't," Mouse told him.

"You know, you ain't very reassuring sometimes."

"I'm sorry. It's not easy to predict how reality is going to behave under present circumstances."

"Something moving." Burnfingers pointed forward.

Tall, gangly figures were emerging from some of the ruins flanking the road. People, Frank thought. Or rather, things that might once have been people. A few still resembled human beings. Most were shambling, stumbling nightmares plucked from some demented biologist's fevered brain.

Some of the mutants scuttled about on all fours. Others had no legs and traveled on their turned-under knuckles, like amputee apes. The faces were worst of all because expression is the last refuge of humanity. They'd been gathered up and dumped in a genetic Mixmaster, beaten and pounded and jumbled together only to be poured out still alive. Many wore clothing, though they saw nothing that was not ragged or torn.

Neither attacking nor fleeing, they gathered to gape at the pristine, undamaged motor home. It must look like a figment from a dream to them, Frank knew. He wondered how long ago the cataclysm had taken place and how many, if any, of these poor creatures remembered it. Had they ever seen a functional piece of machinery, much less anything as elaborate as the motor home? Maybe in old books, if any had survived. If reading had survived.

He found himself slowing, not wanting to hit any of them. "What now?" There were dozens of the troglodytes packing tight around the Winnebago. The numbers made him nervous even though he saw nothing more threatening than an occasional club.

"Stop," Burnfingers ordered him.

"Here?"

"We must find out where your family has been taken. We cannot continue simply to follow our feelings. That means we should ask possible witnesses. What is wrong? Does their appearance make you nervous?"

"Damn straight, it does."

"It shouldn't." Burnfingers rose and moved to the side door. "I have spent nighttime at Piccadilly Circus in London. In the tube tunnels beneath the square dwell humans stranger than these."

Frank turned to Mouse. "Do as he says, Frank."

"Can't you still sense which way they've gone?"

"It is thin, very thin. Far better to have their presence here confirmed."

"Have it your way. But I'm staying inside."

He hit the brake. The instant the motor home halted, the crowd of pitiful humanoid shapes surged toward it.

Frank kept his foot on the brake and the transmission in gear, ready to burst forward at the first hint of trouble. He heard the door open, heard Burnfingers Begay talking and something cackle a reply. It didn't sound like English, or any other language Frank could recognize. That didn't slow Burnfingers, who kept chatting steadily with the crowd.

Those who hadn't gathered by the open door surrounded the motor home. A dozen or more stood in front, running their fingers silently over the hood and headlights, caressing and marveling. A few tears dribbled from damaged eyes.

There was nothing to be afraid of here, he decided. Only things that had once been men and women, creatures more deserving of pity than disgust. He wondered what had precipitated the dropping of the Big One on this reality line, prayed the people on his own line could avoid it. The Anarchis's influence, Mouse had hinted. For the first time he began to really understand what was at stake in all this.

Alicia and Steven and Wendy concerned him more than history. The sooner he got them back and away from this place, the better for their health and sanity. Already the children might have suffered serious psychological damage.

The door closed with a click and Burnfingers rejoined them.

"You were able to understand them?" Mouse asked him.

"All language is a variant of some other. You just have to learn to listen close and pick out the significant parts." He bent to point through the windshield. "Your woman and children were taken that way. They were not hard for these people to spot. Operative vehicles are as scarce here as clean drinking water. A mutant named Prake and his gang took them."

"The Anarchis has allies everywhere," Mouse murmured grimly.

"According to the locals this Prake is one pretty tough sumbitch. When I told them we had to go after him they tried to talk me out of it. Civilization may be dead here, but courtesy and humanity survive. There is hope yet for this line."

"Which way?" was all Frank said.

"Keep going north, then there's an avenue that angles northwest. Funny how certain things never die. Like street names. Like the Appian Way." He gestured a second time. "Three quarters of a mile that way, then we turn up Grand. Go all the way to the end of it."

"Got it." Frank moved his foot from brake to accelerator. The sorrowful crowd of mutant humanity parted to make way for him. They moaned and gesticulated, trying to dissuade their visitors from going. Our sheer normalcy must be a relief to them, he mused.

Maybe the locals wouldn't mess with this Prake, but he sure as hell intended to. "Did they actually see Alicia and the kids?"

Burnfingers nodded. "Around here an ordinary human being would attract more attention than this vehicle. They saw them, all right."

Grand Avenue was a mass of broken, twisted concrete. It took them most of the day to negotiate the tormented pavement. The sun was setting by the time they drew near the section of the city that was dominated by Prake and his followers.

They'd also been slowed by a brief but violent attack by a roving band of unfriendly mutants. During the assault the motor home sustained one cracked window. Saving his precious ammunition, Burnfingers had climbed onto the roof and used Steven's baseball bat to knock off the attackers one at a time.

When it was over and Burnfingers had rejoined them, Frank asked Mouse why she hadn't simply sung their assailants away.

"Not everyone or everything responds in the same way to my singing," she explained. "People, even altered people, are not rat-things or demons."

"Different approach for different folks." Burnfingers held a wet washcloth to a bruise over his left eye. The bloody bat lay near the side door. "Hey, don't look at me like that. You're not afraid of me, too, are you?"

"I fear anything I cannot understand," Mouse replied, "because there is so little I do not. You are one of those incomprehensible encounters, Burnfingers Begay. You confuse me, therefore I am wary."

"I confuse me, too." He leaned forward. "Whup! Better slow down, Frank."

"Why? What's the matter?"

"You'll see in a minute."

He did. The cityscape remained unchanged but not the road. Directly ahead, it was submerged beneath a film of scum-laden liquid. No isolated puddle, the water extended between the buildings as far to north and west as they could see, forming a cinnabar mirror that threw back the light of the setting sun.

"I was right," Burnfingers declared. "The lake has risen even more on this line than on ours. It has invaded the city. It may happen on our line, too, some day soon." He put his washcloth aside. "This is the old lake coming back to reclaim its territory. Lake Bonneville. After the last Ice Age it covered all of Utah, reached into Arizona, New Mexico, and Wyoming. Now it is growing again."

Frank strained. "Looks pretty shallow here."

"The whole lake is shallow. Our town friends told me that Prake has himself a makeshift fort out this way, on one of the few high pieces of ground. Used to be a city park, long ago. Now it is an island. That is where we will find your family."

Frank pressed his face to the window. "Water doesn't look more than a few inches deep here. Maybe we should try and drive all the way and run over a few of 'em."

"The depth may change, and there could be submerged potholes full of water. If this part of the city has been underwater for very long the pavement might have begun to disintegrate. If we get stuck we might never get unstuck. I do not want to be afoot in this land." Burnfingers looked to his right. "Lady singer, could you drive if you had to?"

Mouse regarded shift lever and pedals distastefully. "I don't like machines, but under the circumstances all of us have to do that which we do not enjoy."

"Damn right," said Frank sharply. "I've done plenty for you. Now it's your turn to help me, and if that means doing a little driving, you can damn well do it."

She nodded, her reply even. "I guess I damn well can." Both Burnfingers and Frank grinned. "But if I am to drive, what will you be doing?"

Frank's grin subsided. "Yeah. What will we be doing?"

"Having a swim, I think, if the water does not get *too* deep." Burnfingers gestured at the couch. "These mattresses should float long enough to take us where we want to go. You have a flashlight?"

"Should be several. The outfit that we rented from said this tank was completely stocked."

Burnfingers regarded the back of the motor home speculatively. "Let us see what else we can find that might prove useful."

A hundred yards from the motor home the water was barely knee-deep. The two men advanced silently, lying on their bellies on the makeshift raft. Burnfingers had wrapped the three mattresses they'd removed from the master bed in black plastic garbage bags. The plastic provided extra buoyancy while rendering the raft invisible against the dark water.

Frank kicked slowly and steadily, the way Burnfingers had instructed him, easing his feet gently into the water to minimize noise. Occasionally he would kick too hard or they'd coast above a shallow place and a foot would touch bottom.

Hugging the submerged foundations of those structures still

standing, they paddled their way toward the firelight that marked the location of Prake's island. Before long even this limited cover was denied them as they left the last of the buildings behind. Few remained standing by the old shoreline.

Though soaked to the skin, Frank found he wasn't uncomfortable. The water was almost too warm. Nor was it as salty as he'd anticipated. The mineral content of the inland sea had been heavily diluted by its expansion.

Secured to the raft between Burnfingers and himself was another plastic bag. It held a surprise his resourceful companion had prepared for Prake and his gang. Each man carried knives and a flashlight. In addition, Burnfingers had the holster of his pistol slung across his shoulders.

Frank nodded in its direction, whispered, "You think that pistol can stop these guys, if they're as big and bad as the locals say?"

Burnfingers indicated the gun. "This 'pistol,' my friend, is a four-fifty-four. It's loaded with two hundred and forty grain hollow-jacket bullets and packs about a ton of firing power. That's about twice what you'd get out of a forty-four magnum. It'll put a hole through quarter-inch steel plate at twenty-five yards."

Frank just nodded. "Then I guess it'll stop 'em." He tapped the plastic bag that rocked between them. It made a hollow, ringing sound. "If we get out of this, the rental company's not going to believe what we did with some of their stuff."

"Tell them to send me the bill." Burnfingers's attention was concentrated on the firelight ahead. They were close enough now to make out the outline of the island. "Look there, off to your left. And keep your voice down."

Frank complied. When he saw what Burnfingers had pointed to he had to choke down his instinctive reaction to cry out.

A large cage fashioned of scrap lumber and hammered metal strips squatted on the island's west end. Firelight showed clearly the three figures seated within. Alicia was cradling someone in her arms. Probably Steven, but it could have been Wendy. Frank half expected to hear the discordant sounds of his daughter's portable stereo, until he remembered that it had been traded away for room and board in a glitzy hotel on another reality line.

As for the remainder of the island, what they could see of it by firelight against the night was childish ruination, technology become slum. Salvaged sheet metal wrapped crudely around weathered two-by-fours. Plastic paneling made a flimsy barrier against the wind. Of stone there was none.

But the skeletal remains of the original playground equipment remained, bolted to subterranean foundations. A thin wisp of steel had been a curling slide. Lumpish iron spaghetti once served as a jungle gym for children to climb. The small merry-go-round was a battered, wounded giant's top.

Firepits lined with scrap metal blazed in the darkness. Figures crossed regularly in front of the light, and Frank's hackles rose at the sight of the inhuman silhouettes. His companion's reaction, however, was only one of anger and anticipation.

"Those are the bastards who killed me. They are going to be surprised."

"I thought the idea was for them not to see us."

Burnfingers's excitement subsided somewhat. "Yes, that is so. Well, they *would* have been surprised. If not for your family I would go in swinging, so I suppose I should give thanks for circumstance saving me from myself. There is no word in Comanche for 'prudence.'" He nodded. "Let us try to work our way around to the left, behind the cage."

There was a guard, as minimal as it was relaxed. Apparently they believed that isolation and reputation would be sufficient to discourage any possible attack, and with good reason. None of the cityfolk had willingly come close to the island. Despite this, the intruders were spotted—by a tired mutant convinced he saw nothing more threatening than a floating shapeless mass of flotsam.

As they rounded the western end of the island, Burnfingers and Frank had to kick a little harder to advance against a light breeze. Fortunately the wind wasn't any stronger, or it might have pushed them out onto the endless expanse of lake.

Then they were bumping dry land. No trees and only a few forlorn, isolated bushes survived on this part of the island, where once laughing children had played hide-and-seek among lovingly tended landscaping. Frank was cold despite the warm brine on which they drifted. If his neighbors didn't grow up, the same disaster could befall his own reality. Never in his life had he longed for anything the way he now longed for the familiar, friendly confines of his home and office.

They could overhear the mutants talking, their broken English full of post-apocalyptic slang. While he and Begay lay motionless, two of the guards turned and walked off, leaving only one of their number standing in front of the cage. He was five feet tall and weighed two hundred pounds.

It was Wendy whom Alicia comforted in her lap. Steven was kneeling by the back of the cage, tossing pebbles against one another. Frank started to rise and move forward, only to find himself held back.

Burnfingers's eyes burned into his own. "Leave the necessary business to me, Frank."

"It's my family."

"True, but you only *sell* athletic virtue, remember?"

It hurt Frank's pride to admit his companion was right. So he nodded and relaxed, making sure he kept a firm grip on their makeshift raft lest the wind carry it off.

Burnfingers seemed to travel below the surface as he slithered upslope toward the cage. Even though he knew where to look, Frank couldn't see his friend against the weeds and rank grass.

Then he knew where Begay was because he saw Steven stiffen. A hand rose from the darkness in front of the boy's face. He nodded slowly, glanced back toward his mother, and kept silent.

Good boy, Frank thought anxiously. That's a smart kid.

Burnfingers worked his way around the side of the cage. Frank heard Alicia gasp softly as a mountainous shadow rose up before her. The guard heard, too, and managed to turn halfway around before the shadow enveloped him. Then both vanished. Frank thought he'd seen a knife flash once, decided he didn't want to dwell on it.

The next time he saw the knife, it was sawing at the twine and wire that held the wooden bars together. This patient work continued interminably, until shapes emerged from the cage and ran toward him. Steven first, then Wendy. Alicia would require a wider gap to slip through.

His children stumbled into his arms. Wendy was moaning "Daddy, Daddy!" over and over despite his whispered attempts to shush her. When he was finally able to get their attention he used his hands to indicate they were to lie flat against the raft.

"Help me back this off," he whispered to them. They complied, making more noise with their kicking than he'd hoped.

Now that they were free he was finding it difficult to restrain his own impulse to swim like mad for dry land.

Alicia was running to join them, Burnfingers leading her by the hand. With the children's help the raft was off to a good start.

That was when Alicia slipped and fell.

It wasn't much of a splash, but several of the island's permanent inhabitants had larger ears than normal. Shouts began to dominate the conversation around the firepits.

"Dammit! Kick harder!"

"I am, Daddy, I am!" Steven flailed at the water with his stubby legs.

"Please don't let them take us again, Daddy!" Wendy was sobbing. "Please don't. They were going to—"

"Then kick, kick for your lives!" No reason for stealth now that their presence had been detected.

Burnfingers Begay half heaved Alicia onto the raft alongside her husband. There wasn't even time enough for a welcoming kiss. The waterlogged mattresses dipped alarmingly under the family's weight.

Light lit the water around their feet, reflected from an old coal-oil lantern. Louder shouts now, dominated by outraged shrieks. Then a deep, rolling *booooom* that echoed like thunder across the lake as Burnfingers got off a shot from his monstrous handgun. Confusion mixed with the initial outrage at their escape.

Alicia kicked wildly. "They took us. I tried to call out to you but there wasn't time, there wasn't any time at all. They took us away and brought us here."

"They didn't . . . ?" He left the unnecessary unfinished.

She shook her head. "They didn't have time. But they were going to. They touched us and grinned these awful grins." She tried to see across the shallow black water. "Where's Mouse?"

"Back in the motor home."

"The motor home's here?" Mere mention of their mobile refuge was enough to stifle Wendy's crying.

Something landed in the water close by. Spear or club, Frank didn't waste time on a look. It was solid but fell short, just bumping his right foot.

Alicia did look back. "Oh, God, Frank, they're coming!"

"It's all right," he lied. "We got the jump on them. We'll

make it. Once we do we'll be safe. There's nothing here that can catch the motor home.''

"Have to reach it, first," Burnfingers said, adding a moment later, "I didn't think they walked all the way into town."

Now Frank spared a backward glance. Hunchbacked, broken shapes were paddling in furious pursuit on makeshift rafts of their own. Others pushed or pulled these crude crafts through the water while those on board waved their weapons at the escapees. The rafts were fashioned of wood and plastic, not sodden foam rubber. There was no way the fleeing family could hope to outpace even the slowest of their pursuers.

Standing in the bow of the nearest and largest raft was something seven feet tall. Barbaric symbols had been tattooed on its bloated, shiny belly and shaven dome. One massive fist clenched a length of one-inch steel pipe, the end of which had been drilled and fitted with nails.

"Prake," Alicia informed them. "Their chief, or leader, or whatever."

"The people in town told us."

"Daddy, I'm tired," Steven whined.

Frank started to curse the boy, stopped himself to smile grimly. "I'm tired, too, kiddo, but we've got to all keep kicking. We've *got* to."

"Never make it." Burnfingers had been wading alongside, keeping pace easily. Too easily. "Better make a run for it. It's shallower here."

The water was barely up to Frank's knees, but it still slowed them, the children in particular. He wasn't athlete enough to carry Steven more than a few yards. If he'd set a better example at the dinner table, maybe his son wouldn't have turned out to be such a pudgy glutton himself.

"Get them to the motor home!" Burnfingers yelled. He stood there, outlined against the advancing lanterns and torches, as the family abandoned the raft. Frank saw him turn, raise both arms, and fire again. The Casull boomed through the darkness. A pursuing raft overturned, throwing its occupants thrashing into the lake.

"What about Burnfingers?" Alicia gasped as she tried to lift her knees to her belly. "Isn't he coming?"

"He knows what he's doing." I hope, Frank told himself. "Just run!"

The pistol thundered a third time behind them. Then Burnfingers removed something from the big plastic sack in the middle of the sinking raft: a pop bottle with a rag sticking out of its mouth. A lighter flicked in the darkness, catching the rag alight. Burnfingers tossed it:

The Molotov cocktail, filled with unleaded from Hell, struck one of the rafts and exploded into flame. Screams filled the air as its crew abandoned it. Frank tried to watch and run at the same time. A second Molotov fell short, expending itself harmlessly in the water. Burnfingers turned to run.

They could hear the grotesque Prake bellowing commands to his gargoylish clan. The remaining rafts were much closer now, almost on top of Burnfingers. If they were caught there would be no one to save them this time, Frank knew. His lungs threatened to burst and the water clung like liquid glue to his ankles.

Burnfingers caught up with them, his long legs clearing three times the water Alicia could manage at her best. They could have fashioned additional Molotovs, Frank knew, but both he and Burnfingers had been reluctant to sacrifice any more of the motor home's fuel supply.

"They're going to catch us!" Wendy screamed.

"No, they are not, music-girl." Burnfingers let them advance another ten yards before he raised the big pistol a fourth time, took careful aim, and fired. Not at any of their pursuers, but at the abandoned raft. At the big plastic sack that still bobbed in the center.

Frank knew what he was shooting at. "Get down!"

Alicia almost had time to ask "Why?" when the lake heaved beneath them.

As the tremendous explosion echoed away, Frank rose to his knees and turned. Burnfingers was climbing to his feet, the shock wave having knocked him onto his back. A few lingering screams came from the vicinity of the pursuing rafts. Not of outrage and anger this time, but of pain.

The plastic sack had been stuffed with flammable material: paper, napkins, Wendy's rock magazines, anything burnable. Around this had been packed kitchen knives and forks, screws and nails from the motor home's toolbox, and anything else small and sharp. In the center of this mass of kindling and killing, they'd tied the removable propane canister which fueled the motor home's stove. The heavy-jacketed slug from the Casull had set off a homemade bomb of considerable size, square in the midst of their pursuers. Bits of the shredded canister added another level of lethality to the trap.

Bleeding, torn bodies floated on the dark water, drifting out into the lake. Those not dead or unconscious stood or sat in shock in the midst of total devastation.

"Wow!" Steven muttered as his father half dragged him through the water.

Burnfingers rejoined them moments later. "Didn't get all of them. Did not get the one we needed to get."

A quick glance showed perhaps a dozen of the mutants still struggling through the water. In the lead was the gargantuan Prake, roaring and bleeding like a wounded bear.

"They'll catch us, I am afraid. You go on." Burnfingers was panting hard, obviously tired. Frank had come to think of him as some kind of superman. Now he saw he was wrong. The Indian was strong, but he was not indestructible. "I will hold them off. I have a few shots left."

Alicia looked back at him, slowing. "Don't you have enough?"

He grinned at her as he dug in a pocket, bringing out a few more shells. "These bullets are very expensive, earth mother."

She eyed him oddly. "Why do you keep calling me that?"

"I label as I feel. I think it fits."

Frank slowed. His thighs were encumbered with lead weights. "I hear something."

"Splashing. I hear it, too." Alicia stared into the darkness. "Are there big fish in this lake?"

"There aren't any fish in this lake," Burnfingers told her. "Too saline."

It wasn't a fish, but rather something considerably larger. Lights on high beam, the motor home plunged through the night toward them, a metal dinosaur spitting water from beneath six big wheels.

"Mouse." Frank was swaying, fighting to maintain his balance. "Thank God."

The water was up to the big vehicle's hubcaps as it swung around to greet them. The resulting spray from the wheels drenched them all, but nobody cared. They stumbled madly for the door, which was flung wide from inside. Mouse stood waiting, outlined by the cool electric shine from within: an undernourished angel.

"Don't slow down now!" Burnfingers made sure no one was left behind.

Frank half threw his son aboard. Wendy was next up, then Alicia. He followed faster than he believed possible. Even so, Burnfingers was crowding him.

"Go!" Mouse looked forward as she barked the command. To whom? Frank wondered, since she was driving herself.

Burnfingers grabbed the handle and dragged the door shut as they accelerated. None of them saw the huge shape that flung itself at the rear of the fleeing vehicle. Massive hands locked tight on the back bumper.

"Excuse me a minute." Burnfingers turned and strode toward the back of the motor home. Frank heard him slide open the rear window, heard the Casull bellow a last time. A moment later their tall companion rejoined them, a grim but contented expression on his long face. Frank caught his eye.

"No big deal. Some garbage caught on the bumper as we were leaving. It is gone now."

13

ALICIA HAD A TOWEL wrapped around her hair. She handed a dry one to Burnfingers. He smiled at her, took it gratefully, and began drying himself as best he was able. Mouse was helping Steven out of his dripping clothes while Wendy stood waiting her turn, both arms crossed over her chest. Her mother walked over to her.

"Come on, darling. You have to get out of those clothes."

"But, Mom." Wendy looked meaningfully to her left. "Dad is here, and Steven, and..." Her gaze rose.

Burnfingers was wiping mud from his eyes. "Wendy sprite, you are a cute little white girl-almost-a-woman. But I have seen more ladies bare-ass naked than you ever will see similarly of both sexes. If even I was inclined to have a look at you I promise I am too tired right now to look at anything except maybe a hot cup of coffee."

"I'll make you one as soon as we're through here," Alicia promised him. Then her face broke out in a wide smile and she started to giggle. "Oh, I guess I can't. We don't have any propane."

Wendy slowly lowered her arms. "There's the microwave, Mom."

"Yes, that's right. We can make some instant, can't we?" Thoughts of doing something as domestic as making coffee cheered her visibly. "But nobody gets anything until we've all switched to dry clothing." Reluctantly, Wendy began to strip, starting with her shoes.

Burnfingers paused with his shirt halfway up his chest. "By the way, Frank, who the hell is driving up there?"

"I was wondering that myself." Mouse was still helping Steven to change.

A beaming, ruddy face appeared around the side of the driver's chair, one hand clinging to the wheel. A nose W. C. Fields would have been proud of dominated the surprising visage. It was flanked by shiny red cheeks and topped by a head of kinky reddish-blond hair. The eyes, deep-set beneath brows of equally startling hue, were bright pink. The man had a holiday air about him, as though Santa Claus had been crossed with the Easter Bunny.

"Hallu!" One pink eye winked, then the whole torso vanished behind the bulk of the seat.

Frank slipped into the bathrobe his wife handed him, moved forward as he belted the dry terry cloth.

Their driver was seated atop several cushions. This raised his eyes above the dash. A pair of stick-like prostheses were secured to his boots, short stilts improvised out of twine and poles. These enabled him to control the brake and accelerator. They were necessary because the man was barely three feet tall. A voice spoke at Frank's side.

"Say good evening to our new friend," Mouse urged him.

Dazed, Frank leaned against the other front seat for support. "Hi."

"Hi yourself." The little man stuck out a hand. Frank took it automatically. "Flucca's the name. Niccolo Flucca. Haven't had a chance to drive anything without four legs in five, six years. Mouse tells me it's brand-new. Didn't think there was anything brand-new left in the world."

"Not in this one," Frank told him, looking hard at Mouse as he spoke.

"I told you before this started that I was not good with machines. As I was waiting for your return, the curious began to gather around me. Niccolo was one of them. Years ago he wandered accidentally into this reality from another."

"Thought it was a bad dream," their driver said, "and it was."

"Of all who surrounded me in your absence, only he recognized this machine as a vehicle. He offered to help. I am a good judge of people no matter what their origins and I could tell instantly he was large of heart and spirit. So I accepted. Fortunate for you, I think, that I did."

"Prake's bad people," said Flucca.

"I wouldn't want him for a neighbor," Frank admitted.

"Mouse helped me rig up." He indicated the cushions and stilts. "I used to be a pretty good driver. Great to be behind the wheel again. I know all the submerged roads."

"When we heard the first explosions we thought we'd better come looking for you," Mouse explained. "Niccolo assured me we wouldn't get stuck. I thought it would be the right thing to do."

"You thought right, little singer," said Burnfingers from behind them.

"Speaking of right things to do." Alicia put both arms around her husband and kissed him passionately. Wendy stared while her little brother made a disgusted sound.

"Ah, come on, Mom!" he finally pleaded, unable to stand it any longer. His parents parted. Frank had his hands on his wife's hips, smiling at her.

"You been holding back on me all these years, sweetheart? I never knew death and destruction excited you."

She pulled away sharply. "Frank, you're terrible! Can't you take anything seriously?"

His expression turned somber. "I got plenty serious when we found out you and the kids had been kidnapped." He patted her side and she reached out to gently touch his face with the back of one hand.

The children had retreated to the security and quiet of the back bedroom. Leaving Alicia to deal with the pile of unexpected but unbloodied laundry, he walked back to join them. Both children sat on the king-sized bed. Steven was staring out the rear window, no doubt hunting for pursuing mutants. Frank didn't think his son would see any. They were beyond the lake waters now, back in the main part of the city. Flucca certainly knew his way around, and Burnfingers had hung on to a few shells for the Casull. They were safe, at least until the next unexpected attack.

Wendy's sodden hair hung limply from beneath the towel wrapped around her head. Frank sat down next to her. She didn't look at him.

"How you doin', little girl?"

"I'm fine, Daddy." Now she turned to him, her expression twisted. "And I wish you wouldn't call me that."

"Sorry." He smiled, uncomfortable. "I keep forgetting."

She sounded bored and tired. "And don't tell me I'll 'always be your little girl,' either. I'm an adult now."

"Of course you are."

They sat silently, Frank trying to think of something to say and not wanting to commit another paternal faux pas, his daughter obviously uneasy and tense.

It started with a sniffle, which became a sob, which degenerated into tears. She sat on the edge of the bed crying and hugging herself, and she didn't object when Frank moved close enough to put an arm around her and pull her gently down against his shoulder.

"I'm scared, Daddy. I want to go home."

"I know, I know." He squeezed her shoulder. "We all want to go home. But we've kind of got a tiger by the tail and we can't let go yet. Actually, it's a Mouse."

She inhaled and managed to smile at that, and it was easy for him to smile back.

Steven turned from the glass, looking on uncomfortably. "Don't worry, sis. I'll take care of you."

One long, last sniffle preceded her reply, which was raspy but full of familiar filial sarcasm. "Oh, that's great, that's wonderful! We can all relax now. Steven Mark Sonderberg is on the job!"

The boy shrugged, turned away. "Hey, if you don't care . . ."

"No fighting. Not now," Frank warned them. "And you watch your mouth, litt—Wendy. We're all having a tough time."

"Dad?" Steven continued staring out the back window as he spoke. There was no ten-year-old bravado in his voice now. "We are gonna get home, aren't we?" He sounded very small and alone.

"Of course we are. We're just"—he hesitated—"taking a little detour, that's all."

"Yeah, right. A detour." The boy brightened at the thought. "Dad, you shoulda seen some of the uglies that were holding us prisoner. They were *gross*. And that big guy, he was the ugliest one of all. He was bigger even than Andre the Giant!" Frank knew who his son was talking about because as the owner of a chain of sporting goods stores it behooved him to know a lot about activities he really cared nothing about. "How'd you make that bomb, huh? I bet Mr. Begay made it, didn't he?"

"We both worked it out," Frank replied, slightly miffed.

It went right by his son. "Burnfingers sure knows a lot of stuff, doesn't he? I wonder if he's really from Arizona?"

"I don't know, either, but unless we find out otherwise we have to take him at his word."

"Sure, I guess so." When Steven turned back to the glass, Frank glanced down at his daughter.

"You gonna be all right now?"

She nodded, forced a smile as she wiped at her eyes. "I think so."

"Okay, then." He rose. "I've gotta get back up front and see what's going on." He started out.

"Hey!" At the shout he paused to look back at her. "Don't forget you owe me a new stereo."

"Don't worry." He grinned. "Soon as we're back in L.A. we'll go pick out whatever you want."

"I'm not going to let you forget," she warned him.

"That's good." He didn't know if she was feeling better when he left the bedroom, but he certainly was.

Flucca was still driving. "I can take over now if you like," he told the little man.

"Actually," the dwarf told him reluctantly, "much as I'm enjoying this, I am getting tired." He shook his left leg. "The cruise control's no good at these speeds and these straps are starting to bite."

Alicia was seated across from him. "Do you need any help getting down?"

"Not only do I not need any help getting down," he told her with a wink, "I never need any help getting up."

Frank stared through the windshield into the night. "You sure it's okay to stop here?"

"You bet." Flucca let the motor home coast to a halt. "I

know the whole damn city. Nobody comes here. We're near the old industrial district. Locals think there are still hot spots out this way, but there ain't. I used to know a real old guy who had, what do you call it?" His face screwed up in concentration. "A dagger counter?"

"Geiger counter?" said Alicia helpfully.

"No. Something similar, though. He told me this part of town's been cold for years. But superstition keeps the locals away." He removed both makeshift stilts and tossed them aside, then slid down off the pile of cushions.

Frank cleared the driver's seat and settled behind the wheel. In spite of all the heavy driving he'd done lately it still felt good to be back in control again. He readjusted the position of the chair.

And realized he didn't have the foggiest notion which way to go. This was Salt Lake City, which he'd never visited, on another reality line, which he'd also very definitely never visited.

"Which way's your Vanishing Point?" he asked Mouse.

"Off this reality," she told him. "I wouldn't have come this way at all if your family hadn't been brought here."

"Then how do we get back on the right line?"

"You know, I was a cook." Flucca ignored the threatening surroundings. "Best damn cook in Las Cruces, New Mexico."

"Really?" said Alicia. "I'm something of an amateur chef myself. Maybe you and I could do some cooking together." She eyed the now fuelless stove and sighed. "When we get home."

"I'd enjoy that a lot." Flucca sounded wistful. "I miss working with real pots and pans."

"I know a few people in the restaurant business. When we get back I'll help you find an opening. If you're as good as you say you are, that is."

"Better. All I want to drive again are the controls of a gas range."

"It is good to have goals." Burnfingers Begay's eyes scanned the darkness. "However, we should concentrate on the immediate ones for now. Let us begin by leaving behind this city of the dead. Any suggestions?"

Standing on tiptoes, Flucca pointed to his left. "If we go past the pit, I don't think anyone will try to follow us. The highway out that direction's still pretty intact." Frank glanced at Mouse, who nodded her approval.

"It feels right. Or at least, it does not feel wrong."

They found the impact crater, gave it a wide berth as Frank maneuvered the motor home through the damaged intersection and onto the avenue Flucca indicated. As soon as they were sure they were on the right road, Burnfingers and Mouse took Flucca back to introduce him to the Sonderberg children. That left Frank and Alicia alone up front.

"I wonder if it's good for Steven to be spending so much time with Burnfingers?"

His wife frowned. "Why? They seem to enjoy each other's company."

"I know, but Burnfingers keeps showing him how to sharpen knives and handle weapons and things. You know how impressionable Steven is."

"Considering where we are, maybe we could all do with that kind of instruction," she replied surprisingly. "When I was back in that cage wondering if I'd ever see you again, wondering what those awful people were going to do to us, I wished I'd known a little more about fighting myself."

What she said made sense but still left him troubled. He divided his attention between the conversation and the road ahead, which was leading them northward out of the city.

"We're just your average family. We shouldn't have to know how to use knives and homemade bombs."

"We shouldn't be traveling through alternate realities, either, but we are."

"Well, I think you're coping wonderfully."

"That's me." She slid down in the seat, put her feet up on the dash. "I'm fine during a crisis. It's when I'm safely back home soaking in the tub that I'll crack up and get hysterical and throw things. Can't afford the time for that right now."

A new voice joined the conversation. Mouse was staring straight ahead.

"We are back on the right path once more. The little man knew the way better than he himself knows."

"Is there any chance this Anarchis will give up and leave us alone?" Alicia asked plaintively.

"No, but we have successfully slipped its grasp again. It may take it some time to gather its forces for another assault. Chaos is not suited to planning. Forethought pains it."

"Good! I hope it suffers a cosmic migraine," Frank muttered.

Beyond the city limits the road stretched straight and relatively unbroken. Weeds pushed through cracks in the concrete, but there were few impact craters or potholes to slow their progress. As they cruised northward they saw no other vehicles, no wandering humans, hardly anything ambulatory.

Once something that might in a healthier time have been a bat glided through their headlight beams, a distorted lump with wings. Frank didn't try to follow its progress because he might have succeeded, and he didn't want a better look. Except for the isolated flier, the motor home was all that advanced through the devastated night.

"We're drawing near." Mouse frowned at the road. "Yet something feels not right."

"What a surprise," Frank murmured sardonically as he slowed and tried to see farther into the darkness. "Tell our fellow travelers," he told his wife, "to get their butts up here. We're getting close to something."

"Close to what?" Alicia rose from the chair.

"I dunno, but if it concerns Mouse it concerns me. I've learned that much."

Alicia returned a moment later with Burnfingers and Flucca in tow. Frank let their speed fall below forty, then thirty. It was fortunate he did so. Otherwise he might not have been able to stop in time.

Ten yards ahead, the road vanished. So did the ground. Off to the right, the silhouettes of high mountains paralleled the road as far as the same point. There they also came to an abrupt end. To the west the northern reaches of the Great Salt Lake ended in a distant roaring. Frank cracked his window a few inches and the noise filled the motor home. It was the sound of water falling without striking bottom.

The sky remained, along with the stars. Too many stars too close.

"I think I know where we are," Frank muttered. He edged a little nearer the brink, set the emergency brake. There was just enough light for everyone to see the lake waters where they tumbled into nothingness, forming a salty waterfall miles in length.

"The edge of the world. I've seen it before."

Alicia gave him a funny look. "When did you ever see anything like this before?"

"I was out walking when you and the kids were kidnapped. That's when I saw it. There was some of it behind the motel." He didn't add that he'd seen it and understood it in Mouse's company any more than he went on to explain why he and their guest had been wandering through the woods together early in the morning. For once he was grateful for Alicia's lack of persistence.

"So what do we do now?" she mused aloud.

Mouse wore a dreamy expression, her eyes half-closed as she concentrated. "This is the right way. The only way. The road is here. Our eyes are deceived."

"Deceived, hell." Frank continued to stare at the bottomless waterfall. "They're being lied to like crazy. There's no road out there. Burnfingers?"

Begay shrugged. "I know hidden byways. I do not know what lies beyond the edge of the world. Of course, if the little singer is wrong, all we would do is fall. There would be plenty of time to talk things out before we hit bottom."

Mouse spoke up. "Once you trusted Burnfingers Begay when you could not see a road where a road was. This time you must trust me. The road is there, but we will not see it until we trade this reality for another."

"I dunno. . . ."

"We cannot go back," she said firmly. "The allies of the Anarchis will search ceaselessly until they find us. It will be much easier for them to do so if we remain on this line. Others will come in Prake's wake, others more terrible than he."

Frank shook his head doubtfully. "I don't think I can imagine realities worse than Prake."

"That's because your imagination is limited by what you know."

Still unsure, he turned to Alicia. She smiled encouragingly and added that cute little toss of her head he'd always found so endearing. It gave him courage if not confidence.

"All right. What do you want me to do?"

"That which you have done so well all along. Drive on."

He swallowed hard, released the emergency brake, and drove over the edge.

The smooth transition left him breathless. One moment there

was nothing below them, the next they were cruising along a pale ivory pavement that ran through emptiness. It was unblemished and well-maintained. His muscles began to unknot.

"You were right." Alicia gazed admiringly at Mouse. "You've been right all along."

"Well, I wasn't positive," she replied slowly, "but I was reasonably certain."

Frank's head came around fast. "What do you mean, you weren't positive?"

Mouse smiled warmly. "Would you have driven over the edge if I'd admitted uncertainty?"

He started to reply, thought it over, and decided to say nothing.

The reality they'd left behind rapidly faded from view. Mountains, great lake, and old highway consumed by distance and darkness. The road they were on twisted and bent madly, but no matter how steeply it banked the motor home hugged the smooth surface tightly. Frank settled the speedometer on forty, though everyone had the feeling they were moving far faster than that.

"Everyone okay?" he inquired. The response was gratifyingly positive.

"Are we going to be all right now, Mom?" Wendy asked.

"I don't know, dear. We aren't sure where we've been and I guess we're still not sure where we're going."

"At least we got away from the monsters, huh, Dad?" Steven was eyeing Burnfingers admiringly. "We really blew that Prake guy away, didn't we?"

"I did what was necessary." Begay put a hand on Frank's shoulder. "Your father is a remarkable driver. I begin to wonder at the 'coincidence' that inspired him to stop and give Ballad Eyes a ride."

"No big deal." Frank discovered he was embarrassed by Burnfingers's praise. "The driving, I mean. I just put a foot to the gas and go. See, when I was getting started in business I used to drive the delivery truck in addition to doing most of the paperwork. Time being money and all that. Besides, anyone who grew up in L.A. and learned driving there can drive anyplace. There are intersections in L.A. that remind you of the edge of the world and Hell."

Burnfingers looked thoughtful. "It was different for me. As I have told you, driving on the Reservation is not the same as driving in the real world. We have our own speed laws and our own police. Many of the roads are no more than suggestions in the dirt. When the principal mode of transportation is an old pickup truck with a stripped transmission, you learn to drive carefully.''

Mouse was concentrating on the winding road ahead. "Niccolo's choice came from the heart. We are going the right way."

"Glad to hear it," Frank confessed, "since alternate routes seem to be in short supply out here."

Alicia had the back of one hand pressed to her forehead. Her eyes were half closed. "This has all been so wearying."

"Wearying? *Wearying?*" Frank snapped out the words. "What this has been is fucking insane, is what it's been."

She made a face at him. "Frank—the children."

"Let 'em hear. I'm fed up."

"I'm sorry to have involved your family," Mouse told him. "Time and circumstance offered me no other choice."

"Yeah, yeah. So you've been telling us."

"Then if you are intelligent enough to acknowledge the inevitability of what we are doing, why are you angry?"

"I don't know!" He slammed both hands hard against the wheel. "Can't I just be mad? Do I have to have a reason? Christ, I don't wanna save the world. I just want to be able to keep on selling Taiwanese baseball mitts at fifty percent markup. That's my idea of a reality worth fighting for."

"Want me to drive for a while, Frank?"

As he glanced back at Burnfingers, he subsided. "Naw. Just blowing off steam. Call you if I need a break."

"Okay. You may think of yourself as ordinary and weak, Frank Sonderberg, but I think you are one tough son of a bitch."

"Thanks. You got to be to run a business like mine. That's the American way."

"We should have taken some pictures," Alicia pointed out. "After all, we've had some pretty unique experiences."

"Who'd believe us?" Frank punctuated the rhetorical question with a grunt of disdain. "I can see it now. We could have the Blockers and the McIntyres over for a slide show." He raised his voice theatrically.

"Here we are in Hell—notice the demons at the tables? Observe the stuffed children mounted on the walls. Here we are on the highway to nowhere, and this one now, this is the one that takes you off the edge of the world. This place that looks like Las Vegas? It's really on another planet. You can tell by the guy with the root growing out of his head and the lady with the purple fur on her face.

"This dump is Salt Lake City, only it's after they've dropped the Big One, which is why the streets haven't been swept in a while. Yeah, we should've taken pictures." He concluded by making a rude noise.

"Well, *we* could have looked at them," she persisted.

"No thanks, hon. If we get out of this, the last thing I want is anything to remind me of it. I'll be real happy to put it behind me. Way behind me."

"But you won't be able to do that, darling."

"No," he grumbled. "I guess I won't."

Burnfingers leaned close, nodding. "Looks like light up ahead."

A patch of sunlight grew in the distance, which was intriguing since there was no sun in sight. It illuminated an intersection. Frank slowed up as they approached.

It was a sextupal crossing. Signs littered posts or hung in midair. There was also a single homey red stop sign. The rest were unrecognizable. A few were composed of pure light. Others busily rearranged themselves as they looked on. The variety of the display was impressive.

Beyond the intersection lay a large parcel of land composed of sand and gravel. It occupied a circle several hundred yards in diameter. Void abutted it on all sides. In the middle of this patch of suspended grit stood a simple frame structure painted dark brown with white trim. Its tin roof sparkled under the false, sourceless sunshine. A half dozen fuel islands surrounded the main building. They resembled abstract sculpture more than they did gas pumps.

As the motor home stood idling behind the stop sign, what appeared to be a metallic flying fish folded its wings and settled down across from one of the pumps. There was a pause before a small bolt of lightning leaped from pump to vehicle. A creature that resembled a protozoan with legs hopped out of the fish-car, did something to the pump, and then climbed back inside its machine. The filmy wings unfurled, the head of the fish turned, and the streamlined shape shot down one of the other roads so fast only the shock of its disappearance echoed in their memories.

As near as Frank had been able to tell, it had never once made contact with the ground.

A pair of other vehicles stood parked in the lot to the right of the building. One was a large boulder on treads. The other looked like a cluster of titanium bamboo surmounted by a brass bubble encircled by a single treadless wheel. The bubble was big enough to hold an elephant, the wheel less than a yard thick. Frank tried to see how it remained balanced.

Smoke rose lazily from a brick chimney at the rear of the building. As they crossed the intersection they saw that the sign over the entrance changed characters as fast as individual frames on a videotape. One frame read CAFÉ before vanishing in favor of blurred alien hieroglyphs.

"Probably says the same thing in hundreds of different languages," Flucca suggested. "But it's a restaurant. You can smell it."

"Wonder if they can smell us." A check of the gas gauge revealed less than half a tank left. He wondered if he could top off their tanks here. If they sold lightning bolts, maybe he could buy premium unleaded, too.

There was plenty of room to park alongside the giant treadless wheel. He pulled up carefully, set the brake. Fifty yards to the right, sunlight and solid ground gave way to void. It was with considerable relief he gingerly stepped out onto unyielding earth.

Flucca hopped down and hurried past him. "Wonder what kind of place this is and what it's doing here?"

"If this is a reality line it is surely a short one," was all Burnfingers could say.

"A bit of reality apart from any other." Mouse turned slowly, studying their surroundings. "A drifting fragment, held in place only by this intersection. Astonishing."

"Interesting chunk of real estate, all right." Flucca was leading the way toward the entrance. "Wonder what the food's like?"

Thoughts of real food set off a small bomb in Frank's belly. None of them had enjoyed a real meal since leaving behind the Cedar City that was too full of truth to be their reality. He indicated the brass bubble and its neighbor.

"Looks like they have a few customers already."

"Never saw a place yet fond of turning business away." Flucca reached for the handle of the front door.

The café's interior was nothing like what any of them expected because it looked exactly like what they were familiar with. It was no different from any of a hundred similar establishments you would encounter traveling along a rural state highway.

They took a table near a front window with a view of the parking lot and fuel islands. The Formica tabletop was lined on the side with fluted metal strips. Legs solid as railroad iron supported it. There were salt and pepper shakers and a big glass sugar dispenser with a stick of vanilla inside to maintain freshness, paper napkins and cheap metal silverware. A cluster of laminated menus shared a plastic stand with the napkins. Everything looked and felt familiar. Gazing out the window, Frank half expected to see cars whizzing past, mountains and cactus in the distance. But there was only the parking lot, pumps, sourceless sunshine and, off in the distance, the blackness of the abyss.

That's when the voice startled him out of his reverie. "Now, then, whut kin I git for you folks?"

14

THE HEAVYSET WOMAN regarding them patiently was in her mid-forties. Her bleached blond hair was piled in swirls atop her head, a sweeping abstract sculpture. She wore a plain white waitress's uniform. Two pens peeped from the lip of a blouse pocket. One hand held a third, the other a yellow note pad. Gum snapped as she chewed. Her cheeks were pale rose.

"What is this place?" Wendy spoke first. "No—*where* is this place?"

Chicle popped, punctuating each sentence. "This place? Why, this here's the Conjunction. Me and Max, we run the whole joint." She nodded proudly toward the kitchen, from which strange and wondrous odors emanated, not to mention the thick aroma of hot grease. "We've been here for some time. I take it this is the first time out this way for you folks?" She scanned them approvingly. "Always nice to see new faces. We got enough regulars as it is." She hefted pad and pencil, 160 pounds of kitchen computer instantly on-line. "I expect you'd like something to eat."

Frank didn't reply. His attention was drawn to a booth on the other side of the restaurant. Its occupants could only be the drivers of the two extraordinary machines parked outside.

A giant green caterpillar wearing wraparound blue sunshades

sat across the table from a tall, thin creature built of petrified Silly Puddy. Taking up an enormous chair out in the aisle was a walrus-sized quadruped with engraved tusks and hands like a pianist's. He wore dark gray dungarees and waved his hands animatedly as he spoke. Most of his sentences were directed to the caterpillar. The Silly Puddy person sat and sipped silently from a glass two feet tall and an inch in diameter.

"Sorry?" Frank blinked, leaned back in his chair.

"Asked what I could git ya." The waitress started to slide her pencil behind one ear. "I can see you folks are tired. I'll come back in a few minutes."

"No, no, that's all right," Alicia said quickly. "Could I—do you have coffee?"

"Don't see why not. What else we sellin' today?"

"I wanna chocolate shake," Steven told her, "with whipped cream on top!"

His mother bent close to him. "Steven, we don't know if a place like this carries anything like—"

"One chocolate shake." The waitress made a terse notation on her pad, looked up. "You folks gonna have anything to eat, or you just thirsty?"

A numbed Frank picked up one of the menus, opened the laminated sheets. It was as thick as a small book and full of writing that leaped off the page. He couldn't read a word of it. Unlike the sign above the entrance, the words did not change as he studied them.

The waitress leaned over his shoulder. She smelled of cheap perfume. He wondered if it was produced by adding liquid to her skin, or if it was her actual body odor, or if it changed like the sign outside to meet the olfactory requirements of an extraordinarily diverse clientele.

"I forgot: you folks are new here." She straightened. "Max is pretty versatile. You just tell me what you'd like and I'll bet a dime against a dollar he can whip it up."

"Anything?" Frank swallowed, the saliva running inside his mouth like a spring flood.

"Sure. He likes a change now and then. Gets tired of feeding the same specials to the same regulars."

"Okay." One more swallow. "I'd like—a New York strip sirloin, medium well, with grilled onions, baked potato, sour

cream and butter on the side, no chives, and whatever the
vegetable of the day is.'' When he finished he was nearly in tears.
''Can he—can he do that?''

She grinned down at him, suddenly no longer an inexplicable
vision. ''What size steak?''

''Twelve—no, ten ounces. I don't want to overdo it.''

Everyone ordered. Fried chicken for Steven, shrimp salad for
Wendy and her mother. Mouse requested unfamiliar food in an
unrecognizable language while Flucca called for chicken mole
with frijoles and rice. Burnfingers Begay waited until everyone
else had put in their order before calmly requesting tenderloin of
venison filled with trout pâté beneath a sour cream–champagne
sauce, potatoes au gratin on the side, and haricots verts accompanied by a 1948 Bavarian Liebfraumilch. Not to mention rambutan
sorbet for dessert.

''Right.'' Their waitress scanned the long list before walking
back to the kitchen. They could hear her rattling off the orders to
an unseen figure behind the grill.

Wendy was shaking her head. ''Can you believe this place?''

''It's no more impossible than everything else that's happened
to us.'' Her mother was arranging a napkin on her lap. ''I don't
see why we shouldn't believe in it, as well.''

''Got a good location,'' Burnfingers observed.

In a few minutes the waitress returned with their drinks:
coffee, iced tea, wine, and one towering chocolate milkshake.
While they drank, the walrus and his companions rose to leave.
Everyone watched them go.

Frank heard their machines start up, peered out the window to
observe the departure. The wheeled globe belonged to the Silly
Puddy creature. Instead of rolling down the road, it rose six feet
off the gravel and banked sharply to its left. The wheel was
rotating so rapidly around the globe it was less than a blur. The
caterpillar and the walrus left in the other vehicle, exploding up
the roadway opposite the café.

The Sonderbergs were alone in the café with their friends.

Twenty minutes later their food emerged from the kitchen.
Wendy's and Alicia's salads were ice chilled, the shrimp the size of
small lobsters, and everything expertly washed and shelled. Frank's
sirloin arrived on a sizzling steel platter. The first bite was purely

sensuous. He chewed and swallowed two more before he could find his voice.

"Anybody—anybody else use the road we came in on?"

Their waitress frowned as she stacked serving plates. "Now that you mention it, not for quite a while. Guess that section of road's under repair. Usually seems to be." Her gum popped, sounding like a small-caliber pistol.

"Does this place have a name?" Flucca's lips were dark with mole sauce.

"Just the Conjunction." She hesitated, gazing toward the kitchen. "Say, it's kinda between mealtimes right now. Would you folks mind chatting with Max while you eat? Talking to the customers is one of his biggest pleasures."

Frank's defenses went up instinctively, relaxed when he saw Steven smiling back at him. "I guess so. Come to think of it, I'd like to meet somebody who can conjure up a meal like this in twenty minutes."

"Great!" She turned and bellowed toward the kitchen. "It's okay, Maxie! C'mon out and shoot the bull if you want to!"

"Minute!" came the reply from the vicinity of the kitchen. "Just scrapin' the grill!"

They were three-quarters finished with their food and beginning to slow down when the chef finally emerged to join them. His waitress wife was in back of the counter setting places and arranging alien desserts inside a tall glass cylinder.

Max was almost as tall as Burnfingers Begay, and much beefier. He had a permanent five-o'clock shadow and thinning black hair. His wide apron somehow stayed in position without the aid of shoulder straps. As he approached the table he was wiping both huge hands with a dirty towel. On his bare right shoulder Frank identified a tattoo of a naked woman entwined with a snake beneath which rode a banner and two hearts. Beneath it, in florid script, was the word MOTHER. The other shoulder displayed a tattoo which traveled from elbow to neck. It resembled nothing on Earth.

"Everything okay, folks?" Each word ended in a grunt, giving Max the sound of an educated hog. He smiled as he listened to a barrage of compliments. "Thanks. Eileen says you folks haven't been through this way before."

"We're trying to fix something that's broke," Steven blurted before anyone could stop him.

Max just nodded. "Trouble with the threads of reality?"

"How did you know?" Mouse was instantly on guard.

"We feed a lot of truckers in here. They know just about everything that's goin' on anywhere. You look like the fix-it type. Wish you all luck. Hope you put reality to right. Chaos is bad for business."

"As an independent businessman myself," said Frank as he gestured with a forkful of steak, "I can go along with that."

"What sorta business you in, buddy?"

"Sporting goods."

"No foolin'?" The cook was delighted. "That's great! Used to be big on sports myself until I found out I had this other talent. I was pre-med in school. Gonna be a designer molecular engineer until I discovered I liked slingin' hash better." He jerked a thumb toward the counter. "Eileen didn't want to go world-hopping anyway, so when we found this place up for sale it was a natural for us. We'll never get rich here, but you can't beat it for gettin' to meet interesting people."

"I can imagine." Alicia sipped her perfect blend of Colombian and Kona coffees.

"We need to top off our tanks, too," Frank told him. "I don't suppose you carry premium unleaded out here?"

Max scratched beard stubble. "Oh, I reckon we got just about anything you need. Not much good tryin' to run a business if you don't stock what the customer wants."

"That's exactly how I feel about it." A sudden thought make Frank frown. "I don't know how we're going to pay you. Do you take credit cards?"

"Hell, we take anything." A big hand dug into a pocket beneath the stained apron, emerged holding fragments of metal, plastic, and crystal. Some of the crystals burned with bright internal fires. Max displayed the handful before shoving it back in his pocket.

"You run a place out in the boonies, you better get used to acceptin' some funny money."

"If you'd prefer, I think we can cover the bill with cash."

"Hey, since when did anybody turn down cash? That steak done right?"

"Absolute perfection. Tastes of mesquite. Where do you find mesquite?"

Max shrugged modestly. "I got my suppliers. Truckers, they get everywhere." He nodded toward the window. "There goes a regular right now."

Everyone turned as a blast of passing air rattled the windows and something the size of the Queen Mary with wheels thundered through the intersection beyond the gravel parking lot.

"Wow!" said Steven softly. There was a faint smell of burned caramel in the air. It faded rapidly. "What was that?"

"Don't know for sure," Max told him. "Can't tell where everybody's going or where they're coming from. But a lot of 'em stop here." He was quiet for a long moment. "There is somethin' you could offer that'd be better than money, though I'll take that, too. Call it a tip."

"Like what?" Alicia asked hesitantly.

He looked down at her. "Personal contact. Oh, not what you'd call intimate. I simply want to touch you." Seeing the expressions on their faces he explained further. "Call it a hobby if you will, but one of the pleasures of running this place is knowing the folks you serve."

"This won't hurt, will it?" Wendy asked him.

"No, little lady," he replied, laughing softly. "It won't hurt at all."

Frank shrugged. "God knows you've earned a bigger tip than anything we could leave. If that's what you want. . . ." He stuck out his hand. "Pleased to meet you. I'm Frank Sonderberg."

"Just call me Max." The chef extended his own paw.

It was an ordinary handshake they exchanged, except for the faint lingering tingle Frank felt as he drew his fingers back. Without a second thought, Alicia extended her own hand.

"I'm Alicia."

"Charmed." Max turned her hand over and kissed the back. Frank wondered if his wife felt more or less of the subsidiary tingling as a result.

Everyone shook his hand: the children, Flucca, then Begay. The chef's eyes widened perceptibly as he gripped Burnfingers's equally large hand. "Well, well: a Traveler."

"I get around. Hitchhike, mostly."

Max was just staring. "I'd like to talk with you at length."

"Be glad to, but I'm with these folks and they're in kind of a hurry. Sorry."

"I understand." Max let the Indian's fingers drop. For a split second, less than the blink of an eye, Frank thought he saw half a dozen steely green digits attached to the chef's wrist. Or maybe they'd been silvery tentacles. Two localized hallucinations in less than a second. Before he had time to digest his eyes' deceptive information, Max's hand was a normal hand once again.

"That's the trouble with folks. They stop here for a fill-up and a quick bite to eat, and then they're off again, sometimes for the last time." He turned to Mouse, extending his hand a final time.

She lifted her own tiny hand to meet his. Frank wasn't sure exactly what happened next, but the first contact produced a bright blue flash and a crackling in the air. He nearly fell out of his chair. Wendy squealed and covered her face.

When he'd recovered from the shock, a cloud of blue smoke was already beginning to dissipate above the table. Their host was lying against the counter, legs spread, shaking his head like a man who'd just taken a solid uppercut. Mouse was standing by her chair, her eyes even wider than usual.

"I didn't mean to do anything," she was saying over and over.

"It's okay. It's all right," Max told her. Eileen was leaning over the counter, staring at him and still chewing her gum.

The chef used one of the counter stools for support as he rose. Then he turned his gaze not on Mouse, but back on Frank. "You got any idea who you're travelin' with, buddy?"

Frank stared at Mouse, who wore her usual enigmatic expression. "A musician?"

"Musician, yeah." Max wiped at his pants, straightened his apron, and chuckled. "Right: a musician." He inspected his hand, shaking it loosely from the wrist while supporting his elbow with his other hand. "Quite a handshake you got there, miss."

"Just call me Mouse."

"Miss Mouse, I haven't had contact like that since"—he glanced back at his wife, who was looking on from behind the counter—"well, let's just say it don't happen often."

"You okay?" Even as he asked, Frank wondered what Mouse had done to the much bigger man. There'd been a spark, a ripping noise, and he'd been thrown across the floor as though he'd been shot from a cannon.

"Sure, I'm okay."

"I didn't mean to do anything." Mouse was openly apologetic. "I'm usually very careful."

"You were careful," Max told her. "I should've mentioned that I'm an open receptor. Usually I just get a sip of everybody who comes through here. I wasn't prepared for a deluge. Most folks don't put out more than a trickle." He took a deep breath. "That'll be a memory to savor. Thanks." He looked around the table. "You can thank the lady here for your meals. On the house."

"You sure?" Frank fumbled for his wallet. "You should let us pay you something. I still have to fill up."

"Go ahead."

"Then you have to take some money." He extracted several bills without bothering to check the denominations. "Here. Take this and give me whatever the change is."

Max frowned at the paper. "What's that?"

"Money." Frank started to put it back in his wallet. "If it's no good . . ."

"No, no. Currency? Let me see." Frank passed him the bills. "I'll be damned. Eileen, have a look at this! You won't believe it. *Paper* money. Intentionally transitory currency." He turned back to Frank. "You don't often meet someone who comes from a society that makes a virtue of insubstantiality."

"Not all of it's insubstantial," Frank protested. "We use coins, too. Metal."

"Oh, that stuff's common." Max was examining the bills avidly. "Not even charged or bonded. Remarkable. Could I have one of each denomination? The images are so exquisitely bombastic."

"Well, sure," said Frank uncertainly. There was nothing in Max's hand larger than a twenty.

"We'd best be going." Mouse was looking out the windows. "We're losing time."

"Yeah." Frank took back the excess dollars.

"Wonderful," Max was murmuring. "Paper money."

His wife was filling sugar shakers. "See something new every day, doncha, honey? Listen, you folks ever come back this

way, you be sure and stop in for coffee and danish or something,
okay?''

"Sure," Frank told her, "if we ever come back this way."

Max was holding a ten up to the light. "Unbelievable. Such a
feeble material for a unit of exchange." He blinked, followed
Frank and the others as they headed for the door. "Kinda hard to
see through, though. I'm supposed to get new lenses in a week or
so.''

Frank hesitated by the exit as his family filed outside. "I'm
not sure I can handle those pumps. They look a little funny."

"Oh, you'll find one that fits," Max assured him. "We
monitor dispensing from in here. Just go ahead and fill 'er up. And
remember next time you're back this way: the Conjunction never
closes.''

"I'll keep that in mind.''

Frank followed his family across the gravel, staring through
the intersection at the starry void on the other side. As Max had
promised, hidden among nozzles with peculiar shapes and open-
ings was one that closely resembled a standard gasoline filler. As
he lifted it from its support hook the word UNLEADED appeared in
glowing letters on the metal of the pump housing. There was no
visible meter: no digital readout, no rotating numbers. He shrugged,
flicked open the filler cap cover, removed the cap, and shoved the
nozzle in as far as it would go before pulling on the trigger. Gas
began to flow. It stank like ordinary unleaded.

As he filled the tank he watched his family climb inside.
Mouse and Burnfingers waited till last.

"Do you know this place?" he asked suddenly. "What's this
Conjunction, anyway?''

Mouse paused on the steps. "I imagine it's just what they say
it is. A conjunction." She looked thoughtful. "A place where
different strands of reality come together." She smiled and followed
Alicia inside. Burnfingers winked at him.

"Think of it that way, anyhow."

"I'd rather not think of it at all." The pump clicked off,
indicating the tank was full, and Frank slipped the nozzle back
onto its hook. As he was securing it he found himself looking
back toward the café. The continuously changing sign over the
entrance was a blur of icons and glyphs and letters.

He thought he saw a figure standing by one window. It was

eight feet tall, completely covered in a glistening bronze fur, and wore a white apron. As he stared, it extended coppery cables from one arm to lift a sugar shaker off a table. The shaker turned into a tiny glass hydrant full of blue bubbles. Frank shook his head, looked again. When his eyes refocused they saw something like an anemic bear wearing a florid turquoise jumpsuit. It was clutching an armful of purple popsicles.

He could have looked again but decided it might be bad for his eyesight. Not to mention his sanity. Instead, he worked his way around to the front of the motor home and concentrated on checking the oil and coolant levels. It was with difficulty and determination that he kept himself from turning again toward the café.

Back inside, he slid down into the driver's chair and distastefully studied the gravel lot. Beyond it lay half a dozen ephemeral roadways bordered on all sides by impossible emptiness.

"Which way?"

"Back onto the road we were traversing," Mouse told him firmly. "That's the way. That's the path."

"Seems to me I've heard that before." With a sigh he started the engine and pulled out of the lot.

As they left the pumps behind, another vehicle pulled in behind them. It looked like a broken sequoia and went *whisper-whisper* as it settled to the ground beside the row of pumps. Out of it drifted eyes attached to a thin body and gossamer wings. It removed a black wire from a pump and stuck it into the tree trunk. The odor of rotten eggs and fried pineapple filled the air behind them.

Frank didn't even breathe hard as they sailed off the sand onto the highway that stretched out into nothingness. At first he found it hard to concentrate on the road because he was constantly glancing at the rearview mirror. The Conjunction did not vanish abruptly, as if in a dream. Instead, it faded slowly like an ordinary roadside pullout, a bright beacon of light and friendship and consciousness. The last of it to disappear from view was the mysterious many-tongued illuminated sign, flashing its simple welcome to everyone and anyone, a cosmic lighthouse in the middle of the Great Abyss.

Sorry as he was to leave it behind, he felt better than he had in quite a while. The motor home's tanks were full of honest gas and their bellies full of honest food. He wondered if he'd ever again enjoy so fine a meal served by such congenial hosts.

He drove for an hour, two, before the road ahead began to lighten. At Alicia's shout everyone crowded forward.

They were leaving emptiness behind. Sky appeared and beneath it low hills covered with trees. Piles of dark volcanic rock formed gullies and arroyos on both sides of the road that shut out the void. They had arrived somewhere.

Not home, though. The rocks appeared normal enough but the trees were distorted parodies of healthy growths. Their branches twisted and curled in defiance of gravity, which was not so surprising since none of them were rooted in the earth. They floated just above the surface, their roots dangling in air. Nor were they fixed in place. Each moved with extreme slowness, propelled by the feathery waving of fine rootlets. Occasionally they bumped off each other like birds flying in slow motion.

As they stared, half a dozen fish came flying by. They were about a foot in diameter, black with silver stripes. As the motor home approached they suddenly veered leftward, their fins and tails rippling as they vanished into the distance. Alicia's eyes were wide and Frank clung grimly to the wheel. He had to because the roadway was rippling beneath them, having turned the consistency of taffy. Somehow the motor home clung to the surface, the wheels hanging on with deep tread instead of fingers. Or maybe the rubber had grown claws. Frank didn't look because he was afraid of what he might see. And it was imperative they stay on the road. He firmly believed that if they wandered off the pavement, the motor home might start drifting like the incredible hovering fish, a steel bubble floating forever through an unstable reality.

Another school of larger fish swam lazily across the road in front of them. A family of little round heads atop bodiless legs scrambled into a protective gully. Frank thought he could hear them bleating as the motor home went past.

Whether benign or malevolent, at least every reality line they'd visited thus far had exhibited the familiar constants like air, gravity, and internal logic. It was the same in Pass Regulus as it had been in Hades or at the Conjunction. Now they found themselves on a line somewhere between reality and chaos, where the simplest laws of nature appeared to have been repealed.

"What kinda place is this?" Steven's face was screwed into an expression of distaste and puzzlement.

"I am sure I don't know." Mouse was as intrigued as any of them.

"Maybe we'll get through it quickly." Alicia glanced hopefully at her husband, found no reassurance there. Unable to come up with any explanations for his own questions, he had none to spare for her.

They drove past a grove of upside-down trees. These balanced themselves on delicate branches, their roots hanging in the air like the hair of an old woman. They grew among rocky outcrops that drifted above grass, which in turn grew half an inch above the soil. A flock of raucous birds erupted from the ground beneath one tree, assembled briefly on its roots, then dove beak-first back into the earth.

"Too weird," Wendy muttered.

The engine chose that moment to sputter and miss. The motor home shuddered. Then the electronic ignition refired and they lurched forward.

Frank found he was sweating. If the engine died here they might never get it going again. In a place like this, where natural law seemed to be on a permanent vacation, a familiar internal combustion device might decide to start putting out ice cubes instead of heat. The word for this reality line was *subversive*.

"I've never been anyplace like this," Mouse was saying.

"I've never *imagined* anyplace like it." He kept resolutely to the pavement.

A tapping at his window brought his head around sharply. Three large angelfish drifted just beyond the glass, keeping pace without visible effort. He checked the speedometer, which read sixty. The fish in front was black with yellow stripes, while its companions were orange and white. The leader was tapping on the glass with a fin. Frank hesitated, then cracked the window a few inches. The fish drifted up to the gap.

"Pardon me," it said in perfect English, "but I don't think I've seen you here before." Its fins rippled smoothly as it swam alongside.

"We're just passing through." After all they'd experienced, it seemed almost normal to be conversing with a fish. If this variety fell in the water, he wondered, would it drown? "We're on the right road, ain't we?"

"You're on the only road," the fish assured him. Silver-dollar-sized eyes pressed curiously against the glass.

"Peculiar creatures," opined one of the orange swimmers. "Strange habitat. Could we come inside? Just for a quick visit. We won't stay long."

"I don't know." Frank glanced back at Burnfingers.

"Some of my best friends are fish," came the reply. "Fishy, anyway."

Why the hell not? Frank wondered. He rolled the window down all the way.

Given their speed, the entering fish should have been accompanied by a stiff breeze, but there was no wind at all. They came in wiggling their fins. They poked curiously at everything and everyone, but they couldn't do any harm because they had no hands.

"A nice shape," one of the orange visitors decided. "Next week it might be different, but right now it's a nice shape."

"We're very big on streamlining, you know," its companion declared. "It's hard to be both elegant and streamlined."

"A machine," the other announced with satisfaction. It was poking at the stove like a bottom feeder hunting for worms. "We haven't seen machines in—actually I can't remember the last time I saw a machine. Or if I ever did."

"It's nice to have visitors," said the first. "We don't get many. This isn't a very busy road."

"I can see why," said Frank fervently. "You might arrive looking like one thing and leave looking like something else. Or nothing else."

"It's possible but not likely," said the black and yellow. "Just looking at you I can tell you're all too tightly bonded for that. Your request self will never assert itself. At least not right away."

Frank was tempted to press a little harder on the accelerator but didn't dare. The one thing they could not afford to do was lose control of the motor home. This was no place for reckless driving.

Flucca was keeping a wary eye on the floating fish as he spoke to Mouse. "Are you sure this isn't Chaos?"

"Chaos?" The orange fish laughed, a bubbly, watery sound. "Goodness no."

"Well, you don't seem very organized here."

"Existence is wasteful without flexibility," the black fish told him. It made an effort to smile. "This isn't Chaos. There are the Free Lands. Freedom is not Chaos, though there are similarities."

One of the orange floaters nodded. "Freedom is just Chaos with better lighting."

"It's all in how you perceive reality." The black spun in a tight circle. "Best not to examine too closely the underlying truths. They can be upsetting. Speaking of which, you all are so nervous and uptight. Any stomach pains?"

"No," Alicia responded. "Actually I feel fine. It's just that we're in a hurry to get somewhere and these detours are kind of trying."

"No detours here, unless you want to take them." The orange fish were swimming toward the open window. The black hurried to join them. The unlikely trio exited together.

"Machines," one of them muttered disapprovingly.

"Wait, wait a second!" Frank waved anxiously. "How much farther does this road go?" There was no answer. The three angelfish were already falling behind as they swam in stately formation toward the floating mountains that dominated the distant horizon.

"Well," Alicia observed after some time had passed, "at least the natives are friendly."

"And maybe good to eat," said Burnfingers undiplomatically.

"I wonder what they look like when they're not being fish?" Wendy mused.

"I don't know." Frank kept his eyes resolutely on the road ahead. "But let's not ask for any demonstrations. Uh-oh." He braked, disconnecting the cruise control. The motor home began to slow. Mouse moved up for a better look.

"What's the matter?"

"Maybe it isn't Chaos, but there's a little too much freedom ahead."

They were coming to a split in the road. Not a fork or another off ramp. A hundred yards in front of the motor home, the pale pavement degenerated into a tangle of possible pathways. Some curved skyward at impossible angles. Others plunged into solid

ground. A few curled round and round like endless corkscrews. If
he drove onto one of those, Frank wondered, would he fall off
when the road turned upside-down, or would they just keep on
going?

In any case, he had no intention of plunging headlong into
that mass of multidirectional spaghetti. There was no one in front
of him, no one behind. He slowed, pulled off onto what he hoped
was a paved shoulder, and stared.

"Did you ever see anything like that?"

"Sure. Lots of times," said Burnfingers. "On the reservation. Sheep guts." Behind him, Wendy made a face.

"How do I know which one to take? There aren't any signs.
Leastwise nothing I can read."

There were a good three dozen possible routes, provided one
took into account suspension of certain natural laws. Objects
floated around, over, and through several of the roadways. Some
were even recognizable.

"We could ask the fish," Wendy suggested, "if they'd come
back."

Her father looked to the side. A school of silvery shapes
glided through the air half a mile distant. They showed no sign of
moving closer.

"Maybe if we just wait," Alicia said hopefully, "someone
will come along who can give us directions."

"Sure, and maybe we'll all come apart like toys."

"Or turn into fish!" Only Steven was excited by the possibility. "I wanna be a tuna."

"You like to eat tuna," his mother reminded him gently, "but
I don't think you'd like to be one."

"I would if I could fly."

"Nobody's flying anywhere," his father said sternly, "least
of all in this motor home. This is our anchor, the one stable thing
in this whole crazy place. Nobody turns into anything unless we
all do so together." He looked at his wife. "I think you're right,
hon. I think we stay here until we can get or figure out directions,
even if we have to ask an oak tree in Bermuda shorts."

But nothing much came by, certainly nothing likely to offer
directions. Once a school of large sardines swam over the top of
the motor home. They giggled ceaselessly while ignoring the
bipedal entities trapped inside.

"Wish we hadn't used up all the propane," Frank muttered as he nibbled on a sack of Doritos.

"We did not have much choice," Burnfingers reminded him. "We could not make a partial bomb. As for myself, I am enjoying the cold snack food. For a long time all the food I had to eat was hot."

"You think we'll ever get out of here?" Flucca asked him.

"Of course we will." Burnfingers chewed on a pepperoni stick. "We have gotten out of every other place we've been."

"I wish I had your confidence." Frank stared morosely at the impossible interchange frustrating their progress.

"Don't worry, sweetheart." Alicia patted his arm. "We'll make it. Hand me that box of raisins if you're finished, will you?"

"Sure." He complied, found she was eyeing him strangely. "Something wrong?"

"I don't know."

"Then what are you staring at?"

"Your arm."

"What's wrong with it?"

"Nothing, I guess. Except you used to have only two."

He frowned at her, then down at himself. A third arm had grown from one shoulder. He raised it, watched the fingers respond to mental commands with a mix of fascination and horror.

"The fish." Mouse was staring at him, too. "The fish said something about our 'request' selves."

"That's neat, Dad," said Steven. "Can you grow another one?"

"What are you talking about? I don't know. I don't want to." As he finished, a fourth arm emerged, then two more. He tested them all, wiggling the fingers, the arms bending and moving gracefully. "This could be handy, except when you needed a new shirt."

"You always were the grabby type," Alicia told him.

"Don't get funny. What about you? If I'm gonna look ridiculous I don't want to do it alone."

"All right." She closed her eyes and strained. Her arms did not multiply, but a faint pink aura appeared in the air surrounding her, a rose-hued mist. "I'm sorry," she said. "I guess I can't do it."

"But you did something else," Mouse told her. "Try again."

Alicia took a deep breath and concentrated. Soon a tremendous feeling of health and well-being filled the motor home, wiping away fear and concern, relaxing them all, reassuring and warming. It radiated from Alicia, a pure femininity encompassing sensuality and maternal affection. Frank recognized it right away. He'd felt it before, only nowhere near as powerfully. It was one of the things that had first attracted him to his wife. She'd always had it. The difference here was that instead of concealing it within, she could let it spread outward like a bracing pink wave.

She slumped, blinking. "That felt good, even if I didn't grow any extra arms."

"It made all of us feel good." Mouse was smiling. "That's a very special ability, Alicia. Maybe more than roads intersect at this place."

"Hey, look at me, everybody!"

They all turned. Flucca stood in the middle of the motor home, gesturing excitedly. "Watch this." As they stared, two Fluccas ran toward each other and melted together, like a trick on television.

"Do that again," Burnfingers asked him.

"No problem." Snapping his fingers for effect, the dwarf executed a neat pirouette. One of him jumped left, the other to the right, and once more there were two of him. The first jumped on the second's shoulders. Four stubby arms extended parallel to the floor.

"I always knew I was a normal-sized person. But there was only half of me in the real world."

"Maybe more than half," Burnfingers suggested. "Try it again."

"Really? You think so?" Both Fluccas spoke simultaneously. It was purer than stereo. Both snapped their fingers at the same time, jumped—and the back of the motor home was occupied by four very short Mexican chefs.

"That's enough," said Frank. Looking at the four Fluccas hurt his head.

"The unending Niccolo." Burnfingers's voice had fallen to a whisper. "I wonder how many of him there really are?"

"More than meets the eye, which is what I've been telling people for years." Like the cards in *Alice* he jumped back together until only one of him stood before them. "Always was my own best company."

"What about you, Mouse?" It was Alicia who posed the query. "What can your secret self do?"

"I am a singer. I am a singer here, I was a singer in your reality, I would be a singer on any reality line. Nothing more or less."

Disappointed, Alicia looked past her. "Then what about you, Burnfingers?"

"I do not know." He peered back at Flucca. "What should I do? Snap my fingers, or turn a circle, or hold my breath?"

"Try and let your inner self emerge," Mouse told him. "I think that's what the fish meant."

"All right. Hey-ah."

He stood up, smiling. A serious smile this time, not sappy or half-cocked. As they looked on, he began to grow. Slowly at first, then more rapidly. His head bumped the ceiling.

"Maybe I had better go outside."

"I dunno." Frank hurriedly checked the windows.

"The fish are not going to carry me away." He opened the door and stepped outside.

As he grew, his body diffused. The ground did not splinter under his weight. In minutes he was a thousand feet tall and several hundred wide. It was possible to see through his vapor-thin feet.

"That's enough, Burnfingers!" Alicia had rolled down her window and leaned out to watch. Now she yelled worriedly. Frank crowded behind her while the children, Mouse, and Flucca spread themselves from the door to the rear windows.

A thin voice drifted down to them from up among the clouds. "I can't stop. I cannot stop myself."

"You gotta stop!" Frank shouted.

"Please, Burnfingers! It's not funny anymore!" Alicia screamed.

"It never was very funny." They couldn't see his face anymore. "But it sure is enlightening."

Then he was gone. Or it seemed he was gone. They argued about it. Neither Frank nor Alicia could see anything, but Mouse insisted Burnfingers Begay was still standing there, his position unchanged.

Frank straightened. "I knew he shouldn't have gone outside. I

knew it. The only reality we've got left is in here. As soon as he
went out, that was all she wrote. No more links with his own
reality."

"He's still there," said Mouse, disagreeing fervently.

"Yeah? Where?" Frank made a show of studying the terrain
outside. "I don't see him."

"He kept growing," she insisted. "As he grows, he becomes
more spread out, until the atoms of his body are so far apart it's
the same as if he's become transparent. Now he is an echo of a
shadow of an outline."

"Solid like a brick," Frank muttered.

"Say, rather, less than an echo but more than a memory." She
stood in the open doorway, staring at the strange land beyond.

"What do we do now?" There was sadness in Alicia's voice.
Though at first suspicious of him, she'd grown quite fond of
Burnfingers Begay, and not only because he'd risked his life to
help rescue her and her children from the mutants of a devastated
Salt Lake City. She'd come to like him for himself.

"We stay here until we're sure which road to try or until our
food runs out, whichever comes first. That's all I know how to do.
Mouse?"

She didn't reply, just kept staring out the open door.

15

THEY WAITED IN VAIN for a sunset. If there was a sun hereabouts it worked longer hours than their own. Rather than coming from a source in the sky, the light of this country was evenly distributed, like particles suspended in water. Eventually they slept despite the ceaseless illumination.

Frank was dozing when Steven's excited voice woke him.

"Dad, Mom, everybody, wake up!"

Frank's eyelids rose ponderously. "What is it? What's the matter, kiddo?"

"It's Burnfingers! He's coming back!"

"Steven, no!"

Ignoring his mother, the boy threw open the door and dashed outside. Everyone in the motor home rushed for the windows.

Steven stood on the grass that grew half an inch above the ground. He had his head tilted back as he stared skyward, using his cupped hands to shield his eyes. Everyone else looked up as the body of Burnfingers Begay seemed to coalesce out of thin air.

As they watched, he shrank and solidified. Soon he was no more than an Everest-sized Burnfingers, then hillside-size. His legs became opaque as he filled up the space where he'd been. Finally he was as he'd been before. He picked up Steven and tossed him into the air, catching him easily. Steven was still laughing as they walked back to the motor home together.

"I got big," he said in response to the questions on their waiting faces. "I just kept growing and growing and spreading myself out." He glanced at Frank. "Better to grow extra arms, I think."

"We thought you'd evaporated or something," said Alicia relievedly.

"Or come apart," Flucca added.

"Nope. I just got bigger. Than this place, than this world, than this whole reality line. I got so big I could see several reality lines at once. There's a lot to see in just one reality. I got so big I could see right into our own reality. It looks real fine, let me tell you, and damned if it didn't make me a little homesick.

"When I started to come back into myself I made sure to take a good look at part of all the realities I could see. Particularly the roads." He turned and nodded toward the windshield. "I know which line leads to your Vanishing Point," he said to Mouse.

"Did you see anything else?" she asked him intently. "Could you see how the Spinner was doing?"

Burnfingers shook his head. "I guess that was too far up the road. All I could see was that it was the right one. All the roads led to the same place, but this was the one that got there the quickest."

"All realities end there," she murmured. "That's why it's called the Vanishing Point. Are you sure that's what you saw?"

"Sure I'm sure. It was impressive, let me tell you. Enough to drive a person insane. But since I am already crazy it did not bother me at all."

"I'm just glad you're okay." Frank extended a hand. Burnfingers slapped at it and Frank returned the high five. He didn't even mind when Alicia gave their startled guest a surprise kiss and hug.

"All right, then. We know which way we have to go to get where we're goin'. Let's go there and get this taken care of."

"What is really amusing," said Burnfingers, "is that the road to the Vanishing Point leads right back through Los Angeles."

"Now that's funny." Frank was feeling better than he had in some time. "That's the last place in the Cosmos where you'd think reality would be strong."

"A matter of perception," Mouse commented. "Many realities twist back on themselves. I'm not surprised I have to return to where I've been in order to get where I wasn't. It may even be possible for me to leave you at your home and continue the rest of the way myself.''

"Let's not worry about that now.'' Alicia patted Mouse's hand reassuringly. "We've come this far together. If we have to we'll see you through the rest of the way, too.''

"Don't promise so quickly. Once back among familiar surroundings you may not be so eager to give them up.''

"One thing at a time. Let's get back to L.A. first.''

Alicia looked past Mouse and Burnfingers. "Wait a minute, Frank. Don't forget Steven.''

"That's right.'' Wendy retreated to look out the door. "He's still outside, Mom. I'll get him.''

She walked to the doorway, stopped to stare. Her little brother was standing again where he'd gone to meet Burnfingers, but he wasn't alone. He was talking to angelfish. A whole school of them. They swam in close formation around him, a whirlpool of orange and black and red and yellow fins and scales. They were talking to him, and he was talking back.

When Wendy said nothing, Alicia finally rolled down her own window. As soon as she saw what was going on she leaned out and yelled, "Steven! Get back in here! Right now!''

Frank leaned over his wife, the small hairs on the back of his neck rising when he saw his son engulfed by fish that were swimming in air instead of ocean. He rushed to the door.

"Steven! You heard your mother. Get over here!''

The boy turned toward the motor home, peering between the circling fish. His tone was apologetic. "Sorry, Dad. I can't. See, I've been talking to my friends and I've gotta go with them.''

Frank stood frozen in the doorway, gazing in dumbfoundedly at his precocious, overweight son. "This isn't a game, kiddo, and we don't have time to play. We've got to be on our way. We've got to get home.''

"Oh, I know that. You guys go on ahead and I'll catch up.''

"Catch up? What do you mean, catch...''

The sentence died away. He found himself standing and staring, without a net of reason to support him. Ascending at a sharp angle, the school of angelfish climbed into the western sky. Wearing a broad, innocent grin, Steven dog-paddled furiously after them.

"Steven!'' Alicia had left her chair and crowded in the

doorway beside her husband. "Oh my God, what's happening! Steven, this is your mother! You get back here right now!"

The boy had caught up to the school, was surrounded by softly waving fins. He called back apologetically. "I can't, Mom and Dad. I'm really sorry, but I *have* to go." He was at once astonishing and comical as he hung there, treading air. "See, these guys are my friends. They wanna help me find something. Something important."

At any moment Frank expected his son to plunge earthward. He was a hundred feet above the ground and had to shout to make himself heard.

"See," Steven was telling them, "this is the place where everybody finds out what they can do, what they're really about. Dad, you can grow extra arms, and Mom, you're just Mom, only more so. Mr. Flucca can copy himself, and Burnfingers can get as big as he really is, and Wendy just stays scared a lot, and Mouse—Mouse sings, just like she's been telling us all along. Now it's my turn, but I've got to go with these guys." He gestured at the milling, impatient school. "They've promised to show me the important stuff, but I have to go with 'em."

"Steven, you aren't flying anywhere with a bunch of maybe-fish to see anything." Frank tried to make himself sound stern and threatening, but he was too frightened to do a really good job of it. "We're going right now, and you're coming with us."

The boy shook his head. "Sorry, Dad. It's okay, they're friends. I'll catch up. I've *gotta* go with 'em. I'll come back as soon as they've shown me how to do the stuff."

"What kind of 'stuff'?" Alicia didn't really want to know but didn't know what else to say. There was no way for her to go and get him.

Steven's grin got even wider. He sucked in his belly and puffed out his chest. "I can obulate!"

With that he turned and resumed his dog-paddling as the angelfish convoyed him in steady procession toward the clouds.

"Steven, Stevie!" Frank jumped out of the motor home and started running, trying to chase the fleeing flock—or was it school?—on foot. "Steven, come back here!"

"It's all right, Dad." The little-boy voice was confident but very faint now. "Everything's gonna be okay. You guys go on.

Don't worry about me, and tell Mom not to worry, too. I'm with my friends.''

It didn't take Frank long to run out of breath. He slowed, stopped, bending over and sucking air as he rested on the grass that grew above the ground. He lifted his gaze and stared until the school became tiny specks surrounding a slightly larger speck. Then there was only a single speck.

Then there was nothing.

Forcing down the lump in his throat, he turned and walked slowly back to the motor home. They were all waiting for him, silent. He ignored everyone's eyes but Alicia's.

''We have to go after him,'' she said softly.

''How?'' It was a frustrated growl. ''This is a Winnebago. Not a spaceship, not an airplane.''

''Well, we have to do *something*. We can't just leave him here.'' She was looking past him toward the horizon.

He leaned against the doorjamb. ''What do you suggest we do?''

She had no reply to that. It was left to Mouse to comment. ''We must go on.'' The words were painful in the stillness of the day. ''Remember: if we linger too long in any one place it will enable the Anarchis to locate us. Then all will be lost.''

Frank turned to her, his tone bitter. ''What about my son?''

''Little warrior did not look to be in danger.'' Burnfingers too was staring into the distance. ''He said they were his friends. He was very certain. I think they are, and I think they will take care of him.''

''But he'll be marooned here if we drive off! He'll be stuck on this reality line with no way of finding his way home.''

''He seemed sure he would.'' Burnfingers looked down at his distraught companion. ''Always children have to trust their parents. I think maybe this time you are going to have to trust him.''

''Trust him? Trust him to what? A bunch of refugees from some airborne aquarium?''

''I think they are more than what they seem.''

''What,'' asked Alicia numbly, ''is 'obulating'?''

No one knew. No one even had an idea. Not Burnfingers Begay, not even Mouse.

''It must be something really unique or special for him to leave his parents over it,'' Flucca observed.

"He's just a kid," Frank snapped. "He doesn't know what's going on here. He doesn't know what anything's about. To him it's all a big game."

"No, Dad." Wendy put an arm around her father's shoulders. She was looking out past him, in the direction her brother and his friends had gone. "He knows it's not a game. Steven's, like, a pain sometimes. I guess all little brothers are. But he's pretty smart. He didn't think Hell was a game, and I know he didn't think that place we just left was a game, when we were in that cage, and I don't think he thinks it's a game now."

She was interrupted by a distant rumbling, the throaty purr of something darker than hunger on the prowl. Flucca scurried to the rear of the motor home to peer out the back window.

"It's getting dark in back of us, folks, and it doesn't look like nighttime that's coming up on us."

Mouse looked. "The Anarchis. It's too close, much too close." She turned bottomless eyes to Frank. "We must go now. If we're trapped here it will be the end of everything, including hope. The end of my mission to help the Spinner, of your chance to see your son again, of all of us. Do you know anything about the Unified Field Theory?"

"Huh, what?" Frank shook himself, blinked, turned away from the far horizon that had swallowed his boy.

"The Anarchis is kind of a unified field. It's Chaos and Evil personified. If we don't get away from here fast we won't do your son any good at all."

"But if it's coming this way," Alicia said, "and Steven's still here . . ."

"I think he's gone." Mouse nodded toward the horizon. "With his friends. And I don't think he's coming back to this spot whether you're here or not." It was a cold thing to say, but with the entire sky behind them blackening rapidly Mouse had no time to lavish on tact. "He's gone away with his friends, obulated or whatever it is they do. The only way you can help him now is by helping yourselves. We must go on."

"All right." An uncaring numbness had taken hold of Frank. His son was gone. Having accepted that, he found he didn't much care what happened anymore. Not on this reality line or anyone else's. All he wanted was his boy back.

But he was intelligent enough to realize he was out of his

depth, caught up in a maelstrom of implausibilities beyond his or anyone else's experience. Without any knowledge or ideas of his own he had to rely on people like Mouse and Burnfingers Begay to tell him what to do. Mouse said they had to go on. So he would go on. He climbed inside and moved purposefully toward the driver's seat.

Alicia followed closely. "Frank . . . ?"

He shook off her hand, grimly inspecting the instruments. "Mouse says we can't stay here. So we've got to go."

"If we leave this reality he'll never find us. We'll never see him again, Frank."

He looked up at his wife. He couldn't smile. His mouth wasn't working properly. But he tried to sound reassuring anyway. "We don't know that. Just like we don't know anything else here." He started the engine. At least something responded to his wishes, he told himself.

"Frank, he's only a ten-year-old boy. If he doesn't know where he is now, how will he ever know where to find us?"

"Maybe the damn fish will show him. How the hell do I know?" Seeing the hurt on her face, he softened his tone. "Look, sweetheart. We don't have any choice. We can't stay here. Even if we could, I don't think the kid's coming back right away anyhow."

"Dad's right, Mom." Wendy tried to comfort her mother, who was on the verge of tears. "I don't like leaving the little brat here, either, but like Mouse says, we don't even know if he's here anymore. This is the craziest place we've been yet. Maybe— maybe he's on his way home already. Maybe that's where the fish took him. He might even be waiting for us." She made herself sound cheerful. "What if that's what obulating is? Finding the way home?"

Alicia tried to reply but choked and could only nod.

Frank put the motor home in gear, spoke without looking back over his shoulder. "Which way, chief?"

"Straight ahead. First turn to the right," Burnfingers told him calmly.

Hoping Alicia wasn't watching, Frank leaned slightly forward and looked to his right as he pulled out onto the road. There was no sign of Steven or his patrimonial pisceans. Tricky little bastards, he thought furiously. They swim aboard, act curious and friendly, then make off with his kid.

No, that wasn't right, he told himself forcefully. Steven had left with them voluntarily. His friends, he'd called them, and seemed to mean it. He'd always enjoyed flying. Frank prayed fervently that wherever his son was and whatever he was doing at that moment, he was enjoying himself.

It was very quiet inside the motor home. As they accelerated, the ominous thunderheads and querulous lightning shrank behind them. Mouse stood in back watching the clumsy, deadly Anarchis recede. It was tenacious but undisciplined. They could not go around it, but as long as the motor home functioned they could outrun it. It only suspected their presence here, smelled their intentions. Like a blind killer, it would follow remorselessly, intent on stamping out the hope they represented. They had to continue to stay two steps ahead of it. One wrong step and they would all perish.

Along with everything else, she knew.

The Sonderbergs sat side by side, speaking little. They kept their attention on the road ahead, no longer interested in their constantly changing, surreal surroundings. They thought solely of their vanished son.

He'd sounded so relaxed, so confident, Frank mused. Much more sure of himself than any ten-year-old had a right to be. In spite of Mouse's and Burnfingers's reassurances he still had to wonder if he'd ever see his boy again. He found himself regretting all the times he'd yelled at him, usually over little things, inconsequentialities. Now he'd lost him to a world of permanent inconsequentiality.

The highway climbed a grassy knoll before splitting on the other side into a second tangle of curls and twists. Burnfingers Begay confidently pointed the way, remembering the view from his earlier near-cosmic vantage point. Frank drove on, through holes in mountains that weren't solid, avoiding solid holes that drifted in the midst of insubstantial mountains. Climbing vertical lanes that passed between clouds and dived down into dark earth.

They drove a corkscrew of a road, around and around, making half a dozen loops without falling from the summit of each before the highway straightened out. Mist began to close in around them. Frank switched on the motor home's fog lights. They helped some, but the poor visibility forced him to slow. There'd been no sign of the Anarchis for several hours, but he had no intention of stopping and waiting for the soup to lift. Besides, there was no place to pull over. There was only the road and the fog.

Long thin shapes with multiple wings were dimly glimpsed rafting through the grayness. They had bright yellow bodies stiff as rulers and tiny, unmoving black eyes. They didn't so much fly as paddle through the sky. Later they passed a pair of cow-sized creatures that resembled the deep-sea nightmares Frank had once seen in a National Geographic documentary: all mouths and guts. But they had no teeth. They were consuming the fog, taking huge gulps of the stuff. Wherever they bit, a perfect sphere of clarity appeared. They paralleled the motor home for ten minutes, eating lazily, before falling behind.

The road commenced a gradual descent. It also narrowed, which forced Frank to shift into low and kiss the brakes repeatedly as they negotiated one tight turn after another. After a while he could smell the burning brake shoes, a sharp acrid odor which drifted up through the center console.

"Better get to the bottom of this soon, or find a place to pull off," he grumbled. "We have to let the brakes cool down."

"Maybe there?"

Alicia pointed. The fog was rising. Trees materialized out of the mist surrounding them. They looked like normal evergreens. Their roots were planted firmly in the ground, not an inch or so above it. As the mist thinned further they could make out a sweeping panorama of high snow-covered peaks and deep tree-lined canyons. A noisy river rushed down the gorge that paralleled the road. The pavement beneath the motor home's wheels had given way to dirt somewhere back in the fog, Frank didn't recall when or where. Now it straightened and turned to two-lane blacktop.

As he accelerated tentatively, another car whizzed past in the opposite lane. It held another family. Buick, Chevy, he couldn't tell. They were all so interchangeable these days, and it went by fast. Not too fast for him to make out a mother, father, and a couple of kids in the back seat. It might have been the Sonderbergs, except all four were five years younger.

It was followed in a couple of minutes by a battered pickup. Each bruise and paint scrape was a wound of reality. The fog had almost dissipated completely.

"Which way?"

Burnfingers's eyes narrowed as he surveyed the intersection ahead. "I don't know. I did not see this place. My concern was to find the right road, but I did not have time or vision to follow it to its end."

"Turn right," Alicia said suddenly.

Frank eyed her in surprise. "Don't tell me *you've* developed some kind of special sensing ability."

"N-no." She hesitated. "It's just that right feels, well—right."

When Burnfingers said nothing, Frank shrugged. "What the hell. I've taken everybody else's advice."

He made the turn, found himself back on concrete highway. In a little while they found themselves atop an overlook. The road continued on, descending to the vast basin ahead in a series of neat switchbacks. A large truck was grinding its way laboriously up the steep grade.

Ahead lay a vast alkaline lake. A thin ribbon of white, the highway skirted the southern shore before disappearing between two volcanic slopes, like a bit of dental floss cutting between a pair of molars. Something was wrong, Frank told himself. Everything looked too right. His brain was still unwilling to trust his eyes.

Alicia was equally contemplative, but Wendy was bouncing up and down by the time they pulled into the little town that clung to the highway beyond the lake. She read every sign and advertisement aloud, as though claims for fishing lures and ads for chicken dinners were declarations of conquest.

It was so heartbreakingly ordinary it left Frank dazed. He walked through the dream in comparative silence, pumping gas from a real pump, downing fast food at a McDonald's. The teen who took their orders marveled as they polished off three normal dinners apiece. The sole objection came from Flucca, who was disappointed they hadn't been able to find a Taco Bell instead.

"Don't worry," Alicia told him as she finished her second Big Mac and drained the last of her vanilla shake. "I'll introduce you to the right people once we're back in L.A."

"A dream," the dwarf mumbled around a mouthful of fries. "My own reality, the city of the holocaust, all a dream. Only this is real. I proclaim it so!"

"We can all relax, then." Frank wasn't too tired or relieved to be sarcastic. He tapped his fingernails on the Formica, inhaled the smell of salted potatoes and hot grease. "It's real, all right. It's hanging on too long for it to be anything else. We're back. We made it back. Back to reality, *our* reality. Back to normalcy.'' He smiled at Alicia, then looked to his right. His smile faded. "Only you aren't normal. Are you, Mouse? Or whatever your name is.''

She sipped daintily at her Coke. "What is normal?''

"Why do you have to answer all my questions with another question? I hate that.''

"Steven's not here,'' Alicia reminded him. "That's not normal, either.''

"No. It's not normal and it's not right.''

"When I reach the Vanishing Point,'' Mouse told him, "everything will be made right again.''

"Meaning Steven'll come back to us? You can promise that?''

She just looked at him. It was not an answer.

They learned they were in Lee Vining, a little tourist town that catered to fishers and hikers. It sat on the eastern slope of the Sierra Nevada, not far from Yosemite National Park. A straight drive of six to eight hours would put them back in L.A. Back home.

It meant driving through the desert again, a different part of the same Mojave they'd traversed when starting out, so long ago, on their interrupted journey to Las Vegas. They would pass uncomfortably close to Barstow, to the beginnings of bad memories and disconcerting images. No one paid any attention to them as they exited the restaurant and returned to the motor home.

"What will you do when we reach Los Angeles?'' Alicia spoke as she settled back into her seat.

"Continue on my way, with or without you,'' Mouse replied. "We have shaken the Anarchis for a while. I feel confident.''

"When we picked you up you were going *away* from L.A.,'' Frank reminded her.

"Sometimes to get where you are going you have to return to where you have been. Traveling a Möbius strip, you would call it. Not all roads take familiar turnings.''

"I don't understand,'' said Alicia.

"I barely understand myself. The way is difficult and complex. The Vanishing Point does not lie on a map, but rather beyond it.'' She put a hand on the other woman's shoulder. "Do not worry about your son. He's all right. I'm sure of it.''

"I wish I could believe that. I wish I could believe you. I'd feel better if I knew what this obulating was."

"Someday I think he'll explain it himself."

Only exhaustion prevented Frank from driving straight through. After what they'd been through, what they'd experienced, it was a joy to eat ordinary food, to use plain cash and receive change in kind, and to talk with people who looked back at you out of eyes that did not glow. Even Burnfingers Begay, who insisted he needed no sleep, confessed to being tired.

So they spent the night in the town of Mohave, luxuriating in the sappy, reassuring programs and loud commercials on the TV in their room. Not even the rattle of the freight trains that rumbled down the tracks that paralleled the main street could prevent them from sleeping deep and soundly. Nor could Frank's unease at closing his eyes one more time in the desert.

He awoke with a start, to what he thought was growling outside their door. It was only a couple of college students starting up their aged, reluctant sedan. He slipped out of bed and cracked the door of their room. The morning smelled of desert dampness, old boxcars, oil and grease and coffee. All was as it had been when they'd turned out the lights and gone to sleep, with the addition of sun. He felt almost human as he gently woke Alicia.

He made himself linger over breakfast. Waffles and bacon, eggs and hashbrowns and toast. Burnfingers offered to pay for his own, but Frank grandly refused the proffered doubloon.

It was evening when they finally entered Los Angeles. A bad time to be on the road, but Frank didn't mind. There were only two kinds of traffic in L.A. anymore anyway: rush hour and not quite rush hour. He delighted in the sight of the overloaded eighteen-wheeler that crowded him from behind, cheered the Corvette that cut him off in the slow lane. The freeway at rush hour was an old friend newly revisited, harbinger of normalcy, a great rough pet sucking in the sharp odor of unleaded gas and exhaling huge gouts of smog. The lungs of the city breathed around him, and he knew he was home at last.

All that was missing was a familiar, whiny, complaining face from the back of the motor home. Steven's continued absence was proof that memory and imagination were not the same. Everything he remembered had happened. In his mind's eye he saw his son happily paddling away into the sky accompanied by a school of oversized angelfish. Not the last image one expected to have of one's youngest child.

What had been so fascinating? What pull had been strong enough to draw him away from his family? The fish? Obulating—whatever that was? Steven's farewell had been a confident one. "I'll be okay!" he'd insisted. How could he be so certain? What ten-year-old knew anything of the future and its prospects? Frank wondered if he'd ever see the overweight little rug rat again.

Of course, he reminded himself unsparingly, they could all four of them just as easily be dead. Or worse, if Mouse's stories of the Anarchis were true. At least father, mother, and daughter were alive and together instead of chained forever in Hell, imprisoned by thugs in an otherworldly casino, or undergoing the torments nuclear-devasted mutants might devise.

Not at all the thoughts to have while cruising down Artesia Boulevard on a bright, sunny summer morn.

16

I T WAS MIDDAY when he left Sepulveda for the Peninsula road. How reassuring to see the Pacific once more, an endless expanse of steel-gray water stretching toward Asia. They cruised past the neighborhood shopping center, its tile roofs sweating in the sun. Malaga Cove was crowded with surfers. Then up into the Palos Verdes hills.

The openers for the electric gate that guarded the driveway were in the family cars. Frank had to exit the motor home and activate the iron barrier with a key.

"Quite a place you got here," Burnfingers observed approvingly as they drove toward the house.

"Couple acres." Frank was unduly modest. "I do pretty good. Work for it."

Flucca stood by a window. "This is what it looks like on my reality line. The architecture's different. I wonder what other realities are like? Maybe there are gardens full of unicorns and griffins."

"Or like the old days when antelope and deer roamed the hills, unrestrained by fences, uncounted by game wardens." Burnfingers bent to survey the well-tended grounds that formed a green California necklace around the single-story house. "Where men counted coup with clubs instead of H-bombs. Do you know, little singer, where you are now?"

Mouse shook her head. "I've never been here before. It lies on a path I must take for the first time."

It was a rambling ranch-style structure. Lawn, bushes, and flower beds had all been recently trimmed. That meant the gardeners had been here within the past couple of days. They had only cutworms and beetles to battle, he mused. Hibiscus and geranium bloomed profusely. Iceplant turned one steep hillside facing the ocean a bright pink. It was all soothing and relaxing. He discovered he was looking forward to getting back to work with messianic intensity.

Sara wasn't inside. The maid usually left after lunch. Alicia insisted on taking care of her home to the full extent of her abilities, hence they engaged only part-time help. It was just as well. Sara would have been surprised to see them back home so far ahead of schedule.

Frank set the brake, then joined the others in front of the main entrance. Burnfingers was eyeing the still open gate.

"I expect I will be on my way now."

"Nonsense! You come right inside and rest." Alicia took his arm. "You too, Mr. Flucca. I promised I'd call some people on your behalf and I'm going to do exactly that, just as soon as we've all settled down a little."

"Just show me the kitchen." Flucca was rubbing his hands together in expectation. "It's been so long since I've had a chance to cook with proper utensils I'm afraid I may have forgotten how. Leave dinner to me."

Mouse was gathering her dress around her, tightening the silken folds. "And I must be on my way. My time is no less precious here than elsewhere."

"You'll make better time if you have a good night's sleep and start fresh in the morning." Frank knew that tone. His wife would not be denied. "We'll pay your plane fare if necessary."

"You forget. I cannot travel by plane."

"Oh? Do planes upset you?"

"No." She smiled. "Something about me tends to upset planes. I must continue on the ground. Still, you are right. A meal and shower would be refreshing and speed me on my way. I am more confident now. The Vanishing Point cannot be far. I have managed to turn time and place back upon themselves. I am near enough to sense the Spinner's presence now. Its agitation increases, but if I am not challenged or delayed further I believe I'll be in time to do the necessary work.''

''Then it's settled.'' Alicia was pleased. ''We have guests.''

Recently scrubbed and polished by Sara, the house smelled faintly of lemon oil and disinfectant. Wendy vanished into her room while Alicia and Flucca headed for the kitchen. Frank was giving Mouse and Burnfingers Begay a tour of the house when the tall man spotted the big swimming pool out back.

''A swim and a bath.'' He sighed appreciatively. ''Those are two things I badly need. You will have to excuse me from the rest of your tour.''

Frank had a moment of uncertainty over the ''bath'' part, then was deriding himself for his hesitation. If Burnfingers wanted to take a bath in the pool, or go swimming in the tub, or set fire to the furniture, he'd more than earned the right to do so.

He did not expect, when he returned from changing into clean clothes, to see the Indian and Mouse floating side by side in the shallow end of the pool, completely naked. Wendy was still in her room while Alicia was helping Flucca make dinner. So there was no one to prevent Frank from standing in the hall and staring as Mouse emerged from the water. He half expected to see tiny wings attached to her shoulders, but her body was perfect. Not a blemish or wrinkle marred her sleek torso. In pretty good shape for someone thousands of years old, he told himself. He was unaware of the grin that had spread across his face.

He watched motionless for a long time, drinking in the sight of her as she dried herself. Once he found himself wishing he was ten years younger. It took a moment to remember who and where he was, and what he was not. Then he headed for his office, a converted bedroom at the back of the house.

It required him to pass his son's room. The door was shut. Frank found himself slowing, forced himself to hurry past. Concentrating on making it back to L.A. had helped him to forget a little. Now that he was safely home, emotions forcibly shunted aside returned in a rush.

Alicia had kept her composure by making constant small talk and by avoiding this part of the house. As for himself, despite a strong constitution, he knew that if he opened that door and saw the model spaceships dangling from the ceiling, the nature posters and charts on the walls, and the small but carefully labeled rock collection that filled its own bookcase, he'd lose control. So he didn't slow down until he'd reached his office.

His desk was spotless, surrounded by work. Piles of paper and magazine articles were neatly arrayed on the carpet. Frank had a perverse fondness for using his desk as a place to rest his feet and the floor as a desk.

Slumping gratefully into the high-backed leather executive chair, he hit the first button on the telephone, waited impatiently for the autodialer to connect him to his company vice president's private receiver. There was a click. The familiar, lightly accented voice that spoke sounded bored.

"Yes."

"'Morning, Carlos."

The voice turned instantly attentive. "Frank? Where the hell are you, man?"

"Home." He sighed deeply, aware that the speakerphone would pick it up as clearly as any word.

"What do you mean, 'home'? I thought you'd be spread out by the pool by now, with a cool drink in one hand and some dark shades so you could watch the *muchachas* parading by without Alicia noticing."

"It just didn't work out. *Comprende?* Anyway, I'm home."

"Not much of a vacation, boss."

No, it wasn't, Frank thought to himself. You'll never know the half of it, my friend. Aloud he said, "How's business?"

"You haven't been gone long enough for any crises to develop. Everything's under control."

"I know that. You run the outfit better than I do, anyway."

Carlos voiced a polite protest while Frank continued to praise him. It was an old game the two men played, and a comforting one. They'd been friends for nearly two decades. Carlos was one of the first men Frank had ever hired. Together they'd filled the back of a rented truck and gone door-to-door peddling aluminum baseball bats and used mitts and uniforms to city parks, Lions Clubs, and Little Leagues.

"Gimme a quick rundown anyway."

Carlos proceeded to do so, efficiently and without hesitation. As Frank suspected, there was nothing requiring his attention. He thought a moment, then straightened in the chair.

"I'm comin' in for an hour or two anyway."

"*Bien*. Should I warn people?"

"Naw. Surprise inspections ain't my style. I'm not looking to catch anybody out."

"I know. Hey, I may not be around when you arrive. I've got an appointment with a Voit rep downtown. Some problems with restocking. You remember? They want to double a few prices."

"Yeah, I remember. Go ahead."

"We're doing lunch." Carlos sounded uncertain. "I can cancel out if you need me."

"No sweat. See you tomorrow."

"Yeah, sure. Hey, Frank, you sure everything's okay?"

"You bet. We just decided to skip Vegas this year."

"Your choice, not mine."

The phone clicked and the speakerphone whined over the loss of signal. Frank silenced it, then leaned back in the chair. The surroundings didn't prevent him from thinking of his son. Maybe Mouse would come across him in her journeying and send him home, or maybe he'd return on his own. From wherever it was he'd got to.

Feeling almost human again he returned to the kitchen. Burnfingers and Mouse still drifted in the pool. The insistent chirp of an electronic keyboard emanated from behind the door to his daughter's room.

Alicia and Flucca were filling the kitchen counter with dishes, utensils, and spice bottles. Flucca stood on a step, mincing vegetables. Oil simmered in a pan on the stove. His wife was hacking at a huge block of frozen hamburger.

"Just called the office."

"That's good, dear. Everything okay?" There was just the slightest edge in her voice.

"A-okay. I'm gonna drive in for a bit."

That made her turn, putting the meat aside. "Oh, Frank, we just got back."

"It's something I want to do. Maybe I'm not sure we're back yet. I just want to check in, look around." He smiled. "Won't be gone long. You'll be all right." His arms went around her waist. "Burnfingers Begay is still here, and Mouse."

She finally managed a nod. "Niccolo, too. I guess I'll be okay. Why shouldn't I be? We're *home*."

He made a show of inhaling deeply. "Mmmmm. Guarantee you I'll be back in time for supper."

"You better be, Mr. Sonderberg, or I'll be damnably disappointed." Flucca waved a butcher knife at him.

As he left the kitchen for the garage, Frank was humming to himself. The Jaguar started cleanly and he didn't give it much time to warm up, pulling straight out onto the driveway past the motor home. Habit made sure he shut the electric gate behind him.

There was little traffic on the Peninsula drive. At the base of the palisades he could see surfers and tanners intersecting at the waterline. Not much surf today but plenty of sun. Like everyone else in Southern California he'd dreamed of riding the waves. Never tried it, though. As a kid he'd considered roller skates an invention of the devil. He was not now nor had he ever been built for any kind of athletics. Maybe that was what had driven him to enter the sporting goods business. Ironic, like so much of his life.

He cut away from the beach, taking a main surface street and avoiding the freeway. Today the parade of fast food restaurants, discount stores, gas stations, and shopping centers was anything but boring. His company leased the top third of a twelve-story glass-sided office building in downtown Long Beach. More impressive offices were to be had in West L.A. or along Wilshire, but the tax situation was better in Long Beach, it was closer to where he wanted to live, and this way he could personally inspect every shipment that arrived from overseas. Besides, he liked the smell of the sea. From his top-floor office he could just see the big container ships entering and leaving the harbor.

A card raised the gate that barred entrance to the underground parking garage. He found his space and backed in. The elevator lifted him to twelve and he exited onto thick carpet. The receptionist greeted him in surprise. Everyone knew the big boss was off on vacation. All she could manage was a startled, "Welcome back, Mr. Sonderberg."

"Thanks, Ellen." He prided himself on knowing the first names of as many of his employees as possible, from executive on down to the boys in the mailroom.

He strode past her into the administrative offices, drawing a few startled glances from behind computers and desks. No one said anything. If the president of the company wanted conversation he'd let them know.

His own office was situated in the back of the building, with a fine view of city and harbor. His long-time secretary wasn't at her desk, though it showed signs of recent occupation. In the ladies' room or on afternoon break, he told himself. No matter.

His office was as he'd left it a few days earlier. Once seated behind the big desk he flicked his own terminal on, calling up facts and figures and spread sheets to review what had taken place in his absence. There was very little, just as Carlos had told him. He was relieved to see that nothing untoward had occurred in this reality while he'd been racing wildly through several others. Figures were constants everywhere. They never panicked the way people did.

The refrigerator beneath the bar yielded a cold seltzer. As he sipped straight from the bottle the intercom buzzed for attention.

"Yes?"

"Mr. Sonderberg? What are you doing back?"

"It's okay, Nina. We cut it a little short."

"I'm sorry, sir." His secretary's voice sounded slightly hollow over the intercom's speakerphone. "You were so looking forward to it."

"We just decided we'd be better off taking it easy at home. Is there anything I should look at while I'm here? I'm going back home in a few minutes."

"Well—there are some papers . . ." She rattled off a string of comfortingly familiar names.

"Bring 'em in." As long as he was in the office he might as well do some work. Alicia often told him it was impossible for him to relax anymore, that he'd forgotten how to take it easy. Her scolding troubled him because he knew she was right, but when you're running a business with thousands of employees and millions in daily transactions you just can't write it out of your thoughts.

Another ten years and he'd retire, quit with more money that he'd ever be able to spend. Then maybe they'd take that round-the-world cruise Alicia was always talking about. He'd show her how to relax!

Nina entered, a sheaf of paper in one hand. She was every inch the model executive secretary, confident enough in her ability to let her hair turn gray where the auburn was beginning to age. She wore a brown business suit, a white ruffled blouse, and another of those antique brooches she collected.

"I can't say that I'm sorry to see you back, sir."

"Don't give it another thought, Nina. We just cut everything short."

"I'm sure I don't know why, but that's your business, of course." She laid the papers on the table before him.

He was still studying the readout on the amber screen. Not wanting her to think he was ignoring her, he looked up to give her a parting smile.

And froze.

Every drop of blood in his body went as cold as the ice piled inside the executive bar. His secretary of nine years smiled back at him. Nina, Mrs. Defly, his efficient intermediary between this office and the cacophony of the outside world, smiled back at him.

Her eyes were lizard-like slits set against light red pupils.

"I have to go downstairs for a minute, Mr. Sonderberg. I'll be back soon if you need me." She hissed distinctly and a long, thin tongue emerged briefly from between her lips. It was at least eight inches long and forked at the tip.

Frank stared at the door after she'd exited, unable to move, cold sweat gluing his shirt to his back. He'd seen it, no doubt about it. By now he was an expert on the difference between what was real and what imaginary. He told himself it was a freak moment, a tiny final nick in the fabric of existence and nothing more.

Slowly, very slowly, he swiveled his chair and stared out the tall glass windows. Had it grown darker outside since last he'd looked? Difficult to say since the tinted glass deliberately muted the sometimes harsh Southern California sun. Was it muting reality, as well?

It still looked abnormally dark outside. The sky was cloudless. He turned resolutely back to the computer screen.

Gone were the neat rows of words and figures, the reports from cities with difficult diphthongs in their names, the charts and graphs. The amber screen was filled with crawling things. They looked like little green bugs and they were cannibalizing themselves.

He did not think of madness. He did not think of insects. Chaos, he thought.

With both hands on the edge of the desk he shoved his chair away. Tiny yellow squirmy shapes were emerging from the screen, which flowed like amber gelatin. They humped and twisted around the edges of the plastic. Handfuls of them spilled onto his desk, began gnawing at the wood and plastic. Bright yellow worms burrowed rapidly into the structure.

The bottom of the computer cracked open and the machine fell on its side. Smoke began to rise from the jump cables in back. Frank threw up his hands to shield his face as the electronic innards blew.

When he looked back there was only a plastic box with a gaping hole where the screen had been. Black smoke and yellow worms poured out of the opening. Keeping a wary eye on the ravenous burrowers, he abandoned the chair and moved to the far wall where the auxiliary phone was mounted. It was definitely too dark outside now. He punched in the number for building security.

Laughter instead of the musical acknowledgment of Touch-Tone dialing filled his ear. It was inhuman and insane. Then a click followed by a recording of a female voice:

"When you hear the tone, the world will have come to an end."

More laughter. He dropped the receiver, letting it bounce against the wall. Red worms began oozing from the handset and smoke from the housing.

"It's here," he mumbled dazedly to himself. "In Los Angeles. The Anarchis."

Maybe not. Maybe it was just the turn of this reality to come apart as the threads of its existence started to unravel. His reality was twisting, snapping all around him. He fancied he could hear it groan. Screams and shouts and other less pleasant, less human voices were coming from the outer offices. He ran to the door and flung it wide.

Madness had advanced further and faster here. High-pitched yowls and inhuman gruntings rose above the noise of broken terminals and whining phones. Overwhelmed ceiling sprinklers deluged the whole floor with tepid water.

The inhabitants of the building were no longer recognizable. Some had grown enormous chests or bellies and had split their clothing. Others sported horns or long curving fangs protruding from prognathous jaws. Very few looked passably human.

They were doing battle with one another and with the machines. Guts and intestines exploded from computer terminals. Wires and conduits flailed wildly, searching for something soft to grasp, suckers pimpling their formerly smooth surfaces. Blood and black slime covered the floor, making footing uncertain as he stumbled blankly toward the hallway.

Two abominations that had once been human crashed past him, locked in each other's grasp, tearing and ripping. They snapped at each other with sharp teeth an inch long.

Frank had to duck behind a still intact desk as they tumbled by, torn by their own frantic, demonic energy. He didn't see the ugly yellow eye staring at him. Once it had been the innocuous faceplate of a calculator readout. Now it turned with a malevolent sentience. Black, rubbery conduits rose and reached for him. He sensed movement and threw himself aside as they smashed the desk to splinters in a violent, spasmodic attempt to clutch and rend.

He crawled the rest of the way, trying to hug the wall, barely thinking but knowing that he had to get out, get away. There was no sign of Nina Defly, or anyone else he might recognize. They were taken, transformed, damned.

He rose to his feet and staggered out into the hallway. It was a little quieter beyond the offices. The nightmarish conflagration had not yet spilled this far. The receptionist's desk was a shambles. Gasping for air he leaned on the wood for support.

"Ellen? Ellen, you back there?" He looked toward the overturned chair.

A blue-green snake as big around as a man's thigh looked out from its coils and prepared to strike. He screamed and stumbled backward. The head rose on its muscular neck to stare back at him. It was of undeniably feminine cast. One hiss, a single flick of the long tongue, and it struck.

He threw himself toward the elevator and the gaping jaws missed. A hand slapped wildly at the call button set in the wall. Again the monster struck. Frank rolled and the fangs bounced off the steel doors. He could hear the cables rattling in the elevator shaft and prayed the cab was only a floor or two away.

He nearly threw himself inside when the doors parted and just barely caught himself in time. If it hadn't been for the soft, chuckling growl he wouldn't have hesitated.

In place of the empty elevator cab was a huge, rectangular mouth, all soft and pulsing wet. Scimitar-like teeth lined a dark narrow throat leading to unimaginable death. The elevator roared and reached for him. As he turned, a tooth the size of a gallon bucket caught his sleeve. He felt himself being dragged downward. Fear lent strength to his legs as he fought for purchase on the slick hall carpet. As his shirt tore free, the sliding jaws of the elevator slammed shut like a couple of compact cars meeting head on.

At the same time, the snake-thing was striking anew. It shot past Frank's head and turned, only to shriek once as the elevator jaws caught it behind the skull and bit through. Headless coils lashed the walls with frightening energy.

Frank flung aside the door that led to the emergency stairwell and paused at the top of the steps. Below lay only concrete stairs and an iron railing painted bright yellow. He plunged down, taking two steps at a stride. Once he stumbled badly, feared he might have broken an ankle. It was only a cramp. Struggling erect, he braced himself against the railing as he continued his mad descent, checking each new level carefully before hurrying on.

When he reached the fire door that opened onto the second floor, he stopped. Horrible noises came from the other side and blood began to ooze beneath the barrier. It poured across the landing and down the stairs in a crimson flood. Taking a deep breath, he cleared the landing in a single bound. Nothing burst in upon him.

He reached the bottom, ripped open the door that led to the main lobby. Blood flew from the soles of his shoes as he stumbled out into the well-lit atrium. The security guard wasn't at his circular station. In his place was a writhing silicon hydra. Each head consisted of a dislodged security video terminal. They wove hypnotically at the ends of heavy-duty cables like parts of some berserk alien anemone.

Every one of the decorative plants which had adorned the lobby had sprouted teeth and claws. Roots erupted from constraining pots and planters as palms and ferns dragged themselves across the floor to rip and rend their neighbors. Two of the security-terminal hydra's cable-tentacles clutched pistols which had belonged to building security. Frank winched as he heard one go off, saw the bullet score the marble pavement off to his right. He expected more shots, but none were forthcoming. Evidently the monstrosity had emptied the magazines of both guns prior to his arrival.

Frustrated, it threw the empty guns at him. One struck him in the ribs, making him arc in pain. The movement carried him close to a palm with blade-like leaves. It swiped at his neck, just missing the jugular.

He ran the feral floral gauntlet all the way to the main exit and reached for the gleaming brass handle. Tendrils clutched at his legs. They lined a glistening green-black maw that made sucking movements in his direction like some perverted flesh-eating gourami. Before they could reach him, he yanked the door open and stumbled out into the dim, unwholesome daylight.

It was worse outside the building. Smoke and flame billowed unrestrained from several structures across the street. Living things leaped or were thrown from shattered windows. A confusing metallic pileup jammed the center of Beach Boulevard. Some of the broken, crumpled vehicles had undergone the same hellish change as his employees. Steel and aluminum hulks crawled about on flexible tires or rubbery, uncertain legs, chewing and tearing at anything within reach. Gasoline and diesel mixed with blood in the gutters.

As he looked on dazedly, half a dozen newly sentient automobiles pawed the remains of what had been a big tractor-trailer rig. Now it more closely resembled a beached humpback whale being torn to shreds by a pack of killer whales. The rig moaned in agony—a chilling, grating, mechanical cry. Frank turned away, his stomach churning.

The street was full of mangled, broken bodies, some of which were still recognizable as human. Others were bloated or distorted like the raging occupants of his own building. While he stood staring, a man and woman tried to cross the street, angling for the safety of an alley. They were instantly run down by a car whose wheels were still round, but whose headlights and grille had been transformed into a cold inanimate face. Both hapless pedestrians went flying. They bounced off the pavement and lay motionless. As Frank looked on in horror, the car-creature ran over them repeatedly, until little remained save darker stains on an already mottled street.

An iron juggernaut came clanking around a far corner. It was green with black stripes and spots. Originally it had been a skiploader. Now it was crunching the sidewalk across from him, sucking up people and smaller mobile machines with a forty-foot-long tongue, drawing them into a mouth the size of a sports car. A broken fire hydrant spewed blood skyward. Drops of it coated Frank's face and shoulders. The horrid downpour did not stir him because he was already in shock.

Blood ran in a steady stream down the gutter, to vanish into the nearest storm drain. Not all of it was red. Green and orange fluids completed the viscous torrent. The stench of death and burning flesh was worse than any of the sights, overwhelming his senses and threatening to make him faint.

This is it, then, he thought numbly. The End. What happens to reality when the fabric of it finally unravels. Reason was giving way to madness.

Bodies and structures continued to metastasize as he stood there, machines and people changing into ever more grotesque forms. Long Beach Boulevard was now a painting by Bosch, a Claymation film gone insane, with smells and sounds to match.

Halfway up the street a car that was still a car stood parked at the curb. He made for it like a drowning man for a life preserver. It was unlocked, but the ignition was empty. Could he jump the wires? He'd seen it done dozens of times on TV, but he'd never tried it himself. He plunged inside. As he slammed the door behind him, something landed on the hood.

Its pupilless eyes glowed bright orange. Once it might have been a big, friendly dog: a Dane or a Saint Bernard. Now it was a fanged skull fronting a horribly emaciated body. It tried to howl but managed only a feeble choking sound as it dug at the window with stubby, broken claws. Teeth broke and bled as it tried to bite through the safety glass.

Frank tried to ignore the thing as he bent beneath the steering column. A tangle of wires swam into view. They were all color-coded, but which ran to the ignition? Using the tiny pocketknife attached to his keychain, he cut through the whole bundle, praying he wouldn't get shocked. Above and outside the car something moaned.

So far he'd been too busy and too stunned to wonder what might be happening up on the Peninsula, what Alicia and Wendy might be going through. Maybe, he told himself desperately, the unraveling was localized. Maybe up in the hills overlooking the ocean everything was still normal and undisturbed. Could he drive out of this maelstrom of madness even as they'd driven out of other distorted realities in the motor home?

He couldn't go anywhere unless he managed to start this car.

The dog-thing had vanished with a yelp as something larger and more vicious had carried it off. It was better without the moaning. Frank started crossing wires. Once a spark stung his cheek, but the engine remained silent.

Then the front door was torn from its hinges.

He scrabbled against the floor and seat, kicking away from the steering column as something like an immense black slug peered in at him. It had arms like licorice cables. Ropy fingers grabbed his left foot and started pulling him out of the car. He heard himself screaming. As his hips slid over the doorway he threw both arms around the steering column and tried to pretend they were made of the same Detroit steel.

He could feel his arms being slowly pulled from their sockets. Then the awesome grip on his ankle relaxed. Sobbing from the pain, he loosened his convulsive lock on the steering column and turned onto his back.

The shuddering, slug-like mass was quivering in pain. Steam rose from the curve of its bulk. Frank managed to sit up and look out. The boulevard was full of running water. It mixed with the blood and gore briefly before sweeping it away. The rising torrent was rushing up the street from the south. Frank didn't have to taste it to know it was saltwater. Sea water. It ran two inches deep and rose as he watched. That's when he sensed the subtle but steady trembling in the earth.

The land was subsiding, the sea invading a sinking reality. Practically every building still standing was smoking or on fire. The bank across the street shuddered and collapsed, dumping tons of concrete, steel, and glass into the ravaged boulevard. At first he thought the subsidence was the cause, but it might as easily have been a change in the reality of the structure itself.

He bent to work on the wires again and this time was rewarded with a rumble as well as a flash. As he rose he hit the accelerator with his right hand. The motor raced encouragingly. Settling himself behind the wheel he put the car in gear, pulled out into the street. The undercarriage cleared the rising water, but not by much.

Up to Anaheim Boulevard where he turned left, not trusting the lower lying Pacific Coast Highway, which might by now be completely inundated. Water invaded storefronts and homes all around him. He peered grimly over the wheel. If the car held together, in ten minutes he'd be climbing the Peninsula. His home stood several hundred feet above sea level.

So intent was he on watching the rising water and the flooding of the city that he didn't see the truck until it slammed into him. They struck at an angle which sent him spinning two full circles before he came to a halt. Blood trickled from his lip where he'd bit himself. Worse, the front of his vehicle was smashed in. Smoke rose from the engine compartment. When he tried to restart, all his desperate efforts generated was a feeble squeal from the alternator.

The truck had come to a stop nearby. A delivery vehicle of medium size, it had been only slightly damaged by the collision. The Ford emblem on its hood hung askew and there was a long gash on its flank, but otherwise it looked functional.

He stumbled outside and straightened—only to find himself confronted by the truck's occupants. They all wore fancifully decorated uniforms, probably scavenged from some deserted surplus store. Braid and medals and ribbons hung from sleeves and pants legs as well as chests. Some of them were remotely human, but most had metamorphosed completely. Angry animal and mutant faces glared at him. Every one of them carried a club or worse.

A couple grunted to each other as they stood regarding him, grinning nastily. Looking left and right he saw he was almost surrounded. So he jumped on the hood of the broken car and made a break for the only gap in their ranks. As he cleared the roof something struck him painfully in the ribs.

He landed hard in the water-filled street, tried to rise but got no farther than his knees. Inhuman chuckling and laughter came close. With a sob he sat up and clutched his throbbing side, knowing it was all over, finished, done for. No mistake about it this time. He tried to cushion himself with warm memories of his family, especially of Steven. Around him, only the ocean was unchanged. He inhaled the salt air, thankful his last sensation would be a sane one.

They closed in around him, laughing no longer, seriously discussing his demise. He saw each weapon as an individual instrument of death. Cold gray blurs rose over him. Maybe he'd be lucky after all, he thought. Maybe the first blow would be a killing one. The idea of a prolonged beating or dismemberment discomfited him. Closing his eyes tight, he waited for the pain.

Thunder rolled down the street, making him open his eyes and jerk in its direction. He didn't recall seeing a gun in the hands of any of his assailants.

It was such a friendly, natural sound, pure and clean in the smoky air, unaffected by madness and death. As he sat dumbly with the saltwater burning his skin, it echoed a second time. The creature preparing to smash his brains out, which looked like a cross between an ape and a Chinese warlord, spread its arms wide as it was knocked backward. The right side of its skull vanished, blown to bits like a Christmas piñata. The sight did not sicken Frank. He'd seen much worse in the previous half hour.

A third boom was chased by a couple of sharp pops from a smaller caliber weapon. The cordite conversation continued until the last of his tormentors had fled or been flattened. Still clutching his injured rib, Frank gazed in disbelief at the inhuman corpses surrounding him.

The survivors piled frantically into their truck. A ratcheting noise came from the half-stripped transmission as it spun its wheels in the water before rumbling off in the direction of burning downtown Long Beach. Frank followed it with his eyes until he was sure it wasn't coming back. He tried to stand, failed, sitting down hard in the bloody water.

Take it easy, he told himself. Whoever it is, if they want you, they'll get you.

Saltwater, blood, and tears blurred Frank's vision, but he was able to isolate two figures hurrying toward him. Two beasts lucky enough to have found working weapons had slaughtered his attackers. Now they were coming to claim their kill. Doubtless they'd kill him as well, when it suited them. They were only two. Maybe he could get away. With so many bodies to gather maybe they wouldn't waste a precious bullet on one more.

He struggled erect, turned, and tried to limp in the direction the fleeing truck had taken. He thought he heard a final shot but couldn't be sure as his legs gave way beneath him, sending him tumbling again into the shallow water. It was a good six inches deep now, he mused. The whole of Los Angeles/Long Beach Harbor would be submerged.

It was a good final thought to cling to: the unaltered sea rising to reclaim the land. The water would drown the abominations that now inhabited it, put out the fires that tormented the ruined buildings. Too bad he wasn't up on the Peninsula. From the palisades he would be able to watch it all with his family.

A hand grabbed his shoulder and turned him. He expected to see the muzzle of a gun and wasn't disappointed. But the tunnel-like barrel of the big pistol wasn't aimed at him.

"Man, I was afraid we would never find you. You have got balls, and they are not all on the shelves of your stores."

Somehow Frank managed to grin through the pain. "Hi, Burnfingers. Looking for a job already?"

"**C**OME ON, LET'S MOVE it!" Frank recognized the other voice as well. It was high and determined. The .22 looked larger than it was in Niccolo Flucca's tiny hand. "Before we run into any more playful citizens."

"Coming, little kitchen wizard." Burnfingers put a massive arm around Frank and lifted him to his feet. The rib screamed and Frank bit into his lip.

"Can you walk?"

"I dunno, Burnfingers."

"You have to try. I cannot carry you and aim at the same time."

"Then I guess I will walk, won't I?"

He did it by rote, putting one foot ahead of the other, chiding the laggard to follow until it was alongside. Burnfingers helped as much as he could. Flucca walked on the other side, his stubby legs kicking up saltwater, his eyes missing nothing.

"Alicia. Wendy," Frank gasped.

"They are fine," Burnfingers told him. "Your house was unchanged when we left to come look for you and it is well above the rising water." The huge Casull gleamed in the smoke-tinted light. In Burnfingers's fist it looked big enough to blow away the Anarchis itself.

That was another unreality, Frank told himself unhappily.

They were fighting their way toward an island of metal, of sanity. It stood unaltered amid madness and devastation: the motor home. Several new gouges scarred the trim where something had tried to break through. The metal had resisted. A little of the pain in his side and shoulders went away at the sight of it.

"If we survive this I'm gonna buy that damn machine. Alicia can turn it into a planter or the kids can make a rec room out of it. I'll take off the wheels and put it up on blocks, but I'm not giving it back. It's saved my ass too many times."

"It has not saved anything yet." Burnfingers manipulated the keys with one huge hand until he found the one that fit the door lock.

He and Flucca had to help Frank in. Water continued rising around them. What looked like a giant salamander came wriggling through the water toward them. Burnfingers kicked it aside. The contact produced a feeble, gurgling squeal. Tiny dark eyes peered mournfully up at them out of deeply sunk eye sockets. The face was faintly human.

Once inside, Frank headed for his familiar place behind the wheel. Burnfingers gently but firmly eased him into the other chair.

"Not this time, my friend. Now I drive whether you like it or not." Frank was too exhausted to argue.

"All clear!" Flucca yelled as he closed the door and dogged it tight.

Burnfingers turned the motor home around, accelerated slowly so as not to soak the brakes. The water was halfway up the wheels and still rising. Fortunately, the motor home had higher clearance than any automobile.

After a few miles, the road began to ascend, climbing from the industrialized harbor area into the suburban knolls of Rolling Hills Estates. Looking back the way they'd come, Frank saw a ten-foot-high wave advancing across the city. No ordinary surf, it was more like a bore tide. The solid wall of water rushed up the city streets from the harbor to crash against burning buildings. Anything less than a story high was submerged.

Riding the crest of the irresistible tide was an army of nightmares from the depths, all pulsing red gills and snaggle teeth and poisonous spines. Flat, silvery fish eyes burned with an unnatural intelligence. Even at this distance Frank fancied he could hear the bloated bubbling sounds the aquatic invaders made as they began to feed frenziedly on the drowning carcasses of the inundated city dwellers. Hills and trees soon blotted the horror from view.

The Peninsula appeared deserted. Any surviving families were probably cowering inside their homes. There were no other vehicles moving. Palos Verdes had become a Gibraltar-like island anchoring the southern corner of the sunken Los Angeles Basin.

For the moment they were safe, though the land continued to subside. The fabric of reality was unraveling around them faster than ever. At any moment the remaining dry land might sink beneath the hungry waves or be torn asunder by a new earthquake. Gravity itself might end, sending them spinning into space, choking and gasping for air as the planet's atmosphere dissipated rapidly around them.

As they continued to climb he saw that the Pacific had reclaimed all the lowlands. The only evidence of former human habitation were the tops of office towers and luxury condominiums along Wilshire and downtown, and the occasional top lane of some freeway interchange to which crowded cars clung like ants trying to escape a flood.

Burnfingers shifted out of low as the ground leveled off. They drove past denuded eucalyptus, oak, sycamore, and bottlebrush. Even the evergreens had been stripped of their needles. As they crossed the Peninsula and turned south toward his house, they saw the ocean once more. It was bubbling and heaving like a boiling pot. Waterspouts danced across the tormented surface despite the absence of wind. The long brown silhouette of Catalina Island was missing entirely from the western horizon, having vanished completely beneath the waves.

His house still sat intact on its acres, the iron gate guarding the entrance unbroken. Flucca borrowed his key and opened the lock, admitting them to the circular driveway.

As they entered, a vast shadow darkened the motor home. Frank leaned forward and looked skyward, flinched as the monster attacked. It was all teeth and claws and dripping toxins. The motor home rang like a bell when the thing made contact with the roof, but the metal held and they managed to remain upright.

Flucca darted outside, popping away with his tiny pistol. Frank followed, then Burnfingers. The Casull bellowed once, twice. Nothing tumbled to the ground and there was no answering scream, but the shadow vanished.

"It will be back." Burnfingers holstered the now empty hand cannon. "Along with mother knows what else. The world is going crazy."

Frank leaned against the comforting side of the motor home, breathing a little easier. He felt a lot better now than he had when his friends had dragged him from the collapsing city below. The throbbing in his side was starting to relent.

"Nothing's stable no more," Flucca avowed, still scanning the sky. "The fabric of existence is really coming apart." Satisfied that the clouds shielded nothing more than an errant pigeon, he looked over at Frank. "We're running out of time, we are. That's what Mouse told us before we came looking for you."

"That's what she's been telling us all along."

"I was beginning to wonder if we could make it all the way to your office," Burnfingers told him. "Then we saw you lying in the water with that bunch preparing to do you."

"Five more minutes." Frank straightened, able now to stand on his own. "No, I didn't have that much. Three, maybe."

"We have to get her to the Vanishing Point quickly. She is the only one who can stop this."

"You get her there. You and Nick. I'm all out. I'm staying here. I want to die in my own house surrounded by what's left of my family. If things keep worsening at this rate you'll never make it, no matter how close the Point lies."

"That is not like you, Frank Sonderberg." Burnfingers put a big hand on the other man's shoulder. "I have been in worse spots and it has always worked out for me."

Frank was shaking his head. "How would you know if it worked out for you or not? You're nuts, remember? Besides, how can you cope with a situation that changes from day to day, minute to minute? How do you cope with a new reality every time you turn around?"

"You change with it."

"Burnfingers, I ain't like you. You've been some weird places and done some weird things. Me, I'm strictly middle-class straight and normal. I can't take this anymore. *I can't take it*. I'm not the hero type. I knew that when I was growing up, I knew it

when I was going through school, and I knew it when I was
starting my business. I still know it. It's just not in me, understand?''

Burnfingers replied solemnly. ''Sometimes, my friend, we are
forced into situations we don't like, that make us uncomfortable,
that we think we haven't a chance in hell of coping with. But
people cope, Frank. They cope all the time. From what I have seen
of you these past many days I believe you can cope, too. No more
talk of dying in your hogan. This is not the day for it. If you do go
down, we all go down together fighting, if it be against the
Anarchis itself. People were not made so they could cower in their
beds when there was work to be done.''

''You heard the man.'' Flucca headed for the front steps.
''Let's get the others out of there.''

''What about it?'' Burnfingers jerked his head in Flucca's
direction. ''He has half your size and twice your guts.''

Frank hesitated, took a step forward. Too late, he knew he
was committed. But according to Mouse, he'd been committed
since that morning when he'd stopped to pick her up. So why the
hell was he beating himself to death worrying about the inevitable?
When he took the second step, Burnfingers Begay smiled.

''That's better.''

Halfway to the front door the big hibiscus bush on the left
wrapped leafless branches around Frank's waist. He let out a yell
as the branches pulled him toward a mass of leaves that concealed
something wet, green, and threatening. What they needed was an
ax or machete. Instead, they had to make do with Burnfingers's
butterfly knife. It sawed through the branches as the remaining
landscaping began to rustle alarmingly around them. More muta-
tions, more changes.

''See, it's hopeless,'' Frank muttered as he brushed himself
off. ''Pretty soon we'll be fighting crabgrass and bugs.''

''Mankind's always fought crabgrass and bugs,'' Flucca
reminded him. ''Let's get inside.''

The rose bushes were the worst because of the thorns. By the
time they reached the door all three of them were scratched and
bleeding. Burnfingers flailed at the clutching vines while Frank
and Flucca pounded on the door.

''Wendy, Alicia, open up! It's me!''

The door was wrenched inward and he almost fell. Alicia
caught him. She was crying.

"Frank, Frank—I thought we'd never see you again."

"Same here, sweetheart." He held her close, not wanting to let her go.

Only Burnfingers's size and weight allowed him to shut the door against the press of rose bush and hibiscus which a degenerate reality had turned carnivorous.

Wendy stood in the center of the hall, staring blankly toward the door. Her expression was as lifeless as was possible for a sixteen-year-old to muster. Frank tried to manage a smile.

"How ya doin', kiddo?"

She blinked, focused on him. "Daddy. What's going to happen now, Daddy? I thought it was all over and it's only gotten worse, it's gotten worse."

He moved to embrace her. She hardly had the strength left to hug him, having cried herself out earlier. Branches and vines beat a staccato tattoo on walls and roof as the vegetation went berserk all over the Peninsula. They weren't strong enough to penetrate the walls.

"Got anything in the way of large and sharp?" Burnfingers inquired, feeling it was time to interrupt the reunion. "An ax would be nice."

Frank looked back at him, Alicia under one arm and his daughter beneath the other. "This isn't exactly a mountain cabin. What would I be doing with an ax?"

"Thought you might have a fireplace."

"Two of 'em, but we have wood delivered in the wintertime. We don't cut it ourselves." He remembered something else. "Hang on. There are garden shears in the garage. I mean, we have gardening service but we do keep a few tools and—"

Burnfingers was gone already, racing for the garage. Alicia peered up at her husband. "If we have a minute or two, would you like some coffee, dear?"

"God, I'd love some. If it runs normal and doesn't bite."

Mouse greeted him when he entered the kitchen. He waved or said something meaningless—he wasn't sure. Everyone sat down at the dinette and stared at the green carnage taking place in their yard. The double-paned glass kept the rampaging plants away from them but not from each other.

Decorative bushes ripped and tore at each other in eerie silence, the only noise the sound of breaking wood and leaves being shredded. Even the big elm by the back wall had gone mad, flailing away at its smaller neighbors until it found itself locked in a wrestling match with the eucalyptus nearby. Meanwhile, smaller branches and vines flailed wildly at the roof and walls of the house.

The smell of fresh-brewed coffee was a physical presence in the kitchen, its taste wonderfully invigorating. A few things hadn't changed. His family was still human, his house still a sanctuary in a world gone mad.

Certainly Mouse's presence helped. She was leaning against a counter, sipping tea.

"It is getting out of hand. The condition is becoming chronic."

"Now there's a news bulletin," Frank muttered. The coffee was balm to his throat, his stomach, his soul. "The whole city's gone."

"Gone?" Wendy stared at him, eyes wide. "You mean, like, everything?"

"Like everything, kiddo. The sea's come up a hundred feet. Catalina's not there anymore. First the people went nutso, then the machines, and now the land itself. It's all underwater. You didn't see any of it?" His gaze flicked to his wife, who shook her head negatively.

"We haven't been outside since Burnfingers and Niccolo went looking for you. They told us to stay in and keep the doors bolted."

Frank grunted. "Sound advice."

"What's going to happen now, sweetheart?" She was playing at drinking her own coffee, but her hand was shaking so badly she had to set the mug down until the trembling subsided. "What's going to happen to us?"

"I dunno. Our reality's shot regardless."

"Perhaps not," Mouse said calmly.

He stared sharply at her. "Don't you of all people go trying to make me feel better. I've been through hell the last hour and I'm in no mood to be patronized. I know my own reality when I see it. This is my house. I was in my own office, among my own people, until it all turned into something out of a real bad horror movie. Whatever happens now, nothing can change that. Our world is gone."

"Are you so absolutely sure this is your world, then? Your

reality? There are millions of reality lines, Frank Sonderberg. The slightest of differences would be sufficient to distinguish yours from one very much like it.''

He put the coffee down. ''So how do we know if this one is ours?''

''Once the Spinner has been soothed and the fabric of reality made whole again you will return to your one true reality. Only then will you know if this line is yours—or another.''

''And if this one isn't ours, where are the local equivalents of us?''

''In Las Vegas, enjoying your vacation, I should imagine. Provided Las Vegas still exists on this line.''

''You mean, if this ain't our reality and we hang around here long enough we might run into ourselves?''

''Nothing is impossible when reality lines cross.''

''That's enough!'' Wendy rose from the table, screaming and clutching her head. ''That's enough, that's enough, that's enough! I can't understand any more!''

Frank rose to grab her, pull her close. She kept raving. What was he supposed to do, slap her until she quieted? That was what they did in the movies, but this wasn't a movie. This was his daughter who'd suffered too much he was holding in his arms. He couldn't hit her to help her.

So he just rocked her gently and kept telling her everything was going to be all right and, as it developed, that was exactly what was required.

A clattering sounded in the hallway and everyone turned sharply, but it was only Burnfingers Begay returning from his foray to the garage. His hands held the garden shears Frank had remembered seeing hanging on a wall hook. Also two small tree saws and a pair of hand clippers.

''No chainsaw, but these will help. We should take all the big knives, too.'' He looked over their heads. ''Where is Flucca?''

Frank turned a circle. He didn't remember when the dwarf had disappeared. His return coincided with Burnfingers's own.

''We're all here, then.'' Burnfingers nodded to himself. ''We will fight our way out together, as we have done since the beginning. I am glad I will be with white-eyes who have learned how to fight.''

''Fight? Our way out?'' Alicia sounded despondent. ''Frank,

we're not leaving again, are we? Not from here, not from our house."

"It may not be our house," he told her grimly. "Burnfingers is right. We can't stay here. We have to go on until there's an end to all this, no matter who wins. And if this does turn out to be our reality, I don't want to stay here anyway. Not with the whole damn city drowned. At this rate the rest of California's going to go, too. Maybe the whole planet." He looked over at Mouse. "I wish to hell I'd never set eyes on you."

"I'm sorry, Frank Sonderberg. Right now I'm the only reality you have left."

"Yeah, I guessed." At that instant he understood everything better than at any moment since they'd left Barstow. Small comfort at best. "Let's go."

"No, Daddy." Wendy took a step away from him.

"Honey, we have to. We've come too far to stop here. Don't you see? We don't have any choice in the matter. Probably haven't had for some time. Besides," he finished quietly, "if we don't go with Mouse I have this powerful feeling we'll never have a chance of seeing your brother again."

"What makes you think we have any chance anyway?" she replied bitterly.

"Because I believe we do. I believe it because I have to."

Mouse was smiling that thin, enigmatic smile he found so maddening. "I knew you were the right one when you stopped for me, Frank Sonderberg."

He whirled to face her. "How about you shut up for a while?" His anger surprised him. Since he had the strength in him he took the opportunity to rail at God, the fates, and whatever other agency might have played a part in the disintegration of his pleasant, contented life. What he really wanted to do was fight back, but in this war there was nothing to strike out against except the shapeless, ill-defined nemesis Mouse called the Anarchis.

That didn't prevent him from cursing the Cosmos, which he proceeded to do loudly and fluently. When he was finished he gave his wife a hand up from the table.

"We're stuck, sweetheart. We can't go back and we can't stay here, so we have to go on. So we might as well give it our best shot. Whaddaya say?"

Her smile was full of love. "That's how we've always lived,

Frank. I guess I'm too set in my ways to change now even if I want to.''

"That's my gal.'' He kissed her lightly, then turned to Burnfingers. "I think we're ready.''

"I know it is so, my friend. Now, everyone grab something useful. Knives, cleavers, food, bottled water, juice—anything we might need.''

They loaded themselves down, filling pockets with food and medicine, arming themselves with makeshift weapons. Mouse carried more than her share, but she was so full of surprises Frank didn't even blink at the size of the sack she slung over her shoulder.

As they assembled supplies in the front hall, preparatory to making a dash for the motor home, Frank saw Burnfingers emerge from the garage carrying a double armful of unexpected devices. He nodded in their direction as the Indian began shoving them in an empty suitcase.

"What are you gonna do with all that stuff?'' The small propane torch made some sense: what they couldn't cut or stab or shoot they might be able to burn. But the rest struck him as peculiarly useless.

"You will see. At least, I hope you will have the chance to see.''

Frank considered, trying to look past the present moment at something else. "You know, we sell a lot of hobby stuff in our stores.'' He nodded at Burnfingers's package. "Steven used that for a little while, then got bored. Funny it should be lying around. I wonder how much of what's happened here lately is coincidence and how much of it something else. That Mouse—I get the feeling she can do a few tricks with the threads of reality herself.''

Everyone assembled in the front hall, loaded down with bags and suitcases. Flucca insisted on being first out the door. "If they aim for your heads, they'll miss mine. Besides, I'm used to working with vegetables.'' Alicia's biggest cleaver dangled from his right hand as he turned.

Burnfingers stood ready to back him up as he flung the door wide and the little man dashed outside, weapon held high. He didn't have to use it. The plants' blind fury had burned itself out.

The front walkway was littered with debris. It looked like the aftermath of a hurricane. Branches and leaves were scattered

everywhere, a fine carpet of brown-green which was just beginning to decay. Only a few growths remained standing. All were
broken and torn, ripped to pieces by their neighbors. A few of the
smaller plants which had been ignored in the greater carnage
reached weakly for the refugees, but their roots and leaves were
too short to span the walkway pavement. Flucca and Frank cut
them to bits anyway, glad of a chance to strike back at something.

Taking the suitcases and heavy bags from the women,
Burnfingers tossed them through the motor home's open door, then
helped them inside. A shadow the size of a 727 passed overhead,
but when Frank tilted back his head and shaded his eyes he saw
nothing. He wasn't disappointed. Whatever it had been might be
coming back, and he was relieved when it was his turn to enter.

"Sure you feel well enough to drive?" Burnfingers asked him
as Frank settled himself behind the wheel.

"You kiddin'? I'm looking forward to it."

They took their seats and he headed for the gate, not bothering
to close it behind them as they barreled through. Whether this was
or wasn't their own reality, he doubted they'd be coming back.

He slowed as they approached the first intersection. All the
streets were carpeted with shredded vegetation. The remaining
stripped growth stood motionless as the dead all around them,
having spent their energy in that earlier hour of cannibalistic fury.
Only a few of the taller trees that lined the streets jerked spasmodically. None reached for the motor home. Not another vehicle
appeared as they sat idling behind the stop sign.

"Which way?" He looked back over his shoulder.

Mouse stood by a closet, eyes closed tight. Either she was
thinking hard, or else inspecting something none of them could
see. Then her eyes snapped open and she looked to her right.

"That way?" Frank sounded dubious. "That way's down.
Nothing there anymore except ocean." Come to think of it, he
reminded himself, there was nothing in any direction except
ocean. He shrugged and pulled on the wheel, putting the motor
home on the drive that wound like wire around the ragged edge of
the Peninsula.

Soon the ocean came into view. Catalina was still gone and
there were more waterspouts and whirlpools than before. Immense
brown-red shapes the size of small ships battled in the raging
water. Behind them, the sun was setting. Even it was different: a

swollen, unhealthy-looking yellow globe. Frank was sure he could
make out individual solar prominences flaring hellishly from the
edge of the bloated disk. Was it an optical illusion or had it really
grown? Would it go nova on this reality line while they were still
driving in circles? He fancied he could see dark sunspots crawling
across the nuclear surface, forced himself to turn back to the leaf-
and branch-paved road.

The coast drive descended sharply toward a small suburb
called Hollywood Riviera. Redondo Beach was the first major
community up the coast.

Except Redondo Beach wasn't there anymore. There was only
the agitated green sea, which stretched as far north as the Hollywood
Hills. A few taller structures still thrust their uppermost floors
above the waves, now that the rate of subsidence seemed to have
slowed. East and north, the towers of Wilshire Boulevard rose
above the water like a line of violets. He applied the brake.

"What now?"

Mouse nodded calmly. "This is the right path. Continue."

"But we can't," Alicia pointed out. "The road goes under
the water."

The other woman smiled at her. "Reality is what you make of
it. Keep going, Frank. I'll tell you when to stop or turn."

So this was it, he told himself tiredly. They could turn back to
the empty house in the devastated neighborhood and wait for the
ballooning sun to fry them, or he could listen to Mouse. Tiny,
elfin-faced, beautiful, enigmatic, irresistible Mouse. She'd followed
as often as she'd led, these past crazy days. Now she was telling
him to do the impossible.

But was it really so very much more radical than sticking
one's foot over the edge of the world, or driving blind on a
highway that ran through ultimate void past a veil of stars? If there
could be roads through nothing, why couldn't there be roads
through something? Water, for instance? Slowly his foot came off
the brake.

"Frank . . . ?"

He turned to his wife and smiled, surprised at his own
indifference to what might happen next. "There's nowhere else to
go, sweetheart. Not here, not on this line. So we might as well go
on."

She looked at Mouse, who smiled reassuringly. Then she sat

up straight in her seat, her hands gripping the armrests tightly. "Okay. I don't know why, but okay."

"There is only one other problem." Burnfingers was staring straight ahead as Frank started down the slope, the motor home picking up speed as it headed for the water.

"What's that?" Frank heard himself shout.

"I cannot swim."

The motor home did not leak. Not even a little bit. Nor did it show signs of leaking as they plunged deeper and deeper into the resurgent sea. By law they should have come to a halt. At the very least, water should have seeped into the engine compartment and shut them down, or the air they continued to breathe should have made them too buoyant to cling to the increasingly rough seabed. Laws, however, no longer seemed to apply to them, natural ones least of all.

Mouse continued to give directions and Frank obeyed, too far beyond astonishment to object. He tried to pretend they were out for an afternoon drive on the San Diego Freeway, but it was hard to ignore the fish and other denizens of the deep who swam curiously up to the windshield and windows. Something was keeping the water out, and it wasn't a pressure differential or air-tight seals. It defied reason—which meant that in the context of the past several days it was perfectly logical.

"Just don't open any windows." Mouse's eyes alternated between open and shut. Frank wasn't inclined to ask why. "We are safe within a fragment of your reality, which you have carried about with you the way a diving spider carries its air supply. Now is the time for you to make use of it."

"How long will it last?" Alicia asked softly, marveling at the increasingly dark landscape.

"Long enough."

"It better, little singer." For the first time since they'd made his acquaintance, the big Navajo was showing symptoms of fear.

They had a hard time driving through the kelp forest that clung to the narrow continental shelf. A pair of mutated things that looked like sharks with hands inspected them closely before swimming away. Frank wondered how their protective bubble of reality would respond to a direct attack. Would any assailants bounce off, or would they be able to penetrate?

As time passed and the air inside the motor home remained

breathable, he found he was able to relax a little. They were so deep now that if their protection did collapse it would all be over in a few seconds. They rolled down an increasingly flat and featureless bottom until he came to a steep dropoff. He wasn't even surprised to discover that the brakes still functioned.

"Keep going," Mouse instructed him.

"What, over that?"

"It's the way." Her eyes were only half open, giving her a slightly sinister look.

Frank turned to his wife. They exchanged one more kiss. No need for words anymore. Not in a here and now that wasn't.

He switched from brake to accelerator. As they went over the cliff he instinctively shifted into low. The slope was almost seventy degrees, but they didn't fall. Somehow he kept control.

"Reality is sticky stuff," Mouse told him with a sly smile.

Feeling almost jaunty, he switched on the headlights. The twin beams pierced the blackness for forty feet. Schools of small silvery fish swam into the lights, hung as if paralyzed for an instant before dashing away in fright.

Their descent seemed to continue forever. When the cliff did terminate, the end was abrupt and unexpected. The ground leveled off. A broad, flat plain stretched endlessly before them. It looked like mud and sand, but the motor home progressed across the uncertain surface without any trouble at all. Except for the small area lit by the headlights, it was pitch-black around them.

"Wow, did you guys see that?" Wendy was sitting by a big side window, staring out into the darkness.

"See what, dear?" her mother asked.

"Something *big*. It had teeth and fins and it looked like a neon sign!"

"Didn't know we were *that* deep." Frank spoke without turning. "You sure we're goin' the right way?"

"We are going the only way," Mouse assured him.

"Pressure down here must be hundreds of pounds a square inch, or however the hell they measure that stuff."

Whatever the pressure was, the motor home cruised along unaffected. The roof did not crack, the joints did not groan. It wouldn't take that long, Frank knew. If their protection went, the motor home and everything within would be flattened like a tin can beneath a tank.

Other phosphorescent monstrosities gradually became visible. Things with stomachs bigger than their bodies, with heads bigger than their stomachs, all needle-sharp teeth and bright electric eyes. The motor home's lights froze them briefly before they jerked or darted back into the eternal night that was their home.

Other creatures, infrequent but active, scuttled out of the motor home's path, stirring up mud and silt as they fled. Once something like a fifty-foot flounder exploded out of their way, stirring up so much muck they never got a decent look at it.

Frank glanced down at the speedometer. With the accelerator pushed to the floor and no obstacles to slow their progress, they were doing slightly over a hundred miles an hour, right up near the motor home's limit. He saw no reason for caution. There was nothing down here to run into and in Mouse they had a guide more efficient than any sonar.

Only once did she direct him to deviate momentarily from their course. As they did so he saw the plutonic glow of subsurface vents off to their left. Five-foot-long worms clustered close around whirling plumes of Earth's breath. Bacteria clouded the water, feeding on hydrogen sulphides. It was all real, and more alien than anything they'd yet encountered.

After several days of this Frank found himself wondering if it was Mouse's intention to circumnavigate the globe underwater. They were making excellent progress and the fuel level fell with inexplicable slowness, but their range was still finite. She assured him repeatedly that they were not driving aimlessly, but toward a definite destination.

There was no propane to cook with, but the motor home's microwave worked fine. Assisted by the imaginative Flucca, Alicia managed to conjure up remarkably nutritious meals from their declining food stock. Only Burnfingers was unable to relax and enjoy the impossible ride. Knowing that tons of water pressed tight all around them, held back only by a thin strip of transient reality, he kept to himself and said little.

"We're getting close," Mouse finally said one day.

Frank was doing his stint at the wheel. Now he took a deep breath. He'd begun to despair of ever hearing those words despite her repeated reassurances.

She was crowding close, her perfume distracting him from his driving. "Turn here. No, more to the right. That's it."

He complied, marveling once more at how the motor home responded under what should have been not only impossible but deadly conditions.

"Now straight."

A loud bump came from beneath and Frank's blood went cold for an instant. Then he realized they hadn't lost their seal of reality. It was only the sound of the front shocks adjusting as they began to ascend. He shifted back into low.

The grade was as steep as the one they'd descended when leaving Los Angeles but the motor home climbed with all the agility of a four-wheel drive. Several hours passed before Wendy let out a shout.

"Dad, turn the lights off! It's getting light outside!"

Sure enough, the blackness through which they'd traveled for days was giving way to a velvety purple color. Soon brightly hued schools of tropical fish were swimming around them, darting for cover among rocks and coral as the motor home advanced.

Paradoxically, Frank found he was more nervous now than he'd been at any time since leaving L.A. They'd come a long way under unbelievable circumstances. But if anything went wrong now they could drown just as easily twenty feet beneath the surface as two miles down.

He was worrying needlessly. The motor home continued to ascend into water clear as crystal. Doubly gratifying was the fact that all the fish looked normal. They saw no mutants, no bizarre shapes, no twisted bodies. Only color and form.

They had to drive for a while before they found a break in the jagged reef. Once beyond the coral wall, the surface hung placidly only a few feet above them. The radio antenna broke through, leaving a small wake behind it as they advanced. Frank found himself driving across a gentle bottom paved with white sand.

Come on, he found himself urging the motor home. Just a little farther. Another couple hundred yards and we can breathe free again. A little longer and we'll be there.

Be where? he asked himself. Be where, beware. He found he could smile, however grim the humor of it, now that the pressure induced by their abyssal excursion was almost gone. What strange territory had they reached after days of hard driving? Would this land prove as blasted and doomed as the Los Angeles they'd fled?

Or would it be as peaceful and normal as the coral and fish surrounding them?

They began to emerge from the sea, waiting tensely as the water fell first below the level of the windshield, then past the hood, and finally to the tires. Frank drove out onto a wide crescent beach. Dry sand slowed the motor home no more than had the abyssal muck. Reality, he'd long since concluded, was a wonderful accessory to have on a long trip.

There was a gap in the line of palm trees that fringed the beach. He didn't need Mouse to point the way. The opening revealed a paved highway two lanes wide. A faded, intermittent yellow stripe ran down the middle.

It was getting hot, but he held off activating the air-conditioning. The gas gauge was hovering perilously near empty.

Alicia rose abruptly and marched toward the door. "I'm going outside."

He rose and caught her before she was halfway to the exit. "No way. We don't know what's out there."

"It should be safe enough." Both of them turned to Mouse. Her eyes were open wide now, lavender beacons. "We're free of the water and back on the right reality line. Your own—or one barely distinguishable from it."

"'Barely'?" Frank clung to his doubts. "That's what you said about the one we just fled."

Flucca was standing by the door. "I'll go first, if you like."

"Not a chance, Small Chef." Burnfingers brushed him aside. Frank was startled to see that the big man was hyperventilating. Apparently he'd stood the confinement as long as he was able.

Before anyone could stop him, which would likely have been an impossible task in any event, he pushed the door open and jumped out. Air rushed through, sweeping aside the staleness of the previous days. It was rich with the aroma of saltwater, green growing things, and comforting warmth. It drew them to the doorway.

Burnfingers was doing a dance ten yards distant, hooting gleefully and kicking up sand. "It is all right, it is good!" Ignoring their stares, he knelt to grab a handful of sand and rub it over his face. Then he toppled slowly onto his back, arms spread wide, eyes regarding the clouds.

"Is he dead?" Alicia wondered fearfully.

"Naw." Frank used the handgrip to ease himself out, thrilled to be standing on solid ground once more. "He's just enjoying the sunshine."

Wendy followed her father. Alicia exited next, inhaling the fresh air. Frank watched her breasts rise and fall, marveling at the thoughts that can occur to a man even in times of serious crisis. Mouse was standing alongside his wife, and his subsequent thoughts embarrassed him deeply.

Burnfingers hadn't budged. While the others joined him in relaxing for the first time in days, Frank spent the time giving the motor home a thorough examination.

There was ample proof that their deep-sea drive had been anything but a dream. Rank saltwater was still dripping from the roof. Bottom-dwelling fish and crustaceans unlucky enough to have been caught in the axles and bumpers were starting to decay in the sun. Some had exploded messily under the pressure change. Flucca wandered over to help him with the cleanup.

"Look at this one." The little man held up a three-foot-long fish with minuscule fins. The body was barely an inch in diameter. Two feelers as long as the body itself protruded from the skull. It twitched once in Flucca's grasp.

"We've been through a lot of madness, but this last has to be the ultimate. We all oughta be as dead as that eel thing. And this," Frank said as he tapped the metal side of the motor home, "should be scrap."

"Some things they still build well," was all Flucca could think of to say.

After circling the vehicle one last time to convince himself it was still intact, Frank and Flucca rejoined the others.

"Isn't this a beautiful spot?" Alicia was surveying the little bay where they'd emerged from the sea, shading her gaze from a tropical sun. "Maybe when this is all over we can come back here."

"If it's on our reality line, yeah." There was a harshness to his tone he hadn't intended. He turned to Mouse. "You said we were 'real close.' You've been spouting that line ever since we picked you up."

"Distance is a relative matter, Frank Sonderberg. North we must go a little ways farther yet."

"What happens when we get there?" Wendy asked her. "To this Vanishing Point, I mean."

"When we get there? When we get there, child, why then you will hear me sing."

"But we've already heard you sing."

Mouse shook her head slowly. "No. You haven't heard me sing. Really sing. Not yet." She continued to stare northward. "But I think there is yet time for that. Yet time."

"Then let's get moving." Frank turned toward the motor home.

"I know we have to find Steven," Alicia said to him, "but don't you think you should rest a little?"

"We'll rest when this is done. In our own reality, which we're not sure this is yet." He trudged through the sand toward the only reality he'd known for days. Reluctantly, his family followed.

"Not home." Burnfingers Begay brushed sand from his pants and sleeves. "Hot enough, but the palm trees do not belong. Arizona has plenty of beach. Just no ocean."

Wendy laughed and Alicia smiled, but not Frank. His sense of humor was stuck on another reality line. He wouldn't laugh again until his family was back together and Burnfingers Begay and Mouse and Niccolo Flucca and the Anarchis and Chaos had all been jammed back into the unimportant corner of his mind where they belonged.

The motor home balked when he started the engine. It jerked forward, hesitated, balked again. The exhaust pipe spat water and dead fish all over the pristine beach. Gritting his teeth, Frank kept trying it until the engine cleared. By the time they pulled into the northbound lane of the narrow road, it was running smoothly again.

The terrain was a patchwork: emerald outcrops of dense vegetation consisting of palms, ferns, and brilliant flowers alternating with barren fields of rough dark lava. As the road crossed a narrow spit that extended out into the ocean, they came into view of a towering active volcano. It reminded Frank too much of the first stop on their odyssey through alternate realities.

Mouse's reaction was very different. "The place!" she declared excitedly. "The marker. The smoking harbinger. Very soon now, very soon." She was standing between his seat and Alicia's, staring intently forward.

Soon they were driving along a thin strip of road with ocean on one side and sheer cliffs on the other. Rocks lying in the road kept Frank glancing nervously at the plant-choked wall of stone on their left. The road had been sliced from the sheer rock at great expense, yet no one seemed to use it. Since leaving the beach they hadn't seen another vehicle, another sign of life.

"Wherever we're going we'd better get there soon," he muttered. "I don't know how it's lasted this long, but we've about run out." He indicated the fuel gauge. The digital readout rested on empty. "We're down to emergency gas, if there is any. Must be, because we're still goin'."

"There! Turn there!"

It threw Frank for a moment because it was so rare that Mouse shouted. He hit the brakes harder than was necessary, then crept forward until they reached the turnoff she'd indicated.

The steep, narrow dirt track occupied a cleft in the rocks. Concealed as it was by thick ferns and other growths, it was all but invisible from the main road. He would have driven past it a hundred times without suspecting its presence. Reluctantly, he turned into the opening. It was barely wide enough to admit the motor home. Occasionally the metal sides scraped rock.

Tropical flora closed in around them. It was as if they were traveling down a long, green tunnel. At times the ferns packing the open space in search of scarce sunlight were so thick they completely blocked the windshield. Frank had to drive slowly and by feel, praying there were no sharp dips or unexpected bends or drop-offs ahead. Soon the road itself disappeared. They continued to advance up the stream bed, which had cut the canyon. A trickle of water ran down the center, disappearing between their wheels and re-emerging in their wake.

After half an hour of driving across terrain that the motor home had never been designed to handle, the tunnel opened onto a much wider but equally steep-sided canyon.

Walls of volcanic rock towered hundreds of feet above the canyon floor. In places they were nearly vertical. Everywhere was dense vegetation. It looked like films Frank had seen of New Guinea or the South Pacific, though there was no reason to believe they were anywhere in either vicinity, or even on the same reality line where such familiar places existed.

Mouse stood close by, nodding and murmuring incomprehensibly to herself. In the absence of further instruction he kept going.

The stream bed filled up and became more like a road again, silt muting the bumps and bounces. The squeaking, complaining suspension gave every indication of failing utterly at any moment.

They topped a small rise in the middle of the canyon valley. Ahead, the by-now awesome walls enclosing them on all sides came together. Almost. Where they nearly met, a thin sliver of sky showed clearly. Everything ended at that place. Or extended from it, Frank thought. The canyon, the vegetation, the little stream, even the sky and sunlight all angled toward that narrow passage.

Mouse sighed heavily. "There it is."

"There what is?" he asked tiredly.

Her smile was wider than ever. "The Vanishing Point."

18

HAVING COME SO FAR the hard way, they all sat and stared for a long time. Even the motor home seemed to idle easier.

"What happens when we get there?" Wendy finally asked, breaking the silence. "Do we vanish, too?"

Mouse brought herself back from some faraway place to smile at Wendy. "No. It is the insubstantials that disappear at that place. Space, time, reality: that's what a vanishing point is all about. It's where everything goes when it's not here, a place all its own, at once a part of yet outside the real cosmos. It's the focus of real and of time."

"What do we do when we get there?" Alicia wondered.

"It is where the Spinner lives, weaving the fabric of reality. Presently it lies uneasy, as does reality itself. By soothing it we shall regulate its spinning and thereby restore reason to the worlds around us. I will sing to it and it will be healed." She paused. "At least, that is what I hope will happen."

"Then we'd better hurry and get there." Frank resumed his cautious advance up the stream bed.

Ever since they'd left the beach, strange muted sounds had been coming from the vicinity of the rear bedroom. Now they were joined by a sharp metallic odor. He had to speak without taking his gaze from their path, but he couldn't restrain his curiosity any longer.

"What's goin' on back there? Where's Burnfingers?"

Flucca piped up from his seat halfway back. "Working, I think. In the bedroom."

"Working on what?" Alicia's nose wrinkled as she inhaled the acrid odor. "Smells like something's burning."

"Ask him what he's doing," Frank snapped.

Flucca slid off his seat and headed rearward. The door opened slightly at his call. Frank could see him whispering to Burnfingers. After a couple of minutes the door shut and Flucca came forward.

"Some kind of ceremony he's into. Says he can't be disturbed. He's not burning anything up."

"Well, if he's not doing anything dangerous then I guess it's okay," Alicia said dubiously. Frank grunted. If Burnfingers was up to something peculiar they could hardly stop him by force.

The stink from the back grew worse as they climbed the gently sloping, rapidly narrowing valley. Once Wendy tried to peek in on Burnfingers, only to discover that he'd locked the door from the other side. Frank wasn't thrilled with all the secrecy. What did they know, really know, about Burnfingers Begay, anyway? He'd confessed to madness. Was he going to try and prove it somehow?

He tried to concentrate on the road and ignore whatever was happening in his bedroom. It wasn't difficult, given the congeniality of the surroundings. Exotic blooms and brilliantly hued growths of every description crowded close around the stream bed. Orchids hung from trees and insects darted in and out of trumpet-shaped blossoms the color of children's laughter. Vines wore coats of tiny purple flowers. In its way the valley was the exact antithesis of the first alternate reality they'd stumbled into. Instead of fire and brimstone they drove past crimson and yellow blooms.

Wendy spoke up excitedly. "Look, Mom: hummingbirds!"

Frank took his eye off their course long enough to spot the tiny, metallic-hued creatures as they darted among the leaves and branches like winged crystals. In a short while they were enveloped by them. It was like driving through a giant beehive, so sonorous was the beating of thousands of wings. He'd never heard of hummingbirds living in dense flocks.

But as the little fliers drew near it wasn't their myriad colors that provoked murmurs of awe from the occupants of the motor home. That was reserved for the ones who rode them.

They were people, or human, anyway. Though little larger than a thumbnail, each was perfectly formed in every detail. They clung tight to hummingbird reins and secured their feet in hummingbird stirrups. A few carried harps and other miniature musical instruments. Frank wondered how they could hear them over the beat of so many wings. They were almost too tiny to think of as little people. He could see them talking to one another in voices that were less than squeaks.

It took him a moment to realize that they weren't talking. They were singing, and Mouse was singing with them. She'd opened a window and her face was against the screen. He could see her lips move but, strain as he might, could not overhear a single word.

Only when she straightened and rejoined them did Alicia ask the question. "Who are they? They're precious!"

"They wouldn't think so." Dozens of hummers and riders were darting back and forth in front of the glass. "This is their home. They live on the tip of the Vanishing Point. We're related, a little, because they too are musicians. For them a ballad lasts only seconds, a cantata a few minutes, an epic less than one of your hours. They've sung like that since the beginning of time. They cannot share with others because their music is as intense as their lives. Too much for people like us to handle." She turned and gestured back the way they'd come, back down the stream bed.

"The other inhabitants of this land suspect their existence and have told tales about them for centuries. Most people do not believe in the tiny ones, which suits them well. They like their valley the way it is. Visitors, even friendly ones, would despoil it and interfere with the music."

"What land are you talking about? Where are we, anyway? Besides close to the Vanishing Point, I mean."

"What lies behind us no longer matters. All that matters is what lies ahead. Have a care from now on for what exists beyond reality." She lowered her voice. "The crucial time approaches. We must be careful lest this changes, too."

"This?" Alicia was all but nose to nose with a dozen hummers and their exquisite, perfectly formed riders. They hovered outside her window, easily keeping pace with the motor home. "This couldn't change. This is too beautiful."

"It is exactly that, which is why so few people have seen it. But there are no absolutes in the cosmos, Alicia. Truth and Beauty exist because people invent them. When a tree falls in the forest it makes a sound whether anyone is present to hear it or not, but it is not beautiful unless someone is there to look upon it."

Frank tried to drive around a good-sized rock, failed and winced as a tire kicked it up under the chassis. "Just so long as you're right about us being close. I'm tired of ending up on highways to nowhere."

Mouse nodded ahead. "We are almost there. Thanks to you, Frank Sonderberg, I think everything is going to be all right."

He glanced back toward the rear bedroom. "If Charlie doesn't burn us down or blow us up first."

"He's talking to his yeibichais."

"What?"

"His spirits, his gods. I've known for some time he's not alone back there. They're all working on something together. He doesn't want you back there because he knows you couldn't handle what you might see. I gather it's a very sensitive business."

"So you don't know what he's up to, either?"

She shook her head. "I trust Burnfingers Begay. He's an unusual man, besides being a Traveler."

It was harder than ever for Frank to keep his mind on his driving. "Hardly enough room back there for two people, let alone a bunch of gods."

"There are large gods and small gods, and the proportion of them has nothing at all to do with physical size. I think Burnfingers's gods are very big indeed."

The canyon walls closed in around them until for the second time that day there was barely enough room for the motor home to pass between them. The narrow passage was suffused with an eerie, slightly orange sunlight. Vines and orchids, ferns and palms, vanished, leaving only the cold stone. Frank edged the motor home forward, finding he missed the comforting hum of the birds and their riders. This was a place where a song was needed, even one he couldn't hear.

There was a sharp *spang* as the sideview mirror on the passenger side was snapped off by protruding rock. Frank cursed, corrected imperceptibly to the left. Alicia rose to put a comforting arm around her daughter, who didn't like enclosed places.

If they wedged themselves in here, Frank told himself as he sweated the drive, they'd never be able to back up.

Overhead, the walls of the canyon towered hundreds, maybe thousands of feet toward the sky. Then suddenly they opened up, parting, literally falling away on both sides. Frank breathed a sigh of relief as they rolled out onto a wide, flat plateau covered with bright green grass and inch-wide yellow flowers. He decided the latter were close cousins to dandelions.

"Stop," Mouse quietly instructed him. "Stop here."

Frank put the motor home in park, turned to look back at the cleft from which they'd emerged. Surely it was far too narrow to have passed the Winnebago. At the far end of the slit of a canyon the light was faint and hazy. It was like looking toward another world.

"This is it," Mouse was saying. "We've done it. We're here." She strode past Wendy and her mother to open the door. Frank hastened to follow.

Now that the engine was off, they could hear it clearly: a vast sighing, the rush of immense bellows—eternity breathing. Mouse was walking through the grass and yellow flowers toward the edge of the plateau. Beyond lay turquoise sky. With each step tiny black things jumped out of her path and the flowers inclined curious heads toward her ankles.

The Sonderbergs followed, along with Niccolo Flucca. Frank held his wife's hand. As they neared the drop-off, Alicia sucked in her breath and Wendy gasped. Flucca murmured something inadequate in a foreign language.

The Spinner hung in the bright blue air, stretching to infinity. Clouds broke against the unending golden body. Some were tinged with red, others with yellow. Lightning flickered beneath the Spinner's epidermis, which was not skin but something indefinable. As the body rippled like a long Chinese kite, thousands of legs busily twisted and worked against one another. From each pair of legs a silk-like thread emerged, to drift off into immensity. The sky surrounding the Spinner was full of rippling silvery mats, and reflected in each could be seen entire worlds, whole universes. Each thread was a different reality, and there were thousands upon thousands of realities.

Anyone could see something was amiss. Holes showed in some of the mats, and in places there were no mats at all where proximate threads had been broken or become entangled. There the spinning legs jerked spasmodically, uncertainly. Realities became entwined, or roped together. There was great confusion, but not chaos. Not yet.

Though Mouse had referred to it as such, Frank hadn't really expected the Spinner to be an actual creature. Somewhere in the archives of man there was doubtless a creation myth which got it right. If so, it was one he'd never heard.

"Behold the Spinner," Mouse instructed them, one arm lifted gracefully in its direction.

Two eyes stared blankly from the near end of the immensity. They were an impossible distance away. Distance had no meaning here. The gap might be measurable in miles—or in light-years. Each orb was a limpid blue sea the size of Lake Superior. The Spinner hung in cloud-stuff far away and below the rim of the plateau on which they stood. Frank cautiously looked over and down. If there was a bottom, it could not be seen.

"It's clear that it's ill." Mouse pointed out the rips in the fabric of existence, the broken threads with which legs toyed helplessly. "It suffers from an emotional instability that will only become worse—unless I can soothe it with song. Even something as great as the Spinner can suffer." She turned to Wendy. "If you wouldn't mind, dear child, I will need a really big glass of water."

"Okay, sure!" Wendy turned and dashed back to the motor home. When she returned with the glass, Mouse took a long swallow of the contents before handing it back. Wendy stepped aside without having to be asked.

Suddenly Mouse seemed taller, stronger. She cleared her throat once, twice, while resting both hands against her lower abdomen. Without appearing to exert much more effort than she had on similar previous occasions, she began to sing.

It was a wordless song, a song of power, and it poured out of her like a torrent in an endless fortissimo. Frank had to put his hands over his ears, and Alicia, too. They listened in awe to the incredible volume of sound issuing from that seemingly frail body. The music was simultaneously calming and exhilarating, reassuring and ennobling, soothing and strength-bestowing.

As they looked over the edge of the plateau, they saw that the rippling movements of the Spinner's body were becoming more pronounced, like waves traveling across a golden beach. It was starting to move, not in uncertain, hesitant jerks, but smoothly and in time to the rhythm of Mouse's song.

She sang for a long time, longer than should have been possible, before her lips finally came together again. She wore the strain of the song like a scar on her face as she turned and smiled weakly at Wendy.

"I'll have another sip, I think." Dumbstruck, the girl handed her the glass.

"Wow—if I only had my tape recorder."

Alicia was taking in the vastness that was the Spinner. "Is that all? I mean it's over? You fixed it?"

"I do not know."

Frank frowned at her. "Whattaya mean, you don't know? After all we've been through you mean to say you can't tell if it's been worthwhile?"

"I believe I have stabilized it some, but not completely. Did you think this would be so easily done?" She passed the water back to Wendy. "I must continue. It is not finished."

Throwing back her head, she let loose an entirely new and different tsunami of sound. The irresistible musical avalanche swept out from the plateau to wash the place the Spinner lived. This time it seemed to have no effect. The expression Mouse wore when she concluded the song showed she was not pleased.

"Still not there. Something is wrong and I know not what."

"I do."

Surprised, they all turned. Burnfingers Begay regarded them, proud and exhausted. Sweat streaked his face and his black hair lay flat against his skin. In his right hand he held a two-foot-long golden cylinder that glowed with internal fire.

Alicia stared at it in amazement. "Where did you ever find that?"

"Did not find it. Made it. In your bedroom." He grinned at Frank. "With your hobby tools, my friend."

"What the hell is it?"

Burnfingers held it up so the clouds could have a good look at what he had wrought, like a father proffering his newborn son for approval.

"It is a flute. *The* flute."

"Doesn't look like any kind of flute I ever saw," Frank replied uncertainly.

"It is not the kind of flute you would find in a symphony orchestra. This is a Native American flute. The best kind of flute. From it comes the music of prairie and grass, of butte and sandstone, of the wind and the waters. This flute will breathe Four Corners music." His eyes glittered; perhaps with his madness, perhaps with something else.

"I made it out of the gold I have saved and collected. Gold of Spanish doubloons and Colombia and the Yucatan. Gold from the Andes and the Sierra Nevada. Gold from the shallows of Brazil's rivers and from great museums where I have worked and studied."

"You stole it?" Alicia asked him.

"Stole it?" He lowered the unique instrument to regard her intently. "I did not steal it. I liberated it. This is piece and fragment of all the gold the white men have ever stolen from the Amerindian, from the tundra to the plains of Patagonia. I did not know at the time why I liberated it except that it made me feel good to do so." His gaze rose, to settle on Mouse. "Then I met the little singer and learned of her journey, and I knew what I would do with the gold when the time came for it to be of use.

"When I told you that I was crazy you should have guessed I was a musician."

Mouse was nodding knowingly, like one who'd just found the missing piece of the puzzle under her chair. "And I thought you were only a Traveler."

"All musicians are travelers, but not all Travelers are musicians," he replied merrily. The glint in his eyes had become a twinkling. "It takes more than the right song to soothe the Spinner. It take the proper accompaniment." And putting the gleaming flute to his lips, he began to play.

So Mouse, inspired, sang a third song, and they all knew it was the best yet, better than ever before. But when it was done she declared herself still unsatisfied, and the Spinner, though obviously much improved, still heaved and buckled alarmingly.

"Still something absents itself." She was thinking hard, staring at the ground. "Burnfingers Begay, your music has helped much, but I fear it is not enough." She glanced so sharply at Frank that he twitched, startled. "Frank Sonderberg, can you play an instrument?"

"Who, me? You've gotta be kidding. None of us can. . . ."

"Hey, Dad. Dad?"

Father and mother looked at Wendy. Frank readied himself to say something, and then he remembered. Back in the reality that had claimed his son, where each of them had demonstrated a special talent, a unique characteristic, only his daughter had simply sat and stared, displaying nothing. Now here. . .

"Are you sure, sugar?" He hadn't called her that in quite a few years. It came back easily and felt good. "I mean, *really* sure?"

"I can try, Dad."

He nodded, smiled, and indicated the motor home. "Go and get it, then." Eyes shining, she turned and sprinted past Burnfingers Begay.

Frank turned to Mouse, unable to vanquish the pride in his voice. "My little girl, when she puts her mind to it, can play the harmonica."

"I don't know." Begay was doubtful. "It is not a noble instrument."

"The nobility lies in the performer, not the instrument," Mouse informed him. "We must try and hope."

Wendy rejoined them, panting hard. In one hand she held a shiny silver concert harmonica. Next to Burnfingers's solid gold flute it didn't look like much, but Mouse didn't appear disappointed. She came forward and put both hands on the girl's shoulders.

"Just listen and try to follow. Let your thoughts flow and be one with the music."

Burnfingers raised the flute to his lips. "Now it is time to let your heart sing."

Wendy nodded. "I'm ready." She put the instrument to her lips.

It was not what Frank normally thought of as music, when he thought of it at all. The golden flute was akin to bubbles in champagne while his daughter's harmonica sounded more like the foam atop beer. Somehow it all came together, carried forward by the power of Mouse's song. And enveloping them and adding to it all was the almost palpable projection of maternal affection and warmth that emanated once more from Alicia.

Frank looked on and listened, and much as he was amazed by it all he discovered he was feeling very left out.

A tug at his arm made him look down. Flucca stood there. "Don't let it get to you, mate. Me, I couldn't carry a tune in a bucket." He winked. It shouldn't have made Frank feel better, but it did. He straightened as he turned back to the improbable concert.

The Spinner was reacting. Bursts of sun-sized lightning now ran not only along its back but through its entire body. Legs which had been twisting and jerking against one another gradually relaxed, until they resumed weaving in unison. The alignment commenced near the head and spread slowly toward the unimaginably distant horizon. As he looked on, the gaps and rips in the silvery mats that formed the fabric of innumerable reality lines began to close up. The image that resulted was one of vast beauty and regimentation. Frank felt an overwhelming sense of peace and contentment.

Mouse's voice was the soothing strength, the cool sound of Burnfingers's flute was her support, and Wendy—Wendy's herky-jerky harmonica provided an odd sort of harmonic glue that bound the whole together. The resonance of reason, he thought, marveling that his own daughter could be a contributor to such an endeavor.

So entranced was he by the performance and the effect it was having on the Spinner that he was unaware he was rocking back and forth in time to the music. Unaware, that is, until he felt Flucca tugging anxiously on his wrist.

He'd been asleep while awake. Now he frowned down at the smaller man, who turned and pointed back toward the canyon.

The narrow slit of light was no longer visible as a bright dividing line between the towering cliffs. Now only darkness lived there, intensifying as he stared. A rumbling began to sound in his ears, in his bones.

The others noticed it as well. Mouse looked worriedly back over her shoulder even as she continued with her song. Frank didn't have to ask the significance of the advancing darkness.

Relentlessly pursuing across alternate realities, the Anarchis had finally caught up with them.

"Will she finish the song in time?" he muttered aloud, trying to divide his attention among the trio, his wife, and the oncoming nightmare.

"She has to," said Flucca. "As I understand it, if she's

interrupted before her therapy's been completed, then all our efforts will have been for nothing. I don't' see how this Anarchis could do harm to anything the size of the Spinner, but it doesn't have to. All it has to do is stop the healing process.''

Frank turned away from the singers to study the canyon that formed the outside tip of the Vanishing Point. Only the narrow confines prevented the Anarchis from advancing faster. It had to compact itself, squeeze down to fit through.

''I guess we've got to stop it.''

Frank's lower jaw dropped as he regarded Flucca. *"We?"* The dwarf was already racing for the motor home. Frank fought to catch up with him. ''What are we supposed to do? Throw rocks at it?''

''We have to try something. We have to buy as much time as we can.''

''Maybe we can reason with it.''

Flucca was shaking his head as he mounted the steps. ''Can't reason with an agent of Chaos. That's a contradiction in terms.''

''The story of my life.'' He piled in behind the little man.

Flucca scrambled into the passenger's seat. This time it didn't feel so good to be sitting behind the wheel, but Frank knew his friend was right. They had to try and slow their unreasoning nemesis, had to give Mouse as much time as possible to complete her work. He wondered if Alicia had seen him leave. The warmth she projected was as vital to the Spinner's therapy as the music. Just as well if she didn't notice his absence. But it would've been nice to have had a chance to say good-bye.

''Maybe we can slow the damn thing down, or at least give it a bellyache,'' he growled as he started the engine. ''If it doesn't like reality, a few tons of Detroit iron oughta give it pause.''

The wondrous music of the trio continued to reach their ears through the motor home's walls, raising their spirits as it soothed the Spinner. Frank swung the motor home around, raced the engine, and then slammed his foot on the accelerator. No dragster, the Winnebago picked up speed gradually, but in a couple of minutes it was thundering toward the canyon at a very respectable velocity and gaining more every second. Whatever it struck would know it had been hit.

He wondered if they'd make contact inside the Vanishing Point or out in the real world, and if it would make a difference.

His fingers tightened on the wheel. Probably wasn't his world out there, anyway. In his world the Pacific hadn't invaded the land and monsters didn't run rampant in the streets of Los Angeles. Despite the gravity of the moment, he found he could still grin. Not south of Sunset Boulevard they didn't, anyway.

Flucca kept an eye out for possible obstacles; rocks or logs. There were none on the perfectly flat plateau. There was only grass and flowers, which sprang back with unnatural vigor in the wake of the motor home's heavy tires.

They could see the Anarchis squeezing through the Vanishing Point, like black toothpaste boiling out of its tube. It was driving a swirling cloud of terrified hummingbirds and little people before it. As they neared the roiling mass Frank was able to identify individual shapes held tightly within. There were the devils and demons from Hades Junction, off to the side the shifting hulks of the alien thugs who'd tried to steal Burnfingers Begay's precious gold at Pass Regulus, and behind them the armed and raging mutants from the fringes of a nuked Salt Lake City. Mixed in and among these more familiar evils were the killers and gargoyles which had frolicked amid an inundated Los Angeles.

It rolled toward them, expanding as it emerged from the canyon. Bulging eyes and barbed tongues flared from its surface, as unstable and ever-changing as the Chaos that was its master.

"I'm only sorry you never got the chance to taste my cooking," Flucca murmured solemnly.

"Yeah, me too." Frank closed his eyes. *Good-bye, Alicia. Good-bye, Wendy. Good-bye, Steven, wherever you are.*

Plowing into the center of the writhing black storm, the motor home scattered teeth and eyeballs, mutants and devils in every direction. Frank's eyes opened involuntarily, to reveal that they were driving through a substance like thin tar. Then the Anarchis began to recover from the shock of being struck by so much relentless reality. Evil and darkness closed tight around them, thick as molasses. They could no longer hear Mouse's exhilarating song.

Sly tendrils of night began to ooze into the motor home, seeping through imperfect joints, working their way beneath the weather stripping that lined the windows. The bubble of reality that had held back tons of sea water was unable to halt the invasion.

Frank wrenched at the wheel with one hand as he used the

other to swat at the cloying darkness. Maybe they could swing clear and come around for another run. The darkness recoiled from his flailing hand like a live thing, insubstantial tentacles searching for just the right opening. Flucca fought the feral probes with a frying pan.

The motor home rumbled clear of the cloud, evil trailing behind like a clinging black contrail. Swinging around, Frank saw between coughs that they'd slowed but not stopped its advance. Mouse and the others continued with their song as though oblivious to the danger crawling across the plateau toward them.

"Hang on!" Frank yelled.

For a second time they smashed into the storm front that was the Anarchis. This time it was ready for them. Penetration came faster, the tendrils reached for them without hesitation. Frank thought the smoke laughed, a hideous, unpleasant chuckle. Coils of it encircled his arms, then his wrists. Another that had slipped up through the heating elements contracted around the foot he kept resolutely jammed to the accelerator.

He tried to bring the heavy vehicle around for a third attack, but he could feel himself losing control. Hands were firmly disengaged from the wheel as his foot was lifted from the gas pedal. Flucca made a dive for it, only to run headlong into a wall of dark, pulsing smoke.

A thin tendril wrapped itself round his forehead and dipped down to arc up his left nostril. Frank coughed, tried to choke it out, knew instinctively that if it crept down inside it would fill his lungs and throat with unbreathable horror. He cut through it with the edge of one hand only to see it re-form instantly.

The light inside the motor home was going out, together with the light that was his life. He hoped only that he and Flucca had bought the others enough time to complete the work.

Drifting through the darkness came a dinner plate. It had eyes and stripes, though whether it was black with white stripes or black on white he couldn't tell. Lack of oxygen was impairing his vision. As it drew near he added fins and tail to his final catalogue of proximate observations.

"Impolite," it ventured coolly.

"Quite," said a similar voice.

The three angelfish floated in the center of the motor home. The Anarchis tried to swallow them as it had swallowed the motor home and all its contents. Each time a smoky tendril made contact with shining scales it recoiled as if in pain.

Frank waited for the third fish to speak and complete the tripartite hallucination. It might have done so had it not been superseded by yet a fourth voice.

"Hi, Dad."

An unfelt wind swept the strands of the Anarchis from the motor home's interior, though blackness still enclosed them on all sides. Frank hastily grabbed the wheel and hit the brake. Not even an impossible rescue could save them if he drove over the edge of the plateau. Claws and rasping tongues scratched at the windshield in frustrated fury. Only a few isolated puffs of darkness remained inside the motor home, and the angelfish were methodically herding them outside. Frank gaped at the tall young man standing behind him.

"Steven?"

The unanticipated visitor smiled. Only then did Frank recognize his son.

"Sorry I took so long to get here, Dad, but it was a long way and I wanted to be sure I could do something when I got back."

Instead of the overweight, slightly porcine ten-year-old raised on a steady diet of junk food and junk television, the Steven leaning against the back of Flucca's chair stood six-three and weighed a compact two twenty. He'd aged along with his inexplicable growth. Frank would have guessed him to be twenty-seven or twenty-eight.

He was clad in a sheepskin vest with the fleece facing outward, over a red and blue pearl-buttoned Western shirt. Below were jeans, snakeskin belt, and leather chaps beneath which boots flashed. Boots and shirt tabs were capped with gold. His Western hat was dusty brown encircled by a second reptilian band. Ivory-handled Colts rested in holsters slung from his belt, along with a shining lariat fashioned of something other than hemp. Always the would-be cowboy, Frank mused.

"I've heard about kids who grew up too fast," Flucca commented, "but this is ridiculous."

Steven smiled at him. Gone along with the fat was any suggestion of hesitation or uncertainty. He'd been transformed emotionally as well as physically.

"Nothing's ridiculous about obulating."

"What the hell is that, anyway?" his father demanded to know.

Steven pushed his hat back on his forehead. "It's kinda hard to describe. You might think of it as experience attained through travel. It's like reading a book only you're in it for real. Helps you mature in a hurry."

"No kiddin'."

"I've been through a lot of realities, Dad. It was a help to have guides." He indicated the three hovering angelfish. "On the other hand, I'm afraid I'm overqualified for Little League now." He gazed out the front window. "Looks like the crisis has come. All reality's at stake. I've learned a lot about reality, and unreality. I figure I've acquired enough experience to be of some help."

"Someone sings," said one of the angelfish, "and sings beautifully."

"It will restore the Spinner's rhythm," said one of the orange fish, "but only if she is given time to finish. We must restrain the Anarchis a little longer."

"That's what we've been trying to do." Frank kept a wary eye on the angry darkness beyond the glass as he spoke. "It's like trying to fight smoke."

"You have done well," the other orange fish told him. "Steel is good for weakening Chaos. Aluminum is better still. Now we can help, too." It was drifting less than a foot from Frank's face now, regarding him from the bottom of flat black eyes. Disconcerted, Frank looked past it toward his son.

"What can I do?"

"Drive on," said one of the other fish.

Despite his fears Frank was more than happy to follow

instructions for a change. For a second time the motor home burst clear of the Anarchis. As soon as they emerged he saw they were more than halfway across the plateau. Dark tendrils the size of trees were reaching for the three musicians performing perilously near the edge. Alicia's self-confidence might hold it back for a moment or two, but no longer. Then they would find themselves enveloped, together with reality's last hope.

Frank drove a little nearer oblivion than he would have preferred, but they needed the additional room. Already the Anarchis reached skyward, obscuring the cliffs from view and expanding to cover the entire plateau. As it advanced, the little yellow flowers closed up and grass wilted. The cloud of desperate hummingbirds and riders were forced into a steadily shrinking portion of plateau.

The door slammed. A moment later Steven appeared in front of the motor home. He climbed up on the front bumper and unlimbered the shining lariat.

Frank stared as his son whirled the rope over his head. It grew and grew until a sound like that of an approaching freight train filled the Winnebago. With a quite credible *ya-hoo!* Steven let the immense loop fly at the oncoming wall of darkness. It settled neatly around the entire gigantic bulk.

As he began pulling it tight, the Anarchis let loose with a roar powerful enough to make worlds tremble. Steven began whistling, drawing in the loop like a deep-sea fisherman fighting a record marlin. He didn't stop until the Anarchis had been compacted by the lariat, reduced to a cylinder of pure Chaos barely a couple of yards in diameter. It was as black and shiny as polished obsidian and it fought with a relentless, wild strength.

Steven used one hand to grip the radio aerial, wrapped the lariat twice around his wrist. "Let's go, Dad!"

"Yes. Time to go," the angelfish chorused.

"Go? Go where?"

"Back the way you came." Another fish gestured with a fin. "Back to reality, which the Anarchis cannot stand. Back through the Vanishing Point."

Frank eased down the accelerator. "It'll break free. He *can't* hold it." His son stood on the bumper, clinging to rope and aerial as the motor home started forward. "It's just one little rope."

"Little rope?" said an orange angelfish. "Don't underestimate your son or his tools. His rope is a superstring."

"What the hell's a superstring?"

"I forget how primitive is your reality line," said one of the other fish. "A superstring is little more than an atom wide, but it's billions of light-years long. The gravitational strength it exerts is beyond your comprehension. All superstrings were formed during and are left over from the creation of the Cosmos. They're very useful for tying things together. Some are even stronger than the Spinner's reality lines. It takes someone very special to make use of them."

"Like you?" Flucca wondered.

"We have neither hands nor inclination. Your son has always had both."

"Cowboy," Frank murmured.

"Expert obulator," the third fish corrected him. "He's been a fine pupil."

The Anarchis bellowed and thundered. It slammed into the canyon walls, sending rocks the size of skyscrapers flying. But it could not break the superstring. By this time Frank saw that the string itself was invisible. What they could see was the energy it radiated in the immediate visible spectrum. The silvery fluorescence he'd thought was the lariat itself was only its ghost.

Gritting his teeth, adrenaline surging through his veins, he hung tight to the wheel as for the third time the motor home slammed into the body of the Anarchis. He thought he saw it contort violently as it tried to strike at the individual holding the end of the lariat.

The sunlight turned silver. At the same time, Mouse's song, which had been overpowered by the bellowing of the Anarchis, swept over them in a great wave of sound. He flung up his arms to protect his eyes.

The rear wheels rose from the ground first. Then the entire machine was blown forward as if by a tremendous gust of wind. At the last instant Frank saw the true eyes of the Anarchis, yellow like contaminated water. They flew at the very face of Chaos.

A calmness filled him, the knowledge that he'd done the right thing. That Mouse had at last come to the end of her song. The cry of despair that rang in his head came not from the musicians or his strange companions or from his precariously positioned son but from the intensely evil thing wrapped around the front of the motor home.

The cry and the music still echoed through his brain as he regained consciousness. The seatbelt held him upright in the driver's seat. A concerned face gazed into his own.

"Frank? Hey man, you all right?"

He blinked at Flucca and tried to straighten. At the Farmer's Market in L.A. there was a big taffy machine that ran round the clock; pushing and pulling, pushing and stretching. He felt like it had been working on his body. Only when he was reasonably confident he wouldn't fall over in a dead heap did he permit himself to unsnap the seatbelt.

"Pretty slick driving, Dad."

It was Steven, looming larger than ever. The fancy cowboy outfit was gone, replaced by clean jeans and a short-sleeved shirt. Easy for an obulator to change clothes, Frank mused. Could be that everything would be easy for Steven from now on. Anyone who could learn how to swap youth for age and fat for muscle could surely manage a quick change of attire.

"Where are we, kiddo?"

"Back where we belong, Dad. On our own reality line. That's what Mouse says, anyway, and I'm inclined to agree with her."

"Me, too." He looked up sharply. "The Spinner?"

"Spinning smoothly, soothed and rhythmic. All's right with the Cosmos again."

"Frank?"

He recognized his wife's voice. Steven moved aside to let her through. She glanced in wonder at her mature son before moving to hug her husband.

"It worked, Frank. Thanks to you and Niccolo and Steven and Wendy and everybody else, it worked. Mouse finished her song."

"Just in time, too." He looked past her, reluctant to disengage from her arms. "Where is she?"

The motor home was a wreck. Food and linens, dishes and utensils were scattered everywhere. Not unnatural, since they were lying in the old stream bed at a thirty-degree angle. He turned and peered out the window on his side. The glass was cracked but still in place.

A few hummingbirds flitted from flower to flower. Hard as he tried, he couldn't see any little people riding them. However, one flew right up to the window and stared in at him for a very long time before it turned to dart back into the trees.

"Finished the song on a rising note," Steven was saying.

"I heard that note. That's when everything blanked out."

"The Anarchis went with it. With the Spinner soothed, its reason for being in that place was no more. It's gone back beyond order and logic to lick its wounds for a while." He grinned. "Still got my lariat wrapped around it. It's gonna have a hell of a time ridding itself of all that excess gravity. I don't think it'll trouble any reality for some time."

"You always did like fooling with ropes and cowboy stuff—when you were a kid."

"I'm sorry, Dad—Mom. I know I didn't give you much of a childhood, but I think I make a much better man than I did a boy. I'm gonna try to make it up to you."

"Just warn us if you're gonna do any obulating in the house," Frank told him, "and don't ask to borrow the car."

Wendy was standing in the doorway, staring out at the green canyon that lay on the right side of the Vanishing Point. "I hope she makes it back home. Mouse, I mean. She said I had a future as a musician." She looked back at her parents. "Me, can you imagine? But she told me to try another instrument."

"I'm sure she'll get home okay." Steven moved up behind his formerly big, now little sister. "She's probably on her way to another concert already, to sing to something like the Spinner or maybe just to the stars. I wonder if we'll ever see her again?"

"I hope not."

Alicia eyed her husband in surprise. "I thought you liked her, Frank?"

"She's okay, but she's also trouble. I don't want any more trouble."

He rose from the seat, his muscles throbbing, and went to talk to the rest of the wayward band. Burnfingers Begay was standing in a bed of tropical blossoms, chatting with Flucca. Both turned to greet him.

"How does the Grand Prix driver feel?" Burnfingers inquired solicitously.

"Like he ran into a wall." Frank grimaced. "Felt real enough." He turned to study their situation.

The motor home's wheels were buried deep in the sandy bed of the little stream. They'd need a diesel truck tow just to budge it.

Behind them, where the narrow strip of light marking the location of the Vanishing Point ought to have been, there was only solid rock, a stone cul-de-sac. A small waterfall tumbled over the top of the unbroken cliff to feed the rivulet that ran beneath the motor home. Frank was about to ask if it had all been a dream, there at the last, when his eyes caught the faint glint of light on gold. Burnfingers Begay's remarkable flute protruded from his back pocket, catching the sunlight like a long golden straw. Not a dream, then.

Certainly Steven wasn't.

"Looks like we walk," he said simply.

Burnfingers eased the burden of the long hike by tooting cheerily on his instrument, mixing Native American tunes with jazz and classics.

"You know," Frank said to his son, "the one thing I still can't figure are those damn fish. They didn't look particularly clever and they didn't act especially helpful."

"Angelfish, Dad. *Angel*fish."

"Oh. Yeah."

He was still mulling that over when they reached the highway. It was the same highway they'd turned off a short eternity ago. It was also still deserted.

Frank turned and gazed back the way they'd come. Ferns and palms obscured the narrow canyon, making it invisible from the road. Alicia's voice jolted him out of his memories.

"Which way should we go from here?"

All of a sudden he didn't care. Sporting goods stores, television, gambling no longer struck him as important to the scheme of things as hummingbirds, small yellow flowers, and having his family around him.

"We were headed north when we turned off here." Burnfingers started up the pavement. "Might as well go on that way."

They hadn't walked far when a low rumbling noise sounded behind them. For a bad moment Frank thought of telling everyone to scatter among the few trees clinging to the rock wall. His panic proved unjustified.

The big Dodge van slowed as it drew near, stopped in the far lane. The puzzled driver rolled down his window and leaned out for a better look at them. His hair was black and curly and he wore a bright red shirt imprinted with flowers.

"What you folks doin' out here? You on the wrong side of the island."

"Our motor home broke down a ways back," Frank told him truthfully.

"What motor home?"

"Back up the canyon. About a mile back down the road."

The man frowned. "No canyon here. Just rock and cliffs." Then he smiled and shrugged. "None of my business nohow. But it too damn hot to be hitchhiking. I'm on my way in to work. Why don' you folks come aboard?"

"We'd appreciate a lift," said Steven.

"I'll take you all to the hotel. You do what you want from there. Motor home, you say?" He shook his head in disbelief. "Didn't know there were any motor homes for hire on the island, but that not my business neither."

"We'll be glad to pay you for the ride," Frank told him as he climbed in.

"No way, frien'. I'm always picking up folks out this way. Not too many people realize how empty the back country is. Mostly they just stay in Hilo or one of the big resorts." He eased back out onto the highway.

"Daddy," Wendy whispered to her father, "we're in Hawaii!"

Cars began to appear, not many, but enough to be reassuring. Frank felt like a moviegoer who'd spent a year inside a film, only to finally have climbed back down off the screen to resume his seat in the real world. He leaned against the bench seat.

"Burnfingers, how about giving us a tune?"

"Sure, my friend." The Navajo extracted his flute, set it against his lips, and began playing. It was an invigorating song, alive with jaunty triumph. A thousand trumpets playing fanfare at a royal coronation could not have been more thrilling.

In a few minutes they were all singing or humming along, including the driver. Off in the distance the world's tallest active volcano, Mauna Loa, smoked threateningly but otherwise behaved itself.

Frank found himself watching the waves that broke against the rocky shore. It was a rhythm he recognized, the rhythm of the Spinner. His heart kept time with the waters, all entwined with the breeze whipping past the speeding van, with the pattern of the volcano's breath fashioned in the clear blue sky. All were part of one and the same thing: volcano, heartbeat, wind, and wave. One world, one reality, one song.

Probably Mouse could have put it better, could have explained what it all meant, but she was on her way elsewhere. Home, or to another demand on her special talents. A singer she'd called herself, and a singer she was, though on a scale no words existed to describe.

In spite of everything it had cost him, he found that he was glad he'd been invited to the concert.